I0658985

# Blood Upon the Snow

A Novel of the American Revolution

*Martin R. Ganzglass*

A PEACE CORPS WRITERS BOOK

## ALSO BY MARTIN R. GANZGLASS

### Fiction

*The Orange Tree*

*Somalia: Short Fiction*

### In the American Revolutionary War Series

*Cannons for the Cause*

*Tories and Patriots*

### Non-Fiction

*The Penal Code of the Somali Democratic Republic
(Cases, Commentary and Examples)*

*The Restoration of the Somali Justice System, Learning From Somalia,
The Lessons of Armed Humanitarian Intervention,
Clarke & Herbst, Editors*

*The Forty-Eight Hour Rule, One Hand Does Not Catch a Buffalo,
A. Barlow, Editor*

Cover: Detail from The March to Valley Forge by William B.T. Trego.
Used by permission of the Museum of the American Revolution.

*For Evelyn*
*For everything*

Blood Upon the Snow
A Peace Corps Writers Book.
An Imprint of Peace Corps Worldwide

Copyright © 2016 by Martin R. Ganzglass
All rights reserved.

Printed in the United States of America
by Peace Corps Writers of Oakland, California.

No part of this book may be used or reproduced in any manner
whatsoever without written permission except in the case of brief
quotations contained in critical articles or reviews.

For more information, contact www.peacecorpsworldwide.com
Peace Corps Writers and the Peace Corps Writers colophon are
trademarks of PeaceCorpsWorldwide.org

This novel is a work of fiction. The historical figures and actual
events described are used fictitiously. All other names, characters,
places and incidents are products of the author's imagination.
Any resemblance to living persons is purely coincidental.

ISBN 978-1-935925-72-9
Library of Congress Control Number
2016935527

First Peace Corps Writers Edition, March 2016.

*"[I froze] to see such horror and distress, blood mingling together- the dying groans, the garments rolled in blood.*

*The sight was too much to bear."*

*Sergeant Joseph White*
*Massachusetts Artillery*

# Part One
# Trenton and Princeton

# Chapter 1 - The Taking of Trenton

Corporal Georg Engelhard was exhausted, worn down by the incessant rounds of night sentry duty, shivering in small huts and makeshift outposts, and the daytime patrols through the snow-covered fields and thick forests where they could be ambushed by the Rebellers at any moment. On Christmas Eve there was no respite. They were awake all night under arms and ready to muster at any alarm.

Even when the Hessians of the Seckendorf Company were officially on relief duty in their barracks, the soldiers were ordered to sleep in their uniforms with their cartridge belts strapped on. The old three story stone building was almost as cold inside as out. At breakfast in the common room on the ground floor, the fire barely warming those fortunate enough to sit close by, the men were only permitted to unbutton their jackets. Their muskets, bayonets affixed, were at the ready, stacked on worn wooden racks, near the entrance door. Georg longed to undo his knee high black gaiters but it was forbidden. They pinched his calves as he sat on the rough-hewn bench, next to his friend Christoph.

"This has truly been the worst Christmas week, I have ever spent," Georg said. "Since we buried Andreas I sleep fitfully. I see his face before he died as we carried him to the wagon."

Christoph nodded. They both remained silent, thinking of their last patrol with their friend, the rifle ball coming from the murky dark woods, Andreas crumpling to the ground, his white waist-coat quickly soaked red with his blood, and dying slowly in agony from his stomach wound.

Andreas had often expressed his desire to be captured or to desert in the confusion of battle. He had encouraged Georg and Christoph to join him. Georg refused. It offended his sense of honor and jeopardized his remittances to his parents. He wanted to win the war and go home. All it would take would be to cross the frozen Delaware, a half a day's march to Philadelphia, capture the Rebeller's capital, gather up loot and plunder and return to Hesse, richer than his family could imagine. No, he would not leave his comrades and desert to the ragged, ill-disciplined mob of farmers and tradesmen who ran when the Hessians charged them, bayonets at the ready.

"Shh," Christoph hissed, quickly glancing at the other soldiers bent over, seated around the table eagerly spooning porridge from their bowls to their mouths.

Georg was so tired, he was unaware he had spoken. He tried to remember what he had said.

"Georg. You must. . ."

Christoph's words were interrupted by the sound of musket volleys in the distance. The soldiers looked at each other confused, awaiting orders. There were shouts in the street.

"Heraus! Heraus! The Rebellers. The Rebellers. Turn out. To the alarm posts. Hurry, hurry."

The men scrambled to their feet and ran for their muskets. The kettledrums beat urgently for them to form up. Outside, it was sleeting. The wind, gusting down from the top of the town, picked up already fallen snow and swirled it around them in clouds, obstructing their vision. Georg, as the Corporal in charge of the first two lines, got his files of men in order. His Company, led by Lieutenant Reuter, quick marched in ranks on the snow- covered lane from the barracks to the bottom of King Street. It was one of two broad and long cobblestoned streets that sloped the length of Trenton, down to the bridge at the bottom where the road led south to Bordentown. Their alarm position was less than a hundred yards away, in the field past the Presbyterian Church and below the apple orchard. As they crossed King Street, Georg looked to his left. The men of Colonel Rall's Regiment, distinctive in their mustard colored breeches, were falling in midway up the street, outside the brick buildings that served as their barracks.

At the top of the hill, where King Street met the Pennington Road, through the wind blown sleet and snow and the smoke of musket fire, Georg could barely see figures of soldiers. They seemed to him to be an indistinct mass of blue-coated troops. His Company turned on to Queen Street. From here, Georg could more clearly see the Rebellers at the top and some at the junction with the Princeton Road. Georg thought there were too many of the enemy for a harassing raid. He heard the volume of musket fire increase but whether it was the Rall Regiment returning fire or the rebel force, he could not tell.

"Will. Bring the gun over here," Lieutenant Hadley cried, pointing with his arm to a level area among the soldiers. Will urged Big Red forward. He leaped off the horse and ran to detach the traces. Isaiah, Levi and Baldwin, unlimbered the six-pounder and together they turned it around. Will joined them as they rolled the gun forward through the soft snow. They were at the top of a wide street. Below them was the town. Some of the troops formed up around them, and fired a volley toward the Hessians midway down the street. Others raced through the snow-covered fields behind the buildings seeking to get closer and fire into the enemy's flanks.

"Aim low. Keep your muskets low. Leg them. Leg them," an officer nearby shouted to his men before they fired another volley. The smoke from their muskets blew down the street, blending into the nearly horizontal sheets of sleet and snow.

"Sergeant Merriam. Hurry, man. Bring your gun to bear," Hadley shouted. Will and Levi unloaded grape canister from the side box. With the cannon aimed down the street and the wind behind them, there was no danger of snow going down the muzzle. Sergeant Merriam pried the touch-hole cover off with a knife and immediately covered it with his thumb.

"Baldwin. Come here," Merriam shouted over the wind. Baldwin ran to the left side of the cannon and thrust his leather thumbstall over the touch-hole. Will kept the lid on the powder box until he sensed

Chandler was about to withdraw the sponge. He flipped open the hinged lid, grabbed a charge, slammed the lid down with his boot and handed the canvas bag of gunpowder to Levi. Will stood near the muzzle ready with the cylindrical bag of grape shot. Chandler rammed the load home. Merriam inserted the quill in the touchhole. Lieutenant Hadley, his sword drawn, pointed down the street and shouted "Fire." Merriam leaned over the touch-hole, lit the quill and made sure it had caught. "Give Fire," he shouted and took two quick steps back, stumbling as his bad ankle turned beneath him. The grape shot tore through the clustered ranks and several of the Hessians fell. More went down as the second cannon in the battery fired.

"Quickly now, men," Merriam called, as Baldwin sealed the vent with his thumbstall to block air from escaping and prevent the hole from getting wet. They rapidly loaded and got off another round as the Hessians retreated. The noise of musket and rifle fire increased as the Americans broke into buildings lining the street. Once inside they dried their flintlocks and fired at the Hessians from behind windows and doorways. The Hessians, having discharged a few volleys, now found their muskets misfiring due to the snow and sleet.

"It is cannon balls now lads," Hadley cried, pointing at a group of Hessians unlimbering two guns midway in the street below them. Will handed the smooth ball to Levi and heard the metal sphere rolling down the barrel. Isaiah rammed it home, the gun was primed and their shot struck in front of the Hessians and plowed into a horse still attached to the gun. Even with the wind blowing from behind them, the wounded animal's piercing cry of pain carried up to their position.

"Again." Hadley shouted. "Have at them again. Before they set up." The other two cannons in the battery fired. Will heard a horse neighing, perhaps it was the same one, or another. It didn't matter. He had to keep the powder dry, timing taking it out of the powder box to give the canvas the least exposure to the driving sleet and snow. He knew Baldwin would protect the touch-hole. The danger of a misfire was greatest when Merriam ignited the quill. If the slow match was blown out by the wind they would have a live charge in the barrel and no way of knowing if a spark was working its way down the quill to the powder bag.

Will heard a boom and was surprised by the whooshing sound of a cannon ball passing their battery. The Hessians were firing up at the Americans, although blinded by the wind whipped sleet and snow swirling down upon them. The Hessian's aim was wide but next time they would sight in on the American's muzzle flash. If their gun crews lasted that long. More and more troops were inside homes on both sides of the street, firing from close range at the Hessians massed in ranks in the middle. Other troops, running through the fields behind the brick houses on King Street, would soon be behind the Hessians.

Tyler finished worming, turned and took the charge from Will, brushed the snow flakes from the top of the canvas, and shoved it down the muzzle. Chandler rammed it home, waited for the cannon ball to roll down and leaned on the rammer again.

"Give fire," Merriam shouted, Will heard the blast of their gun. Seconds later, a Hessian cannon ball struck the ground in front of them and bounced past their emplacement.

Something was terribly wrong. Their cannon was off kilter and lower to the ground. At first, Will thought the Hessian ball had hit them. He looked frantically around to see if anyone was bleeding or decapitated. Isaiah and Levi had dropped to the ground behind the six-pounder. Will feared they had been wounded.

"The axle tree is broken," Levi said, crawling out from behind a carriage wheel. The cannon lay in the cradle created by the vee shape of the oak beam. "It must have cracked in one of the ravines right after we crossed the river." The two other cannons in the battery fired down the street and Will heard a cheer from one of their crews. The grape shot had downed the Hessian gun commander and several of the men, leaving only a few survivors to man their cannon.

"There is the gun for us," Hadley shouted, pointing with his sword down the street to the Hessians, forty yards away. "Capture it men. Forward. Now." Will leaped over the powder box and rushed down hill, behind the Lieutenant. He lost his footing on the sleet slick cobblestones, slipped but caught himself as one hand touched the icy ground. He ran low in a crouch straight toward the small malevolent looking mouth of the Hessian three- pounder. Hadley was in front of him waving his sword and shouting words that were lost in the gale.

Soldiers in blue coats emerged from the side streets and rushed toward the Hessian gun. Everyone was screaming, shouting in fury. Will yelled too, unaware of what he was screaming, only that his throat was raw. The sound of his own voice filled his ears.

They were almost there. Seven or eight Hessians struggled to load the gun. In a panic, Will suddenly realized, he was unarmed. He had no sword, musket or bayonet. He was charging an enemy gun battery empty handed. Desperately, he looked for anything to use, saw a half shattered wooden bucket, grabbed at it and wielding it like a hammer, he jumped up on the side box and swung it at a Hessian, knocking aside his musket with its long, evil looking bayonet. Hadley slashed at a gunner with his sword, opening a large bloody gash on his shoulder. One of the Americans, an officer, short, slight framed, looking more like a young boy, fired a pistol point blank into the face of one of the Hessians, who threw up his hands and fell backwards. Musket fire from the adjacent buildings hit another soldier who fell on to the snow bleeding from a neck wound, and the rest fled down the street.

"Turn the gun around," Hadley shouted. Will grabbed the tiller of the carriage and together with Tyler and Chandler positioned the cannon facing the fleeing Hessians. The gun weighed half of their six-pounder and felt like a toy. Will opened the powder box. Inside, it had a leather flap over the canvas charges to keep them dry. He left it in place as Levi rolled the sponge in the snow to get it wet and then plunged the pole down the barrel. The cannon ball felt light. Almost no weight to it at all. Will handed it to Levi, Isaiah rammed it home and they were ready. Down the street, Hessian troops had emerged from between buildings and had formed up in ranks facing the cannon.

"Where is Sergeant Merriam?" Hadley cried, looking around. Will looked back up King Street and saw the Sergeant limping and hobbling as best he could to join them. Will dashed back, put Merriam's arm around his shoulder and together on three good legs they scurried forward to the Hessian gun. Will glanced down the street. The Hessians were marching toward them, braving the heavy fire from the adjoining buildings.

Merriam removed a quill, inserted it in the touch-hole and lit it. "Give fire," he shouted. Will involuntarily flinched, moving away from the gun. Nothing happened. For a split second he thought the Hessian cannon would misfire. The sudden blast sent the ball down the cobblestones, bouncing into the three deep massed ranks, leaving a gap in their line. They hesitated. Will saw a Hessian officer raise his sword and point toward their gun. There was a volley of musket and rifle fire from the buildings and the officer and several others fell. The Hessians broke and retreated rapidly down the street.

"Follow them, men," Hadley yelled, pointing with his sword. "Take the cannon and follow them."

Will was surprised how maneuverable the three-pounder was, even with the side boxes. He pushed against the studded carriage wheel with his shoulder. Baldwin and Levi manhandled the tongue and two more were on the other side. The cannon bounced over the cobblestones as they descended into the lower part of town. They careened down the slope past the wounded Hessian troops, some still alive and moaning in pain, others missing limbs, lying dead in the pools of their own blood staining the snow around them. The cannon wheel rolled over a severed leg, crunching the bone underneath. Will shuddered as his bare hands touched the pieces of flesh and bone on the wheel when it rotated into his grasp. Quickly, he wiped his hands on his breeches. The next time the wheel came around, he consciously grabbed the spokes instead.

The Hessians retreated from King Street, marching left off to the side and disappeared behind the brick buildings. At the bottom of the street American troops swarmed after them. Hadley ordered the gun crew to halt. [1]

—⚍—

Georg heard the Regimental drummers and haute boys sound the advance. They marched up Queen Street, the heavy snow accumulating on their brass caps and shoulders. The Rall and Von Lossberg Regiments were ahead of them, flags blowing stiffly in the strong winds. The three Regiments would counterattack into the center of Trenton. The Rebeller riffraff would not withstand their disciplined bayonet charge. He was glad his powder was wet. There would be no pausing for musket volleys. They would use the bayonet and drive these inexperienced shopkeepers and farmers before them, back to the river and then annihilate them. He saw the two Regiments disappear through the back lots and lanes of the town toward King Street. To Georg's surprise, they did not follow. Led by their Major, the Knyphausen Regiment stomped through a snowy field paralleling Queen Street. Georg thought they would veer left and hit the Rebellers higher up, trapping them between the three Regiments.

Instead, they marched through the snow-covered fields, passing behind the Friends Meeting House and clambering over the stone wall below an apple orchard. To his left, from the center of town, Georg heard the booming of cannons and musket and rifle fire. They headed uphill. The storm had intensified with the wind blowing directly into their faces. He couldn't see it but he knew the Princeton Road was less than a quarter of a mile up the slope. As they advanced, a few men in the front ranks fell, downed by rebel marksmen. Georg grimaced. The Rebellers aimed for the officers, then the Sergeants and Corporals. No matter. Once they got close enough, they would spit these cowardly riflemen on the end of their bayonets before they could reload.

Suddenly, ahead of them, from behind the buildings lining Queen Street, the men of the Rall and Von Lossberg regiments burst into the orchard. Georg could see from their depleted ranks they had sustained substantial casualties. He heard the drums signaling them to reform and the troops wheeled and marched back toward Queen Street. He had no time to think about them. Muzzle flashes from enemy rifles winked at them from the stone wall marking the high end of the orchard. The company ahead of them, knelt and fired a volley at the Rebellers. The sound of only a few muskets blew back to Georg. Their powder and flint were wet and most of the guns had misfired. Georg knew the same was true with the men of his Company. He waited for the order to charge and use the bayonet. That would be the only way to fight in this snowstorm. Several men around him fell, wounded from flanking fire on their left. Georg turned toward the buildings, in time to see a rebel rifleman in the first floor rear window withdraw his long barreled gun to reload.

"Retain your ranks," a Sergeant bellowed as the men halted their advance. A riderless horse, panicked by the battle, raced down the hill, plowing through the soldiers in its path.

"The Major has been shot," someone yelled. The drums sounded the retreat. Despite the confusion, the men retained their discipline, and as if on a parade ground, wheeled and turned back toward the lower part of town.

Georg's company was the last to leave the frozen orchard. Above them, the survivors of the Rall and Von Lossberg Regiments, beaten back for a second time from the center of town, were surrounded in the apple orchard. Rebel troops kept up a steady fire from the back of buildings off Queen Street, as did the troops protected by the stone wall at the top of the orchard. Georg thought he heard shouts in German of "Throw down your arms, throw down your arms," but with the howling of the wind, he wasn't sure. How could the Rebellers be speaking German? Then, he remembered, Andreas had told them he had met a farm family in New Jersey and had conversed with them. He shook his head, still thinking the wind was playing tricks with his hearing. [2]

They marched downhill, this time with the wind at their backs, taking sporadic fire from homes at the lower part of town. Georg knew from previous patrols, there was a millpond and creek at the southern end of Trenton, a narrow bridge and then the road to Bordentown. If they made it to that road they could escape.

Lieutenant Holmes led his company past a stone bridge and along the creek bank until he found a place where they could cross below the east side of Trenton. Behind them, other Mariners together with General Sullivan's troops held the narrow bridge across the creek. Any retreat by the Hessians down King Street was blocked by another regiment of Sullivan's division.

Holmes spotted a shallow gravel bottomed location where the two banks were low and closer together. This was the place to ford. He would have preferred to dig entrenchments on the southern bank and wait for the Hessians to attempt to cross. However, his orders were to cross the creek and confront the Hessians as they emerged from the town. They waded three or four abreast into the thigh deep frigid water holding their muskets above their heads. The men splashed quickly through the icy stream and up the opposite bank. The bitter wind froze their wet canvas breeches to their legs. For the first time since the battle had begun, they were facing into the strong winds that blew sleet and snow straight at them.

Adam was in the first column. He peered through the storm and made out a mass of men in blue uniforms marching toward them, their flags blowing toward the Americans. At first he thought they might be some of their troops coming to join them. Their gait, discipline and the length of their bayonets, gave them away.

"Lieutenant. There are Hessians ahead," Adam shouted, pointing with his musket. Holmes ordered the two columns to spread out to block the enemy's intended route to the creek. The Americans' battery on the slope above the bridge opened fire. Two balls plowed into the mass of Hessians who hesitated and then regrouped.

"Give them a volley," Holmes ordered. "Let them know we are here. On my command." Adam had protected his flintlock with his jacket cuff and was reasonably certain his musket would fire. He knelt in the snow, oblivious to the wet slush under his knee and the stiffness of his frozen legs.

"Fire," Holmes shouted. The men got off a ragged volley and several of the Hessians in the front line fell. Adam saw an officer on horseback, knocked out of the saddle but whether it was from their fusillade or the American troops on the Hessians' flanks, he could not tell. He reloaded, although this time he had little confidence his musket would fire.

"Ready bayonets," Holmes ordered. Adam steadied himself. They were barely fifty paces apart. It would be a short run uphill, into the storm and then hand-to-hand fighting. Next to him, Solomon, his long arms bare at the wrists protruding from his uniform jacket and his thatchy eyebrows covered with snowflakes, stared grimly ahead. He shifted his musket from one hand to the other, as if weighing it for the first time.

"I would rather have a pike or even a Durham pole for this business," he said to Adam. A pike would be nice, Adam thought.

"Hold. They are striking their colors," Holmes said. It was true.

Adam watched as the Hessians let their regimental flag staffs fall on the snow in front of them. Those in the forward ranks turned their muskets downward and stuck them in the ground by the bayonets. Others simply threw their guns down.

The Mariners advanced in a rush and motioned for the Hessians to back away from their colors and the pile of muskets. The Hessians took three or four paces back in unison.

"Lieutenant," Adam said. "I speak some Dutch. They will understand." He cupped his hands to his mouth and shouted, Handen om hog. Hoger. Hoger."

The Hessians raised their hands over their heads.

"Watch out," someone shouted. "They still carry their swords."

"Tell them to unbuckle their swords," Nat said. Adam shouted at them and a few began undoing the straps across their chests and throwing the short swords on to the snow. One tall Hessian took a step forward, slowly and insolently undid the strap and said something to Adam. Quick as a cat, Adam stepped forward and with two hands viciously jabbed his musket barrel into the man's stomach. As the Hessian doubled over, Adam clipped him with the butt on the jaw.

"He called me a black dog, Sir," Adam said by way of explanation.

Nat grinned at Adam. "Well, by making an example of one it will improve the attitude of the rest and teach them they are our prisoners."

Holmes bent down and picked up the Knyphausen Regiment's flags and colors. "And now time for another lesson." He looked around, motioned for Solomon, Jeremiah and Titus to step forward.

"March smartly and present these captured colors to General Sullivan. With the compliments of the Marblehead Mariners," he shouted. The men cheered as their three comrades headed through the snowy field toward King Street. [3]

—⚏—

Georg waited his turn to step forward. The stocky black man in uniform, the one who had felled Sergeant Dorner, had ordered them to take off their brass hats and knapsacks. Georg's hair was drawn back tight from his head and tied with a pigtail ribbon. Bare headed he felt exposed. He had a few personal possessions in his knapsack, a pipe and a bit of tobacco, his razor, and a small knife he had taken from Andreas' kit to remember him by. He would have liked to have kept that at least.

At the thought of his dead friend, Georg began to cry. Sobs wracked his body as he stood in ranks waiting for whatever the Rebellers had in store for them. Andreas had urged them to desert or hoped they would be captured. Then the war would be over for them. They would become laborers on some farm. When the war officially ended, they could stay and by hard work earn title to good farmland. That had been Andreas' dream. If he had lived one more week, he would have seen what he wished for come to pass. Georg's shoulders shook as he was overcome with grief. How strange God's plans are for we poor human beings, he thought. Why could not Andreas have lived to be a farmer. Was it too much to ask?

He felt an arm on his shoulder. It was Lieutenant Reuter.

"You are a good and brave soldier, Corporal Engelhard. I share your sense of shame in being captured by such a rabble and ordered about by a black man. And another black slave carries off our sacred battle flags." He squeezed Georg's arm. "Bear up, Corporal. Remember you are a soldier of the von Knyphausen Regiment."

Georg gritted his teeth. His Lieutenant took that as an expression of resolve. Instead, Georg was thinking what a pompous ass you are Lieutenant Reuter. As a prisoner of war, you will live a comfortable life in good quarters as a gentleman and officer, until you are paroled to New York where you will sit before a warm fire drinking brandy, still thinking these Rebellers are rabble who could not beat us. But they did. Because you and our other officers did not do your duty to prepare us for this attack. And I will live a miserable existence in some cold Rebeller prison, sick, starving, freezing and maybe dying before this cursed war is over.

Bare headed, in long plodding columns, flanked by the troops who had captured them, the Hessians marched up Queen Street, down a lane and into the Presbyterian Church. Georg hardly noticed when different soldiers assumed guard duty. He pushed aside a pile of discolored straw, releasing the pungent ammonia smell of horse urine, and collapsed on the cold stone floor. He was thankful to be out of the storm. He was thirsty. He reached for his canteen, before realizing he had surrendered that too.

—⁓—

"See what these heathens have done to this Church," Merriam said gesturing vaguely. Will looked around. The pews had been stripped long ago and burned for firewood. The altar was gone. Piles of dried horse manure and straw littered the floor. It was obvious the Hessians had converted it to a stable.

"These are not God fearing men but savages without restraint of religious teachings of morality," Merriam said angrily. "They pillage, rape and desecrate at will." Wisps of his grey hair stuck up from the sides of his battered tri-corn. He looked up at the Church spire, as if appealing to Heaven. "If I had it within my power, I would leave only the Hessians in the Church they have destroyed, bar the doors and call upon God Almighty, to smite them down for their heinous crimes."

A wounded Hessian cried out in pain. Will turned to see the man, bleeding profusely from a shoulder wound, as one of his comrades leaned over him trying to staunch the blood with a torn shirt.

"Sergeant," Isaiah said, bringing Merriam out of his religious fulmination. "We have orders to move the wounded. To the Anglican Church." Merriam nodded, almost absentmindedly counting the number of wounded. "Organize the able bodied Hessians to carry the wounded. I need volunteers to escort them."

"I am terrified you will call down lightning bolts upon this House of God," Levi Tyler said, wiping the melting snow from his hair with his bare hand. "It will be safer for me to be outside in the storm with these bleeding Hessians." He looked around to see if any one else enjoyed his joke.

Isaiah ignored him. "I will go," he said and walked over to several Hessians who seemed uninjured. He motioned for them to get up and pointed at the wounded lying about. By gestures and shouts, they got the Hessians to help the thirty or so wounded who were able to walk or who could be carried out the arched double door and back into the storm. Those too seriously wounded to be moved, were left where they lay, pools of blood seeping from their uniforms onto the stone floor.

Will stood in the Church door and looked back at them. They would probably die before any surgeon came to help them.

The Anglican Church had been converted into a field hospital. Outside, a pile of severed limbs, the blood frozen to the sawed off stumps, tendons and flesh, stained the snow-covered graveyard. The walking wounded, supported by their comrades, hesitated at the grim sight, then lowered their bare heads and entered the Church. Inside, it was clear the Hessians had not desecrated this place of worship. The pews were intact and had been pushed off to the sides to make room for makeshift operating tables of doors and planks resting unsteadily on chairs. The soft groans of those in pain, lying on the stone floor, awaiting their turn, were drowned out by the intermittent screams of agony as the surgeons sawed through tissue, muscle and bone.

A Hessian lay on the plank table, his shattered forearm hanging by a single strip of skin to his hand. Will felt the acid bile rising from his empty stomach and fill his throat. He backed out the door. The mixture of snow and sleet that had fallen all morning during the battle had changed to rain. Will forced down the urge to dry heave, sucking in large breaths of icy cold air.

Victorious Continentals strode up King Street, stepping around the frozen bodies of dead Hessians, whose lifeless bodies were partially covered by the freshly fallen snow. The American troops carried Hessian brass helmets, swords and bayonets. Some wore overcoats and blankets on top of their worn uniforms. A boy ran uphill, his old regimental drum strapped to his back, and his newly acquired brass Hessian drum proudly worn on his front. Will wondered if the Hessian drummer boy was alive. He shuddered at the memory of the small crumpled body of the Hessian lad, cut in two by their musket fire, his drum lying by the side of that narrow road leading from Pelham Bay. He could handle death during the fighting. It was the bloody aftermath that bothered him. A horrible, long agonizing scream came from inside the Church. Will realized he could not go back inside.

"There is rum to be had," one passing already inebriated soldier shouted at Will, waving an open canteen. "Hogsheads of good Jamaican rum," his companion added, tipping back his head to drink. The Hessian brass hat fell off his head into the slush.

Isaiah emerged and took Will by the elbow.

"I have seen enough amputated limbs for one day," he said. "Come. There is no need for us to remain here." Together they walked back to the Presbyterian Church. Inside, several bodies covered with blankets, lay neatly arranged near a side door. Sergeant Merriam waved Will and Isaiah over to barrels of salted meat and hard biscuits.

"Tis not much better than our fare."

"It tastes better when washed down with rum," one of the company said offering his canteen. "There is plenty more where that came from. Down near the old stone barracks."

"None of that now," Merriam said sternly. "Our orders are clear. The prisoners, under guard, will bury these dead in the Churchyard. The rest of us are to bring our cannon and the brass three and six-pounders taken from these Hessians to the Trenton Ferry. Lieutenant Hadley said we will cross the river again before nightfall."

Will walked through the ankle deep slush back up King Street, fighting the strong wind and rain. He shuddered as he passed the dead horse of the Hessian gun crew, it's hind quarters torn off by a cannon ball. He found Big Red where he had left him, in the copse of snow-covered evergreens, a little ways up the Pennington Road. The horse whinnied as he approached. Will brushed the sleet from his shaggy mane and scratched Big Red's rough chin. He leaned his head against the horse's neck. He thought he was relieved to see Big Red unharmed, but realized the relief came from having survived the battle unscathed. He had acquitted himself well. Of course he had, he thought smiling. What other soldier attacks an enemy gun crew with a shattered wooden bucket?

Once back in town, he and Isaiah hitched two of the six cannons captured from the Hessians to Big Red. At Will's insistence, he helped Sergeant Merriam, still nursing his weak ankle, up onto the horse, and walked up King Street, leading Big Red by the reins. The other two gun crews followed, each horse pulling one cannon. The Hessian prisoners pushed the remaining artillery pieces, guarded by the jubilant men of the Massachusetts Regiment. Part way up King, the column veered west onto a broad, rutted, frozen road paralleling the river, until they arrived at the upper ferry about a quarter of a mile beyond the town. They loaded the cannons and some of the prisoners on the flat-bottomed ferries and waited, exposed to the wind and rain from the northwest.

"Tis better to go by ferry than to retrace our route by foot," Levi Tyler said.

"Yes and this time, you have proper boots, I notice," Isaiah observed, pointing to the black shiny calf high boots on Levi's feet. "They look like they came from a Hessian officer."

"He no longer had any use for them," Levi replied without elaborating. "I have a pair of shoes in my haversack. They are well made and serviceable. Two pairs of gaiters as well. And once we get these miserable prisoners to their new home, they will have no need for footwear. They will have wooden working clogs instead. For my part, I care not if they go barefoot."

Will only half listened to their talk back and forth. With his back to the river and facing the road, he was the first to see the Mariners arrive. He smiled and hallooed loudly as he recognized Nat, Adam and Solomon, Jeremiah and Titus, and others he knew when he had stayed in their barracks in Cambridge. They arrived with a few hundred Hessians, walking bare headed and hunched down, looking much smaller and less formidable than they had last summer on the Brooklyn battlefield. Will dashed down the plank to shore and embraced Nat first and then Adam.

"It is about time you arrived to ferry us across. The Hessians have not killed us but this weather will freeze us to death before long," Will said.

"You must be patient a little longer," Nat replied. "Others are to ferry you across. We have an eight-mile march ahead of us with these prisoners to retrieve the Durhams. If the ice is not too thick, we can pole down river to our camp on the Pennsylvania shore. If it is," he shrugged, "we will have to make land and march down. It matters not."

"Why so?" Will asked.

"Our term of service is over at the end of the month. Colonel Glover has informed us he will lead us home."

"Yes," Adam said smiling. "After that, no more marching.

We will go back on the water."

"As privateers," Solomon exclaimed. "Where money can be made far beyond a soldier's pay in Continentals."

"Nat. Will you be a privateer?" Will asked, remembering his friend had told him the British hung privateers as pirates, when they captured them.

"Not immediately. Anna is expecting our child in January. With Providence's blessing, after I see her safely through childbirth, I expect to be Captain of my own vessel. This marching is not for me, Will. I am done with it."

They clasped each other by the shoulders. "I will see you on the Pennsylvania shore," Will called, as the Marblehead Mariners marched north on the river road. "Do not leave without saying goodbye," Will yelled. Nat turned and waved farewell.

After a long, wet slog of a march, the Mariners reached the ice encrusted Durhams in the late afternoon. The tie lines were rigid and the water in the holds had frozen.

Holmes divided the prisoners into lots of fifty each. With much gesturing and prodding with bayonets at the end of muskets, the first twenty-five struggled over the jumbled mass of ice floes on the shore and clambered over the gunnels. They stood in the hold shivering, their lips quivering uncontrollably.

"Tell them to jump up and down," Nat said to Adam.

"Jump," Adam shouted. "Afspringen," he yelled in Dutch. The Hessians understood.

"Ja. Springen, springen" several of them said nodding. They began jumping up and down in the hold breaking the ice under their feet. Adam laughed. The other Mariners around him broke into hoots and guffaws. The Hessians made a comical sight. The frozen tied tails of their hair stuck straight out behind them, stiffly moving up and down as they jumped.

"They do not appear now as menacing and fearsome as they did in on the road from Pelham Bay," Holmes observed.

Adam bent down, grabbed a chunk of ice and threw it overboard. He motioned for them to do the same. The Hessians grabbed the ice in their bare hands, emptying the boat of the additional weight.

"Now," Adam said in Dutch. "Up here on the walkways." He motioned for some of the Hessians to climb up. A few gingerly joined him, slipping on the ice-covered wood. "Afspringen," Adam commanded again, showing them how. The Hessians gingerly jumped only a few inches, cautiously maintaining their balance. With some practice, one and then another jumped higher or stomped their heels on the thin ice sheen, until the walkways were clear.

"Back down into the hold," Adam ordered. Solomon had untied the Durham and the Mariners pushed the boat off into the swirling river.

—m—

Georg stood in the freezing ankle deep water of the black boat. His teeth were chattering. Hatless, with only his uniform jacket to protect him from the chilling wind and rain, he was as cold as he had ever been. The only warmth came from the men on each side of him, huddled together for the crossing. He prayed to God on high, the boat would not sink, crushed by a giant ice floe, or that he would not freeze to death in the frigid waters. Georg thought of the Regiment's terrifying crossing of the North Sea. Their pastor had led them in the Psalms. He looked at Christoph, next to him and the men beyond. Every man's lips were blue. The chins of some moved up and down as if controlled by some force outside their bodies. Georg lifted up his voice in song, recalling the words of the Psalm. Fervently, the Hessians bent their heads and sang the sacred words, which were carried away by the roar of the wind and grinding of the ice in the river.

—m—

Let the Hessians sing, Nat Holmes thought, manning the steering sweep. They would be on the Pennsylvania side soon enough. Then, fresh troops would guard the Hessians and take them to wherever. He did not care. He was exhausted. The Mariners had been on the move continuously for more than thirty-six hours, starting from their camp at four in the morning the previous day. They had covered eight miles to McConkey's Ferry, poled the Army across the Delaware, marched another eight miles to Trenton, fought and won the battle and marched back to the landing site with their prisoners. All he wanted was warm quarters, a hot meal and dry clothes. After that, he would not mind if he had to walk to Salem, to Anna and their baby yet unborn, even if it stormed the entire time. He was ready to go home.

# Chapter 2 - Keeping the Enemy at Bay

The early morning fog had lifted. They were on the Princeton Road, Bant estimated maybe seven miles north of Trenton. He avoided the deep mud brought on by yesterday's thaw and trotted quickly on the grass beside the muck to keep up with the advance patrol of long legged riflemen of Colonel Hand's Regiment. He held his five and one half foot long rifle in his right hand, his palm warm on the smooth wood, his fingers tight around the cold metal of the barrel pointing in front of him. The rifle's eight pounds were no more a burden to him than his own arm and he took comfort from its familiar feel.

The other men were mostly from Maryland and Pennsylvania, backwoodsmen armed with their long rifles, hatchets, tomahawks and knives, clad in deerskin hunting shirts, leggings and moccasins, with all sorts of headgear made from animal heads, tails and skins. Bant fit right in with his hunting frock but was one of the few wearing a tri-corn. He and a dozen others from New Jersey militias had been accepted by Colonel Hand, desperate to refill his Regiment's ranks, seriously reduced by battle and disease. After the victory at Trenton, hundreds of new recruits had eagerly joined local militias, enticed by the broadsheets trumpeting the great battle- one thousand Hessians killed and another thousand captured, hogsheads of rum for the taking and a share of the captured plunder, rumored to be dozens of cannons, kegs of powder and the entire payroll chest for three Hessian Regiments.

Bant had joined Hand's Regiment for the opportunity to kill more British. Even the ten dollar bonus for re-enlisting, payable immediately upon signing up, and in sterling or Spanish hard dollars, was meaningless to him, as was the half of a gill of rum. [1] If the army was now going to carry the fight to the enemy, he was willing to leave the local militia and ambushing small patrols and pickets. Here was a chance to pick off cavalry and field officers. To take revenge for what he had seen and still saw in his nightmares. To assuage the guilt that was always with him.

"You move well for a little man," the rifleman to his right said, coming closer to Bant to skirt a long muddy stretch of the road. He was taller than Bant, a few inches under six feet, all sinew, tendon and muscle, with leathery brown skin, large knuckled hands and dark, sunken eyes, hidden under a protruding bony forehead, like two lumps of coal sitting under a bat cave's overhang. His chin curved outward in an aggressive J, that gave his entire visage a determined, pronounced forward thrust. Bant grunted, acknowledging the compliment without inviting further conversation. The man had introduced himself last night when he and Bant had volunteered as one of twenty plus advance skirmishers. James McNeill, he said from some place in western Maryland. Bant had forgotten where.

"'Tis a good omen on the first day of this new year we are marching toward the British with our army massing in Trenton," McNeill continued. "If we defeat them here, less likelihood this year will be the one of the hangman for us." [2]

Bant froze in mid-step at the mention of hanging. He pretended he had slipped on a clump of grass and regained his footing. Ahead, on a large elm, its bare branches silhouetted against the grey sky, Bant again saw the bodies of the militia men, swinging from ropes, their eyes bulging, their tongues extended from their mouths, blood dripping from their nostrils. And him hiding up a tree while the British troopers looked for him, before hanging the others. He shook his head and the image disappeared to be replaced by a Redcoat on his horse under the tree, directing the hanging of another three men.

"Have you seen a ghost?" McNeil asked, staring at him. "You are as pale as a new canvas tent."

"Demons," Bant muttered and instantly regretted it.

"What demons?" McNeil asked, looking at the small man strangely.

"It is nothing. They come and go. I still see clearly enough to hit a charging cavalry man in the throat," he added defensively.

McNeil continued to ask him questions but Bant stubbornly refused to respond. He stared off into the distance, concentrating on the target of an imaginary Dragoon riding toward him before Bant's rifle ball blew him off his horse.

That night when the group of skirmishers had finished eating two geese, that some of the men had "liberated," from a farm they had passed earlier, it became obvious to Bant, that McNeil had mentioned his demons to the others. He did not mind. Ignoring the strange looks they gave him, he moved away from the fire, his tri-corn pulled down tightly over his small curled ears. He wrapped himself in a blanket and fell asleep leaning against a thick tree trunk.

He was awakened by the loud noise of thick rain drops pelting the ground. Bant sat up, gathering his legs closer to his chest and remained shivering in the darkness before dawn. His nightmares had returned with a vengeance, disturbing his sleep with contorted purple faces, pleas for mercy, the thud of bodies being dropped to the ground with ugly red rope marks on their bare dirty necks, and the overpowering smell of human shit, released from the bowels of the dead men. He wrapped his blanket more tightly around his shoulders and sat up blinking. He gagged at the smell of shit and shook his head to make it go away. He was no longer dreaming. He was awake. He heard a loud fart. A soldier emerged from the woods close by. The pickets had dug a shallow pit as a field latrine, oblivious to Bant's presence or perhaps deliberately placing it near where he slept. Stiff and cold, Bant raised himself up and moved closer to the dying fire and away from the stench.

At breakfast, McNeil, to make amends, offered Bant some coffee. "More bark than beans," he said apologetically. Bant held out his cup. It was hot and he nodded in appreciation.

By mid-morning, the skirmishers were hidden one hundred feet on either side of the road where it dipped into a small creek. Someone said it was called Eight Mile Run, but whether that meant eight miles to Trenton or Princeton, Bant did not know. He found a place along the southeast side of the Run, away from where the road crossed the creek. It was well protected by brush and logs. He rested his rifle on a thick fallen trunk and smoothed the ground next to him. He would fire, roll to his right parallel to the log, reload, roll to his right again and aim and fire. Behind him, the woods were thick with shrubs and brambles, enough to slow any cavalryman foolish enough to enter.

Bant looked up at the sun and guessed it was between ten and eleven, closer to eleven he thought. The day was unusually mild for the second one of the new year. The temperature was well above freezing, an unexpected warming that was uncommon for January in New Jersey. It would be a muddy slog on the roads, he thought. Better to retreat through the woods and fields, when the time came. [3]

He shuddered, recalling McNeil's words- 1777-the year of the hangman. Now that he thought of it, the number seven did resemble a gallows. One did not need a properly constructed gallows. His nightmares reminded him that a gnarled tree limb, high enough off the ground, served just as well to hang a man.

He removed the black gaiters he had taken from a dead British soldier and folded them into his haversack. He could run faster without them. He had no trouble waiting. It was only a matter of time. The Colonel had said the British would march down this highway from Princeton. Their Regiment would be the first to draw blood and make the British and Hessians pay in dead and wounded the entire way before they even confronted the American Army digging in at Trenton.

The road leading to Eight Mile Run was straight for several hundred yards. It was muddy so there was no telltale sign of dust but Bant saw the horsemen in the distance approaching from Princeton. At first, they were mere dark specks. They turned into red splotches on horseback and finally individual troopers of a cavalry screen for the army that was following. Bant thought there were around forty of them, trotting leisurely, three abreast. He could not distinguish an officer from a trooper. No matter. He would let them come to within one hundred and fifty yards and from his angle to the side, pick off the rider closest to him in the second row. After he reloaded, if the cavalry remained on the road, he would aim for another further up the column.

They were a little more than two hundred yards away. Bant calmly sighted down the rifle's three foot long barrel. As the cavalry came closer, Bant could make out the death's head insignia on the black front plate of the trooper's brass helmet. The helmet, with its red crest, covered the middle of the rider's forehead. Bant aimed for the exposed bone just above the man's eye. He waited patiently, carefully gauging the distance. At approximately one hundred and fifty yards he fired. The trooper fell back on his horse, his black booted feet trapped in the stirrups. Several other shots rang out, as Bant rolled to his right, removed his ramrod and cleaned the barrel. He tore open a cartridge with his teeth, primed the pan, covered it, poured in the powder followed by the ball, rammed it home, reattached his rod, and peered over the log. In the less than a minute it had taken him to reload, the riflemen's first volley had emptied a dozen saddles. The frightened riderless horses among the forward ranks milled around, blocking any forward movement on the road by the remaining cavalry. Three troopers spurred their horses into an open field and riding low in the saddle galloped toward Bant's position. A shot from a rifleman brought down one horse, causing the horse of another to shy away. Bant had a shot at the trooper from the side. He pulled back the hammer to full cock, aimed for his temple and fired. He watched with satisfaction as the man's head exploded in a blood red spray. He stood up as the few remaining dragoons retreated up the road and the masses of red-coated troops still marching toward them.

The skirmishers fell back, loping silently through the woods, crossed an open field, avoiding the deep mud from the melted snow and took shelter among the trees at the far end. They rested there briefly, before continuing south paralleling the road. Behind them, they heard cannon fire from British artillery, spraying the woods with grape shot where they had ambushed the cavalry. Bant decided he would like to pick off an artillery officer if the opportunity afforded itself.

He and the other skirmishers passed through their Regiment's pickets and took up positions on the south side of a larger creek. Bant appraised the place. It was a dense pine and cedar forest, with an occasional clump of bare branched oaks and maples. There were no paths for cavalry to enter and stout fallen trunks and thick brambles provided excellent ground cover. The British would either have to follow the road and wade across the creek where the bridge had stood before being torn down by Colonel Hand's men, or fan out in open fields and ford the creek where they could.

Bant knelt down behind a fallen tree. The deep shade of the forest was cooling. He brushed the remaining unmelted snow off the log and rested his rifle on the wet bark. With his hand, he dug away the soft earth and reddish fiber pulp from the decomposed tree to make a comfortable depression for his right knee and waited. McNeil was to his immediate right about four feet away. On both sides of them riflemen were spread out in a line, well hidden from view. Several cannon were in position near the place where the woods met the road.

Colonel Hand moved slowly and calmly from one group of riflemen to another. In the early afternoon heat, he had removed his tri-corn, revealing his high forehead and bald pate, like a pink cap stopping at his ears. He was a tall, lean man and when he reached Bant and the others around him, he towered over the kneeling riflemen. Hand gestured there was no need for them to stand.

"Men," Colonel Hand said, coolly, as if addressing them before a rifle competition. "The entire British Army is coming down the Maidenhead Road. Their intention is to attack our troops in Trenton. Our orders are to delay their advance until nightfall."

He unbuttoned his blue jacket and rested a hand casually on his sword pommel. "We will let the Redcoats come within close range and fire together. I will give the order. Major Miller on the left side of the road will do likewise. Surprise and ambush will make the British break ranks. Remember, no one fires until I give the order." Several of the men grunted their understanding.

Bant remained kneeling and thought about the Colonel's words. He would have preferred to pick them off at a distance but he would follow orders. This time, he was excited. The entire British Army. Let them come. Maybe he would bag a General.

—⁓—

It seemed odd to be crossing the Delaware without the Mariners manning the boats. Yet, on the first day of the new year, having said farewell to Nat, Adam, Solomon, and the others, Will held Big Red's reins and stood on a flat bottomed scow, along with Sergeant Merriam and others from the gun crews. They left Beatty's Ferry on the Pennsylvania shore, swiftly crossed the river and crunched through the thin ice at the Trenton Ferry landing.

"Give me a hand, lad," Sergeant Merriam asked as they disembarked. "I fear the mud will grasp my swollen ankle and pull it from my leg."

"Please, sir. You rode Big Red out of Trenton after our victory. Tis fitting you ride him back into town." Will helped Merriam place his good foot into the stirrup and gave his ample butt a push as the Sergeant hoisted himself into the saddle. With a groan, he eased himself forward as Will nimbly swung up behind him. Big Red plodded up the muddy slope, pulling a captured Hessian brass six-pounder and carrying the two riders.

Slowly, they rode down King Street, the sight of the bloodiest fighting less than a week ago. The studded wheels of the gun carriage clattered on the cobblestones. Big Red shied away and nervously tossed his head at the stench from the remains of the dead Hessian artillery horse, lying where it had fallen. The head and chest were all that remained. Crows perched on the blood stained rib cage, picking at morsels of flesh, oblivious or unafraid of the men marching by. Will looked away as a crow hopped onto the dead horse's head and pecked at the eye socket. He was thankful the dead Hessians who had lain twisted and frozen in the bloody snow were gone, as were the severed limbs that had been stacked like cord wood outside the Anglican Church.

When they reached the open fields at the end of town, Will saw thousands of troops on the rising slopes across the stone bridge over Assunpink Creek, furiously digging and constructing protective dirt barriers. The earthen works were in three parallel lines rising up the slopes running for more than two miles along the creek, with the Delaware River on the Army's left flank. Because of the steepness of the slope, the troops behind each earthen work could fire simultaneously, without shooting into the backs of men in the line in front of them.

Hadley was on the lower part of the slope at the first earthen works. He waved his tri-corn to attract Will's attention. Will clicked his tongue and urged Big Red forward. The horse's massive chest strained as he pulled the cannon, shot and powder up the muddy slope, made more slippery by the feet of the many soldiers who had preceded them.

"Bring that gun in position over here," Hadley shouted. Will guided the horse through the lines and slipped easily from the saddle to the ground. "Your cannon will be part of this three gun battery loaded with canister to greet our British and Hessian guests when they assault the bridge." Will assumed he was talking to Sergeant Merriam.

"You, Sergeant," Hadley said to Merriam, who had moved back to occupy the entire saddle, "will be up the top of the slope with a twelve- pounder. We need your skill to lob cannon balls at the enemy when they establish themselves in the town's brick buildings."

"So, Will." Hadley said smiling, "May Sergeant Merriam ride your horse to his position? You are to be gun commander of this cannon."

Will protested. "I cannot command a gun crew," thinking of how well he and Tyler, Chandler, Webb and Merriam worked together.

"As a soldier you are forbidden to disobey an order," Hadley said affecting a brusque tone. "For your bravery in helping to seize the cannon on King Street, you have been promoted to Corporal and made commander of this fine captured Hessian piece. Tis by order of Brigadier General Henry Knox, himself promoted by General Washington following our victory at Trenton." He removed his tri-corn and affected a mock bow. "I too was promoted to Captain Lieutenant," Hadley said with some pride. "For that very same encounter with this cannon." He patted the brass barrel running his fingers over the embossed coat of arms of the Landgraf of Hesse.

I do not know how to command men, Will thought. Why would they follow me? He began to protest again but Hadley would have none of it. He handed Will a leather pouch with a shoulder strap. "These are your quills, the pricking wire and slow matches. Try one match out to time the burn." He put his hand around Will's shoulder.

"General Knox has confidence in you. Your crew are all experienced men from our own Regiment. They know their roles. Do several dry runs to get them comfortable with each other and you with them. When the British arrive, wait for orders to fire." He patted Will on the shoulder. "You will do fine."

Will tried to smile, to say he would do his duty and live up to the General's expectations of him. But all he could think of was he was now responsible for aiming and firing the cannon. Chandler would have told him to keep busy and concentrate on what needed to be done. Fear and worry would be overwhelmed by the tasks immediately at hand. [4]

His cannon, one of three in the battery, was in the center, at the first line of defense. Looking down, Will saw it was well placed to cover the narrow stone bridge across the creek. The guns could also easily be turned to fire on any of the enemy who sought to wade across the Assunpink on either side of the bridge. The three cannons were set about ten yards apart with no earthen works in front so the muzzles could be adequately depressed. To his right and left, there were other batteries of three guns each. He counted a total of twelve cannons that could be brought to bear on the bridge.

"This battery will fire only grape shot. You will need to give the cannon balls to the batteries higher up," Hadley said, addressing Will, Sergeant Otis and another Corporal Will did not know. "Take any spare canister from those batteries. Get your powder boxes and side boxes situated, then sight in on the bridge," Hadley instructed.

Sergeant Merriam leaned down from the saddle and beckoned Will closer. "There is nothing to the aiming, lad," he said quietly. "You will be firing grape shot. The canister will spread out and do its bloody work for you, like shooting a fowling piece at ducks." He clicked his tongue to get Big Red to move. "Tell your horse to be gentle with an old man," he squealed in fright, turning awkwardly in the saddle. "I cannot afford to be thrown before the British arrive."

Will watched Big Red pick his way sure-footedly up the steep path, with Merriam leaning far forward over the horse's neck, fearful of sliding backwards. Will turned to his crew. "You two. Take one side box with cannon balls. You," he said pointing to a short thick-set man, in a ragged blue uniform, "and I will take the other. Up to the next line and exchange the balls for grape shot. First pair down, start digging an earth wall for the powder boxes." He turned without waiting to see if the men were following his orders and grabbed the rope handle of the side box. They moved past the lines of soldiers steadily digging into the soft muddy earth. Will estimated it was almost two in the afternoon and there was much to be done.

—ᚥ—

Bant exhaled slowly to steady his arm. He was used to firing at distances of more than one hundred yards. He could feel the men on either side of him tensing like snakes coiled and ready to strike. Fifty yards away, the green clad Hessian Jaegers, with their short barreled rifles, followed by whole companies of British redcoats had crossed the creek in a broad line and were angling forward to reform on the muddy road. He watched several soldiers in front of him slog through the brown slop that came midway up their calves. They were almost thirty yards away. As they struggled through the muck, their lines became ragged. Now, they were closer to twenty yards. He could see the pewter buttons on their jackets. Bant sighted on the forehead of one Redcoat and tightened his finger on the trigger. With relief, he heard the shouted command and fired.

The noise of almost six hundred rifles exploding simultaneously together with the roar of the cannons was deafening. Bant reloaded as quickly as he could, terrified a Redcoat would appear on the other side of the log and spear him with a bayonet. When he looked up, the British forward ranks had disappeared. The field was littered with the twisted bodies of men, the red of their blood indistinguishable from the cloth of their coats, some still moaning in agony, others lying grotesquely contorted and maimed in death. Through the smoke he saw the remnants of the advancing troops. They had fled back across the creek and onto the road, breaking up the crisp units of the oncoming marching troops.

But in less time than Bant thought possible, the British had brought up artillery. Their cannons emitted darts of orange flame surrounded by puffs of white grey smoke as the British guns engaged the Americans batteries. Ignoring the incessant roar, Colonel Hand walked calmly among the men of the Regiment.

"The artillery duel will give us a respite. After that, the British will form up in battle order and march at us again. Wait for my order," he said softly. He paused in the midst of a cannonade from the American guns. "We will begin firing at seventy five yards. Pick off officers where you are able. Reload and fire at will but harken for the order to fall back. We will retreat through the woods and make another stand closer to Trenton." The men nodded and Bant found himself doing so also. He felt he was part of the Regiment now and no longer an outsider. He looked to his left at McNeil who gave him a small smile. Bant acknowledged with a slight nod.

After what seemed to Bant only a brief passage of time, the cannons fell silent. Fresh British regiments formed up in battle order in the open, muddy fields on either side of where the bridge had been. Bant heard the drums beating, the high-pitched tone of the fifes and a strange wail of a noise as the Redcoats advanced. Beyond them, along the road, stretching back for miles, Bant could see soldiers and cavalry, and behind them wagons, all waiting to descend on Trenton. He had never seen so many troops before.

The Redcoats waded across the creek and advanced in perfect order, their regimental colors limp in the windless warm afternoon. Bant caught sight of a mounted officer on the side of one of the marching companies, about one hundred yards out. He could make the shot, but decided to wait. He was sighting in on the officer's throat when the man threw up his arms and fell backwards off his horse. Bant had not heard the order to fire and another had beaten him to the kill. There was more sporadic rifle fire and a few others fell. Whether or not they were officers, Bant could not tell. He held his fire until the front line was around sixty yards out and took out the flag bearer, a huge man with the wooden staff held snug in the leather cup of his white cross straps and a large sword on his waist. Bant watched with satisfaction as the man went down as if he had been poleaxed. The Regimental colors fell in the mud. Once again, the British retreated across the shallow creek.

They reformed again and sloshed through the creek water in

a long extended line. Even Bant could see the Americans would be outflanked and surrounded. There simply were too many of them. Colonel Hand ran along their line.

"I need volunteers as skirmishers to delay their advance. The rest of the Regiment, fall back through the woods."

Bant stayed behind with about two dozen others. He shot one of the advancing Jaegers, probing to discover if the Americans were still there in force. The other skirmishers fired off a round and the Hessian scouts retreated. Together with McNeil, he scampered back through the woods, found an impenetrable bramble of bushes overlooking the road and hid. They ambushed another scouting party, killing two before dashing off through the woods again.

They found their Regiment dug in on the south side of a fairly steep ravine. Bant, McNeil and the others filled in the line in the woods and waited. Behind them, less than half a mile away, were the houses of the upper part of Trenton. To their left was a battery of artillery and beyond them, behind a rail fence in an open field, more American troops. The air had turned colder as the sun dipped lower in the clear sky. Bant thought it was somewhere near four o'clock.

The British came down the road. Their extended column of troops and baggage train of wagons, stretched for miles, intermittently blocked from Bant's view by trees and curves in the road. But as far as he could see in the distance, there was a red mass of uniformed men progressing slowly but inexorably toward Trenton.

The American cannons fired first at the lines of troops within range. The battery of six guns was at an angle to the road. The round shot tore huge swaths among the men down the length of the column. The British retreated briefly, reformed in a broad battle line and waited. Bant watched as their field pieces were brought up, laboriously dragged through the mud into position and began firing on the American battery. The front lines of Hessians and Regulars began to advance on the American lines, firing their muskets in steady volleys. Behind them, more troops formed up in the fields, flanking the American position. Bant picked off one Hessian who he thought was an officer, and another in a conspicuously clean uniform.

While he was reloading, Bant heard the order to fall back. He replaced his ramrod, stood up and was surprised to see the Hessian front line was within thirty yards. He scurried back through the woods, past others soldiers forming a rear guard, and onto the muddy road. At the top of the town he glanced back. The advance units of Hessians, Jaegers and red-jacketed Light Infantry were sprinting forward, followed by columns and columns of troops. He raced down one of the broad main streets, a few paces behind McNeil and other riflemen. Continentals moved forward to meet them. They formed a line, three deep and as Bant and the others from Hand's Regiment passed through, they fired their muskets in a concentrated volley, briefly halting the oncoming Hessians.

The Continentals and the troops of Hand's Regiment mingled in a rush through the fields at the bottom of Trenton to escape across the creek. Bant heard a cannon ball fired by an American battery strike the end of the paved street behind him and bounce on the stones, plowing into the enemy's ranks. His last glimpse up the street was of a black-frocked civilian being forced out of a house by several Hessians at bayonet point. Bant scurried onto the bridge, slightly wider than a wagon, the citizen's scream chasing after him. He was jostled against the west rail of the stone sidewall by the crush of troops eager to reach the safety of the American lines. [5]

The men of Hand's Regiment, clambered up the muddy slope above the creek. Cannons further up the incline fired at British troops massing on the flat and muddy fields on the American's right flank. Bant looked down and saw they were directly opposite the stone bridge. Colonel Hand moved among his men, instructing them to fill in the first line of Continentals, hidden behind the freshly dug earthen walls. Bant looked for a place where he could have a good sight line on the bridge.

"Bant." He heard a voice call his name. Looking up, he recognized Will Stoner, the artilleryman who had rescued him at the Raritan. Together they had buried poor Jacobus Brouwer at Kingston before Bant had joined a militia to raid British posts scattered in southern Jersey.

Will was standing next to one of three polished brass cannons, directly opposite the bridge and along the line of the newly dug trenches. Bant felt uneasy being too close to the artillery. They would attract the counter-fire of British batteries. He tentatively raised his hand in greeting and took his place on the line. Two Continentals from another regiment were an arms length away on either side. He saw McNeil's familiar face, two men down on his right. The line was less than forty yards from the bridge. Hopefully, he thought, they were far enough away from Will's battery.

In the dusk of the late afternoon, the British Army stretched before them, concentrated opposite the American lines from the Delaware River to well beyond the bridge. They stood in silence, their Brown Bess muskets at shoulder rest, regimental flags waving in the front line, drums beating slowly and ominously. The soldiers were several rows deep in the lower fields bordering the creek. Their well ordered ranks filled the pastures and grounds behind the houses of the town on both sides. At the top of Trenton, red-coated soldiers stood in full view, in dressed ranks, massed and awaiting orders. The only movement was from the artillery, as the British crews unlimbered the guns and orderlies took the horses to the rear.

"There are ten thousand of them, at least," one of the Continentals said softly. [6]

"And many more coming down upon us from Princeton and beyond," another replied.

Bant, who had seen the long columns of troops, horsemen and artillery stretched out on the road earlier in the afternoon, was struck by how much larger the enemy army seemed when massed in front of them. They were more lethal and menacing. The American lines seemed thin and sparsely manned in comparison. Bant twisted and looked back up the slope. He took some comfort there were two more earthen works to retreat to if the enemy should get across the creek.

"They must attack soon. The daylight is almost gone," one of the Continentals said.

As if in response to the soldier's spoken surmise, the Hessian drums began to beat, the high-pitched hautboys sounded their notes and the powder blue squares of Hessians marched resolutely for the bridge, followed by two broad columns of red-coated British infantry. Bant sighted on the bridge and waited for the order. The Hessians quickened their pace and with a sharp disciplined maneuver, narrowed their solid columns to fit the width of the bridge.

Bant flinched as the American cannons fired, the explosions so loud they seemed to be inside his head. The lead Hessians were mowed down by the grape shot. As those behind them stepped over the bodies of their fallen comrades and reached the middle of the bridge, every rifle and musket within range opened fire. Bant fired at an individual Hessian's head, but the man disappeared in a mass of fallen soldiers. Bant was not sure his shot had brought him down. The Hessians and Redcoats retreated off the bridge and began reordering their ranks in the pasture below the town. This time, instead of wasting a shot on the mass of Grenadiers, Bant aimed for one of the officers reforming the Hessians' ranks. He was a tall mustached man with dark eyebrows. Bant sighted on the man's forehead, just below the brass plated cap and fired. The officer fell backwards, as the Grenadiers began another determined assault on the bridge. They charged forward in disciplined lines, bayonets lowered, quickly covering the short distance to the bridge.

—m—

Will stood to the left of the touchhole. The gun had been swabbed, wormed and loaded with another canvas sleeve of grapeshot. The Hessians and Regulars were attempting their second assault on the bridge. He was aware of heavy musket fire to his right. He resisted the temptation to look north up the creek and see if the British had forded the Assunpink and were turning the line. He forced himself not to panic. He pricked the powder bag and inserted the quill.

"Primed," he shouted, unsure the crew had heard him over the roar of Sergeant Otis's cannon or the volley of musket fire. He lit the slow match, inserted it in the quill and yelled, "Give fire." The brass six-pounder recoiled slightly. The smoke blew away to show a mass of thrashing blue clad bodies in the middle of the bridge. The Hessians retreated a second time.

Spontaneously, the Americans erupted in a loud shout, many of them standing up with their muskets raised above their heads. Will joined in, shaking his fist at the retreating Hessians and the British troops still threatening them from the Trenton side. He was shouting in defiance, daring them to come on and attack, determined to fight. He was not afraid of their masses of uniformed troops, regimental flags, officers on horse and cannons. Then, he realized as gun commander he was acting unprofessionally. He grinned sheepishly at his crew, who were brandishing swabs and wormers and bellowing along with everyone else. [7]

As the gun was being wormed, Will glanced up the line to his right. Clouds of gun smoke blew away from the American side, obscuring the British troops attempting to ford the creek, at a shallow, narrow point. It was getting darker, close to five p.m., he guessed. The Americans had dug in close to the creek bank and were firing almost point blank at the British soldiers.

He was jolted out of his idle observance by the simultaneous whooshing sound of a cannon ball and the screams of agony, as the ball plowed through the soft earthen embankment and into the troops sheltered behind it. The Hessians had set up two cannons next to the last stone house at the bottom of town and were engaging his battery. Their next shot would be more accurate. No time to send a messenger to the batteries further up the slope to concentrate on the enemy artillery. All he could do was hope Sergeant Merriam or some other gun crew would notice and redirect their fire.

Will saw Bant in the trench to his left, crouching down and reloading. He left his cannon and ran along the line of troops.

"Bant," he said breathlessly. "Can you pick off the gun crew?" He pointed at the Hessians hastily reloading. Bant looked down the slope.

"It is less than sixty yards," Bant replied. He gestured to two other riflemen and pointed at the enemy cannon. They nodded and eased their long rifles over the embankment. Columns and columns of British light infantry were rapid marching on the muddy road leading toward the bridge. Will raced back to his brass six- pounder, as one of the gun crew rammed home the grape charge. Will took the long thin wire from his pouch and pricked the canvas charge, inserted the quill, remembered to yell, "Primed," and waited until the first line of infantry was on the bridge. He kept his eye on the advancing troops but in his mind, he tensed himself for a cannon ball from the Hessians.

For the third time, the British charged forward, climbing over the wall of dead and dying Grenadiers. They reached the middle of the bridge when Will lit the match and yelled "Give fire."

The grape shot from his cannon and those in the other batteries and the concentrated hail of musket balls tore into the oncoming troops. It blew the front line away and the next and the one behind that, until the bridge was covered with a mass of thrashing, red-coated bodies. The survivors retreated, many being shot in the back and falling on the road and in the field beyond.

Will glanced over at the Hessian cannon. Five men lay on the ground around it. Only one was moving, his arm flapping across his chest, like a fin of a fish out of water.

It was dark. And silent, except for the occasional musket or rifle shot, preceded by a yellow-orange muzzle flash. Pinpoints of light appeared in the buildings of Trenton. Higher up the slope, fires were lit, indicating where the British troops were encamped. An occasional cry for water or help came from the darkness of the bridge, over the soft constant collective moan of the dying enemy soldiers.

The battle was over. Behind Will, dots of flame appeared as the Continentals lit cooking fires. Will directed the crew to secure the powder boxes before lighting any fires of their own. He walked up the slope, threading between exhausted and hungry groups of soldiers, some lying flat, some sitting with their heads between their knees, simply waiting in the quiet darkness. Tomorrow, the British would attack again, in greater force and with more determination than today. There could be no retreat. There were no boats to carry the Army across the Delaware this time. Besides, the river was choked with huge ice floes. He shivered, whether from relief, the oncoming cold night, or the thought of facing the British army in the morning, he did not know. All he wanted to do now was report to Captain Hadley and find some feed for Big Red. [8]

# Chapter 3 - A Cold Night March

Bant lay barely off the damp ground on a narrow fencing plank, with his feet facing the large bonfire. He clutched his long rifle to his chest, the stock against his shins, the barrel protruding past his head. All around him, the troops had torn down nearby fences and set the cedar rails ablaze to ward off the cold air that had descended on Trenton. A strong northwest wind caused the flames to dance and dissipated their beneficial heat in the darkness. It was the first time he had any rest since awakening early that morning in the woods several miles up the Trenton-Princeton Post Road.

From his uncomfortable resting place, he could see orange pinpoints of light along the slopes at the top of the town and in the fields adjacent to the stone buildings. The sounds of the British army settling down for the night, drifted across the distance separating the two camps. He sensed there were enemy pickets and sentries closer to the bridge and the creek, a little over forty yards below their lines. No matter. He pulled his worn blanket to his throat, made sure his rifle was safe on top of him, tugged his tri-corn tight on his head and closed his eyes. He was desperate for sleep but afraid of the nightmares he always had. Exhausted as he was, he knew they would come.

He awoke struggling to pull away a bony, grimy hand covering his mouth. It smelled of ingrained gunpowder, dirt and smoked meat. "Be still," McNeil hissed. "Your demons have got the better of you. You were screaming in your sleep."

Bant looked up at his companion's weathered face and slowly sat up and looked around. The fire was still burning but lower now. He was not sure how long he had slept. Men were stirring, moving from where they lay.

"The orders are to form up at the far right of our line," McNeil whispered, lowering his head to Bant's ear. "The watchword is silence."

"Where are we going?"

"General Washington did not consult me on his intentions," the tall man replied. "Nor has our Colonel confided in me. Maybe we are to hit the British in the rear with a night attack. Maybe we are off to somewhere else. Until it is clear, I would not trust my pack to the baggage train." [1]

Bant shouldered his knapsack, grabbed his long rifle and followed McNeil up the slope. Others from their Regiment joined them as they moved away from the Delaware, instinctively crouching as they passed behind the bonfires of other troops, so as to cast a smaller shadow from the prying eyes of British pickets. They scurried along in a single line, one behind the other, until they reached a woods. Below them, a few large bonfires burned brightly and beyond their own lines, the Assunpink Creek. They stood and waited silently, leaning against trees and stomping their feet against the cold. The ground was hard beneath Bant's feet. He wiggled his toes in his moccasins. It had dropped at least twenty degrees since he first lay down, he thought. He glanced up at the sky. There was no moon. Only a few stars were visible.

Following a whispered order, they proceeded walking two abreast along a narrow path. It was almost impossible to pierce the impenetrable darkness of the forest. Bant relied on the sounds of the men in front of him to follow along. Feet crunched through the thin ice that had formed over ruts. Hacking coughs, sneezes, spitting of snot or phlegm, and the occasional string of farts punctuated the wordless march as they threaded through the blackness. Bant walked into a freshly cut tree stump, about two feet high, and groaned as he barked his shin. McNeil chuckled softly. "Watch the man in front and see when he steps high or over," he said softly. Bant concentrated on the legs of the dark form in front of him, barely able to distinguish the shape in the gloom.

They crossed a shallow run, the water icy cold up to their ankles. Bant sensed they had turned east but was not certain.

After several minutes, the men bunched up and came to a halt. McNeil grunted and turned on the man behind him. "Shoulder your rifle," he hissed angrily. "You will poke a hole in my back the next time."

They waited in silence, standing in place. A few men tried to lie down and rest but were pulled up by their comrades. One rifleman fell asleep, leaning against a tree and had to be roused as they resumed trudging in the cold. Bant was tired but alert. His fear of nightmares kept his drowsiness at bay. Now that they were well past the British lines, the men spoke in normal tones, although they still moved cautiously through the woods.

"It is not a night attack on the British at Trenton," McNeil said. "We have gone too far for that." There was some commotion ahead and they slowed their pace. A cannon was blocking the road, it's axle jammed against the thick stub of a cut tree, the gun crew trying to back the piece off while the horse, still in its traces refused to move.

"You men, over there. Give us a hand."

Bant, McNeil and a few other dark shapes moved forward and grabbed the lever bar between the spoked wheels. With several of them on each side they lifted the carriage over the stump. Bant stumbled as the horse pulled the cannon forward with a jerk. He turned around and returned to the tree where he thought he had left his rifle. It was not there. Panic-stricken, he looked back at the path, trying to get his bearings.

"Over here," McNeil called and handed Bant his rifle. "It has nice heft to it," he said.

"It suits," Bant replied, offended the man had taken his gun. He brushed the dirt and pine needles from the base of the stock.

"Now that we are far beyond the British lines, you must talk to me as we march," McNeil said. "I am terribly sleepy and fearful I will fall down and be left behind." Bant looked at the tall man to see if he was making fun of him and decided he was not.

"The others behind us will step on you. That will awaken you soon enough," Bant said. He was not a talker and although he felt a sense of comradeship with McNeil, it was not enough to make him a blabber.

"Those behind us, in our regiment are just as tired as I am and would not even notice," McNeil said. "And I heard in camp we are attached to a Pennsylvania Militia unit that made a twelve mile night march from Bordentown. Let us see how awake they are for today's commotion."

Bant let McNeil talk on about the different units he had seen after the battle: tradesmen and artisans from Philadelphia, the remnants of a Maryland Regiment that had served in Brooklyn and retreated down through Jersey, an untried and overeager militia from Mount Holly in southern Jersey. He grunted or coughed occasionally to keep up his side, relieved he did not have to do any more talking. McNeil fell silent and when Bant glanced at him, the tall rifleman was walking forward but angling toward a tree. His eyes were closed. Bant grabbed him by his sleeve and pulled him back onto the narrow path. McNeil looked down at him. His eyes seemed to have sunk further into their sockets beneath his prominent brow.

"You were walking with your eyes closed," Bant said.

McNeil snorted. "The perfect soldier I am. I can march and sleep at the same time." Strange as it seemed, McNeil was actually refreshed after the incident. They passed through the woods, across runs and climbed over fences too numerous for Bant to count or remember. They made good time on a frozen hard road, the ruts solid ridges as if they had been made of stone.

"We are definitely going to Princeton," McNeil said. Bant had thought so since they reached the road. The dawn's light confirmed his sense of direction. It would be a clear day but promised to be even colder than it had been during the night. They crossed an old stone bridge shortly after dawn and followed other troops on to an even wider road. The grass on the flat rolling hills was covered with frost and in places reflected the sun's rays off frozen droplets on the bare shrubs and branches. The sounds of cannon and musket fire broke the peacefulness of the early morning. McNeil pointed to a long low cloud of white powder smoke arising ahead and to their west, less than a mile away.

"There is the beginning of this day's battle," he said, watching the smoke float slowly upward into the sharp blue sky. They waited on the road, listening to the volleys and counter volleys, the booming of cannons and the shouts and piercing cries of men fighting and dying.

—◊—

John Stoner had begun the day pleased Lieutenant Chatsworth and the 16th Light Dragoons were leaving the relatively small garrison at Princeton and joining the entire British Army in Trenton. Every Officer was of the opinion this would be the end for the Rebels and the reinforcements from Princeton would probably arrive too late to participate in the rout. From there, after disposing of the American army trapped near the Delaware, it would be on to Philadelphia and he, John Stoner would make sure he was in the vanguard of the troops entering the Rebel's capital. He would protect the Crown's interests of course, but there would be ample opportunity for self-enrichment in that city, known for the brick mansions of its wealthy merchants.

Chatsworth was riding up front, his horse prancing next to Colonel Mawhood, who, to John, looked ridiculous riding a small brown pony with his two mottled English spaniels darting back and forth across the Post Road to Trenton. A solitary dragoon raced across a field, joined the Colonel, and pointed to the southeast. The column of infantry halted. Mawhood, accompanied by the Dragoon and Lieutenant Chatsworth, rode to a slight rise overlooking a distant woods. They galloped back to the road and suddenly, the entire column turned back toward Princeton, the Light Dragoons racing ahead, the infantry, grenadiers and highlanders all running in quick-time in good order behind them. John was barely able to move his horse off to the side before the Dragoons swept by him shouting about a large Rebel force on their left. He followed as they caught up with the baggage train. The drivers laboriously turned their teams around toward Princeton, partially blocking the road. The Dragoons dismounted, tied their horses to the backs of the wagons, grabbed their muskets and headed on foot, along with the infantry off the highway toward an apple orchard. [2]

John decided the safest place for him would be with the baggage train. He positioned himself so the wagons acted as a screen, blocking the Dragoons' vision of him and watched as the men took positions behind the orchard's fence. The American force was advancing from the lower part of the field. That was enough for him. He rode among the wagons, trying to appear inconspicuous, fearful his bright red coat and clean buff britches would attract the attention of a senior officer. Behind him, the musket volleys and cannon fire intensified.

—⸿—

Bant watched as a cluster of officers, riding hard, galloped down the Saw Mill Road, away from Princeton, toward the sounds of battle. He thought he recognized Colonel Hand but was not certain. The riflemen stood impatiently in the cold. It mattered not to Bant whether they continued on to Princeton or fought the British here. All he wanted was to be in place to kill the enemy. While they waited they were issued half a gill of rum, sprinkled with gunpowder.

Bant had never seen this drink before. He sniffed at it suspiciously.

"It is supposed to give courage," McNeil said, downing the contents of his wooden cup and placing it back in his pack. "I have gone into battle after having the drink and fought when the ration was not issued. It does not seem to matter." Bant shook his head and handed his pewter mug to a rifleman who had left his haversack behind in Trenton. The drums beat the quick advance and they left the road, marching in ranks through a snow-covered field. Ahead, puffs of smoke marked the line of the British troops behind a fence at the edge of a pasture. Remnants of the American troops fled before them across the open ground toward the road. Behind them, other Americans formed up and advanced toward the British. Bant's regiment would strike the Redcoats on their left flank. He unstrapped his pack and left it in a neat line with the others and continued advancing.

At forty yards, on a given order the riflemen stopped, dropped to one knee and fired. Bant was certain he had blown the head off a grenadier, his high bear skin cap seemingly suspended in air for an instant, without the soldier's skull to support it. The British soldiers in front of them, assaulted from this unexpected quarter caved in toward the center of their line and then hastily retreated across the field and toward the bottom of an orchard.

"After them men. Hunt them down. Hunt them down." Bant recognized Colonel Hand's voice but needed no further encouragement. Relentlessly, he and the other riflemen pushed forward, picking off the fleeing Redcoats, pausing to reload behind leafless, barren apple trees, their trunks freshly scarred by musket ball and canister, the ground littered with twigs and branches knocked down by the heavy gunfire.

As the riflemen approached the top of the orchard, where the British had overrun the American lines, they abruptly stopped in dismay. Ahead of them, the blood of the dead and wounded slowly flowed down hill toward them, moving like red rivulets over the smooth surface of the sheen of ice. [3]

McNeil muttered an oath of disbelief under his breath. "This is the devil's very work," he said, raising a hand to his face to ward off the image. Bant gingerly skirted the eerily shimmering streams of blood and climbed through a partially dismantled fence. They passed the corpses of American troops, lying partially hidden behind shattered gun carriages and carts. Many had multiple bayonet wounds and bashed in heads, evidence of no quarter having been given by the British. [4] At the sight the dead American troops, the riflemen pursued the fleeing Regulars with a grim determination. It was now a ruthless hunt for revenge. Ahead of them, the remnants of the British Regiments fled across the snow-covered fields, slipping and scrambling on the ice to escape. Occasionally, a group would form up, turn, fire a volley and then resume their retreat. The pause in their flight, simply gave the riflemen a better opportunity to sight and fire at stationary targets and more time to reload. Bant thought he killed one officer and two Regulars in this fashion. Now Hand's regiment was almost to the Post Road.

Ahead, a Highlander, using his long broadsword as a crutch, was hobbling toward the safety of a stone house to the right of the road leading toward Princeton. Bant aimed first at the sword, intending to knock it from the large man's hand and watch him fall. Instead, he targeted the man's neck. The Scotsman pitched forward and lay still.

The sword would be good booty to sell after the battle, Bant thought, but there was no time to collect it now.

Some of the riflemen pursued the fleeing British across the road and into the wooded fields. Bant, McNeil and others, turned right and raced down the road toward Princeton, eager to cut off the Redcoats before they reached their artillery on a hill, less than a mile from town. Methodically, Bant shot two more, at a distance of less than fifty yards. The British artillery was withdrawing to Princeton. Bant had hoped to get a shot at an artillery officer. Instead, thwarted by their hasty retreat, and absent any other orders, he trotted back the way he had come to retrieve the Highlander's sword.

Will felt trapped. The three gun battery, instead of being in the forefront of the troops, as at Trenton, was blocked by the ranks marching down the Saw Mill Road. Behind them, he heard sporadic musket and rifle fire. Ahead, from his vantage point on Big Red, he could see a massive four story building with a central spire and numerous chimneys. Puffs of smoke from the long rows of windows, their expensive glass shattered, marked the location of British troops inside firing down at the approaching Americans. Two cannons were already deployed in front of the building. As the men on the road spread out on the grounds surrounding the building and prepared to assault it, Will rode Big Red through a wide opening in the fence, quickly dismounted, and together with his crew unlimbered the brass six pounder and wheeled it into position. They were still carrying canister in the side boxes and loaded a charge. It would only be of use, Will thought, if the British soldiers within emerged from the Hall and attacked. Will waited for further orders, unwilling to take it upon himself to fire grape shot at a brick building. Someone shouted the command "Give Fire," and the two cannons already in place in front of the building boomed and white smoke blew toward the building.[5] Will watched in horror as one ball rebounded off the exterior brick and narrowly missed an American officer on horseback. The other shattered a window shutter. American troops stormed the entrance way and almost immediately, white sheets appeared at the windows.

The men cheered as the British troops emerged, stacked their muskets and were marched away under guard. Will guessed there were less than fifty of them, scowling and surly in their countenance, distressed by the curious stares of the Continentals and militia who had poured through the fence and into the compound's yard.

His gun crew had disappeared. They probably had entered the building looking for food, Will thought. He should have maintained control and dismissed them. They were as hungry as he was so he could not blame them for not waiting for his order. He was disconcerted by how the battle had ended, elated watching the captured British soldiers being led away, but uncomfortable with not having played any role in its outcome. He had never even come under fire. For Will, the attack on Princeton had been a series of skirmishes, out of his sight, the noise, gun-smoke and shouted battle cries, always in the distance. The fighting had been either in front or behind him as he rode Big Red pulling the brass six-pounder, which had never been unlimbered until the very end. It all seemed very strange to him. Not at all like the engagements on Long Island, the focused attack down King Street in Trenton, or yesterday, commanding the gun in the long entrenchments on the slopes across from the narrow stone bridge.

The mass of Continentals and militia surged around the large hall and broke into the fine two story building adjacent to it. The men, who had within the last hour, wheeled in formation at a drum roll and advanced in orderly ranks, were now a milling mob, raising mugs full of rum, rolling barrels of flour in the street, flaunting cloaks, hats and jackets of British officers and carrying pieces of furniture plundered from suspected Tory homes.

Will heard a familiar voice calling his name over the noise of the boisterous troops. Captain Hadley, sitting on his chestnut mare motioned for Will to join him.

"I have in mind to pursue the baggage train which left Princeton as we entered, and perhaps capture some necessities for our forces. Are you game?"

Will nodded. "Where are the others?" Will asked looking around.

"The two of us will suffice. More can join us if they wish." He reached into his saddlebag and handed Will a pistol. "It is loaded.

You have one shot. The wagon drivers will not put up a fight and the soldiers are defeated and have no stomach for more action." Will hoped Hadley's assessment was correct. This was his only weapon. His musket was strapped to the gun carriage.

Will spurred Big Red into a trot and they rode through the village and emerged on the post road to Brunswick. Their passage attracted two more from their Regiment and the four of them galloped toward the tail of the British baggage train, visible less than a half a mile away.

—⁂—

John Stoner was at the rear of the long line of wagons, the drivers flogging their oxen, driven by the fear of pursuit by the victorious Rebels. Colonel Mawhood, having escaped with some of his Regiment had found Stoner at the front of the three-mile long caravan and ordered him to be part of the rear guard to protect the baggage train. John had reluctantly left the safety of the lead, cursing the impetuous Colonel under his breath and ridden as slowly as possible along the train back toward Princeton. Why had not they simply proceeded on to Trenton that morning and then with a superior force returned and annihilated the rebel force? No, he thought angrily. Colonel Mawhood with his self important sense of honor had taken on the entire American Army, and now ordered John to place himself in danger. Upon reaching the end of the baggage train, John was surprised to find there were less than a dozen soldiers, shivering and battle weary, riding on the backs of the wagons, their shoulders sagging and heads nodding on their chests. He would not command them to march in ranks. If he did, he would have to lead them and make himself a prominent target. Instead, he turned his horse and positioned himself on the right side of the road, several wagons ahead of the last one and prayed for the train to move faster toward the British garrison in Brunswick and safety.

—⁂—

Captain Hadley led the three of them at a gallop, rapidly closing the distance to the trailing wagons.

"Shout lads. Make it seem as if the furies are coming down upon them."

Will guided Big Red with his knees as he pulled the pistol from his coat and cocked it with one hand. Hadley led their charge at a wagon piled high with new tents, their bright white canvas as clean as the snows in the fields beyond. It was six or seven from the end of the train. The three soldiers on the rear most wagon jumped off, fired their muskets wildly in their direction and ran off into a field, discarding their guns and packs in their panic stricken flight. The others formed a single short line, fired a ragged volley and dropped their muskets and raised their hands in the air. Hadley passed them and he and Will pulled their horses up at the wagon carrying the tents and ordered the driver to halt. The thin, frightened looking Redcoat, quickly dropped the reins and lifted his hands in surrender as Captain Hadley pointed a pistol at his head.

"Turn this wagon around and return to Princeton," he ordered. "You are our prisoner." As the driver turned the wagon, Will saw a red flash of a mounted uniformed figure hidden by the next wagon. Hadley was looking down the road toward Princeton. The lone British trooper edged his horse from behind the wagon, pistol drawn and aimed at Hadley's back.

"Captain. Watch out," Will yelled kicking his heels into Big Red's flanks. His intention was to get between the Redcoat and Captain Hadley. The trooper hesitated, jerked his horse's head and fired an instant later, before fleeing up the line of the baggage train toward Brunswick. Will caught a glimpse of his brother's frightened face beneath a black tri-corn trimmed with a gold band. In an instant, Will gave chase consumed by a fierce anger. John had killed Captain Hadley. His brother drew another pistol from his saddlebag, glanced over his shoulder and without taking careful aim, fired a shot in Will's direction. The distance was closing rapidly. John turned around to see if his pursuer was still there and this time recognized Will. He lowered himself on his horse's neck and desperately beat at its flanks with his whip. Will pressed on, oblivious that he was riding up the line of the train toward its head where there would be more troops. He saw the startled faces of the wagon drivers as he thundered by on Big Red, and glimpsed one of them aiming his musket. He heard a shot, followed by another. He tucked his head low over his left shoulder and saw

Captain Hadley behind him and the crumpled body of the red-coated driver lying sideways on the plank seat.

"Turn back," Hadley shouted. Will reined Big Red in and took one last look at his brother racing ahead, still frantically whipping his horse. He now realized the danger he was in. There were at least fifteen wagons between Will and the one with the tents, each with a driver armed with a musket and fully aware the two Americans were alone. Hadley had drawn his sword and was waving Will forward to him. Big Red easily jumped the two rails of the cedar fence on the side of the post road and he and Hadley galloped across the snow covered fields toward the rear of the baggage train. Puffs of blue smoke appeared along the line of wagons, followed by a dull boom from the Redcoats' muskets. Their fire was ineffective at that range, more a futile gesture of defiance and anger, than a meaningful threat.

They caught up with the captured seven wagons, driven by Redcoat prisoners and escorted by the two others from their Regiment.

"Well, we have put the King's spaniels to flight," Hadley said, as they trotted alongside the rear most wagon. "'Tis a pity we cannot pursue them to their kennel in Brunswick. Those drivers have now discharged their muskets and not yet reloaded. We should return and ask them to also accompany us to Princeton." Will felt a jolt of fear in his stomach that did not entirely fade when Hadley laughed. "No need, Will. We have done enough for one morning."

"That was my older brother." There was a tremor of anger in his voice.

"Who?"

"The one I was chasing. The one who fired at your back."

"You were after him? What were your intentions?"

Will thought for a moment. Hadley slowed his mare and looked at him, waiting for an answer. He realized he had intended to ride alongside and shoot John, not take him prisoner. As he put his thoughts into words, he was surprised his saying so did not disturb him. John was a turncoat and traitor.

"There is no longer any bond of brotherly affection between us. If we meet again, I would not hesitate. If his aim had been better, he would have killed you and then me."

"Fortunately for me, you were there to thwart him." Hadley tipped his tri-corn in salute. "I thank you for that." He reached over and squeezed Will's shoulder. "Do not feel badly. Remember that yours is not the only family divided by this war," he said gently. Will thought perhaps the Captain remembered his long evening talks with Miss Mercy van Buskirk in Morristown. There had been many skirmishes, retreats and battles since those quiet nights before the warmth of the van Buskirk hearth.

In Princeton, all was haste to load the wagons with as much of the captured stores and supplies as possible before the advance units of the British Army arrived from Trenton. Already, the sounds of skirmishing a mile or so down the Trenton-Princeton Road signaled that the Jaegers and light infantry were approaching. Hadley found a building that had served as the mess hall for the British garrison. They pushed their way through a mob of boisterous soldiers gathered around casks, hurriedly filling their canteens with rum. British fare of baked bread, butter, cheese and roast beef, littered the rough hewn wooden tables, having been picked over by the hungry and victorious soldiers. Will wolfed down as much of the beef and bread as he could, stuffed some cheese and bread in his haversack and followed the Captain outside as the drums continued to beat the long roll. They made their way through troops rushing to form up.

He hitched Big Red to the brass six-pounder still standing in the compound of the multi-storied spired building where he had seen the British troops surrender. Together with the rest of the artillery and soldiers from a New England Regiment, Will left Princeton on a road leading northwest from town. Behind them came the wagons carrying the wounded followed by others loaded with wooden boxes of musket and cannon balls, tents, blankets, shoes and cured hides, and barrels of gunpowder, flour, salted pork and beef. The remainder of the army, in good spirits from the rum that also insulated them from the cold wind, straggled out of Princeton. Some troops remained as a rearguard at Stony Brook on the Post Road, to contest the crossing and impede the Redcoats' progress. Another small contingent in Princeton had started bonfires and were burning the captured British supplies the Americans could not take with them. [6]

Will looked back at the thick black column of smoke snaking upward into the cloudless clear blue sky. He wished they could follow the remnants of the British Army toward Brunswick instead of retreating from Princeton. He wanted another opportunity to confront his brother.

# Chapter 4 - The Education of King George

"Get up you Hessian bastards. Raus. Raus." Georg blinked at the militia guard barking at them as daylight streamed through the open cell door.

At least fifty of them shivering in their wet uniforms, hungry, despondent and exhausted by their day long forced march from the Pennsylvania side south of the ferry landing, were crammed into a small room of a brick prison. The rough stone walls were so like frozen blocks of ice, the men could not bear to lean against them for long. They were without blankets or food. Their only source of warmth was to huddle together. The room was dark and men constantly groaned and cursed as others stepped on them. Those able to find a place to lie down did not remain still, but incessantly, almost insanely, scratched at their thighs and stomachs. Worse than lice, the thawing wet wool of their breeches and shirts created a ferocious itching that was not relieved even when their broken finger nails drew blood. The floor was covered with a thin layer of straw and in one corner was a chamber pot, which by dawn was overflowing. The soldiers closest to the pot sat or lay in the excrement of their comrades, too weary or cold to care.

Georg stood up and flexed his stiff knees. His toes were numb in his worn square black shoes, his bare ankles chaffed raw against the inside of his canvas gaiters. He was certain the skin of his feet was cracked and covered with congealed blood. He hoped he would not lose his toes to frostbite. The thought of them being amputated scared him and he wiggled his toes vigorously to keep the blood flowing. As the prisoners stumbled into the clear light of early morning, the militia by gestures and angry commands directed them to line up in files, in preparation for the morning march. Some of the men, who knew a few words of English, shouted for bread. Georg added his voice, although his throat was dry and scratchy. "Brot. Brot," he heard himself squawk. "Und wasser," he added. Others took up the cry. Soon, all two hundred of them were calling in unison for bread and water.

The militia escorting them encircled the prisoners and made a show of fixing their bayonets and aiming their muskets. Georg saw his friend Christoph. He pushed through the shouting men until he reached him.

"They treat us like dogs," Georg said, over the yelling. "This is not what Andreas dreamed of. Surrender indeed. For this? What a fool he was," he said of their dead friend.

Christoph pointed to an ox drawn wagon lumbering toward them over the ice encrusted cobblestones. One of the militiamen jumped up on the back of the wagon and began throwing loaves of bread onto the snow covered ground. The prisoners broke ranks and rushed forward, scrambling eagerly for the food. With no officers to restrain them they were an undisciplined mob. Georg as a Corporal felt an obligation to attempt to maintain some sort of order.

"We are not animals," he shouted. "Form lines," he yelled at the men around him. The hungry prisoners ignored him and continued to fight each other for the bread. Some who had snatched a loaf shared with their close comrades. Others held on to the precious food for as long as possible, wolfing down as much as they could before they were knocked down and the bread ripped from their possession.

Christoph had a chunk of bread in his hands. He tore it in two and offered half to Georg. The bread was stale and crawling with weevils. It had a heavy musty odor. Georg forced himself to chew slowly and swallow it.

"Wasser.Wasser," the men cried. One of the militia pointed at the muddy snow on the ground. He bent down and scooped it up and made a gesture of eating it from his hand. As a few of the prisoners picked up the snow, the militia man made a point of dropping his pants and pissing on a relatively clean white patch in front of him. He laughed and tied his breeches, joking with the other militia and pointing from the yellow stain to the Hessians eating snow.

They left the town, surrounded by their guards and led by three militia officers, mounted and proudly prancing ahead as if they had captured the Hessians single-handedly. Their buff colored breeches were clean and the brass buttons on the pristine fabric of their dark blue coats were as bright as gold coins. It was obvious to Georg these militia officers had never been in the field. After a half hour, they were ordered off the road and permitted to rest on the cold frozen ground. Georg collapsed against a tree and tucked his bare hands under his armpits to warm them. Christoph leaned against him, furiously scratching one leg.

"What will happen to us?" Christoph asked. "Will they shoot us?"

"If God has not forsaken us, we will remain prisoners for the duration of the war. Where we will be held is my concern. Do the Rebellers have prison ships? I could not bear to be kept in some dark hold below the water line, my feet gnawed at by rats, never knowing whether it was day or night out."

"I wish someone had a bible. Mine was in my pack, taken from me at Trenton."

Georg looked at Christoph. He had not been one of the more religious men in their Company, more prone to taking the Lord's name in vain or complaining about the length of the compulsory services. Hardship changed men's characters, even their beliefs, he thought.

More Hessian prisoners, these from Colonel Rall's Regiment straggled up the road, prodded by the bayonets of the militia escorting them. Some limped along, others who seemed too weak to walk on their own, had their arms draped over a comrade for support. All looked bedraggled, dirty and defeated. If Colonel Rall could see his proud Grenadiers now, Georg thought, he would weep with shame. He had heard the Colonel had been killed at Trenton. Better fortune for him. He wondered bitterly if the other captured Hessian Officers were enjoying the hospitality of Rebeller Officers before a warm fire in some nearby town.

He heard shouted commands of "Raus. Raus," followed by the familiar English words he had learned since being captured, "you Hessian bastards." The men struggled to their feet and joined the soldiers from Rall's Regiment on the road. What a piteous procession of silent beaten men we make, Georg thought. And there are so many of us.

After an hour's march the prisoners at the head of the columns passed the word back they could see the spires and rooftops of Philadelphia, the grand city of the Rebellers. We were that close, Georg thought. Instead of winter quarters in Trenton, if our Officers and the British General who paraded so pompously before the Rebellers' artillery on the banks before Trenton had led us properly, we could have crossed that narrow river and captured this place.

As they entered Philadelphia, large crowds of its citizens packed the main thoroughfare, gawking and pointing at the Hessians. Additional regular troops formed a barrier between the people and the prisoners. The populace did not seem hostile but simply curious to catch a glimpse of the Hessians. Georg looked around at the fine three story brick buildings on the broad streets and the people along their route, the men well-dressed in long black coats with silver buttons, the women in cloaks, some with fur collars turned up against the cold wind, their hands hidden in woolen muffs

Christoph gave voice to Georg's thoughts. "There would have been plenty of booty and plunder in this place," he said ruefully. Georg thought back to his Regiment's rampage in Brunswick and the entry in the Quartermaster's ledger of his share for that, as well as the Rebellers' captured cannons and supplies in New York. It was all gone now. He would not return to his homeland a wealthy man, that is if he survived and returned at all.

They made a right turn on to a narrower cobble stoned street, as the men from Colonel Rall's regiment continued straight. The column bunched up and Georg heard shouts ahead. A group of women, less prosperous looking than those the prisoners had passed entering the city, strands of their gray hair protruding from under their bonnets, screeched at the Hessians as they shuffled by, pelting them with filth and kitchen garbage and an occasional stone. Georg was in the file closest to them and raised his arm to fend off a barrage of fish heads, offal and rotten vegetables. The militia seemed unable or unwilling to quell the women's anger, their only reaction being to hurry the prisoners along. One woman easily eluded a guard, hurled the contents of a chamber pot at the head of a Hessian and then, still not satisfied, let loose a huge gob of phlegm catching him in the ear. The prisoner plodded on, not even stopping to rub the filth from his uniform. Georg could not understand any of the shouted words and wondered why these women hate them so? [1]

They stopped in front of a long low building, surrounded by a four-foot high rusting iron fence. It was a warehouse by a river. The metal gates were thrown open and the one hundred or so prisoners were herded into the yard. After the gates were closed, they discovered the building's doors were locked. There was no other choice but to sit on the ice-covered ground, their backs against the brick walled building and wait. Four militiamen stood at the closed gates, occasionally drinking from their canteens. From their laughter and joking, Georg knew they were drinking alcohol. He wet his lips, recalling the taste of the brandy coursing down his throat and warming his innards that they had been given in Trenton with their last hot dinner before the Rebellers' attack.

By late afternoon, as the sun set low in the winter sky accompanied by a bitter chill to the air promising a brutally cold night, Georg was convinced the Rebellers intended to starve and freeze them to death. He was angry at his Officers and angrier still at the men around him, as stupid and docile as dumb beasts of burden, shitting where they stood or sat, listless with no spark of human intelligence on their weary, grimy, expressionless faces.

"This will not do," Georg muttered and gestured for Christoph to follow him.

The two of them walked around the yard, peering into the eyes staring out from the unshaven faces of the men from their Regiment. Georg was searching for those who had good strong voices. He assembled eight of them in a curving row in the center of the compound facing the building. They began to sing. They sang the Psalms they all had sung during the terrifying voyage across the North

Sea to overcome their fear. As their voices rose and echoed off the building wall, a few of the prisoners staggered to their feet and joined in. More did the same, until there almost all one hundred of them were standing, some with bowed heads, praising the Lord in words they had known since childhood. The few Hessians remaining on the frozen ground were too physically weak or too defeated in spirit to make the effort.

In the middle of one Psalm, the men facing Georg and his makeshift choir, fell silent. A few pointed at the gates. Georg heard the high-pitched grating as the cold metal squeaked in protest at being opened. Several wagons loaded with straw and barrels entered the compound, accompanied by their militia guards and two mounted officers. One dismounted and unlocked the padlocked doors to the building. The militiamen, by gesture and shouts, directed some prisoners to unload the straw and carry it inside while others rolled the barrels into the dim long room.

Torches were lit. The building was empty except for large stones stored at one end. The Hessians spread the straw laterally down both long walls. The barrels were set upright in a row and left at the entrance. The prisoners, as directed by the militia, lined up in the center on the dirt floor path between their straw bedding and the barrels. They were ordered forward in groups of ten. This time, under their guards' watchful eyes, there was no mad scramble for food. Each man was given hard biscuits and a piece of salt pork and every five men shared a ration of watered cider from a single mug. That night, again without blankets, they slept on the straw covered floor, shivering in the cold dank moisture of the warehouse.

By Georg's count, they remained in their makeshift warehouse prison for three nights. During the day, they were permitted to walk around the yard. At night the doors were barred from the outside and militiamen were posted at the gate.

On the first full day after their arrival, at mid-morning under a clear but cold winter sky, several women approached the fence. Their heads were covered with white embroidered caps under the hoods of their dark cloaks. Their skirts were a plain black. They carried baskets. They pulled back the cloth covers embroidered with colorful patterns of red, green and yellow, to reveal freshly baked breads, chunks of hard cheese, small dried and salted little fish, their eyes glazed at the end of their thin silver bodies, dried apples and even an occasional pie or meat patty. The prisoners, responding to the generous and modest demeanor of the women, lined up along the fence, with their hands outstretched between the metal bars, and waited for the women to divide up the food and place a piece of this or that in each outstretched palm. When it was Georg's turn, he instinctively wiped his hand on his breeches before offering it. When the woman gave him a small piece of bread and cheese, he bowed slightly and said "Danke."

"You are welcome," she replied, acknowledging his thanks and moved on. [2]

The second day more women came, with more food. Now the men smiled and conversed in either German or in broken English. Georg learned from Christoph two phrases, "good morning," and "God bless you," which he repeated to every woman distributing food through the fence.

The nights were still unbearably cold without blankets or a warming fire. They awoke stiff in limb and shivering in their worn uniforms, thinking of the blankets and coats they had lost and the thin, straw filled mattresses of their barracks. At the time, they had cursed their winter quarters in Trenton where the wind blew the powdered dust of deteriorating caulking through large clefts in the stone. Now, they longed for those drafty barracks.

The anticipated visits by the women prompted the prisoners to brush the straw and dirt from their jackets and pants, attempt to tie their pigtails more neatly and to smooth out their ragged mustaches. To Georg, this grooming was a comical but welcome return of the prisoners' recognition of their own humanity. He had no illusions how they all looked. One only had to take a deep breath inside the warehouse to know how filthy and foul they smelled. Still, the women came and the men remained polite and grateful for their generosity.

Early in the morning, on the fourth day, the prisoners were assembled in the yard. Georg stood straight and tall under the appraising gaze of a pudgy man in a rich dark brown wool coat who walked along the line. When he nodded to a soldier next to him, the militiaman would point at the prisoner and beckon him to step forward. Georg was one. He saw Christoph was another. At the end of the inspection, twenty-two men had been singled out. They were marched to a small shed within the gates and compelled to stand outside in the cold. Georg had no idea what they had been selected for. He did not think they were to be executed. The British used the Rebeller prisoners to dig graves and construct defenses. That would not be so bad, he thought, if they were away from any fighting and given proper rations. When it was his turn, he entered the shed. A clerk sat at a small table upon which were a ledger, a quill, an inkstand and a candle. Georg was surprised when the soldier, who he thought was standing guard, addressed him in heavily accented German which sounded more Dutch, asking for his name, rank and Regiment.

Georg replied and the soldier spoke to the clerk who duly noted down the information.

"Craft or trade," the soldier asked. Georg hesitated.

"Tailor? Blacksmith? Carpenter?

Georg shrugged. "Farmer," he replied and sensed that was the wrong answer. If he had named one of the crafts, maybe he thought they would send him to work indoors, in a warm shop in a town. It was too late to change his answer.

"That is all," the soldier said.

"What is this for?" Georg asked. "Where are you taking us?"

"I am not here to answer questions from you. You will find out, soon enough." He waved the back of his hand dismissively and Georg ducked under the low entrance and went back into the yard. He saw Christoph waiting and pretended to stumble as he passed. "Tell them you know a trade or craft," he whispered to his friend, before moving down the line. [3]

—⁂—

James Kierney led Zak, his family's ox, pulling a sled with the two heavy stones he and his father had levered from the snow covered field, toward the log and slat bridge over the little creek that ran below their house. James was almost eleven. He favored his mother's side with his sandy hair, thin bones and bright blue eyes, as well as his eager, quick manner. He saw the wagon in the distance, bumping up the rutted road, being driven by a soldier with two more militia on the plank benches. His keen eyes made out the bare heads of three men on the wagon floor. It must be a bumpy ride, he thought to himself. Everyone knew sleds rode smoother than wagons in the winter.

"They are coming," he shouted exuberantly to his father who was still in the field, selecting more boulders to make the abutments for the new bridge. Thomas Kierney waved to his son in acknowledgment. He was a solidly built compact man, more square then lean, with a broad back, well muscled from the hard labor of farm work. Unlike his young son, who bounded everywhere like a dog on the scent of a rabbit, Thomas moved with measured efficiency, as if he knew by conserving energy, he would have strength in reserve available for the next task. His face matched his physique, strong with black eyebrows over equally dark eyes, a nose like an arrowhead and a stern thin mouth. But at home with his wife and children, the fierceness of his gaze would disappear, his tight lips would loosen into a smile and his eyes would soften into a look of pride and love.

James urged Zak to move faster, anxious to get a first look at the Hessian prisoners. Father had said they needed an extra laborer if they were to get the bridge built by spring. And there was the mill to be constructed. And now, real Hessians were coming. One would be staying with them on the farm until the war was over. James had no idea when that would be but perhaps they could finish the bridge and do most of the stonework for the mill before the Hessian would have to leave.

James had heard stories about them, how tall and strong they were, how they were fearsome soldiers with terrifying mustaches. They used bayonets as long as swords with which they speared the enemy and tossed them over their shoulders as easily as father pitched hay into their bark-roofed barn. General Washington and the army had defeated them at a big battle at Trenton and captured more than one thousand of them. James imagined the General himself riding on his big white horse leading the Americans forward in a furious charge toward the Hessians who threw down their muskets and ran away in panic.

By the time James had reached the road, the wagon, pulled by two sway- backed horses whose every rib and bone protruded under their shaggy coats, was rounding the bend toward their farm. He urged Zak on, and then impatiently left the ox to plod the familiar path on his own, and ran ahead shouting to his mother and sisters that the Hessians were coming. His father came through the field and joined his wife and family who had emerged from their plain dirt floor wooden cabin. Smoke curled upward from the clay and stick wooden chimney he and his father had repaired in the early fall. No smoke leaked from the seams. His father was so good with his hands and knew how to make anything, James thought proudly.

They stood together, his mother, his sister Sarah, who was eight, her arms folded under her wool cloak to keep warm, his baby sister, Rachel, clutching on to her mother's long skirt and peering out from behind her legs, at the wagon jolting up the rutted road.

The soldier who was driving, tipped his tri-corn to Hannah Kierney. The two other militiamen climbed over the sides of the wagon and stretched their legs.

"Be you Thomas Kierney?" the driver asked, rather formally James thought, since he must have known to come up this road.

His father nodded.

The driver unfolded a worn piece of paper from his tunic. "There are three prisoners remaining. You have your choice. One is destined for your neighbor to work in his sawmill. The last one to a farm I hope to reach by the end of the day. I will need you to sign this paper of your acceptance."

The driver stepped down and walked with Thomas to the rear of the wagon. James followed more curious than apprehensive. He felt Sarah slip her hand in his and hold it tightly. Three men were hunched together, cold and shivering. He had expected them to be in uniform. Upon closer inspection, he could see a few pewter buttons on one of the men's jacket that used to be a light blue. Their breeches were torn and grey. The men all had scraggly mustaches that drooped down and wild rangy, uncombed hair. They had no hats and one was barefooted. James was disappointed. He had expected them to be all spit and polish with bright red uniforms and shiny black boots, like the Redcoats he had heard the adults describe.

"To a man, they do not look as if they could hold an axe," his father said, appraising them as if he were purchasing a horse. The driver gestured impatiently to the back of the wagon. "Make your choice. It matters not to me."

"I need one strong enough to do a decent day's work, not a useless mouth to feed in wintertime." He took off his round slouch hat and scratched idly above his pigtail.

"Thomas," his mother said softly. "Remember your bible. These are miserable wretches in need. We must help them and that alone will be our reward. The rest may follow."

"Whether they are strong enough or weak, is not my concern," the driver said. "If you are not so inclined to sign for one, I will be on my way."

James watched his father eyeing two of the Hessians. He motioned with his hands palms up for them to stand. Only one did, grabbing the side-board for support. He stood unsteadily in the back of the wagon, his hands stiff against his thighs. He was tall, taller than Thomas Kierney but so emaciated his hands seemed larger in proportion to his thin forearms. He looked at James' father, then to his mother, the two girls and finally his eyes, deep in their sockets, rested on James. And he smiled, a weak thin smile, but one nevertheless.

"He will do," his father said, reluctantly. James stepped forward and offered the Hessian soldier his hand to help him down. The man smelled worse than the barn before James cleaned it out of the accumulated goose shit and the manure from Zak, Daniel their only horse, and their cow, Abigail. The man declined James' help and eased himself off the wagon. He stood brushing the straw from his clothes and stomping his feet. James saw the blackened toe nails on the prisoner's left foot protruding through his worn shoe.

His father invited the driver inside, first pointing to an iron boot scraper. James followed and he and Sarah brought mugs of hot mulled cider to the two militiamen guarding the prisoners. His mother took down a spare mug and gave it to James to take outside. James carried it to the prisoner his father had selected. The man clutched the warm pewter in his dirt encrusted hands and held it up to his cheek, savoring the warmth. "Danke," he said to James over and over again, taking small sips. "Thank you," he said tentatively pronouncing the "th"as a D. James smiled. "It is thank you." The prisoner held out his mug for more and when James returned with it filled, the man offered it to his two comrades, still lying listlessly in the wagon.

The driver climbed back up on his seat and flicked the whip to get the two horses moving. The Langleys, their nearest neighbor's farm was a few miles away. They had a sawmill and one of these Hessians was destined to work there. At church this Sunday, he would find out from Oliver Langley, who was only a bit older than James, about their Hessian.

"His full Christian name is Georg Frederich Englhard," his father said to the family. The Hessian raised his head and looked at Thomas. "Ja.Ja. Mein name ist Georg."

"I will call you King George." The Hessian looked puzzled. "It is to remind us you were hired by a tyrant monarch to bring war to our land." Thomas Kierney pointed at George's chest. "You have caused us to fight. And now you will work until we are free of King George and his minions." The Hessian shook his head, not understanding the torrent of words.

Thomas turned to his son. "Show him to the barn. He will sleep there with Zak and Abigail for company. He looked at George's flimsy shoes. "Give him the old wooden clogs on the shelf next to Zak's stall. I will be down in the field. We will see if King George can load stones on our sled."

James led the Hessian to where his father was working. The old worn nut brown colored jacket his mother had taken out of their cedar clothing chest was too short and Georg walked awkwardly in the wooden clogs that were too small. Thomas Kierney was using a broad bladed pick axe to dig the frozen dirt away from a large flat shaped boulder in the ground. Once the bottom of the stone was exposed, James would position the iron gripping claw his father had made, attach the rope from the claw to Zak's yoke and while the ox pulled, they would use the tall iron bar to pry the stone out of the frozen soil. He watched as his father handed the pickaxe to Georg.

Georg took several swings, feeling the wooden handle twist in his hands as the blade hit the hard earth. He tried to find a rhythm but he had no power in his shoulders. Sharp pains surged through his stomach and he barely had time to turn away before he vomited. The warm cider that had tasted sweet when he drank it, now was bitter as he bent over and threw up. As he straightened up he felt the surge in his bowels. Quickly, he took a few steps, squatted and a foul smelling stream of liquid shit splattered on the snow.

James covered his nose as his father shook his head in disgust.

"I might have known the prisoners the Army would send as laborers would be suffering from the bloody flux or worse." He scraped snow over Georg's shit with a shovel. "Walk him back to the house, James. Tell your mother King George is sick. She will know what to do."

He took up the pick axe again. "Best to move him into the forge shed for now. Light a fire to keep him warm. Be sure to put down straw first. No need to foul our workplace." He glanced at the grey sky to the west. "If it snows tomorrow, we will be in the forge making nails."

James led Georg to the low slanted roofed shack. He left him standing next to the raised stone rectangular fireplace, ran to the barn and brought back several sheaths of clean straw. He spread them next to the large leather bellows attached to the hole in the stones. The Hessian lay down and closed his eyes.

"Do not worry Georg. My mother knows many cures, and she is especially good with stomach maladies." The Hessian shook his head weakly, to indicate he did not understand.

"I will be back in moment. We need to start a fire. You must stay warm."

James returned shortly with a tin firebox filled with embers. He put the glowing charcoal in the hearth and began feeding it tinder, then small branches and finally medium sized logs. He worked the leather bellows a few times, leaning on the handles with all his weight and was rewarded with bright flames. He glanced at Georg who had clasped the jacket around his throat and was shivering.

Hannah Kierney came in carrying an old worn blanket and a bowl of hot porridge.

"Make sure he eats it slowly, James. It will help him keep the food down."

She moved the rake and hoe that were leaning on the wooden bench waiting to be repaired, and put down a mug.

"Have him drink this after he finishes the porridge. I added more worm seeds and a dash more of whiskey than usual. He is a big man and needs a strong dosage."

After his mother left, James was able by gestures and repeating the word "slowly," to get the Hessian to eat all of the porridge. Then he offered him the mug. He watched the man sniff at it and then look suspiciously at the contents.

"It is whiskey and garlic, and some rhubarb to make it sweet to cover the taste of wormseeds," James said. "Mother gives this to us when we have worms or the bloody flux. I know it tastes bitter but you must drink it." [4]

Georg looked at the contents one more time, tipped his head back and drank it all. He handed James the empty bowl and mug, took the thin blanket and wrapped it around his shoulders and leaned against the fire warmed stones of the forge. "Danke," he said. "Dank you." He closed his eyes and sighed and fell asleep sitting up, probably made drowsy by the whiskey, James thought.

When returned later in the afternoon with Sarah, Georg was lying on his bed of straw, the blanket drawn up close around his throat, his bare feet sticking out below. His soles were caked with accumulated dirt and blood, with irregular patches of pink skin where the scabs had fallen off.

"He is filthy and smells badly," Sarah said, still clutching James' hand.

"Once he is well," James said authoritatively, "Mother will want us to bring the washing tub to the forge. We can heat water here and he can bathe himself clean."

"I am afraid of him. Do you think he will kill us?" his sister asked, peering at Georg's face and closed eyes.

"No. No, he will not. Father would never have brought him here if he thought that."

"Do you think he is dead now?" Sarah asked. "He is not moving."

James watched for signs of breathing. "He is alive. See, his chest. He is weak and sick. Mother will make him well again. She has the skill." He immediately regretted saying that. Sarah had been six when their little brother died. It had been Sarah's duty to take care of Phillip once he was old enough to crawl. She kept him clean, watched over him as he learned to walk and played games with him, while their Mother did her household chores. Phillip followed Sarah so closely he was like her shadow Two winters ago, Phillip developed a hacking cough. It got worse, despite Mother's medicines, and one morning he was blue and dead. They had buried him in the little clearing next to the barn, a few months shy of his third birthday.

"Do not cry Sarah." He put his arm around his sister's shoulders as the tears came to her eyes. "The Pastor says Phillip is in a better place."

"I wish he was back here with us," she sniffled. "I am afraid we will come here and find the Hessian cold and dead, like Phillip was that morning."

In the bitter darkness before dawn, James returned to the forge shed before doing his chores in the barn. He opened the door cautiously, anxious that Sarah's fears might be true. He smiled to see Georg leaning against the warm stones, holding his hands before the low flames and putting them to his face and cheeks. The Hessian waved in greeting and tried to rise, at the same time gesturing he needed to relieve himself. James helped him outside where Georg squatted modestly behind the shed and dropped a stain of liquid shit tinged with blood. James got him settled back on his bed of straw, shivering again under his blanket and built up the fire.

"I will be back Georg. I have chores to do."

James fed and watered Zak, Daniel and Abigail, scratching the cow on her broad bony forehead before milking her and carried the wooden bucket to the house.

"Georg still has the bloody flux," he said to his mother.

"No work for him today, Thomas," she said to her husband. "He is too weak." His father grunted, finishing his breakfast of bread, cheese and egg. "James. Eat your food quickly. We will move stones before it snows and then keep King George company in the forge."

James looked longingly at the iron griddle in the fireplace where he usually toasted his bread, sopping up the lard. Instead, he cut himself a piece off the loaf and wolfed it down cold with a hunk of cheese.

"Sarah," he heard his mother say as he wrapped his scarf around his throat. "Take this bowl of porridge to Georg. I will make another wormseed drink and bring it to him shortly."

James saw the fear in his sister's eyes. He waited outside until she emerged with the wooden bowl, walked with her to the forge shed to show her Georg was alive and then ran exuberantly through the snowy fields, leaping over the stones and brush to be with his father.

That afternoon, as the snow swirled around the forge shed, James operated the bellows while his father heated the nail rods and hammered them to a point. He inserted the glowing rod in the wooden nail header, and snapped it off where he had dented it for the nail's length. The room resounded with the clang of the hammer hitting the still hot metal.

"We are making crimped head nails," James said to Georg, "to use in the flooring for our cabin. We will have a real wood floor soon. We made some planks ourselves this fall and got the rest from our neighbors, the Langleys." He grunted as he lifted the bellows handle and the fire blew hotter for the next rod. "Father can make three hundred nails in an hour's time," he boasted, looking over his shoulder at Georg. The Hessian was sitting up, his face flushed, watching them with interest. It was dark outside when his father stopped and said it was time for dinner.

"See all the nails we have made, Georg." James handed one to the Hessian who took it in his long begrimed fingers, turned it around and held it up to the firelight. James studied his face.

"Nagel," he said to James. "Nagel."

"Nail," James responded. "It is a nail we made. Father and I." He pointed to his father and then to himself. "We made many of them today."

"With all your chatter, James, King George will learn English soon enough."

The Sabbath fell on the third day after Georg had arrived. Before they left for church, James accompanied Sarah when she brought Georg his breakfast.

"My mother makes this special breakfast for us on Sundays," James said. "She said you are well enough to have some." He nudged Sarah who held out the basket and pulled the cloth back to reveal warm baked oval shaped cakes. "Tell Georg how it is made, Sarah."

"He does not speak English. There is no purpose to it," she said petulantly.

"Do it, or I will not accompany you to the forge anymore," James threatened.

"All right." Sarah smoothed her Sunday dress as if she were going to read from the Bible. "It has milk, eggs, sugar, cornmeal and flour. Our mother bakes it on the griddle and it is delicious with blackberry jam. Here, see we brought you some."

"Dank you," Georg said after tasting one of the cakes. He dipped it in the small plate of the dark sweet and nodded in appreciation. "Das ist gutt."

"For the first time you are eating well," James observed. "Perhaps you will be better soon. We must go to church and will be back at dark. There is enough firewood here to keep you warm." He motioned to the stack of small logs in the corner.

Georg heard the two of them laughing as they ran back to the house. It had been a long time since he had heard that pleasant sound. He opened the shed door and stood in the frame, the thin blanket wrapped around his bony shoulders, watching the family leave in a large sled, the man and boy up front, the boy holding the reins for the horse, the mother and the two girls, covered in blankets in the rear.

He knew with certainty, that if he did not get well and make himself useful, the man would send him back. Georg shivered as he closed the door, more from fear than the cold. He would not survive in prison. He lay on his bed of straw, close to the warm stones and thought about this family. He wondered where they were going and then recalled the boy had said it was Sunday. And church. Many of these English words sounded like his native language. If he guessed at their meaning, he could understand more. Church like kirche, Sunday like Sonntag, father like vater. He drowsed off, sleepy from the effects of the whiskey in the medicine the woman made for him.

When he awoke the sun was high in the clear blue sky. Georg squeezed his feet into the clogs, wrapped the blanket around the threadbare jacket and slowly shuffled the short distance on the snow-covered path to the family's cabin. It took much of his strength and he leaned against the door before opening it. He was surprised to see a floral design scratched on the packed dirt surface. Spirals bordered the large rectangular room. In the center, around the stout wooden legs of the two planked tables and benches, delicate patterns of branches and wide oval leaves circled and wove their way across the floor.[5] The fire was low in the large fireplace. Several tongs, pokers and a small shovel for ashes hung from the mantel. One of those long Rebeller rifles, like the one that had killed his friend Andreas, rested on iron hooks embedded in a ceiling beam above the fireplace. George gazed at it for a while. He could flee with the rifle, some powder and ball and perhaps make it through the wilderness to a British outpost in New Jersey. If there were any remaining, he thought. First he would have to cross that river.

And then what? Even if he successfully escaped, all that awaited him was more battles, constant marching, short rations, sentry duty, patrols and ambushes by the Rebellers. The British had left the Hessians in forward positions while they went into comfortable winter quarters in fine brick homes in Brunswick, the large port city of New York and on the Eden-like island where they had first disembarked.

No, Georg said out loud. I have no more desire to fight for these British. He was surprised by the vehemence in his voice. I do not want to hurt people like this family who are taking care of me. He thought remorsefully of the looting he had done in Brunswick, the wanton destruction and slaughter of animals, leaving people with little or no provisions for the winter. No more he said to himself again and felt relieved by his decision and comforted by the domesticity of this simple room, with its evidence of a peaceful farm life. It reminded him of his own home, a humble one room stone farmhouse with a thatched roof, an attached wooden barn, the smell of smoke and his mother's cooking mingling with the earthy odors of their plow horse and cow. What had Andreas said? These Rebellers owned their land. The farm on which his father had built their home and where they worked so hard to plant and grow their wheat and hay barely supported them and could be taken away by their Landgraf. He would ask the man about land ownership, when his English was better.

Georg knew what he must do. He had to make himself useful so the man would keep him as a farm hand. He surveyed the room. A box to the left of the fireplace was half filled. He would bring the split wood he had seen stacked alongside the barn and refill this box. He would do it slowly, bringing only as much as he could easily carry and he would be careful not to disturb the floral design on the floor. Then he would go back and rest in the forge. Afterwards, if he felt strong enough and before the family returned, he would clean the empty stall of the horse and those of the ox and cow as well. And maybe next Sunday, they would take him to Church. Even if it was all in English, he wanted very much to worship in a house of God.

# Part Two
# Winter Quarters

# Chapter 5 - The Happiest Man in Camp

William hurried from the log hut along the snow packed path to Morristown, reluctantly leaving the warmth of the fireplace and the company of the artillery men. Eight of them lived in a cramped fourteen by fifteen foot space with one door and no windows. It was built of notched logs, chinked with clay, stones and moss to keep out the frigid winter air. The first month or so, after reaching Morristown in early January, had been spent in the thick forests, chopping down trees, trimming the branches and hauling logs to the fields allocated to the army outside of the town. Those skilled in the use of axes, like Will, shaped the trunks into beams and rough hewn doors. Others carried stones to make the fireplace and chimney.

With the eaves only six feet and some inches high, the low roofs were put in place quickly and once up, kept the heat inside, as well as the smoke from cooking fires. The soldiers, used to sleeping in the barns and sheds with the animals, or outside in the bitter cold, either in the few dozen tents captured from the British, or under the overhangs of churches, mills and barns, had worked eagerly and moved into the huts before they were completed. Their shelters were randomly spaced in pastures bordering what had been the woods. All that remained of the stands of trees were stumps, some three feet high, like gravestones in a cemetery, marking the death of the forest.

Will had been one of the few to move from better to worse quarters. Newly promoted Captain Lieutenant Hadley had arranged for Will to be with him at the Ford house where they had once stayed when they brought the wounded to Morristown during the long retreat through New Jersey. The Captain, when he was not occupied with staff and other military matters, devoted much of his attention to Miss Mercy Buskirk Ford who reciprocated his interest. Rarely had Will seen one without the other, which left him ample time alone in the room he shared with Hadley to compose letters in his mind to Elisabeth and await the day when he would have paper, quill and ink.

Once he was in his more humble hut, Will actually relished the close, noisy company of the gun crews to the quiet isolation of the second floor garret in the Ford house. He went from sharing a soft bed with Captain Hadley to a hard wooden bunk made of rough planks, one of four stacked in two frames on either side of the hut. With eight men sharing the small space, Will became accustomed to the smells of stockings steaming before the fire, unwashed bodies and clothing, the rot of leather boots and the constant sneezing, coughing and hacking of men suffering from winter colds.

He was pining for Elisabeth and feeling sorry for himself, as well as having a sense of being adrift with no purpose. He wished the Marblehead Mariners were still part of the Army. He missed Nat and Adam, long limbed Solomon, "snaggle tooth"Jeremiah and even morose and taciturn one-eyed Titus. If he had to be in winter quarters for another two months, on scarce rations, it would be better to be with the companionship of others, than to be preoccupied with his own dark thoughts of never seeing Elisabeth again.

Walking on the road, Will recognized Sergeant Merriam hobbling on a makeshift crutch, cautiously proceeding on the well-worn, snowy path from the cluster of huts toward Morristown, a quarter of a mile away. The Sergeant's uniform was cleanly brushed and he sported a sprig of pine in his tri-corn, a symbol of the Army's January victories. The gaiter on his left foot was unbuttoned at the bottom to accommodate his swollen ankle. Will easily caught up with him and linking his arm on Merriam's free side, protected him from the soldiers swirling around the Sergeant as they hurried to the drill field on the town's green.

"Bless you Will, for accommodating an old man," Merriam said in a raspy voice. "I am on my way to see General Knox on a matter of extreme personal importance." He stopped, digging his fingers into Will's supporting arm. He opened his mouth wide and made deep wheezing noises as he sucked in cold air. Folds of his skin hung loosely below his chin like a turkey's wattles, red from the cold and speckled with bloody nicks from his morning shave. "And where are you off to?" the Sergeant asked, catching his breath before painfully resuming his lopsided pace.

"Mr. Ford's barn to saddle Big Red. We are to practice unlimbering guns this morning. In that hilly field west of the town." Merriam winced as he put his bad foot down the wrong way in a frozen rut.

"Do not worry sir. I will walk with you."

"Good lad, Will," Merriam said appreciatively with a smile. "I knew you were from the first moment we met. Do you remember?"

Will was about to say he did, but Merriam went on, speaking between short gasps of breath. "It was in Cambridge. I was invalided from that cannon ball rolling from the poorly stacked pile behind a twelve pounder into my ankle. That was the start of all my misery. And you came with Captain Hadley, he was a Lieutenant then, to the hospital and tended to the men of the Regiment stricken with small pox even though you knew none of us. My own self included."

They were in front of the stone building that served as quarters for General Knox and his staff. Will nodded to the two sentries and holding Sergeant Merriam by his elbow, helped him up the slippery granite steps to the black double doors. The effort of climbing up to the entrance brought on another fit of gasping and raspy noises.

Merriam patted Will's arm. "And now we are together still, in this our winter quarters." He looked back at the path to the encampment. "There is much blasphemy and profaneness, dissipation and debauchery in this camp. The men forget it is the helping hand of Providence which has rescued us from our enemies." Will thought Merriam was prepared to launch into a sermon to the two sentries, but the Sergeant just shook his head, either marveling at how far they had come together since Cambridge or the rampant sinfulness of the men.

"Tis a rough life for an old man," Merriam said to no one in particular before crossing the threshold. One sentry closed the doors behind the Sergeant and winked.

Will traversed the Morristown Green, a large barren rectangular field, the snow now tamped down and dirty brown. Several companies formed up for marching drills. On the opposite side, General Washington had established his headquarters in Arnold's Tavern. It was guarded by the General's Own in their distinctive blue dragoon style helmets, topped by a white feather plume. Eight of them stood in a perfect line, arrayed in front of the Commander in Chief's headquarters in their dark blue regimental coats with buff colored facing, and matching coffee colored vests and breeches.

The ordinary soldiers had complained how the camp had become more spit and polish since Martha Washington had arrived ten days ago, from Philadelphia. [1] She had been brought in an elegant enclosed carriage, drawn by two white horses, accompanied by her black personal maid servant and escorted by mounted volunteers from the city's most prominent patriotic families. The young dandies had strained the already meager resources of the camp, requiring decent quarters and food for themselves and stables and forage for their horses.

A few days later, there had been a dress parade on the Green in Mrs. Washington's honor. The officers had impressed upon their men the need to have their uniforms clean and patched. The men grumbled at being put upon for show but had been assuaged by the arrival of cattle and pigs and barrels of salted fish and eels, flour, rum, candles and tanned hides for making shoes, all donated by the good people of Philadelphia for "their army." The smells of roasting meats and baking breads had wafted from the many log huts and outdoor ovens. True, as Merriam had lamented, many soldiers had over-imbibed at night after the parade and been found too drunk to stand for roll-call the following morning.

Will spent the rest of the short daylight hours working with different gun crews, dashing across a snowy field to a pre-determined position, quickly dismounting, unlimbering the brass six- pounder, and "retreating" from the battle line, while the gun crew unloaded the side boxes, wormer, sponge, rammer and bucket. It was a matter of speed, how fast they made the gun ready to fire, and how quickly they attached the cannon's carriage to Big Red's traces. Captain Lieutenant Hadley rode from one emplacement to the other, urging the men on and noting the crews that worked the most efficiently and those that needed more drilling.

Toward the end of the afternoon, as the sun dipped below the Watchung mountain range, Hadley signaled the exercise was over. Will stretched in the saddle feeling stiff and cold as Big Red pulled the cannon along a well trod path. The gun crews trudged behind them in the churned up slush. Hadley trotted on his chestnut mare next to Will.

"Your horse performs the best of all in the Company. Perhaps in the Regiment," he added. "Others shy away when released from their traces and are difficult to bring back to the emplacements. It is worse with the militia units. Their horses have never been under fire." Hadley hesitated as if debating with himself whether to say more. "General Knox has a plan to consolidate all the artillery and assign the guns, horses and crews to the Regiments as needed. I believe he has you in mind to train the horses, to accustom them to the sounds of cannon fire." He smiled at Will. "He thinks highly of you. I may have spoken out of turn. Say nothing, until our General informs you himself." Will nodded, thinking of how this additional task would help relieve the boredom of these winter quarters and alleviate his pining for Elisabeth.

As they approached the Green, their attention was drawn to the commotion in front of General Knox's Headquarters. A trio of sleds stood in front of the building and a stream of soldiers flowed back and forth, illuminated in the candlelight, carrying trunks and boxes. Two soldiers wrestled with the frozen ropes attached to a long wooden cradle tied to the rear of one of the sleds.

Hadley pointed to the cradle. "Mrs. Knox has joined her husband for winter quarters and has brought their babe," he said. "I believe our General will be the happiest man in camp this evening. Join me tomorrow for breakfast at the Fords and we will go together to pay our respects to General and Mrs. Knox." [2]

The next morning Will was up early, polishing his boots and brushing his blue regimental coat with a stiff straw brush. Ruefully, he regretted there was no remedy at hand for the poorly stitched patches, the gunpowder stains on the buffing or the tarnished pewter buttons. He put on a clean shirt and donned his breeches, noting the ingrained dirt around the knees. They were better than his linen work pants, torn and roughly repaired at the seams. His stockings were more grey in color than white but at least had no obvious holes. He buckled the breeches tight at the back of his knees over the stockings, thinking the leather straps will surely wear out before long. He pulled his double-sided metal comb through his hair, inspecting the narrow tines for evidence of head lice. Thankful there were none, he pulled his hair back and tied it into a tail. Outside his compact hut, he took a deep breath of the cold crisp clean winter air, filled with the scent of smoke from the many fires. This morning, the wind, thank God, was blowing away from the many vaults behind the soldiers' living quarters.

While he appeared presentable from a distance, Will was conscious that up close he smelled of horse, gunpowder, wood smoke, cooking fat and sweat. The General would understand of course, but he was concerned Mrs. Knox would be offended.

Together with Hadley, who was freshly shaven and sporting a white cockade in his tri-corn, they crunched through the thin surface of ice covering the snow on the road from the Ford's home to Knox's headquarters. Once inside the stout fieldstone building, they pushed their way into the already crowded waiting room outside the General's office. Officers, newly arrived from Philadelphia, lounged against the mantle as if posing for a group painting. They warmed themselves before the fire, laughing too heartily at each other's witticisms. Their uniforms were spotless, their black knee length boots highly polished, their burnished silver buttons sparkled in the light from the flames. They exuded an air of smug satisfaction and entitlement. Will felt extremely self-conscious. Hadley, however, was unperturbed. He approached the General's orderly with comradely familiarity and whispered in his ear. The man nodded and when the door opened to permit an officer to exit, the orderly quickly ducked inside. Will heard the General's voice booming from within.

"Of course. Show them in immediately. I have heard enough insipid requests this early in the morning to last me for the entire day."

The orderly beckoned and Will followed Hadley into the General's office, conscious of the scowls and murmurs of annoyance from those still waiting.

"Will, my lad. Good to see you. You know of course my dearest Lucy has arrived. She has brought some books of interest as well as the latest gazettes from Boston and a few of the less recent ones from London. If I recall, your birth date is in February. Perhaps, you will permit me to provide you with a book as a present."

"Sir," Will replied. "There is no need. I …"

Knox waved a hand and interrupted. "Of course there is. Besides, a book is simply a token. I have a much better gift in mind."

"Sir. All I fervently desire is paper and ink to write to Elisabeth."

Knox grunted. "Time enough for that," he said, motioning for them to sit in the plain oak chairs in front of his desk, piled high with ledgers, orders, and correspondence. Will was puzzled by the General's brusque response to his request, having expected it to quickly be granted. He barely listened to Hadley reporting on the state of training of artillery horses.

"So, Will," the General said loudly, looking at him. "There is work to be done. Are you up to the task? Will you assume the responsibility? Of course you must. Captain Hadley is the second person in as many days to recommend you be promoted to Sergeant. It would be unseemly to have a mere Corporal training others how to control their horses and unlimber the guns."

"I will undertake whatever you ask of me, Sir. But I fear I am undeserving of the rank."

"Nonsense, lad. Remember I have seen you on the battlefield. My clerk will prepare a promotion list for posting tomorrow and there will be a ceremony at this Sunday's parade." Knox was positively glowing, his eyes full of mirth as if he was bursting with joy. Will attributed it to the arrival of Mrs. Knox and baby Lucy.

"Sir. I trust your wife and babe are in good health? They were not discomforted from their trip?"

"They are in the best of health," Knox said beaming. "My dearest wife was briefly ill after her small pox inoculation." He frowned at the thought. "But now, my most ardent desires and my written professions of affection have been answered with her arrival at our winter quarters." Will blushed with embarrassment at the General's candor.

It did not seem to disturb Hadley. "I would consider it an honor if I could present Miss Mercy Buskirk Ford. I believe Mrs. Knox will find her a charming companion."

Knox raised an eyebrow and chuckled. "I have heard that you have already succumbed to her charms." Hadley inclined his head in silent acknowledgment of the truth of the statement.

"All in due course. But now, you both must present your compliments to my dearest Lucy and meet our precious infant daughter who has stolen my heart with the briefest of appearances."

The General pushed back his chair, hoisted his huge girth and led them out of the office and into the center hall.

"Gentlemen," he said in his typical booming voice, addressing the waiting officers. "You must excuse me for some time. I hear my dearest wife has summoned me." Hadley and Will followed Knox to the second floor as each pine stair groaned in protest at the General's more than two hundred and fifty pounds.

"I believe we will find the ladies in what we have designated our sitting room."

Knox rapped on the door that opened inward and uncharacteristically, motioned for Hadley and Will to precede him. Mrs. Knox was seated at an oval sewing table, busy with embroidery. The baby was sleeping beside her in a cradle near the fireplace. Lucy was speaking to someone hidden from view by the open door. Will stepped into the room, bowed to Mrs. Knox and turned toward the other person. There was Elisabeth, his Elisabeth, looking more beautiful than he ever remembered.

The General laughed heartily and clapped Will on the back. "This is a most excellent surprise and gift, Will is it not?" He beamed at him. "If you were not speechless with surprise, you would ask how this came to be." Knox did not wait for Will to inquire. "Mr. Van Hooten graciously consented to permit Elisabeth to assist Lucy with our beautiful baby daughter."

"Nonsense, Harry," Mrs. Knox interjected. "Elisabeth has a mind of her own.

She persuaded her father to acquiesce. As I had to prevail upon my own father to permit you, my dearest, to court me."

There were more words between the General and his wife. Captain Hadley said something to Mrs. Knox. All these sounds swirled around Will who heard the words and phrases but was oblivious to their meaning. He only had eyes for Elisabeth. He took two steps toward her and reached for her hand. He felt her soft skin and looked into her blue eyes that mirrored her delight at having surprised him and the obvious reaction of pleasure on his face.

"Well, Corporal Will Stoner. Have you lost your ability to speak since we last met?"

"I have thought of seeing you almost every moment since we parted in New York." She looked radiant to him. A deep ochre colored shawl covered her shoulders. She wore a thin scarf with a flower pattern around her throat.

She tilted her head and raised one eyebrow. "And what about the other moments? Did you not think of me then?" she said, squeezing his hand.

"What young Will means to say," General Knox interjected, "is that as soldiers, engaged in battle, there are moments when we do not and cannot think of our most precious loves because of the precipitous dangers at hand." He stood behind his wife, gently rubbing her shoulders. She reached back and patted his meaty hand affectionately.

Elisabeth looked at Will with concern. "Your few letters mentioned little of the dangers and battles," she reproached him gently. "It is difficult enough to be apart. When we communicate we must be truthful and leave nothing to imagination. If you are silent, I have the most desperate, darkest thoughts."

"I have had similar dark thoughts," Will admitted. "Mostly of never seeing you again."

"Well said," Lucy chimed in, in her delightful lilting English accent. "I have lodged the same complaint against my dear Harry, to no avail. He claimed my safety and happiness, the sole object of his loving heart, deterred him from describing the perils to which he has been exposed. Now we are together and are able to share the joy of love and companionship and the fruition of our union." She gestured for

Will come nearer. "You knew me when I was heavy with child. Now come gaze upon our beautiful daughter."

He felt a slight pressure on his hand as Elisabeth walked with him, her arm locked in his. He stared down at the sleeping infant in the cradle, her wispy brownish hair curling from around a round knit plain cap, her little pink fingers clasping the fringe of her blanket, embroidered with red and purple flowers.

Will was intensely conscious of Elisabeth beside him. He inhaled the clean smell of her skin, the lavender scent of her hair and heard the sound of her silk skirt rubbing against the roughness of his linen regimental coat. He was also keenly aware of his own body smells, ashamed of himself and afraid he might repel her. She gave no sign of discomfort, holding his hand and telling him how little Lucy was such a good child, how she was almost one and could crawl and giggle and how well she traveled and how bright eyed and intelligent she was.

"She is truly beautiful," Will said looking into Elisabeth's eyes. He noticed a few small pox marks on her cheek and neck. She had risked her health and beauty to be inoculated so as to be allowed to join him at the Army's encampment. He gently raised her hand to his lips and kissed it. "I am truly overjoyed to see you again, Elisabeth. If you will stay with Mrs. Knox for the duration of our winter quarters, I would like nothing more than to spend all of my time, as permitted, with you."

Knox cleared his throat. "Will is to be promoted to Sergeant this Sunday and there are some training tasks he will undertake for me. Most important for the efficiency of our artillery."

"Oh, Harry," Lucy interrupted. "What would you have done if my father had required I not visit your bookstore for your fashionable morning discussions and insisted I attend to my duties as daughter of the Royal Secretary of the Province?"

Knox smiled affectionately at his wife. "I was progressing to that point my dear. Of course, despite Will's new duties, there will be ample opportunity for Will and Elisabeth to be together."

A soft gurgle from the cradle signaled that little Lucy had awakened. Elisabeth released Will's hand, bent down and lifted the infant from her crib. Holding the Knox's daughter, Will thought

Elisabeth transcended her own innate beauty. She seemed more lovely and glowing in the candlelight. The General held out his thick, beefy arms and little Lucy giggled and nuzzled into the folds of her father's fleshy neck, while Knox covered her chubby cheeks with loud smacking kisses.

Hadley politely noted it was time they left. They bowed to Mrs. Knox. Will took Elisabeth's hand in his. "I will see you tomorrow and the day after and every day you are here in this camp. I cannot believe my good fortune that you are really here." He kissed her hand, feeling its softness again and vowed to himself to scrub in the bitter cold with snow and shave with ice water if necessary, to make himself more presentable to her.

"Sergeant Stoner," she said looking up at him, her blue eyes gleaming with pleasure. "I also am truly overjoyed to see you well and unharmed. I have had dreadful thoughts of your being wounded or ill. You must tell me of all your experiences, keeping nothing back. If you so promise, I will forgive you for your incomplete letters," she said and squeezed his hand in farewell before releasing it.

Outside the room, Will broke into a broad grin. "Last night you remarked the General was the happiest man in the camp. It is I who takes that prize," he whooped as he exuberantly leaped down the steps two at a time, followed by Captain Hadley.

Four of the officers, dandies who had been waiting for General Knox were standing in the entryway on the right side of the balustrade. They looked up at Will and turned their backs making clear they thought he was not worthy of their attention and continued talking. Will squeezed by two of them toward the front door.

"Have you seen that pretty blond partridge? " one of them said to the other. "Do you think she is the babe's wet nurse?"

"I do not know," the other answered, "but I would most assuredly enjoy sucking on those teats."

In an instant, Will turned, grabbed the officer by the front of his coat and shoved him to the floor, his fists pummeling the fop's face. He grabbed him by the ears and smashed his head against the wooden boards. He heard shouting around him, felt a blow to the back of his skull and lost consciousness.

When he awoke, he was lying under a quilt on a bed under a low ceiling. A lantern burned on the sill, illuminating the crystals of frost on the panes and casting weird shadows on the walls. His coat hung on a peg, his boots were in the corner. He lifted his neck and felt intense pain in his temples followed by a pounding in the back of his head. Gradually, the rest of the room came into focus. It was Hadley's garret room at the Ford house. He lay quietly, aware now his head was bandaged. Gingerly, he raised one arm and worked it around to the base of his skull. His fingers felt the broad raised lump and damp ooze beneath the cloth. Sighing, he put his arm at his side and tried to recall what had happened.

All he remembered was the smirking face of the one officer who had insulted Elisabeth and the feeling of great satisfaction he felt by pulverizing the man's nose and smashing his teeth with his fists. He looked at his own hands. His bruised knuckles confirmed the beating he had inflicted. He would do it again, he thought, proud to have defended Elisabeth's honor.

The door opened and Will turned, groaning at the pain that spiraled in ever increasing paths of agony from the nape of his neck to the top of his head. The light from the one candle in the darkened room hurt his eyes. Miss Mercy sat down on the edge of the bed and applied a cool wet cloth to his forehead.

"You have been insensible for a very long time. Samuel was worried you would not regain consciousness," she said softly.

"How long has it been?" Will asked.

"Almost eleven hours. Samuel carried you here before noon. It is now slightly after ten." She rose gracefully, careful not to shake the bed. "I will tell him you are awake. He is downstairs before the fire in the kitchen." She smiled sympathetically at him and he saw her shadow disappear in the hallway.

He heard the clumping of boots on the stairwell and Hadley entered carrying a pewter candle-holder in front of him. Silently, he put it down on the windowsill, turned the wooden chair around and straddled it. He rested his arms on the top of the curved chair back and lowered his chin on his hands. His face was close to Will's. For a while he said nothing.

"Miss Mercy told me you are awake. The doctor said if you emerged from unconsciousness soon the likelihood is you would recover." He stared at Will in the flickering candlelight.

"I cannot judge whether you have taken leave of your senses because of your infatuation with Miss Elisabeth or you are unaffectedly insane. Do you realize what you have done?" Will started to answer but Hadley did not give him the opportunity.

"You assaulted an officer in General Knox's headquarters. Not any officer mind you but the son of a member of Philadelphia's Supreme Executive Council. You have viciously disfigured Captain Richard Seeley's visage, realigned his nose, knocked out some of his teeth and caused him to suffer a blow to his head. All in front of witnesses. His companion, one Captain Enos Newcomb of the Philadelphia Troop of Light Horse, who by the by had the honor to escort Mrs. Washington to our camp earlier this month, was compelled by your assault to strike you on the back of your head with his sword guard. It was extremely fortuitous he did not run you through. Instead, he grabbed a musket from one of the sentries, and since he alleges he thought you were still assaulting Captain Seeley, he struck you again with the butt."

Hadley shook his head in disbelief. "Your thick skull which has presumably caused your predicament saved you from being killed for your actions."

"But this Captain Seeley insulted Elisabeth. You heard him. He is a dandy and has never seen an hour of battle. He is a parade ground officer not worthy of anyone's respect." Will groaned as the blood rushed to his temples. The throbbing in his head seemed like someone was beating on a kettledrum from inside his skull.

"I do not care if he insulted Martha Washington herself," Hadley said raising his voice. "You are a corporal and you attacked a superior officer. One who is now demanding your court martial. All because you were unable to control yourself. Well, you have boxed us all in a fine corner now."

Will was confused. What did it matter to anyone else? "I would gladly do it again and I will take my punishment for it," he replied angrily. "Remember it was you who taught me to honor all women and treat them with respect." He pointed an accusatory finger at Hadley.

"How would you have responded if this Captain Seeley had uttered lewd thoughts about Miss Mercy?"

"I may have informed him that gentlemen do not speak thusly of ladies and therefore he has proved to all he is not a gentlemen," Hadley said calmly. "I may have provoked him to strike the first blow and then defended myself," he added. "If I were truly incited, I may have even challenged him to a duel. But," he said angrily, "I surely would not have assaulted him in a blind, uncontrollable rage in the General's headquarters."

Hadley remained silent for some time. Will closed his eyes, again seeing the smirk on Captain Seeley's face.

"Will. I have given my honor you will stay in my quarters instead of being held prisoner in the guardhouse. I need you to promise you will not leave this house without my express permission. Is that understood?"

Will nodded.

"You can and will have visitors. I will talk to General Knox. He will be under great pressure to schedule a court martial immediately, but the decision is his alone to make." He ran his fingers through his thick brown hair. "Captain Seeley's father has the ear of others on the Council as well as some members of the Congress. The General risks alienating extremely influential people if he does not acquiesce to the Captain's demands." He paused as if weighing the counter arguments. "On the other side, and in your favor, I suspect Mrs. Knox is your strongest supporter. While you are confined to these quarters, I charge you continue to contemplate your conduct and its consequences."

"If it comes to the worst, I am ready to be court martialed and take my punishment. I can do that," Will said defiantly.

"Is that so," Hadley said exasperated with Will's attitude. "Are you prepared to be stripped of all rank, tied half naked to a tree, flogged before the troops on the Green, and dishonorably discharged from the Regiment? Are you ready to be separated from your companions and the generosity of General and Mrs. Knox and disgraced in Elisabeth's eyes?" He threw up his hands and stood up, loudly scraping the chair on the floor. "Think on it. Only your friends stand between you and that fate which could be the price you may pay for your impetuosity."

As he opened the door to leave, he turned and gruffly said, "I will ask one of Miss Mercy's nieces to bring you some dinner."

Will lay in bed, grateful for the silence after Hadley's tongue lashing. He had been so ecstatic, imagining the days, nay weeks and even months, being with Elisabeth in Morristown. Hadley was right. A speedy court martial would put an end to that dream. He almost wept with despair, knowing that people like Captain Seeley and his family, the powerful and wealthy in society, usually had their way.

Early next morning, Sergeant Merriam came to see him. Will was grateful for his company and mindful of the effort it had taken the old man to climb the steps to the garret. Merriam leaned his crutch against the sill and sat down in the chair with a grunt. He remained there wheezing and gasping until his labored breathing subsided. With some effort he lifted his bad leg with two hands and rested his grossly swollen ankle on Will's bed.

"How is your foot?" Will asked politely.

"Not any better," the Sergeant replied, wiping his dripping nose on his sleeve. He sat quietly with his leg extended, making rhythmic in and out rattling noises in his throat.

"I am returning home," he said abruptly. Will did not understand and thought Merriam was leaving the garret for his hut.

"But you have just arrived," Will protested.

"The blow to your head must have addled your brain. No, it was scrambled before to permit your thoughtless assault on an officer in our beloved General's own headquarters." He snorted and paused, wheezing heavily. "No, lad, I mean home to Boston. To my wife and little ones. General Knox has consented. I am too aged and infirm, both with my game leg and lack of breath, to serve any longer." Will looked at the old Sergeant, recalling the time on Dorchester Heights when Merriam had aimed an eighteen-pounder, The Albany, rescued from the icy Hudson waters, at the British floating gun battery and hit it smack on without a ranging shot.

"You can be of use teaching gunnery," Will said eagerly. "No one in the Regiment has your experience and knowledge."

"Thank you lad but I am determined and I have the General's blessing. I regret I have failed to teach a certain young Corporal to manage his baser impulses." Merriam was seized with another fit. His breath came in sucking, rasping sounds as if his lungs were a bellows filled with water. He held up one hand signaling Will to wait.

"I have more to say. You are a good soldier, Will. I recommended you to General Knox, to be promoted to Sergeant. So I understand did Captain Hadley. Of course that was all before your actions of yesterday. The devil himself must have taken hold of you." He coughed some phlegm, looked for a spittoon or chamber pot and seeing none readily available, spit into a rag tucked into his sleeve and folded it under the cuff.

"It is evident Satan roams this camp ruining the lives of good men. Soldiers blaspheme from morning until night asking God to damn their eyes, tongue and every other appendage and organ, all the while engaging in gaming, pestiferous vices of liquor, sinful congress with women and all manner of vicious habits. And your loss of common sense and exhibition of a wild rage is but a sign Satan has seized control of your mind." Merriam was exhausted by the effort of delivering his sermon. He sat in the chair, nodding to himself, every once in a while, repeating softly, "Satan's power and influence is everywhere."

"What should I do? I am prepared to take my punishment whatever it may be."

"That will only gratify the victim of your assault, a man promoted to Captain not by his own merits but by the influence of high placed relatives. One who is not fit to command a flock of sheep, let alone soldiers dedicated to our noble cause. A man. . ." Merriam was forced to stop by another terrible bout of coughing and wheezing. Alarmed Will sat up in bed, swung his legs down and gently patted the old man's back.

"It has passed," Merriam said softly. "Some days are worse than others." He waved for Will to return to the bed.

"I pray that General Knox will find a solution and your reason will be restored to you. I myself cannot see a way out of this problem. God, in His infinite wisdom will hopefully provide guidance to our General." He lowered his head and closed his eyes, his lips moving silently. His chin fell forward on his chest and he began snored loudly. Will let him sleep. He did not see how defending Elisabeth's honor meant the devil had invested his mind. And certainly, he had never engaged in any of the other sins Merriam had listed.

By the third day, Will was frustrated by his continued confinement in the Ford's home. He suffered severe headaches and pain only when he climbed the stairs to the garret, which compelled him to do so slowly. Otherwise, he idled away the time pacing the rooms downstairs, sitting in front of the fire or prowling around in the kitchen, enduring the worshipful stares of Mr. Ford's young nieces, who giggled and found every opportunity to serve him bark tea or bread and jam and flitted around him like colorful humming birds. He was deeply disturbed that Elisabeth had not been to see him. Captain Hadley returned midday to the Ford house, but he neither had any word from General Knox about the court martial nor had he seen Mrs. Knox or Elisabeth.

Will was sitting by the fire in the main room when Miss Mercy returned from her work at the Presbyterian Church that had been converted to a hospital. She joined him at the dining table and motioned for him to lower his head. With experienced hands, she undid the bandage.

"The wound has scabbed nicely and the swelling seems to have subsided somewhat. Maybe we can fashion a smaller bandage that is not as dramatic looking."

"It is my heart that is bleeding," Will blurted out. "Why will she not visit me?"

"Perchance it is to avoid agitating the situation even more," she said firmly, applying a wet cloth to the back of his head. "She has expressed concern to Captain Seeley over his wounds and assured him she hopes for his complete recovery."

"What," Will shouted, turning to face Miss Mercy. "She has visited the very lout who dishonored her by his lewd thoughts and words?" Miss Mercy shooed away her two nieces who, at the sound of Will's raised voice, had appeared at the kitchen door.

"You really do have a thick skull, Will Stoner. You think all one needs is fists, swords or pistols to resolve any problem. A softer approach may lessen the likelihood of a court martial." She twisted the wet cloth in her hands and applied it to the back of his head.

"After I apply the new bandage stay by the fire. Elisabeth is to call on me this afternoon at four. I suggest you think carefully the words you will say to her. I assure you she has acted only with your best interests in mind."

Despite the pain, Will climbed the steps to the garret, washed his face, combed his hair, carefully avoiding the back of his head, and put on one of Captain Hadley's clean linen shirts. Will's only shirt still bore his blood on the collar and back. Nervously, he slowly descended the steps and pulled two of the oak chairs from the table closer to the fire. He hoped Elisabeth would agree to sit near to him.

He jumped when he heard the door open. The sound of boots on the wood floor told him it was not Elisabeth. Hadley clomped into the room.

"Do not look so astounded, Will. I have not come for my shirt," he said laughing. He took off his coat and stood near the fire turning his hands before the flames. "You are a lucky man to be inside on this bitter cold day. I have been at the field drilling an inept militia unit who barely know a side box from a sponge bucket."

Will grunted acknowledgment. "I would prefer to be at liberty to do my duty as a soldier."

"Your preference may be near at hand. Have patience, Will. First, listen to Miss Elisabeth. Then, I have some news. You have General Knox and especially Mrs. Knox to thank."

Will had not heard the door open or close but suddenly, Elisabeth was in the room. She raised one hand to cover her mouth, her eyes tearing as she saw Will's bandaged head. She wore a long dark brown coat and droplets of melting snow glistened on her blond hair beneath the cowl.

"Oh, Will," she sighed softly, throwing back her hood. "You look so pale. Are you in pain?"

"Not now that you have come to visit me," he said, motioning for her to sit in the other chair. "Your presence is like a balm to my wound. I would take a thousand lashes to see the concern for me on your lovely face."

Hadley chuckled. "Well said Will, but now is not the time for wooing. She must return to Mrs. Knox shortly. They have much to do." He nodded at Elisabeth.

"I am leaving Morristown tomorrow," she explained. She saw the look of despair on his face. "General Knox is concerned for their babe's health. The infant has developed a slight cough. I am to travel with Mrs. Knox to Philadelphia. We will stay with their friends for a few weeks. Then, we will either return to Morristown or General Knox will join his family there."

"And me," Will said with some bitterness. "Am I to come to Philadelphia as well? Now that you have appeared in this winter camp, after I had given up all hope of seeing you ever again, another forced parting is all the more worse to bear."

"Oh, my dearest Will. We will be together again and soon, I promise that." She leaned forward in the chair and took his hand. Will entwined his fingers in hers, warming them and feeling how slender they were. He remembered sitting with her in New York City, the day before the British invasion. He had not seen Elisabeth again for more than eight months. He stared at her intently, yearning to imprint her every feature, every sense of her, to carry with him for what he feared would be another long separation.

The two young nieces, now suddenly shy in Elisabeth's presence, emerged from the kitchen carrying a teapot, cups and a plate with small slices of bread. Directed by Miss Mercy, the girls placed them on a small side table, and curtseyed to Elisabeth. Will remained looking into Elisabeth's eyes, content to have her hands in his, only gently releasing her fingers when she offered him a cup of tea.

"The General too will be separated from his wife," Hadley said. "He has been asked by General Washington to travel to Springfield to arrange for the casting of new cannons. [3] He leaves the day after his family departs for Philadelphia."

Will shook his head in confusion. "What does this mean for me and the pending court martial."

"Your orders are to accompany him to Springfield," Hadley said. "Mrs. Knox left some baggage there to be retrieved and brought to Morristown." He saw the puzzlement on Will's face. "As for your court martial, I know nothing other than it cannot take place while the General is away. He may explain more of his intentions on your journey."

Will understood he would not be permitted to spend the next day with Elisabeth, nor could he even appear outside to wish her a safe journey. This afternoon was the last time he would see her until he did not know when. He saw the same sad realization in Elisabeth's eyes.

"I have brought you a present," she said, with false good cheer. "Mrs. Knox had a neck stock made for the General." She laughed and the sound was so beautiful to his ears, Will almost cried out. "The tailor had to use such a long piece of cloth because of the size of the General's neck, there was some left over to make a smaller one." She drew an elegant three-inch wide dark blue band from her dress pocket. "You see, it has a brass turnbuckle on the back for fitting close around your throat." Will felt the linen strip beneath the wool covering. The cloth had absorbed the warmth from her body. He held it against his cheek, seeking to claim every measure of her heat. "It will keep away the snow and sleet and I will make you a proper wool scarf while I am in Philadelphia. I promise."

After she left, Will sat by the fire for a long while with his eyes closed, fingering the fabric and visualizing Elisabeth when he had first seen her only a few days ago, and now as she had tearfully left the Ford's home.

Early in the morning, he paced the small garret, unmindful of the bitter cold air blowing in the open window, listening for any noise that would tell him that Mrs. Knox, Elisabeth and little Lucy were leaving. He thought he heard the sound of horses, perhaps the escort for Mrs. Knox, but he was not certain. That night, with Captain Hadley's permission, he left the house and walked the short distance to the barn. Big Red looked up as he entered, whinnied softly in recognition and stood quietly, waiting to be fed. Will rubbed him down and leaned against the horse's neck for a long time, his face buried in his shaggy mane. He loaded some hay and oats on the sled for tomorrow's journey and brought his saddlebags back into the house.

The following day, wearing his new neck stock with his regimental coat collar turned up and a tri-corn sitting on the back of his head to keep the wind off his still bandaged wound, he followed the General and his light horse escort north out of Morristown. The well-worn ash runners of the sled easily glided over the packed snow on the road. Will looked up at the sky. Thin patches of layered white fluff obscured the sun. Nat had called them mackerel clouds. What was the fishermen's saying- 'Mackerel sky, not twenty four hours dry.' Hopefully, they would be snug at some tavern or inn before the weather turned bad.

As they approached a cluster of log huts, Will recognized the men of two companies of the Massachusetts Artillery. They had formed in rank and were bidding farewell to Sergeant Merriam, who limped before them, holding himself as erect as possible. Isaiah Chandler, Merriam's old friend helped the Sergeant up on the sled's plank seat next to Will.

"You are to be my driver as far as Springfield," Merriam said, clapping Will on his shoulder. "Perhaps during our journey I can impart some wisdom into that tempestuous mind of yours."

As they passed by the ranks, the men gave three cheers for General Knox and three for their Sergeant and broke into the "Battle of Trenton", a newly composed rousing drinking song, very popular among the soldiers:

> "On Christmas day in seventy-six,
>   Our ragged troops with bayonets fix'd,
>     For Trenton marched away.
> The Delaware see! The boats below!
> The light obscured by hail and snow!
>   But no signs of dismay."

Merriam twisted on his seat and watched the men marching behind the sled, singing their old Sergeant out of camp. They shouted out the last two verses, proudly and defiantly, standing in the snow-covered road, Chandler and a few others waving farewell.

> Twelve hundred servile miscreants,
>   With all their colors, guns and tents,
>     Were trophies of the day.
> The frolic o'er, the bright canteen,

In centre, front and rear was seen
   Driving fatigue away.

"Now, brothers of the patriot bands,
   Let's sing deliverance from the hands
      Of arbitrary sway.
And as our life is but a span,
   Let's touch the tankard while we can,
      In memory of that day." [4]

Merriam wept unashamedly. "I will miss them," he said. "'Tis strange for me, a man who has frequently railed against the sinful excesses of others, to be honored thus by a drinking song." He laughed and wiped his cheeks with his snot rag. "But I am going home to my wife and dear daughters. I have not seen them since April of '76. May Providence grant that I find them in good health."

And may I soon return from Springfield and be with Elisabeth, Will added silently.

# Chapter 6- Hunting the Foragers

Bant was relieved to leave the camp in Morristown. He hated the close quarters of the log cabin, the feeling of the others surreptitiously watching him or staring openly while they ate their meager meals together. More than once in the dark smoky hut, he had been awakened with McNeil shaking him out of his nightmares while the others cursed and growled about the "lunatic" and his demons keeping them from sleep.

Their entire Regiment, a little more than two hundred effectives, led by Colonel Hand, one Major and two Lieutenants on horse back, had traversed through a narrow snow covered pass and then turned in a south easterly direction. Before leaving, they had been given dry rations for five days, powder and sixty cartridges each. The men saved the rations and ate food offered by friendly farmers, or slaughtered and cooked the cattle and geese they seized from Tory landowners. The provisions from the Loyalists' well-stocked larders, which were not consumed on the spot- butter, cheeses, smoked meats and preserves- were sent back to those encamped at Morristown. It mattered not to them that the Tory families were left with few victuals to survive the winter. Orders were to provide for the army, first and foremost.

The riflemen readily broke open the casks they seized, drank the rum and filled their canteens as well. Bant did not participate. That set him further apart from his companions. He had found excessive drinking did nothing to numb the horrors of the hangings he had seen, nor assuage his guilt for causing them. It impaired his skills with the rifle and that he could not abide. For him, only by killing more British soldiers, especially officers, would he overcome his demons and expiate his responsibility for the deaths of the dozen militia men.

On the fourth day out, at a small cross roads tavern, they encountered a unit of New Jersey Militia accompanied by a Regiment of Continentals. Bant found a small shed on the edge of a pasture, some distance away from the soldiers eagerly congregating around the tavern, barn and outbuildings. He perched on a stack of logs under the overhang, warming himself in the waning winter sun, his feet swinging free, glad to be left alone. The Continentals had established a perimeter about one hundred yards out on each road and thrown up makeshift sentry posts. They stood, stamping their feet and clustered close to the fires to keep warm. The Jersey militiamen lounged around in ill disciplined, noisy groups, carousing and drinking.

He heard the crunching on the snow before McNeil appeared from around the end of the barn about twenty yards away. Bant sat still, unsure whether he wanted his company or not and then hallooed to him. McNeil banged one of the logs against the pile to clear it of snow and sat next to Bant, his moccasin clad feet resting on the ground. He offered a piece of smoked ham.

"Traded some rum for it with a militiaman. I would rather eat than drink before a battle. Although they say either is bad for a stomach wound." Bant took the ham from the point of McNeil's deer skinning knife and chewed it slowly, savoring the salty flavor.

"Do you still have your rum ration?"

Bant nodded.

"Pour it into my canteen. I may have some more opportunities to barter. These militia have been raiding Tory homes for a week and are well provided with foodstuffs but have consumed the rum on the spot and are sparse on spirits."

Bant emptied his canteen into McNeil's. Leaving the carved wood stopper off, he walked over to the low roof of the shed and held it under the fresh water dripping from the melting snow. Impatiently, he scooped some of the snow off the cedar shingles and squeezed it in his hands over the mouth of his canteen.

"The Continentals tell me it is 'Scotch Willie,' who leads them," McNeil said. [1] "He has a reputation. I suspect we will see some hot action soon."

Bant shrugged. It mattered not to him which General was in charge. So long as he brought them within range of British troops, Bant would do his part to kill many of them. The idea of imminent combat excited him. McNeil noticed his narrow thin-lipped smile. "You are a strange bird, Bant," he said, rubbing a cold sore on his jutting chin. "You truly are. However, of all the men in the Regiment, I prefer to fight alongside you, because I know you will never abandon the line as long as Redcoats are in your sights."

Colonel Hand's men slept on the hard ground around the tavern and in the adjacent sheds and out buildings and awoke in the morning, stiff from the cold. Led by local scouts, the riflemen marched east with a portion of General Maxwell's Continentals, a force of close to five hundred men. It was a bitter overcast day, made worse by a nasty northerly wind. They forded numerous frozen streams, the ice strong enough on the edges to hold a man's weight and thin enough to break where the water was deeper. Bant's canvas gaiters chaffed his calves and shins. The streams they had crossed once, seemed to maliciously meander around fields and fences and deliberately appear again in their path. In the approaching darkness of the late winter afternoon, they camped in a deep ravine that afforded them some protection from the biting wind. No fires were permitted and the riflemen, for the first time since leaving Morristown, ate their cold rations.

The next morning, they followed the ravine almost due east, until the advance scouts signaled for them to halt. Orders were passed down the line to climb quickly up the south side, find firing positions and remain silent. Bant scurried up the frozen embankment, stopped at a rail fence and peered over at a broad snowy field that gently sloped upward toward his right. Some of the Jersey Militia were dug in and occupied a small knoll at the top of a pasture, their regimental flags ostentatiously flying in the light wind. Several sentries stood in plain sight, scanning the road below the field.

To his left Bant saw men driving a large herd of sheep and cattle before them on a narrow road toward the pasture. His keen eyes detected movement behind them. Redcoats were coming double time up the road while others emerged from a wooded glen to intercept the militia escorting the confiscated cattle. A signal shot rang out and the militia alerted to the danger, hastily left the captured animals and fled uphill through the pasture toward their comrades on the knoll. Bant watched as the British Regiments formed into ranks, preparing to assault the Jersey militia's hilltop position.

Colonel Hand moved along the slope below the fence line in a lopsided bobbing manner, his right foot lower down the hill, his left leg bent at the knee on the high side. His tri-corn was pushed tightly over his bald head.

"Nice and steady lads. And quiet. The Redcoats will undoubtedly attempt to flank our men on the hill. That will bring them close to this fence line." His voice was calm and Bant had to strain to hear him. "Fire only upon a given order. Reload and then fire at will. If it goes as planned, we will chase them all the way back to Amboy or hell, which ever they reach first."

Bant lay quietly on his side, feeling the cold damp of snow melted by his body heat, seep into his hunting shirt and chilling his ribs. He was conscious of a weird wailing sound and indistinct barked orders. McNeil, on his right, mouthed the word "Highlanders," and Bant recalled the peculiar martial music of the Scottish regiments before the pell mell retreat into Trenton. The noise, for he regarded it more as noise than the familiar music of fife and drum, was louder now, accompanied by the uniform cadence of many men crunching through the snow crusted pasture. It would be good to kill some of them, he thought. They gave no quarter and camp talk had it, they cut the wounded to pieces with their long swords.

He looked down the line of riflemen. Colonel Hand was less than forty yards away, almost mid way in their position. He had unsheathed his sword and held it point down toward the ground. Bant pulled back the hammer to full cock, checked the powder in the frizzen pan and waited.

A portion of the enemy troops had passed and were moving up the slope. Bant guessed they were less than thirty yards from the fence line. With regret, he thought he would be firing into the middle of their formation. The officers would be in the lead. Hopefully, if their ranks broke, he would be able to pick one or two of them off, if they hadn't fallen in the first volley. He placed his index finger along the cold metal of the trigger guard and waited. The Colonel raised his sword, catapulted himself the few remaining feet to the top and shouted, "Fire."

Bant raised himself up and quickly sighted. The Highlanders were marching up the slope in neat regular lines, angling toward the knoll where the Jersey militia were dug in. The Scot nearest to Bant had partially turned toward the fence when Bant blew his face away at a distance of less than thirty yards. He dropped back down to reload, bit off the end of the paper cartridge, poured a little powder in the pan and the rest down his rifle's muzzle, dropped the ball down the barrel, pulled out the long ramrod, thrust it home and re-fixed the rod. He knelt again resting his rifle on a slat of the fence.

The field in front of him was a mass of thrashing bodies, red jackets writhing in red blood on the snow. Green plumed black bonnets, muskets and canteens were strewn everywhere. The Scots formed a line to face the riflemen. Bant was almost distracted by their black and green plaid skirts, their red checkered stockings that ended below their bare knees and a peculiar furry looking white bag they wore at thigh level. The Scots moved forward to attack with their bayonets. A musket volley from the knoll felled many of them. The second round from the Continentals and riflemen decimated their ranks. Bant quickly reloaded as he heard the Colonel shouting, "After them men. After them. Hunt them down."

Bant clambered through the fence. He ran past some of the Continentals who had stopped to loot the bodies of the dead Highlanders. Below them, the rear guard of the Scots had formed up on the road and were loading their muskets. Bant dropped down to one knee and aimed slightly below the red and white checkered band on the soft black cap of an officer directing the defensive line with his sword. It was an easy shot, no more than seventy yards. He saw the man fall. The rear guard, further thinned by the accurate fire, wavered and then fled down the road to join their retreating comrades.

Bant needed no further encouragement. Together with McNeil and several other riflemen they loped down to the road. To their left, some of the Redcoats had reached their empty forage wagons, now loaded with their wounded and were withdrawing slowly, pursued by a band of Jersey militia. Ahead of them, across a snowy field, marked by bloody streaks of the wounded, a large group of Redcoats had entered a wood and were disappearing over a hill. McNeil, Bant and the others gave chase. They entered a forest of thick trunked leafless oaks, and beeches a few of them still bearing their oval, light brown ribbed leaves, and ramrod straight ironwoods. The fleeing British were on the opposite hillside. Some scurried up a narrow leaf covered path, others struggled through the deeper snow, disappearing and reappearing amongst the dark grey trunks like giant cardinals. Bant stopped and rested his shoulder against a smooth barked ironwood and slowed his breathing. He focused on a space amongst the trees where the path neared the crest and his line of sight was not blocked by tree trunks. As a soldier sprinted for the safety of the far side of the hill, Bant aimed for his back and brought him down. By the time he had reloaded, the last of the retreating troops were out of sight. He ran down the slope and caught up with the other riflemen just over the hill. Below them, the surviving Redcoats, a band of more than three dozen, struggled through the snow covered fields, angling toward the road in the distance where more of the enemy and their wagons were retreating.

The rest of that winter afternoon followed the same pattern. The Redcoats fled, slowed in their flight by hills and fences, brambles and ditches, icy creeks and snowy drifts. The pursuing riflemen gained ground and once within range, picked off one or two of the unlucky British, before the space between the hunted and the hunters widened again. Until the next obstacle closed the gap and the riflemen resumed their deadly work. In one snowy embankment, they came upon a Redcoat, lying on his back, blood staining his waistcoat from a ball that had entered below his shoulder blades. A red froth bubbling from his lips. McNeil knelt in the snow next to him, and slowly poured rum from his canteen into the soldier's mouth. The man smiled in gratitude. He did not see McNeil unsheath his skinning knife to slit his throat.

"'Tis a more merciful death than drowning in one's own blood or freezing alone this night," he said to Bant. He wiped the knife on the dead soldier's waistcoat, leaving a broad smear on the buff colored linen.

In the distance, they could see smoke rising from the buildings of Amboy. Tired now, they plodded through the windswept snow drifts, following in the steps of the fleeing troops. When they reached the road, they met a Jersey Militia unit resting among a copse of bare branched elm trees around a bend. Bant shivered, not from the cold but from a strange sense of the familiarity of the place. One part of his mind, calm and rational told him this was not where the Dragoons had hung the militia men Bant had traveled with, late in the fall of '76. That had been to the west, closer to Bound Brook and the mountains. But another voice in his head told him it had indeed been here. See the bare trees, the voice said shrilly. Look at the turn in the road, it advised him. And the silence of the woods, just as before the British Dragoons rode up. It is the same place, the voice screamed at him in panic. You have returned to where they were hung because of you, the voice said with absolute conviction. And why did you survive? the voice asked rising in tone to leave the question hanging in his mind. Yes, hanging like the twelve militiamen, he, Bant was responsible for, as if he had hoisted them up himself.

McNeil squatted next to a few of the militia and beckoned him over. In Bant's mind he saw his friend kneeling, a thick grey noose around his neck. The man next to him was holding the rope and looking up at an overhanging tree branch. Bant was overwhelmed by an uncontrollable sense of terror. He screamed in fear and fled from his horrible vision, running down the road after the retreating Redcoats. He heard McNeil continuing to call after him until the sound of his voice faded away. Bant first ran as a man possessed and then, slowed to a steady trot. He had closed the distance to the withdrawing Redcoats. He could see the front of their column approaching the few brick buildings on the outskirts of Amboy. The last of the troops were barely within range, almost two hundred yards away.

Several soldiers at the very rear plodded wearily along behind a slow moving wagon. Bant squatted on the road with his head down, staring at the fractured web like pattern in the ice between his feet, panting heavily. When his breath slowed to normal, he looked up. All was quiet, except for the faint noises coming from the retreating column of Redcoats.

Bant knelt in a rut, oblivious to the cold slush soaking his breeches. Calmly and mechanically he put the smooth walnut stock to his shoulder and rested his left elbow on his knee. The wood against his cheek comforted him. Holding his rifle in firing position calmed his nerves. He pulled the hammer back to full cock and sighted on the back of one of the soldiers. He fired, feeling the instantaneous impact of the butt against his shoulder. As the smoke dissipated, he saw the soldier buckle, clasping his left leg. Two of his comrades quickly lifted him up and dragged him on to a wagon, all the while looking fearfully back down the road.

Not enough powder for that distance, Bant thought. As he turned and trudged away from Amboy, he unconsciously fingered the remaining cartridges in his weather proof bag. There were forty-six left. He was certain each of his fourteen balls had killed a Redcoat. Except for the last one. That man had been lucky. [2]

—⧠—

"This is a military necessity," Lieutenant Chatsworth explained as they saddled their horses in the barn. "We need forage for our animals. Otherwise, our artillery and baggage cannot move and we become immobile." He grunted as he tightened the cinch.

And what would be wrong with that, John Stoner thought, stepping around a fresh pile of steaming horseshit, careful not to soil his polished boots. To remain comfortable in Brunswick for the winter, living a civilized existence. They had food and drink brought down from New York by wagons escorted by a force large enough to scare away any of the irregular rebel bands roaming the countryside. There was enough forage for the animals in Brunswick to survive the winter. In spring, when the weather improved and the grass greened, they could graze their horses. After they had fattened up, would be the time to take to the field, overwhelm the pitiful Rebel army and capture Philadelphia.

John smiled at the thought. There would be some nice quarters in that city as well as more opportunities for improving his position and lining his pockets. No more sleeping three or four to a bed, in some pillaged mansion, the cold wind constantly blowing through shattered, shutterless windows some ignorant Hessians had smashed for the sheer joy of destroying something.

"Colonel Harcourt is absolutely correct in carrying the battle to the rebels. If they will not stand up in the field to our army, we must entice them to attack our foraging parties and annihilate them when they appear." Chatsworth backed his horse from the stall. "Besides, John, we have our new 'fuzees' I am anxious to try when we are on foot," he said, holding a light musket up, bending his arm and sighting down the short barrel resting on his elbow. "I will procure another one. You must ride up front with me. It will be like one of the grouse shoots back home. Too good sport to pass up." [3]

John nodded as if he would like nothing better. Ballocks, he thought. No chance of his riding in the lead. Bad enough he had to ride out at all. He knew some of the cavalry suspected him, if not of cowardice, at least of reluctance to place himself in harm's way. 'Blamed cunning,' he had overheard one of them say. John vowed he would go through the motions, with proper caution as his watchword.

"I saved your life once," he said to Chatsworth. "Let us hope today will not present another opportunity to do so."

The Dragoon Lieutenant inclined his head. "I remain grateful, as does my dear mama to whom I wrote many months ago about that incident on Long Island." The condescending tone of his voice implied he did not like to be reminded about it.

I will do so as frequently as necessary, John thought, so you will put in a favorable word with your influential friends, perhaps with Colonel Harcourt, an Earl's son and a favorite of Lord Cornwallis.

In the fields outside the stables, the Dragoons mounted up in the early March morning darkness. The pitch of the fife and drum signals called to the different companies of infantry and grenadiers. The Regiments massed along the road leading north from Brunswick toward Bonhamtown. The order of march placed the 16th Light Dragoons almost at the head of the column, behind a company of

Hessian Jaegers in their green uniforms with short hunting rifles and one hundred hand picked Hessian Grenadiers. John stood in the stirrups and looked back at the neat squares of marching men, almost two thousand of them, light and heavy infantry, some Scotch Highlanders, three pieces of artillery and many forage wagons. The numbers gave him confidence, although he still was uneasy about his forward position.

True to his word, Chatsworth found a fuzee for him. John strapped it over his left shoulder. It would have come in handy when his younger brother had pursued him outside Princeton. He could have turned on him, fired to wound and not to kill, and brought Will, bleeding to Chatsworth, or better yet to Colonel Harcourt himself. Imagine their surprise, and the admiration they would express for his apprehending his own brother. No more snickering and arrogant comments about his reluctance to join the fray. Be worth a promotion at least, perhaps even a staff position at Headquarters. For him, capturing his younger brother was simply a rung on the ladder of John's quest for advancement and recognition. Sentiments like fraternal affection or even hatred were irrelevant and not part of his calculations.

The long column moved northeast on the road toward Bonhamtown. At sunrise they crossed the Raritan River, narrow at this point before it widened further east at the Amboys. Chatsworth had said the rebel militias were reported to be active in the area, harassing British foraging parties and attacking supply trains to the north as far as Elizabethtown. With daylight, John's spirits lightened. The broad open flat snow covered fields offered no chance of a surprise ambush. Nevertheless, John was jittery, wary of the snow-covered ditches on both sides of the road. No telling when a man or two might spring up and discharge their muskets at the nearest soldier. He pretended his horse had a stone in her hoof, slowed and edged the mare more toward the center of the road, so he was flanked by one Dragoon on each side.

From his relatively safe position, he reasoned the rebels would not dare to confront such a large force. The entire operation would be nothing more than a jaunt in the countryside. The Jaegers had spread out in a long skirmishing line ahead of the column on both sides of the road.

Ahead were the roofs of the brick houses of Bonhamtown. The large force marched through the town to the cheers of a few Loyalists lining the road and added another Regiment, garrisoned there, to their force. By eleven they were five miles north, again in open countryside when the first shots were fired. Puffs of smoke appeared along a fence line that bisected the road. Three rebel cannon to the left fired obliquely at the advancing column. Artillery was brought up from the rear, unlimbered and soon engaged the rebel guns. A Regiment of Highlanders formed to the left of the road, and one of Hessian Grenadiers on the right, in preparation for an assault on the enemy lines. John was thankful the Dragoons were not involved, either as cavalry or dismounted infantry.

The Highlanders and Hessians stepped out through the snow in perfect ranks but were repulsed. More troops were mustered behind them and extended farther to the Highlanders' left, in an attempt to flank the rebel line. John could see the puffs of musket fire moving away across the field and surmised the rebels had added more troops to their defensive positions. Good, he thought. At last, they were going to stand and fight. And there were enough infantry to do the dirty work and leave the Dragoons to mop up afterwards. Chasing down foot soldiers who had discarded their muskets in their panic stricken flight, was something he could do, and with eagerness.

The bulk of the British troops were committed to the fields on the left, stretching the rebel lines and probing for a weakness. The Dragoons were deployed back on the road, waiting in reserve with the few remaining troops not yet engaged. Suddenly, John saw the Hessian Grenadiers on the right give way, as rebel troops pushed them back. At first it was an orderly retreat, but as more and more of the rebels appeared, advancing in good order and firing deadly volleys, the Hessians turned and ran, across the field and on to the road. They drove into the reserve troops whose ranks disintegrated in the confusion. Soon the remaining force was retreating down the road back toward Bonhamtown.

John was about to join them, riding down some of the soldiers to escape if necessary, when Lieutenant Chatsworth called for the Dragoons to rally with the troops as a rear guard. Instead of dismounting with the other horsemen, John drew his sword and rode toward the rear, pointing back toward the battle and shouting for the soldiers to turn and stand their ground. In this way he moved farther away from the chaos and fighting behind him. However, he recognized a new danger as some of the retreating soldiers were falling from accurate rifle fire seemingly coming from every direction. John turned his horse around every which way, fearful he was exposed and would be picked off. He crouched low over the mare's neck, leaning to the opposite side of where he supposed the enemy was, and rode furiously back up the road toward where Chatsworth had established a position. Reluctantly, he dismounted, stumbled forward, unslung his fuzee and fired wildly in the general direction of the advancing rebels.

The Dragoons and a combined force of Hessians, Jaegers and some heavy infantry had managed to halt the onward rush of the rebel troops. Their line was thin and all they could do was fire a volley and retreat slowly, delaying the advance and giving the other troops either time to reform or to escape. John knelt between two cavalry men and hastily reloaded his fuzee, all the while anxiously glancing up to see how close the rebels were. He almost whimpered a cry of relief when he heard the order to remount. He did not remember how he found his horse, or got on it, or how he restrained himself from headlong flight and instead rode with the others back down the road. He leaned forward over his horse's neck, fearful of an unseen rifle ball piercing his body.

Suddenly, a filthy ragged apparition sprang up from the left embankment, aiming a musket straight at him. All he could see in that moment was the man was a rebel, clad in some kind of makeshift uniform with a dirty slope hat on his head. John recoiled back in the saddle, pointed his fuzee at the rebel and fired. His ramrod pierced the man's chest and he flopped back in the snow as if struck by an arrow.

Chatsworth, who had turned at the sound of shot, saw what happened and laughed out loud. "John," he said, "you are supposed to remove the ramrod before firing. Now you have spitted the poor fellow to the ground and rendered your fuzee useless." John smiled weakly, his legs trembling in the stirrups, thinking of how close he had come to being killed. He regained his self control as they moved farther away from the battle ground and the sporadic sounds of musket fire died down. [4]

The story of his killing the rebel with his ramrod made the rounds of the Dragoons. Before they were back in Brunswick, several of them were calling him "Ramrod John" to his face. He accepted it as best he could, but seethed at their ridicule and resented their making him the butt of their jokes. He suspected they understood the real reason he had fled down the road was not to rally more troops for the rear guard. And every one of them, so cool and calm in battle, would not have been so flustered as to forget to refix the ramrod before firing. He was certain they would remind him of that in open and subtle ways at the Company meals. He could bear it in the security of Brunswick, if there were no more of these forays and he remained secure in their winter quarters until spring.

## Chapter 7- Resurrection in the Spring

Will saw very little of General Knox once they arrived in Springfield. For the first three days, the General, in the company of local militia officers and members of the Town Council, inspected buildings to serve as magazines. They surveyed land on the bluffs overlooking the Connecticut River for situating the arsenal, gunpowder laboratories, and the critical open air furnace for the casting of cannons as well as a mill for boring the barrels. Late into the evening, at the Black Bull Inn where they were staying, Knox met with carpenters, blacksmiths, wheelwrights, harness-makers and tin men, questioning them closely about their crafts, for these were the men who would be entrusted with casting the cannons and cannon balls, constructing the gun carriages and making the muskets. [1]

On the evening on the fourth day, Sergeant Merriam, who was serving as the General's unofficial clerk and orderly, gloomily informed Will the General wished to see him. Apprehensively, Will ascended the dark stairway, the mirthful singing and shouting from the Inn's main room with its warm crackling fire receding, as he guided himself by the thin slivers of light shining under the room doors, to the General's quarters.

Over the past few days, uneasily waiting for the inevitable meeting with General Knox, at which he expected to be told he would be subject to a court martial upon their return to Morristown, Will had reflected upon the events leading up to his predicament. At first, when he reviewed in his mind the scene with Captain Seeley at the foot of the stair, seeing the dandy's sneer and hearing his licentious comment, he had seethed with anger again. Gradually, he saw himself more calmly reacting to the crude insult to Elisabeth's honor. His role changed from the hot-blooded gallant to more of a disdainfully calm and deadly adversary, carefully inciting the uniformed fop to strike the first blow or with provocative words, revealing the Captain to be either a coward or no gentlemen or preferably both.

One morning while grooming Big Red, he had realized his initial motivation in joining the Continental Army was solely because he idolized General Knox. He was everything to Will his own father had not been. The General cared enough about Will to provide him with the opportunity to expand his knowledge, lending him books, pamphlets and broad sheets, all to stimulate his mind. Will now saw those readings had another purpose. They provided him with the philosophical underpinning for their cause- the logic and rationale for opposing the Crown and fighting for independence. It was not enough to fight because one was ordered to do so or greatly admired a commander. The General was showing Will, that as a free man, he should choose to fight for the Revolution and to believe in the cause he was fighting for.  But the General had gone beyond that. Will recognized they had included him as part of their little family and both had expressed an interest in his future happiness.

Then, a thought came to him, so obvious he was surprised he had not seen the connection before. The General had deliberately assigned him to go on the mission with Elisabeth's father. Of course he trusted Will to protect Mr. Van Hooten as he set up his network of informants on Long Island. But also he desired Mr. Van Hooten to become better acquainted with Will who was courting his youngest daughter. The General had brought the two of them together to encourage Will's romance with Elisabeth. He was astounded and overwhelmed with gratitude that General Knox would have planned and gone to such extremes for his benefit.

He now realized, by assaulting Captain Seeley, in addition to risking losing Elisabeth, he had betrayed General Knox's trust and the very cause they served. To be drummed out of the Regiment, to be unable to fight for the rights he now believed in, was almost too terrible for him to contemplate. He could always join a militia but having seen their lack of equipment and discipline, their poor training and their inclination to flee a battlefield, he dismissed that option immediately.

He was adamant that he would not leave the Regiment. He could accept anything short of being discharged. He could endure the flogging. He could even accept the disgrace. It would be temporary. He would win back respect, rank and reputation by bravery on the battlefield. Will knew he would have to beg General Knox for the opportunity to continue to serve in the artillery and plead for a lenient sentence. With these thoughts in his mind, he knocked on the door to the General's room.

The General was seated at a small oak table that served as his desk. It was strewn with correspondence and dispatches. An ink well and quill were perched precariously on one corner, dangerously close to the edge. Knox's face was flushed, despite the open window behind him. He was in shirt sleeves, with his great coat, jacket, waistcoat, and neck stock all cast on a quilt covering the four poster bed. His high black boots, spattered with mud from the day's business, stood in front of a closed closet, whose door was blocked by large, bulging saddle bags.

"Come in Will, though it is like a furnace with all the heat rising from the big room below. We could cast cannons here tonight if the floor would bear the weight," he said chuckling and dabbing at the sweat on his forehead with the handkerchief covering the stubs of his fingers on his right hand. "Tomorrow I am promised samples of tin, copper and iron, mined from this area, which I will take to Boston and have them properly assayed. If we are to have well made cannons of brass and iron, the metal from which they are formed must be of excellent quality."

Knox rifled through a sheaf of papers, his high arched eyebrows raised in frustration. "Now, where is that letter," he muttered to himself. "You will not be accompanying me to Boston." Will stiffened in the chair, his feet pressed hard to the floor to prevent his knees from shaking. He could not bear the wait any longer.

"Sir," Will said quickly. "If I am to be court martialed, so be it. I can bear whatever the penalty. But please, I beg of you. Do not have me dishonorably discharged. I want to remain with the Regiment."

Knox looked up, surprised by Will's impassioned outburst.

"My dear lad. I have never entertained the thought of a court martial. I merely thought it necessary to remove you from proximity with Captain Seeley and his fellow officers and to develop a stratagem to resolve this difficulty. Military discipline is often required to maintain good order. Common sense dictates it must never be exercised to remove a brave and courageous fellow from the field of battle. I also rely upon you to teach others how to properly train their horses to maneuver cannons in battle."

He continued rustling the stack of papers and then threw up his hands in defeat. " I suppose I must endure this confusion when trying to maintain correspondence without my usual staff. The letter I look for is to General Mifflin, our Quartermaster General. Anyway, here is the sum of it. You will recall Captain Seeley was waiting for an audience. The young man was seeking a letter from me to General Mifflin commending him for service in his corps. The Captain's father, while himself a man of influence, has not been able to secure his son's appointment. I have written the General myself on behalf of Captain Seeley. The letter will be sent from here with tomorrow's dispatches."

Will did not understand the relevance of this letter to him. All he had heard was the General would not order a court martial.

"In light of my letter, Captain Seeley has acquiesced to my wish and withdrawn his insistence upon your court martial." He smiled at Will, his eyes bright in the candlelight. "My intuition suggests the good Captain smells opportunity for improving his finances by serving in the Corps and therefore his greed overcomes his pride. I have balanced the risk of turning loose a corrupt scoundrel upon the Quartermaster, with the promotion of an able young man to make our artillery more efficient on the battlefield."

"Sir," Will replied. "I am overwhelmed by your kindness. I will do my best to live up to your expectations."

"You already have, except," Knox said raising his index finger and wagging it at Will, before chuckling deeply "for your actions at my headquarters. And do not thank me. My dear Lucy has taken an interest in your career, or more particularly the romantic relationship between you and Elisabeth." Will blushed, hoping the heat of the room concealed his embarrassment.

Knox gestured toward his saddlebags near the closet. "Be a good lad and bring those here. I have opened one of my beloved's trunks and extracted one or two books for our edification."

Will lifted the heavy bags, weathered on the outside from the elements and smooth on the underside from rubbing against the horse's skin. The General undid the buckles, pulled out a leather bound book and handed it to Will.

"This is "The Second Treatise on Government" by John Locke, recently reprinted by Benjamin Edes with whom I hope to do some important business in Boston. [2] I depart tomorrow and anticipate returning in ten days time. In my absence ride out among the contractors, surveyors and others and be observant. At night, read the writings of this brilliant British political thinker and we will converse on his ideas on the journey back to Morristown. And now Sergeant Stoner, if you will excuse me, I must deal with this vexatious issue of Hartford being favored by some in Congress as the location for an arsenal, and complete these dispatches for tomorrow's rider, including an order for you to be entered in the regimental rolls as Sergeant." [3]

Will stood up. "Sir. I only pray I completely fulfill all that you expect of me. I assure you, if I fail to do so, it will not be for lack of resolve or effort."

"I know that with a certainty, Will. I fancy myself an excellent judge of character. You are an intelligent lad who acts with courage and honest conviction. I believe there is much you will accomplish in this world, for you have great potential. But for now," he chuckled, gesturing at the disorderly piles of papers strewn on his desk, "I have my own tasks to complete. Be a good fellow and ask the innkeeper to send up additional candles and more ink. My writing of letters and dispatches will consume much of this night."

The General and his mounted escort rode out of town shortly after daylight, intending to cover the one hundred and sixty miles to Boston and arrive no later than dusk on the third day. A slow moving, small train of wagons departed later in the morning. Will said farewell to Sergeant Merriam, uncomfortably seated on a large farm wagon carrying barrels of cheeses and butter and other preserves for sale at inflated prices in the Boston markets.

He fed and watered Big Red, cleaned out his stall, brushed his rough winter coat and combed out his mane and tail. Then he rode the horse east on the Upper Post Road from Springfield and circled around to the bluffs overlooking the town where some workmen were filling chinks in the bricks of buildings already rented as temporary laboratories for mixing and testing gun powder. Sounds of hammering and sawing came from within, wagons arrived laden and left empty. The entire area was a veritable beehive of activity.

It seemed strange to him the good people of Springfield went industriously about their business as if there were no war. If the struggle of the Revolution had any impact, it was the opportunities presented by General Knox's plans for the arsenal. They seemed generally ignorant and unconcerned about the terrible suffering of the ill clothed, poorly fed and diseased troops shivering in their crude log huts in Morristown. The rumor among the patrons of the Inn was General Knox had asked Congress for $50,000 to finance the building of the Springfield arsenal. There was money to be made and none seemed eager to answer the call for recruits for new regiments, despite the substantial bounty of $86 paid upon signing. [4]

In the chill of the mid-afternoon, Will returned to the Black Bull for dinner. He was favored by the innkeeper because of his association with General Knox and the payment in advance the General had made for Will's continued lodging. He ate ravenously and remained near the fireplace, pretending to doze while listening to the talk swirling around him. It was all idle gossip although he paid attention to the rumors of a privateer and its two prize ships docking in New London, with a cargo of muskets, flints and gunpowder. There was much loud discussion about whether the weapons would be transferred to Springfield, necessitating work on more magazines. The talk did not interest him. Instead, he thought of Nat, perhaps at sea at this very moment, or in New London as the captain of the privateer who had brought the prize vessels into the Connecticut port. That night Will began to read Locke by candlelight in his room.

Will estimated three days for General Knox to reach Boston, three days to accomplish his business, without understanding precisely what that business was, and three days to return to Springfield. Therefore, on the ninth day he took to riding Big Red first to the work sites and then out the Upper Post Road that led to Boston in hopes of meeting the General. The fresh air and the sound of his horse's hooves helped to clarify his thinking about his reading. He avidly accepted Locke's thesis of the necessity of the consent of the governed and was convinced that the horrors of this war were being visited on the colonists because of the Crown's obstinate refusal to recognize their basic and time-honored rights. For Will, that he as a patriot possessed these rights was indisputable.

When an occasional gust of bitterly cold wind caused him to push his neck stock tighter to his throat, he abandoned Locke's philosophy of the consent of the governed and thought of Elisabeth instead. He imagined her sitting demurely with Mrs. Knox and then, as he had last seen her, distraught at his head injury and tearful at their parting.

Riding east from the town, late in the afternoon of the twelfth day, trying to compose a letter to Elisabeth in his mind, he did not notice General Knox and the four cavalry men until they were within hailing distance.

"Halloo, Will," Knox's stentorian voice boomed out over the snowy distance between them. Will looked up and waved enthusiastically. He clicked his tongue, dug in his heels and Big Red broke into a gallop until Will was close enough to see the broad smile on the General's face.

"It is good of you to ride out to greet me, Will. I am truly pleased to see you. It was a most successful trip to Boston. Brother Billy sends his best and has found for me a gift, a treasure I will show to you in the privacy of my quarters."

Will had no idea what such a gift might be or for whom. He assumed it was something for the General's wife.

"Any news from Mrs. Knox about your daughter," Will asked hoping there might also be a tidbit of information concerning Elisabeth.

"I received one letter while in Boston. Our daughter has recovered splendidly. The ladies have enjoyed the warm hospitality of the prominent patriotic families of Philadelphia. Why not a day passes, my dearest has written, but with teas, dinners, concerts and dances from midday until the wee hours of the morn."

Will could envision the teas, dinners and concerts with Elisabeth and Mrs. Knox seated together. The image of Elisabeth at a dance, being fawned over by dandies like Captain Seeley and whirled around the floor in their arms, was upsetting. He managed to discard that disturbing scene from his mind by thinking of her knitting a wool scarf for him, as she had promised.

At the Black Bull, despite the cold, the innkeeper, coatless and in shirtsleeves, stood outside to welcome the General. As one man held the reins of his horse, Knox ponderously swung his leg over, stepped on the dismounting block and from there to the ground, with a loud grunt.

"Ahh. It is good to be out of the saddle," he said, stretching his shoulders. "Will. Bring my saddlebags with you after you have seen to the horses. There are dispatches in there ordering us to make haste and return to Morristown."

Will led the two horses to the barn. When he returned to the Inn, he found the General holding forth from the head of a crowded dinner table of prosperous local merchants and militia officers about the scarcity of materials for the powder laboratory and ordinance and the difficulties of daily life in Boston. Will squeezed in on a bench at the far end of the table, thinking the wealthy farmers and mill owners would barely be able to disguise their glee at the news of food shortages in Boston. He sensed, from Knox's volubility and the fawning and appreciative comments offered by the other diners who were impressed at being seated with an intimate of General Washington's, that more time than food might be consumed. He ate voraciously, careful to avoid the wine and other spirits, drinking only one mug of mulled cider and kept the General's saddlebags firmly between his feet under the table.

It was well past dark when Knox rose and offered a toast to General Washington, the Cause and the brave men of the Continental

Army encamped at Morristown. The Inn's patrons cheered loudly in response.

"And now, gentlemen, you must excuse me. I have dispatches to write and correspondence to read." He glanced around the room, saw Will standing near the fireplace, holding the saddlebags.

"Sergeant Stoner. There you are. Bring those bags and accompany me to my quarters."

Will climbed the stairs to the General's room, the heavy saddlebags slung over one shoulder, knocked and pushed the door open. Knox was seated on the four-poster bed, attempting to bend down over his large stomach and grab the heel of one boot.

"I normally would not request a battle tested soldier of my own Regiment to aid me with my boots, but as you can see, I am in need of some assistance."

The General straightened out his legs and Will knelt and wrestled the knee high black boots off and put them at the foot of the bed.

"There, that is much better," he said rubbing one foot against the other. "It has been a fatiguing and hard ride from Boston. We covered sixty miles yesterday and forty today." He unbuttoned his waistcoat, tugged his shirt from the band around his breeches and breathed another sigh of relief. The spindles of the chair creaked as Knox stretched back in the chair, his legs out protruding from under the table and wiggled his toes through the stockings. Will deposited the saddlebags next to the General and stood waiting between the four-poster and the desk.

"We must leave early tomorrow for Morristown. General Washington believes the British will soon marshal their forces from Brunswick and urgently requests we make haste to return. He is anxious for me to prepare the artillery for the coming campaign." [5] He motioned for Will to sit in the chair opposite him.

"This is the prize I spoke of," Knox said, removing two thick leather bound volumes from a saddlebag and handing them carefully to Will. "It is a gift for His Excellency. General Washington favors books on military matters." Will looked at the gold embossing on the spine and then the engraved title page- 'The Military Engineer: or a Treatise on the Attack and Defence of all kinds of Fortified Place.'

Carefully he turned the pages noting the detail of the copper plates illustrating different types of fortifications. Knox placed them on his desk, away from his inkwell and opened his copy book.

"I will send one of the cavalry tomorrow as a courier to Morristown with a letter, advising His Excellency we are making as much haste as possible. However, I cannot in good judgment, nor in the interests of my own domestic tranquility, leave my dearest's trunks in Springfield in the interests of rapid travel. I can procure another horse to pull the sled if that will be necessary." He looked at Will, a smile forming at the corners of his mouth.

Will vehemently shook his head. "Big Red will pull it and keep up with you and your escort."

"Good lad. Ask the innkeeper to provide you with assistance in loading the sled. We shall depart shortly after dawn."

Will stood up to leave. "And Will," General Knox said winking at him. "My dearest Lucy shall know her books and particulars arrived with us in Morristown due to your efforts."

The days were noticeably longer in late March. They rode south through Connecticut, turned well west of the British ensconced in New York City and down into New Jersey, riding at a fast pace, leaving the inns and hospitable homes of local patriots shortly after sunrise and continuing to well after dusk. The General would occasionally ride alongside Will and query him on his understanding of Locke.

"Consent of the people is the essential basis for political legitimacy," Knox said, at one point after they had crossed the Hudson on a flat-bottomed ferry. "I have turned this idea over in my mind and see no obstacle to its veracity. Will, the only way for you to acquire knowledge of great ideas is to read. You must read everything within your power to do so. Why, I myself learned all about fortifications and artillery from books." He interpreted Will's silence as skepticism. "Well not all," he admitted. "I presumed too much to make the point. Drilling and more drilling taught me the basics of firing cannons. As it has you." Will nodded thinking of how little he had known when first joining the Regiment. Now, he was training gun crews to unlimber cannons and rapidly move them to support the infantry.

They covered the four hundred miles from Springfield to Morristown in seven days. As the General had surmised, "his dearest love," as he openly referred to her when talking to Will, their infant daughter and Elisabeth, were still in Philadelphia. It mattered not to Will. Elisabeth was nearby. He knew he would see her again and soon.

—⁂—

James thought spring was the best time of year. The pastures were covered with a blanket of light green, a promise of the oats and wheat to come. The fringe of forest bordering their newly plowed fields came alive with birds- thrushes, warblers, bluebirds and grosbeaks flitted through the early foliage, their twitters, whistles, peeps and trills filling the early morning air. This spring, they would be working in the evenings by moonlight. His father insisted the bridge over the creek and the gristmill must be finished by harvest time although he did not say why. James assumed it was so that other farmers would use the mill to make flour for which his father would be paid. The bridge had to be completed first so they could transport the large water wheel for the mill and the heavy grist stones to the site.

Despite the hard work ahead, James looked forward to laboring through the spring nights. He liked working under the starry sky, amazed at the occasional shooting star amidst the twinkling points of light. He took pleasure in the scratching, scraping, clicking sounds of the insects and the calls of animals in the woods prowling in the dark, the muskrats, raccoons, black bears and bobcats, the menacing deep cough of a prowling cougar, the shrill cry of the nighthawk rising into the dark sky with a field mouse in its talons or the eerie call of a barred owl piercing the cool air.

Once Georg had recovered his strength, he proved to be strong and capable. Throughout the winter, they had worked as a three person team. James drove their ox Zak pulling the sled with the large rectangular stones to the edge of the abutment. The Hessian levered them with the pry bar guiding them into position as directed by Mr. Kierney. His father then cleverly fitted each stone in place, being renowned in the area as one of the best dry masons. By the end of

February, the bridge abutments rose over the brook and were even with the level of the road.

The first clear spring night, James and his father laid out the seasoned beams for the new bridge's king post trusses, while Georg plowed a nearby field, striding vigorously behind Zak. His father pounded one of the beams into place with the heavy wooden mallet and then handed the beetle to his son. It weighed over forty pounds. James strained to lift it slightly off the ground. He held it with two hands and swung it parallel to his legs, pounding the stringer beam into the pre-cut square in the upright king post. He hit it again taking several shorter swings, and tapped the beam home. James would not admit it but he was relieved when his father took the heavy mallet and handed him the awl to drill the holes for the wooden dowels. James had become proficient in making the "tree nails," long smooth oak pegs to hold the joints together. Now, careful to hold the awl straight, he bored into the seasoned wood, sweating from the effort, even though the night was cool. He had finished the holes in one beam when Georg drove Zak back from the field.

"It is done," Georg said pointing to the field. He looked curiously at the wooden skeleton laid out on the ground. "How does it . . ." he stopped not knowing the words and pointed from the assembled king post and stringer beams to the gap between the stone abutments on either side of the creek.

"We will have help," Thomas's father said. "I have rented ropes for the raising and this Friday our neighbors will come at sunrise. By day's end, it will be up. But first, we have to set the two beams lengthwise across the brook. The three of us and the ox can do that tomorrow afternoon," Kierney said. "Now it is time to stop and eat something before we sleep."

Georg nodded. He understood more English than he could speak. He drove Zak to the barn and walked the short distance from the forge shed, his regular sleeping quarters, to the house. Several candles lit the interior and he smelled the meat on a spit in the fireplace. He had been eating at the house since recovering from the bloody flux and working a full day.

It was the woman who had indicated he should take his meals with the family. She gave him a pewter mug, fork and spoon and a wooden plate. The first time, Georg had been reluctant to use the fork, instead, bending low over the bowl and shoveling food into his mouth with the spoon, or spearing pieces of meat with his knife and biting off pieces. The woman immediately put a stop to that, directing him in a stern voice to imitate the family's manners. They said some kind of prayer before eating food at every meal, bowing their heads and joining hands. He had been sitting between Sarah and James the first time, and the little girl reluctantly had reached out toward him. Her tiny hand quivered like a small, injured songbird in his rough, callused palm and he sensed her fear of him. He smiled at her, saddened that she was afraid in her own home because of his presence. He thought of himself as more pleasant in appearance, having long since shaved his mustache. He could no longer powder his hair, which had grown out and was tied in a tail at the back, like James and his father.

Georg always removed his wooden clogs at the threshold, leaving them outside and bowing slightly before entering. The first few times he had done so, the man had yelled at him and then imitated his bow and vigorously shook his head no. Georg did not understand why his gesture upset the man. It was a mark of respect to the man and his family for providing him with food and shelter. The wife did not seem to mind and the boy, James, and his sister thought it was funny. He persisted in bowing and the man gave up trying to change his behavior.

Sundays, he accompanied the family to church, wedged up front on the narrow seat of the sled between James and his father. There was no farm work performed until after sunset. He listened to the sermons, understanding little, while shivering on the cold wooden benches, and enduring the friendly but curious stares of the other families. However, once he had been to church a few times, others saw his need and brought clothing for him- worn shirts, pants, and even a black woolen jacket with odd brown patches, which was too short in the sleeves and came down to his mid-thigh.

The day after they had assembled the king post on the ground, they hauled the long beams bridging the space between the two stone abutments and fixed the cross pieces into place. While Georg dug a deep hole on either side of the incomplete bridge, close to the edge of the abutments, the man and his son brought thick logs, roughly planed, which they pounded into the freshly dug holes. Georg saw they would be in the middle of the roadway on either side of the bridge. It made no sense to him, but his English was not up to asking for an explanation.

On Friday, they were up before dawn. James fed and watered the animals in the dark barn. After a quick breakfast, Georg and James loaded the long coils of rented rope on a sled and pulled them down toward the bridge construction site. In the early light, Georg saw five figures standing around a wagon on the far side of the creek.

"Our neighbors," James said waving to one of them. "That is my friend Oliver, his two older brothers, their father, Mr. Langley, Mrs. Langley is on the wagon and that is Hope, their daughter with her." He hesitated. "The other man I do not recognize."

Thomas Kierney hailed Robert Langley with a loud halloo and a wave as James dashed across the old bridge to greet Oliver. As the groups came together, Georg held back, as did one of the men with the Langleys. Despite having a white linen patch over one eye, he looked familiar. Suddenly, Georg recognized him and called out in German.

"Christoph? Is that you? Is it really you?"

"Georg. Georg Frederich?" The two former comrades embraced each other. Christoph was thinner and hunched over in the early morning cold. Georg noticed he was poorly clothed, his jacket little more than a thin cloth with sleeves.

"It will not do to have these Hessians jabbering away in their own language," Robert Langley said to Kierney.

"It appears harmless to me," James' father replied. "They are simply happy to see each other."

"If you coddle them, they will seize the advantage," Langley said gruffly, watching Georg and Christoph intensely engaged in conversation.

"What happened to your eye," Georg asked.

"They have me working in the bottom of a saw pit and the dust continually comes down. Something scratched my eye and it has not healed," he said wearily.

"My boys and I have come to assist on raising the king posts for your new bridge," Langley said. He pointed at the thin edge of orange and red peeping through the trees. "We will waste the day away if we do not get to work. Here now," he yelled at Christoph. "Enough of that infernal gargling. There is work to be done."

Thomas tipped his hat to Mrs. Langley and remarked how Hope had grown since he had last seen her. "Hannah and Sarah are up in the house and will be pleased for your company," he said before leading the men to the bridge site.

James, Oliver, Georg and Christoph were sent into the cold creek water. The men on the banks lowered pre-cut long square temporary braces which the four of them raised against the recently installed bridge beams, to push the floor beams upward before the king posts were raised. Once the ropes were firmly tied to the posts, they were run around the upright logs James and his father had driven into the holes on either side of the abutments.

With James' father and Mr. Langley manning the winch ropes, the rest of them, struggled to push one heavy rectangular king post into position. They waited for Thomas Kierney to give the signal he was satisfied it was vertical to the floor beams. Quickly, James on one side and Oliver on the other, hammered the trunnels into the pre-drilled holes to hold it in place. They took a break at noon and trooped up to the house for a meal of warm bread, slavered with butter, chunks of cheese and smoked ham, and washed down the freshly baked pies with hard cider. Christoph was directed to eat outside by Mr. Langley who raised an eyebrow and scowled as Georg sat down at the table next to James.

"I tell you Thomas, you are doing wrong by your Hessian." He pointed his knife at Georg. "A strong hand is all they know and all they need. Remember, they are not family but foreign mercenaries sent to destroy our farms and visit savagery on our women and children."

James looked at Georg to see if he understood. The Hessian sat upright, unblinking, concentrating on cutting a piece of ham and spearing it with his fork. James thought he understood and was showing off his manners to rankle Mr. Langley. He smiled and winked. Georg winked back. Sarah giggled and poked Hope who stared at Georg with wide-eyed curiosity.

"Each to his own methods," Thomas Kierney replied. "How is your apple orchard coming," he said. "Have the grafts taken?" The conversation during the rest of the mid-day meal was consumed with the usual talk of plowing and planting wheat, rye and corn, the weather for the rest of spring, the health of the cows, oxen and horses and the birth of calves and foals, before turning to the war.

"I believe the British will march out of Brunswick in force this very month and by the end of April occupy Philadelphia," Mr. Langley said. "I hear our army is starving in Morristown and depleted by desertions. Why, whole regiments leave when their ninety days have run out."

"If I signed up to fight," John Langley stated, "I would stay for the duration." He was the oldest of the boys.

"You will not enlist in the Continental Army," Mr. Langley said angrily. "I need you on the farm. I cannot allow you to throw your life away for a lost and hopeless cause espoused by those disputatious chukkleheads of a Congress."

James glanced at Oliver who shook his head slightly to indicate it was best to let his father's anger pass.

"Well," said James' father. "I cannot make predictions based on rumors about our Army. General Washington defeated the British before and I believe he will do it again. If the place be right and Providence favorable to our Army and cause." He stood up from the table signaling the meal was finished. "Come, let us complete raising this bridge together and leave the discussion of the war and Congress to another time."

In the warming sun of the afternoon, the men sweated to raise the pre-cut brace beams, forming right hand triangles with the king's post. Once the wood trunnels had been hammered in fast the bridge was complete except for the floor. The women and girls came from the house to watch as James and Oliver clambered up the beams to the top of the king post and tied a small pine tree as a brush to celebrate. The two boys raced each other down, Oliver winning by a hair and shouting in triumph. [6]

In the days that followed, the three of them worked the fields in the mornings and in the afternoons made the planks for the bridge floor. Georg, who showed a proficiency with their large split-axe, halved the seasoned logs, felled the previous fall. Each time he split a log perfectly, the Hessian would stretch his back, grin, examine his axe and exclaim, "Is goot holzaxt."

Thomas Kierney made planks from the half logs, hitting the hard wood wedges with the heavy ironwood beetle. James sawed the planks to length and laid them loosely across the bridge beams. They would be fixed in place later with trunnels, a layer of roadway planks on top, going in the opposite way.

As the days lengthened and became warmer, they worked longer hours, constructing a stone foundation and frame for the mill house and the wooden sluiceway from the pond to where the large wooden mill wheel would be installed. James was atop a ladder, pounding a wooden nail into a roof rafter when he spied the millwright coming up the road. The two oxen team pulled the one-ton heavy wooden wheel on a wagon. James scampered down the ladder and called for Georg to follow him down to the creek. In the warmth of the late spring day, the cool water was pleasing as they splashed through it to watch the wagon cross the bridge.

"We did it," James yelled enthusiastically at Georg. "See, there was no sag at all." He held his hands level in front of his chest with the fingers touching but unbent. Georg caught James' enthusiasm and smiled broadly. "Goot job," he said as he followed the boy up the steep embankment. Together with the millwright and his assistant, Georg and Thomas levered the wheel, made entirely from white oak, into position until its axle rested on the two stone platforms they had finished only the week before. The millwright stayed for dinner and slept on the floor of the main room. The following day he installed the maple wooden gears that would turn the millstones. James released the sluice gates of the mill race and the massive wheel groaned and began to slowly rotate from the weight of the water falling on to it.

In the following weeks, in addition to the usual farm chores, the three of them finished framing the mill house, squared twelve by sixteen oak beams with a broad axe for the interior ceiling for the shafts, made cedar shingles for its roof and boards for its floor and cut trees from the stand of forest behind the barn for a supply of seasoned wood. Georg was more tired than he had been for a long time. He knew the man respected him for his work, his ability with an axe and his strength and stamina. Sometimes, he thought of Christoph and how Mr. Langley treated him and thanked God he had been selected by this kindly family as a farm hand.

One day in late May the mill stones arrived, pulled by two teams of oxen, the bed stone on one wagon and the runner stone on the other. Georg, had been transporting logs on a sled pulled by Zak from the cool of the forest to the mounded hill adjacent to the house. The air beyond the trees was heavy and damp. Sweat stained his linen shirt and swarms of mosquitos attacked his bare neck, face and hands. The boy had explained they would build a cellar to store fruit and vegetables for the winter. He thought with a shudder of the cellars he had plundered as a soldier, searching for wine, rum and cider, taking what he wanted and wantonly destroying what he could not carry.

It took three of them, together with the miller and his apprentice, exerting all of their strength on the ropes attached to a sturdy oak hoist, to lift the massive one ton bed stone into position. Georg assumed the stranger was the maker of the stones. It was he who directed them to situate the other stone and adjusted the distance between the two. Mrs. Kierney and the girls came from the house and joined the men. James was given the honor of raising the slatted wooden dam to the mill race. The water wheel turned, the wooden gears groaned as the teeth meshed and top running stone began to revolve, faster and faster. Mr. Kierney grinned, the girls screamed with delight and Mrs. Kierney affectionately squeezed her husband's hand. James whooped loudly and waved his hand in a circular motion for Georg to join in. He smiled broadly, nodding his head up and down and repeating, "Ja, is goot," over and over. He felt part of them, sharing in their joy and pride in their success.

The mill was now basically complete. The boy told him this Sunday was a special day at their church. Georg assumed it was to celebrate the new mill. He struggled to understand the sermon but the words all seemed beyond him. The boy was bubbling over with excitement as the family returned home. In the June twilight, the entire family walked along the stonewalls and cedar fences which marked their fields, stopping at the corners and boundary stones, bowing their heads and praying.

"We are giving thanks for our land, the trees and crops we grow," James said to Georg. "Tis Rog Sunday. [7] We will meet the Langleys at the far corner of the cornfield. Their land is on the other side." At the sound of the family name, Georg thought he might see Christoph. He would offer his friend a word of encouragement and urge him to persevere. He understood they were walking the land owned by the man and his wife. So it was true. Here they owned the land they worked. Now it made sense, all the effort and labor from dawn to dusk, cheerfully and willingly done. Why construct a mill and bridge if it could be taken away by the Landgraf or some noble? The bridge and mill were the Kierneys.

It was getting darker and a flicker of candle light from a lantern appeared bobbing toward them. The man greeted his neighbor, Robert Langley who gruffly responded. Georg noticed with disappointment that Christoph was not with them. James ran forward to play with Oliver but his friend stood rigid, looking down at the ground.

"Still treating your Hessian mercenary as family, I see."

"He has worked hard and well and is entitled and welcome to celebrate and give thanks with us," Thomas Kierney replied.

"The Bible commands us to help those in need," Hannah added softly.

"The Bible will not protect you when he steals into your home at night and hacks your heads off with an axe," Langley said with a snarl.

"I am sorry you are so troubled tonight on this Sunday of all days."

"This Sunday marks two weeks since my eldest son, John, chose to abandon his family, his filial duty and our farm. He has run off to enlist with that rabble which calls itself an army. Now I am short handed, with a sullen Hessian waiting to stab me in the back and a wife who can only mope and mourn her missing son. There is nothing to celebrate or give thanks for."

Thomas Kierney remained silent as Hannah spoke quietly to Mrs. Langley. The women embraced one more time as the two families quietly resumed their boundary walk. When they returned to the house, as planned they had tea, cider and cakes to celebrate what had begun as a joyous occasion. Mrs. Kierney began to sing a song and soon the children joined in, their laughter and young voices dispelling the gloom disbursed in generous portion by the Langleys.

Georg left them dancing around the table and went to the forge. He returned with a cloth tied with a twined bunch of daisies, bowed upon re-entering the house, stood before Sarah and bowed again, presenting her with the package.

"I make this to dank you all for making me well and giffing work. Dank you," he said again, bowing first to Hannah and the man, and then extending his hand to James. The boy shook it and smiled back at him.

Sarah undid the woven daisy tie and opened the cloth. Inside were eight, highly polished pewter buttons, from Georg's old uniform. In the light from the fireplace, they sparkled like rounded stars. The little girl's eyes lit up with delight. She rushed forward and hugged Georg around his knees, clinging to him for a long time.

# Part Three
# The Campaign Resumed

# Chapter 8 - Return to the Jersey Shore

The letter from Elisabeth was cheery, intimate and troubling at the same time. Will did not know how to respond. It had come together with dispatches from Philadelphia, including copies of the latest issues of the Pennsylvania Gazette and the Evening Post, detailing the business of Congress. Will put these aside and reread the letter, written in her neat, cursive script, each word perfectly formed, the lines as straight as if drawn with a ruler.

She, Mrs. Knox and baby Lucy, Elisabeth wrote, were staying in the well furnished, comfortable home of relatives of Mary White. Mary, who was married to Robert Morris, a wealthy banker, merchant and member of the Continental Congress, with an elegant mansion in the best part of town, had been most gracious in making her relatives' home available. At one dinner, at the Morris' own home, to which she Elisabeth had been invited, General Knox had speculated that General Howe would leave his mistress in New York and join the Army in New Brunswick to begin the campaign to capture Philadelphia. Will wondered how much talk had there been about the British commander's mistress and was such a subject fit for his Elisabeth's ears. She went on to write about an exquisite tea she had attended with Mrs. Knox at the Society Hill townhouse of Edward Shippen, a prominent Philadelphia attorney whose three daughters had been exceptionally kind to her. They had invited her to a play and then to poetry readings, held in the magnificently furnished homes of leading citizens, and best of all, a dance, at the exclusive City Tavern, attended by a few members of Congress, including John Hancock and Robert Morris, among others. Elisabeth had been flattered by the attentions of several young officers of the Continental Army, who provided charming company with their conversation about music, painting and belle lettres, but she missed Will and longed to be in his company instead of these strangers dancing with her until the wee hours of the morn.

Reading these lines again, Will felt her words betrayed the truth was the opposite. She was comparing him to others and finding him wanting. He was after all, only a simple New York farm boy with little or no social graces. It apparently had not occurred to her that he did not know how to dance, and while he did read, he knew little if anything about music or painting. She concluded her letter with the news she had finished a scarf for him, but since the weather was warm, she eagerly awaited the day when she could present it to him in person when he visited her in Philadelphia. In the meantime she and other patriotic women were collecting clothing, bandages and linens for the soldiers of "their" army.

A black despair settled on him. His hut, in the early June evening was stifling with the smell of sweat, smoke and unwashed men. He left without a word to his bunkmates. He walked away from the cluster of huts, smacking angrily at the mosquitos alighting on his neck and hands. No, he thought. It was his plight to remain in camp, carrying out the training tasks assigned to him and if and when he ever got to Philadelphia, his worn Sergeant's uniform and coarse manners would give proof to Elisabeth that he was beneath her and not worthy of her attentions.

He wandered aimlessly, past the Commons, oblivious to the boisterous shouts of drunken soldiers, drowning out the sounds of the insects of the night anxiously seeking mates for their desperately short lives. The stench of the latrines and the fetid odors of animal waste were so strong it pierced his consciousness and he walked more rapidly, until he saw the Ford residence ahead. He suspected Captain Hadley was there. If Miss Mercy was at home, he was sure to be. Perhaps the Captain could help him interpret Elisabeth's letter and suggest how he should proceed.

A servant opened the door to his knock and asked him to wait while his presence was announced. He found Hadley and Miss Mercy sitting across the table from each other, drinking cider and engaged in an intense discussion. Both acknowledged his presence but were unwilling to abandon their conversation.

"I do not understand the logic of your position, Samuel. If, as you say, the right to vote should be restricted to heads of households who own property of a certain value, then your very definition includes wealthy but unmarried women- widows with substantial estates for example. Your New England dominated Congress, when it discusses the issue, should include what we of the fairer sex enjoy in New Jersey under our new State Constitution." [1] She cocked her head as if the point were obvious. "I have written my female friends with whom I correspond, including Abigail Adams in your beloved Massachusetts. Hopefully, she will be able to influence her husband to see the correctness of our position."

"Women by nature are not heads of households," Hadley said raising his voice in exasperation. "My God. Look around you in Morristown. I will wager not one single household is led by a woman," he said, emphasizing his words by poking his index finger on the oak table top. "So, when your New Jersey Constitution, or any document refers to heads of households, it is adopting what one and all know to be the obvious fact- that men are the heads of households. The drafters might have easily as said white males substituting that phrase for heads of household and achieved the same result." [2]

He turned in his chair and looked at Will. "What say you? In Schoharie was there ever a woman as head of household?"

Will tried to recall if he knew of such a case. He was about to reply but Miss Mercy did not give him the chance. "It matters not whether there are examples, here or in New York. It is the words that matter and the phrase in our New Jersey Constitution is inclusive of women. We have the right to vote, we will exercise it and keep it." She smiled pleasantly at Samuel, indicating the debate was over.

"And what brings you to our companionable table tonight," she said to Will, smiling sweetly. "The want of deep discussion on weighty issues that only men think they are capable of having?"

Will explained his misgivings about Elisabeth's letter and blurted out he did not know how to dance and his lack of polish would be evident to one and all, if he ever had the chance to visit her in Philadelphia.

Miss Mercy emitted a bird like laugh and clapped her hands together in amusement. For some reason, it gave Will hope.

"The easy part is learning to dance. Everyone has to at some time. We will teach you, will we not Samuel?"

Hadley nodded, studying Will as one appraises the ability of a horse to jump fences and hedges. "You are reasonably well coordinated and apportioned. I do not see why you cannot learn in short order," he said encouragingly.

"As for your concerns, Elisabeth would not have written you at all, if she did not care for your affections," Miss Mercy said. "Why relate what she is doing, unless she wants you to share in her experiences as she expects you to write about yours. She knows little of artillery drills, unlimbering of guns and the like but wishes you to tell her because when two people are apart, the only way they can share their lives is through letters." Will rested his chin on his hands. Her words made sense.

"Come, Will. Do not be despondent any longer. Elisabeth is an open and well-intentioned person. She writes not to make you jealous but to make you part of her life." She gestured for him to rise. "I will maintain the beat by clapping and Samuel will teach you the steps."

One hour later, Will stood in his stocking feet in the Ford's dining room, sweating profusely, unhappy and confused. Hadley, at first patient and calm had become increasingly exasperated at Will's inability to grasp the most rudimentary of steps and his continued clumsiness. The more irritated the Captain became, the less Will was able to remember what he had been told.

"I swear I could teach Big Red to dance more readily than you," he said after Will had stumbled, getting his feet tangled in attempting to move into the Z pattern Hadley was trying to teach him.

"Now, Samuel," Miss Mercy said sternly. "Swearing will not teach Will the minuet. Nor does your impatience suit you. You are going too fast and giving him too much to think about." She smiled encouragingly at Will. "I will break it down for you. We will start with the honors. Put on your tri-corn and take my hand. Remember. Keep your body tall yet relaxed. You are publicly honoring Elisabeth as your partner."

His shirt clung to his body and he felt his face flushed but he made it through the honors, remembering to bow at the waist, removing the tri-corn so the inside faced Miss Mercy, awkwardly offering her his perspiring right hand while she led him through a pivot so he ended up facing her.

"Good," she said. "Now let us do it again. Then we will conclude this lesson. You practice this part on your own and tomorrow we shall see about a fiddler to play the Congress Minuet, instead of my keeping the beat. It will be more realistic and it is certain to be one of the most popular dances in Philadelphia. " [3]

I will never learn even this one dance, Will thought as he trudged to the barn in the darkness. Inside, he faced in the same direction he had in the dining room and went through the steps by himself, feeling more comfortable with the repetition. It is like drilling to fire a cannon. If one practices enough, it becomes routine and one can do it without thinking, he said out loud. But, at the thought of dancing with Elisabeth, in public before General and Mrs. Knox and the assembled officers, their wives and ladies, he stepped on his own foot and forgot what to do next.

He entered Big Red's stall and leaned against his horse's neck. He imagined elegant uniformed officers, even that fop Seeley, dancing with Elisabeth, touching her hand, the small of her back and whatever other contact was permitted between partners when they performed the minuet. He would learn that damn dance, he said to Big Red, so that at least, for the Congress Minuet, the one who had insulted her honor would not be able to be with her. He went back out on to the dark, straw covered dirt floor, imagined it was made of highly polished broad planks and began to practice the beginning honors Captain Hadley and Miss Mercy had taught him.

—⁂—

John Stoner cursed under his breath as he walked up the gangplank, already slippery with piss and the rounded piles of shit from the horses that had preceded him. His own mount, smelling the sea air in the strong breeze blowing toward shore, and balking at being confined on the ship, let loose a substantial stream of urine.

"God damn it, Stoner. Control your mare," the trooper immediately behind yelled, as John's horse was now rearing on the narrow walkway.

Viciously yanking the horse's head down and moving his hands up until they were almost at the bridle, John reached the top of the ramp and descended on to the schooner's deck. He led the animal down another ramp and into a stall, lined with sheepskins, the wool still on, to prevent the horses from chafing during the voyage. [4] Probably better quarters than we will have, John muttered to himself.

When he emerged from the transport's hold, a light rain was falling. He looked out over Amboy's harbor, filled with brigs, sloops and schooners. Scores of seagulls circled over the ships, waiting for the cooks' boys to throw the fish heads and other treats over the side. Beyond, Staten Island beckoned through a wet mist, with pleasant memories of sunny days filled with hunts and parades and evenings of dinner parties and balls. That was long before the attack on Long Island and the terrible fire that had consumed much of New York City.

The Army was leaving New Jersey after a fruitless two weeks of campaigning. In retrospect, John thought it had been bad luck to begin the night of Friday, June thirteenth, moving out of New Brunswick with their wagons optimistically loaded with long flat-bottomed boats, built in New York to cross the Delaware and capture Philadelphia. Now he thought, there was a city with many opportunities to be had for self-enrichment and to enjoy the company of the bevy of accomplished beautiful young ladies. He would hire himself a groom. No more taking care of his own horse. And a manservant as well, as Chatsworth and many of the officers had, to keep his uniforms clean, buttons bright and boots polished.

John's exhilaration at the thought of being in Philadelphia, a mere day's march once across the Delaware, had dissipated in dismay when the Army set up camp only nine miles from New Brunswick.

Inexplicably, the troops began constructing redoubts- three of them, huge earthen fortifications as if they expected to be besieged. The 16th Dragoons made a few scouting missions into the surrounding countryside, which John managed to avoid. The troopers returned, driving cattle before them, having plundered and burned nearby farms and the green wheat fields and John regretted not having been with them. But only because in the telling, it was clear there had been little risk.

There were reports of skirmishes and pickets being harassed, killed or captured by the Rebels, who refused to meet the British Army in the field. Mostly, he had sat in camp and waited. After a week of probing by large bands of Rebels, harassing of pickets and patrols and one or two larger clashes, orders were given to abandon the redoubts and returned to New Brunswick. [5] The Dragoons quartered just on the outskirts of the town in a solid white brick house, corrupted by the stench of militiamen hastily half buried in the orchard by the retreating American forces. When John awoke at dawn to relieve himself, he shuddered at the sight of decaying limbs protruding from the shallow graves, as if beckoning their living compatriots to attack and seek revenge.

From New Brunswick, the starting point of what had seemed to John to be the beginning of the end for the Rebels, the army began an organized retreat. By mid-morning, John was with the Light Dragoons on the south side of the Raritan. Together with some British infantry, grenadiers and Hessian Regiments they formed the rear guard of the Army trudging down the road to Perth Amboy, ten miles away. He heard shooting, muskets and cannons, and in the distance, clouds of low-lying smoke wafted above the bridge further north over the Raritan. He sensed the Dragoons were eager to charge forward and engage the Rebels. With relief he heard the orders to hold firm and maintain position. After the sounds of gunfire died down, they led the rear-guard the short distance back to New Brunswick, now mostly abandoned of both troops and residents.

Suddenly, the Hessians swarmed past the troopers' trotting horses, eager for one last rampage and chance for plunder. Chatsworth turned in his saddle and grinned at his men.

"No need to dismount. Such base scum who owned these homes could hardly object to our entering on horseback." And with that, he rode his horse up the wide, wooden front steps of a large house and pranced around the porch, smashing the windows with the stock of his fuzee. John spurred his horse forward through the gaping maw of a home whose double doors had been torn from their hinges and joined in the general destruction, knocking plates and dinnerware to the floor with his sword and backing his horse into the side of a tall, glass fronted bookcase, causing it to topple over. He was hindered from entering other houses by plundering Hessians intent on taking as much as possible. They warned off the troopers in their guttural language. To John it was like the sounds of snarling dogs, fighting over a carcass.

Back on the street, Chatsworth rode up to John and handed him a glass oil lamp, the flame of the wick barely visible in the sunlight. "Be quick. And make sure the fire catches. We want to leave Brunswick with nothing to benefit the Rebels."

John found a two-story building with heavy drapes visible through the shattered windows. A person of substance must have lived here, he thought. He dismounted, tied his horse to a pillar of the porch, and holding the lamp high, entered the darkened central hall. The windows on the room to his left, the one with the drapes, had heavily cushioned window seats, burgundy with a design made of golden colored thread. That will be readily combustible, he thought as he carefully set the lamp down on the floor. Quickly, he slashed at the fabric, tearing out the gauzy muslin filling and spreading it under the deep blue drapes. He grabbed another cushion and felt something hard within the fabric. Eagerly, he cut it open and reached inside. His fingers found a dark green silk pouch, delicately embroidered and tied tightly at the top with fine silver colored ribbon. John resisted the greedy impulse to slash the other window seats and see if they contained more treasures. No time. With the silken pouch secure in his waistcoat pocket, he poured some of the lamp oil on the bottom of the drapes, built up a pile of the muslin and smashed the lamp on the floor. As he left, the flames were curling up the drapes toward the ceiling and the fire had caught on the floorboards and was licking at the base of the window seat.

Remounting, he patted the prize he had found, trying to ascertain by feeling the hard shapes what valuables lay inside. That night, while Chatsworth and the others were off carousing, he emptied the contents on his cot and, to his immense delight, discovered a silver ring with an intricate setting that held, he hoped, a ruby, and a pearl necklace of three strands. He wrapped the pouch in a stocking, tied it tightly at the top, placed the stocking inside one of the linen shirts he had taken from some Rebel home, he no longer remembered where, and buried the shirt beneath other clothing in a lower corner of his wooden trunk. He would make certain the trunk was safely loaded on the baggage train in the morning for the journey to Amboy.

Three days later, instead of arriving at the safe haven on the Jersey shore, and the ships which would transport him away from here, John found himself among the 16th Light Dragoons, led by Colonel Harcourt himself, on a quick night ride heading north toward the Rebels. As the troopers saddled up, they were eager, almost impetuously so, for the coming engagement.

"Well, John," Chatsworth said as he cinched his saddle and strapped his fuzee over his shoulder. "At last we will give these scummy rabble their comeuppance. It is time for them to pay for their sniping at our columns from a distance and skulking in the woods."

John tried to fake enthusiasm for the coming battle but he was thinking more of how to avoid being maimed for life or worse killed. "We will drive them from the field," he said with false bravado. One of the troopers snickered behind his back.

As they formed up on the road, he heard one of them exclaim loudly. "See Ramrod John up toward the front? He is ramrod straight at the beginning but when the first shot is fired, his posture is more of a spent prick- wilted and bent over his horse's neck." John reddened at the laughter that followed. By the trooper's code of honor, he should have challenged the man to a duel. No chance of that, he thought seething. Better to survive and be thought a coward. He will have his day once the army captures Philadelphia. There, his talents would be put to good use and he would be in a position to cultivate the officers and not have to endure the slights of others.

The 16th were part of a larger force of Hessian Grenadiers and infantry moving rapidly up a road toward some hills that loomed ahead in the darkness. It was already getting warm when the sun rose to John's right. He heard sporadic cannon and musket fire, interspersed with the sharper crack of rifles. The dragoons halted and then, led by Colonel Harcourt left the main body and rode around a low sloping hill and across a field toward the sounds of the battle. John could see they were on a course to flank a large Rebel body dug in on a bare hill, surrounded by some woods. Hessian troops were making a frontal assault, their bayonets and brass caps glinting in the early morning light. Closer to the Dragoons, British light infantry were also advancing up the slope in the face of heavy cannon and musket fire. [6]

This was the moment John dreaded. Boxed in among the troopers on both sides, only three or four rows behind the Colonel, he was swept along as the Dragoons spurred their horses to a gallop, sweeping up toward the crown of the hill, to the left of the infantry. They were too close to the woods. John saw puffs of smoke from the trees and a trooper next to him threw up his arms and fell back in the saddle, his horse continuing blindly along with the others. John heard a heavy thud and then his horse stumbled, blood flowing from a gaping wound just in front of John's left knee. He grabbed the reins to pull his mare's head up, aware of his own high-pitched scream above the gunfire. The dying horse crumpled to the ground falling sideways. John, unable to free his feet from the stirrups, went down as well, his right leg pinned under the thrashing horse. He felt a sharp pain in his back as the barrel of his fuzee jabbed him below the shoulder blade. Finally, weak from the loss of blood his mare stopped struggling. A red froth drooled from the horse's mouth. The bullet must have pierced a lung. John grabbed his trapped leg with both hands and pulled on his thigh. Sweating profusely in the mid-morning sun, he was barely able to gain a few inches before he stopped and realized there were no more sounds of musket fire. Nearby, a wounded trooper moaned and called for water.

"Help me," John called out. "Help me. I am trapped." He heard the sound of a musket hammer being cocked and frantically turned his head. He caught a glimpse of black shoes and white gaiters and then, he almost cried with relief when he saw the red coat of an approaching British light infantryman. The soldier walked around John, calmly shot the mare through her eye and laid down his musket. He reached under John's armpits and tugged hard. John cried out as a sharp pain stabbed at his shoulder blade, and then went limp lying free on the damp, soft ground.

"My leg. Is it there?" he asked the soldier desperately.

The soldier smirked at him. "I have seen worse. Look for yourself," he replied, with a note of disdain in his voice, as he moved on.

John pushed himself up on his elbows, gasping from the pain in his shoulder and apprehensively looked down toward his boots. His right pants leg was covered with dirt and grass stains, his boot torn at the heel, but his leg was whole. He sobbed gratefully and using his fuzee as a cane, stood up.

A lone horse nibbled on the trampled grass, its rider lying nearby with a gaping bloody wound in his side. John hobbled over to the dead man's horse, untied the canteen and took a long drink. He saw he was on the periphery of the battlefield. The Rebel force on the summit had concentrated their fire on the charging British and Hessian infantry, In their frontal assault on the Rebel's positions they had suffered the most casualties. The sloping hill was littered with wounded Redcoats some writhing in pain, others crawling about amidst those already dead.

Around him, John could see a few troopers and horses had been picked off by the marksmen hidden among the trees. Colonel Harcourt had risked the Dragoons' lives by shielding the charging infantry from the Rebel riflemen hidden in the woods. He had almost been killed as a buffer for the lowlifes who comprised the British infantry, John thought angrily.

He heard the cry for water, weaker now, from the trooper lying near John's dead mare. Slowly, he hobbled over and bent down, peering into the man's face. John thought he recognized him as one of those who had mocked him in their camp. But he was not sure. The wounded trooper was lying on his back, one hand holding his side, from which blood slowly pulsed through his fingers. It looked like a stomach wound, with a side entry point. He knew one should not give water. The trooper begged John with his eyes. It is his decision, John thought. He asked for a drink. It is not for me to withhold it. He lifted the man's head and held the canteen up to his lips.

"Well, John. Good to see you in one piece," Chatsworth said as he rode up with a few of the Dragoons, looking down approvingly as John appeared to be ministering care and compassion to a wounded fellow trooper.

"I had my horse shot out from under me," he replied, pointing to the dead mare matter-of-factly. "Pinned me to the ground, but I managed to get myself out," he said looking around first to make sure the British soldier who had killed his mare and pulled him free was not nearby.

"We had some sport of it, chasing the Rebels down the far slope almost to another hill where they made a stand and we were called back. We captured a cannon or two and some supply wagons. Are you well enough to ride?"

Now that the battle was over and he had survived enemy fire, John affected a swagger. "My shoulder took a bruise when I was pinned, but I am fit to ride. I will take this horse," he said grunting as he put his foot in the stirrup and lifted himself up. As they rode down the sloping hill, which he had galloped up in such fear for his life, he sat ramrod straight, even though it caused him much pain in his shoulder blade. There will be fewer comments behind my back now, he thought.

In the days after the battle, the weather was oven hot. Mosquitos viciously attacked them in swarms and water was in short supply. The horses' were miserable, their eyes festooned with numerous large black flies that sought the liquid and mucus discharge. The Dragoons rode slowly past soldiers, felled by heatstroke and the effects of having drank the brackish water in the nearly dried up creeks. Swarms of Rebel riflemen and ragtag local militias, pursued the long red column at a distance as it snaked through the baked New Jersey countryside, randomly picking off men as if an angry God was casting the dice to determine who should live and who should die.

And now, when they least needed the rain, it had come, to further dampen their spirits as they left Perth Amboy for Staten Island, where they had first landed eleven months ago. In the hold of a schooner, cramped together for the short voyage, John listened to the angry talk among the Dragoons. They recognized a retreat for what it was, no matter how much plundering and destruction had been done on the route to the shore. They cursed the Generals in charge of this debacle. It was an affront to their honor as courageous and brave cavalry men to concede all of New Jersey to this undisciplined rabble of farmers and mechanics, not even worthy of being called an army.

None of this moved John- the bravado, the oaths of giving no quarter when they met the cowardly Rebels again, or complaints of the lack of leadership by the Great Chucclehead, General Howe. Let the Rebels have New Jersey. He was confident the next move would be to capture the grand city of Philadelphia. And he vowed, until then, he would not place himself in any danger in the field. In Philadelphia, he would ingratiate himself with men of title and influence and feather his own nest as well. It was only a matter of time before the Rebel capital fell.

## Chapter 9 - An Independence Day Celebration

Philadelphia, with its contradictions, charmed Elisabeth. The city exuded a sense of purpose and orderliness, with its numbered streets running north-south and the cross streets, named for native trees, running east-west. It was larger by far than Albany and even grander than New York. There were four magnificent city squares and broad streets paved with cobblestones, lined with brick sidewalks and lit at night by gaslights.

Yet, there was an air of unpredictability about it, an almost exuberant chaos, with the unbridled building and bustling excitement at the wharves and warehouses along the Delaware River. There, privateers disgorged their captured goods and smugglers brought French guns and powder from the Caribbean. Near the waterfront, the war had spawned cannon foundries and smelters of lead for making musket balls, nestled amongst the illegitimate tippling houses and other places of nefarious doings in the narrow alleys. In the better part of town, the delegates to the Continental Congress were seen hurrying to and from their endless meetings or continuing their contentious debates in the nearby licensed taverns and local boarding houses. [1]

The social circles of the prosperous and powerful were open to Elisabeth because of her association with Mrs. Knox. Together they made the introductory social calls. Gradually Elisabeth, on her own, was invited to teas, poetry readings, plays and concerts, attended by the young single ladies of society, with ample opportunities to become acquainted with the eligible sons of the city's elite prominent politicians and merchants.

After the relative quiet of the past few days, brought on in part by an unusual chilly wind and driving rain that had kept Elisabeth indoors, all was hubbub and feverish preparation for the grand celebration of the first anniversary of the Declaration of Independence. She heard the booming of cannons from the galleys and ships of the Pennsylvania Navy gaily bedecked with all color of pennants in the harbor- thirteen gun salutes for each of the former colonies and the distant cheers and huzzaing of the celebratory crowds lining the wharves and enjoying the spectacle in the fine mild weather. General and Mrs. Knox were there, together with members of Congress which had adjourned by mid-morning.

Elisabeth looked in on little Lucy, nestled snuggly in her wooden crib in her parents' bedroom. The baby coughed fitfully in her sleep. Just over a year old, and unable to blow her own nose, she suffered from a summer cold, that caused the General and his wife much anxiety over their only child. Elisabeth had willingly consented to stay at home to watch the babe. A grateful General Knox promised she would have a delightful surprise by the afternoon of this Fourth. He said no more, but Mrs. Knox whispered that Will had arrived in Philadelphia yesterday. Elisabeth puzzled over Lucy's words- first they would see only each other and then she would see him but he would not see her. Mrs. Knox was almost as fond of riddles as she was of playing cards. She had taught Elisabeth both how to play whist and to gamble, two traits Elisabeth was certain her father would disapprove of, if he knew.

She glanced at herself in the Knox's full-length mirror and brought her hand to her blond curls. Perhaps she should have had them brushed and pulled. Mrs. Knox's hair for the celebration was in the tall, upswept manner that was said to be the latest style. She had festooned her hair with frilly red, white and blue ribbons. Elisabeth thought it would look foolish on anyone else but on Mrs. Knox it appeared fashionable instead. The only person she had to please, she told Elisabeth was her Harry and she cared not a whit for what others thought or even said.

That was true up to a point, Elisabeth thought. Mrs. Knox, being the youngest of the wives of the senior commanders, certainly wanted to please Martha Washington and Kitty Green. And she bubbled over with excitement, recounting the attention of General Washington, dancing with her at a ball she and her Harry had attended. Unlike the other Generals' wives, she had no family or close relatives in the newly independent nation. Her family all left Boston when the British had evacuated the city more than twelve months ago. There had been no communication from them since. [2]

Elisabeth, despite her youth, was a good judge of character. She sensed Lucy Knox's loneliness and had seen how despondent she became when separated from her husband. She told Elisabeth in confidence she wanted to have many children, to build a real family for herself and Harry. Elisabeth blushed, thinking of the noises she heard through the walls, emanating from the couple's bedroom at night.

She busied herself with her embroidery, pushing the needle slowly through the pattern of heather and thistles while her thoughts turned to Will. She enjoyed the admiring looks of the captains and majors who came to call on General Knox, and the flirting banter of the younger officers who swarmed around the Shippen sisters at their afternoon teas, and even the attentions of the tall sentries when she left their house with Lucy and the baby. It was all harmless, she thought. None of these men talked about the horrors of the war, or sensed the precariousness of the cause or the possible British occupation of the city. They were like preening pheasants, proud of their immaculate uniforms and what they perceived as witty conversation. Will, while younger than some, had a depth of loyalty and seriousness about him that she admired.

She recognized Will was not as glib or quick with repartee. But she knew she could soften his rough-hewn edges. She smiled to herself at the thought that she wanted to. It meant, Elisabeth had to admit, she had slipped into thinking of them as married. Was it due to genuine feelings for Will on her part, or the not so subtle suggestions from Mrs. Knox and the less obvious but supportive estimation of the General?

When the army left winter camp and took to the field, Mrs. Knox had become fretful, and confessed to Elisabeth the most dreadful thoughts of harm coming to her beloved Harry. She had remained in a state of nervous depression until she received a letter from the General, which graciously included a line or two about Will's well being. As the constant companion of Mrs. Knox, Elisabeth had also succumbed to horrible speculation followed by relief of word that he was safe. But was this an indication of true love or merely feminine concern for a friend? Elisabeth did not know.

And when Will wrote her, which was not as frequently as she would have liked, she read and re-read his letters, and on one occasion when his words were so heartfelt and touched her deeply, she carried the carefully folded letter in her bodice for days on end. To her, it seemed like true love, her heart smitten but without any of the courtship or companionship that Mrs. Knox had experienced when her Harry was a bookseller in Boston and she frequented the intellectual discussions held in his shop. Mrs. Knox's account, in embarrassingly intimate detail, of how she had taught Harry French made Elisabeth blush to hear it, even though Lucy and the General were now married.

Focused intently on these thoughts, Elisabeth only vaguely heard the grandfather clock in its massive polished mahogany case downstairs striking half past one. It was followed by the sound of studded carriage wheels clattering on the cobblestoned street below the open window and General Knox's hearty greeting of the sentries. Simultaneously, little Lucy, uttered a soft cry, perhaps awakened by her father's familiar booming voice, or simply she was hungry and finished with her morning nap. Elisabeth was jiggling Lucy in her arms when the Knoxes swept into the room. At the sight of her father, the baby broke into a broad smile of recognition and reached out with both of her little chubby arms. The General snatched her from Elisabeth and held his daughter high above his head, pretending to drop her and then smothering her with wet kisses as he pulled her into his fleshy neck.

"Be careful, Harry. She still has her cold," Mrs. Knox cautioned.

"The best cure is a surfeit of her father's love," he replied, rubbing his bulbous nose against the tiny snot smeared one of his daughter. Little Lucy gurgled in delight and firmly grasped the tip of his pendulous ear lobe.

"Come, my dear," Mrs. Knox said. "We ladies must dress for dinner. You are to come with us to City Tavern. Everyone will be there." She turned and winked at Knox who caught his wife's look before he resumed playing with their child.

With little Lucy safely in the care of another nanny, Elisabeth joined General and Mrs. Knox in their carriage for the short ride to the City Tavern at 2nd and Walnut Streets. She wore a plain linen gown with embroidered green hem and sleeves, trimmed with a modicum of lace around the bodice and an intricate flower patterned shawl. It was more for show than warmth and covered her shoulders while complimenting the blue of her eyes. One of the Shippen sisters had offered to have her dressmaker alter a gossamer gown for Elisabeth. She politely refused. It was too ostentatious she thought, remembering the cold and diseased soldiers she had seen suffering in their Morristown huts. However, she had accepted a stay and bodice that flattered her narrow waisted figure.

They arrived at the Tavern, an imposing three story red brick building and one of the finest in the city. Dinner was to begin shortly before three. Constant pealing of church bells filled the air. A large, cheering crowd pressed forward, eager to glimpse the invited guests. General Knox helped first his wife and then Elisabeth from the carriage. She looked around at the uniformed officers standing stiffly lining the cobblestoned walkway to the Tavern. [3]

"My dear," the General said to Elisabeth. "I have arranged for my aide-de-camp to be your escort for this occasion." And suddenly, Elisabeth found Will next to her, looking tall, lean and handsome in his clean brushed, but worn dark blue jacket with red cuffs and trim. Eagerly, she hooked her arm in his and rested her hand on his forearm.

"Miss Elisabeth. You are most radiant this afternoon." She basked in Will's admiring gaze, pleased that she was not dressed as extravagantly as many of the other young ladies and their uniformed clad attendants entering ahead of them.

"And you Sergeant Stoner? Has your health improved since Morristown?"

"It most certainly has and now I am in the best of spirits in your company."

"I should reprimand you for being part of this surprise but since I am happy to see you, I forgive your subterfuge."

"I did not plot to deceive you," Will said hastily as they followed the General and Mrs. Knox up the steps to the Tavern. "I was summoned by the General to participate in today's military parade and only learned this morning of his plan to appoint me his aide for the celebration dinner."

"It is a delightful surprise," Elisabeth said, tossing her curls with an amused smile on her face. "Now, you must not keep me waiting another minute. Tell me everything that has happened to you since your last letter."

"I would take as long as all eternity if it meant you would listen and be with me," Will said to her. "There is really not much to relate. Life in camp is routine, filled with repetitive tasks, drills and training." Elisabeth smiled at his eloquence and rapid conversion to his usual modest self. She brushed her hand against his as they entered the entrance hall, oblivious to the noise and commotion around them.

The main tavern room, almost fifty feet in length, had been converted into a banquet hall. Members of Congress were already seated at the long table running across the width of the room. Between them and the double front doors, civilians were grouped at tables perpendicular to the Congressional one. Elisabeth recognized a few members of the Pennsylvania Supreme Executive Council and the city's magistrates. The Continental Army officers in town and their guests were seated further back, closer to the entrance.

The three hundred or more celebrants completely filled the hall. Elisabeth had never seen so many people in one room. Servants, in dark long coats with ruffled white shirts, moved among the tables carrying platters laden with food and pitchers, bottles and crocks of drinks. The Knoxes halted frequently as they made their way in, the General greeting officers he knew and being introduced to their ladies. It was slow progress and Elisabeth sensed Will's uneasiness. Her fingers tapped on his hand and he inclined his head so she could whisper in his ear.

"Once we are seated, there will be less of the press of these people."

He shook his head. "It is not that," he replied. "If you observe the officers, there are those with a ruddy, rugged appearance from having served in the field, and then there are those, pale and almost corpse like in complexion, with their powdered wigs, who have not seen a day in either battle or encampment."

"Will. Please do not be negative with your thoughts or so sour in appearance. Be prepared to be courteous and pleasant to whomever we shall meet." He nodded and smiled at her and she was pleased her words had helped to improve his mood.

"But surely you must notice, Miss Elisabeth," he said grinning at her mischievously, "that with the obvious exception of General Knox, we who have come from Morristown are leaner to the point of looking underfed, while those who have remained in Philadelphia favor the more plump and pampered look."

"Then you will simply have to make up at this dinner for your prior meager rations, although I caution you to mind your manners and not act the lean and hungry wolf," she said with mock severity.

"I promise to devour my food with decorum and to eat no more than the General himself." Elisabeth giggled at the thought, having seen the General's tremendous consumption at the dinner table. She was pleased Will was merry again. "I shall only worry about you if you eat as little as the General's brother."

"Is Billy in Philadelphia?" Will asked excitedly.

"I believe not yet. Mrs. Knox mentioned he is expected to join the General shortly and provide assistance as his secretary."

"Tis much better duty to be the General's Aide-de-Camp," Will said grinning at her.

"I am pleased you are but I sense from that remark you do not regard it so much of an obligation as an exercise of free will."

"Free will, yes certainly, but in your presence, this Will is not free but bound to be your humble servant."

Her eyes lit up with delight at his repost. "Very cleverly said," she acknowledged.

They followed General and Mrs. Knox to their table seating sixteen, which was filled with many of the officers of the Regiment, Captain Hadley among them, escorting Miss Mercy. Elisabeth sensed Will's unease among officers of higher rank. She reassured him, commenting it was the General's table and he was entitled to select his company, and he had chosen Will. The sounds of the soft mellow tones of oboes, complimented by a sonorous melody carried by a few fiddles filled the hall.

"Most of the musicians are the Hessians, captured at Trenton," Elisabeth said. The uniformed Hessian band, looking well taken care of in their powdered wigs and blackened mustaches, were ensconced on a raised platform to the right of the Congressional table. "They have played at numerous outdoor concerts in the city this summer and are quite popular and well-liked." [4]

"Their armed brethren are less likely to be appreciated by the good citizens," Will said. "As you have heard, General Howe will begin the campaign with an attempt to capture Philadelphia. There will be a major confrontation for certain before this summer is over." She recognized the truth of his words. While the others around them continued in gay conversation, she became quiet.

"Forgive me, Elisabeth," he said quickly. "I should not have darkened your mood."

"There is nothing to forgive," she responded. "We are still at war, the outcome is uncertain and there are indeed many in this city who would welcome General Howe and his army. Their sympathies lie with the Crown and not with our cause." She reached for his hand under the tablecloth and squeezed it with affection. They held hands for a long time, untwining their fingers only when food and drink were served. Pot pies and dishes of fish and poultry were followed by roast meats, all accompanied by wines, ciders and beers. The meal concluded with baked wine custards, preserved pears, layer cakes and marvelously contrived pastries with claret and madeira served to compliment the sweets.

There were thirteen separate toasts, each offered from the Congressional table, in honor of the country formed by the thirteen colonies, with acknowledgement of the brave heroes present and those who had fallen in battle in their efforts to advance the cause.

Will leaned over and whispered in her ear: "No mention of the soldiers who have not been paid in months, or of the living maimed and missing limbs, unable to work, and with no compensation from these gentlemen now praising their courage."

"I hear there are those in Congress who have used their own personal funds to send to the troops. The women's circle to which Mrs. Knox and I belong collect clothing and engage in sewing to supplement what is in scarce supply. As do others in the city."

She was about to add another thought but was startled by a barrage of rifle fire echoing through the Tavern's open windows. Will put his arm around her shoulder in a comforting gesture. It brought back memories when he had held her on the sled as they crossed the frozen Hudson at Albany. "It is just the running fire of our infantry," he explained as the muskets discharged from one end of the line to the other. "It is in celebration." With each toast followed by such firings, Elisabeth became more accustomed to the loud noise, but she remained in his protective embrace. Despite what she assumed were his best efforts to scrub himself clean, his jacket smelled of gunpowder and horses, as if the scents had been woven into the fabric. She wondered whether his skin smelled the same. She smiled to herself at her risqué thought.

At the conclusion of the dinner, when the members of Congress rose, it was a general signal for the attendees to move around the vast hall and mingle with others. Will immediately stood, for as aide to General Knox, he was obligated to be part of his escort around the hall. He and Elisabeth followed the General and Lucy at a distance. Elisabeth let him steer her through the crowd, aware of the attention she attracted from the young men they passed. She squeezed Will's arm to reassure him she was pleased to be with him. They lost sight of General Knox and when they did locate him, he and Lucy were seated at another table, the General surrounded by a group of officers, and Lucy holding court among several of the patriotic ladies of the city.

Knox was describing the first battle of Trenton as the army approached the Hessian sentries with the blinding snowstorm at their backs. The elegantly uniformed men, none of whom had been part of the army in December 1776 attentively listened to his account.

"Captain Hadley here, now graced by the presence of the lovely Miss Mercy van Buskirk, was instrumental in our artillery supporting the assault," Knox said, gesturing for Hadley to take up the story. Will listened and was carried back to the cold stormy morning, the gun crew working in unison, firing canister to sweep the Hessians clear of King Street.

"And here is another of our brave soldiers, Sergeant Stoner, my Aide-de-Camp," Knox boomed out, pointing at Will. "It was he, who along with the Captain and a few others, attacked the one cannon the Hessians had managed to get into action and captured it for our cause." Elisabeth felt Will stiffen. "Tell them Will of your part in that encounter." Elisabeth feared that Will would be remain silent or not find his voice. She squeezed his arm in encouragement.

"I was not alone. Captain Hadley led a few of us in a mad scramble down the icy street. It was slippery underfoot and in front of us, several Hessians were hastily loading their three-pounder. Their muskets were useless in the driving snow but their long bayonets would serve them well as we approached. It was only when I was extremely close to their cannon that I realized I was unarmed."

"It is a rather poor soldier who forgets to carry his musket into battle," one of the officers standing near General Knox said sharply. He was a slight man with a very high forehead, which appeared more so by the powdered wig perched on the crown of his head. His pale blue eyes bored into Will, daring him to challenge him. Elisabeth recognized him as Captain Seely's friend, Captain Enoch Newcomb, the one who had bashed Will with a gun stock in the fight at General Knox's headquarters. Anxiously, she held her breath, hoping Will would respond calmly.

"Sir, I normally do not carry a musket into battle because I am part of the gun crew in General Knox's Regiment. The cannon is my weapon," he said, as if explaining something so elementary to a school boy. He paused enough to let the lesson sink in. "But you are quite correct to criticize me for lack of preparedness, although I was not entirely unarmed. I seized an empty sponge bucket and clobbered the Hessian gunner with it before he had a chance to lunge at me with his bayonet. I assume Sir, from your own familiarity with battles you are aware that a sponge bucket has many uses." Several of the ladies tittered with amusement and Newcomb's face turned crimson, the color extending up to the line of his wig.

"My experience, as is true of any gentlemen is from the saddle of a horse. I do not engage in bar room brawling with the enemy," he replied. "You on the other hand do not seem to have limited your brawling to Hessians." He was about to explain further but General Knox cut him off.

"Captain Newcomb. There are times when brave soldiers must use whatever means are at their disposal in attacking the enemy," Knox said loudly. "Quickness of mind and resourcefulness are attributes in the clamor of combat to be highly valued. Sergeant Stoner has exhibited those qualities married to cool courage that make him an excellent soldier. I wish our army had more like him."

Elisabeth pressed his arm, signaling Will to restrain himself. "There is no need Will, for you to say more," she whispered softly.

"Gentlemen, while I would much prefer to provide more first hand accounts of our battles with General Howe's minions, we are required by the occasion to present ourselves for a parade before the city's populace. My dear," he said turning to Lucy and kissing her gently on her upswept hair, "please excuse me. Our absence will be brief." He moved through the crowd, creating a path where there was none, followed by the officers of his Regiment.

"Well," Lucy said cheerily, "let us fill our glasses with sherry and adjourn to the upstairs where we can observe the parade from the front rooms." There was the scraping of chairs and rustling of skirts as the women left the main hall and mounted the narrow stairway.

Elisabeth stood, at the window next to two Shippen sisters and a few other young women she had met at their afternoon teas, poetry readings and parties. From the corner of the window she had a clear view of the direction the parade would come. Below them, crowds three deep lined Second Street, jostling for position.

"You must have a handkerchief to wave at your beau," Peggy Shippen said, pressing hers into Elisabeth's hand. "He seems well spoken and very much taken with you. I would vouch he barely took his eyes off of you for the entire dinner."

"Except to respond to Captain Newcomb," another young lady observed. "And even then, with your hand on his arm, it seemed as if the two of you were one," she said, raising her eyebrows to elicit a comment from Elisabeth.

"Sergeant Stoner and I correspond regularly. General Knox graciously appointed him his aide for the Tavern dinner. That is all there is to it."

"Oh, Elisabeth. Do not be so modest. It seems you have captured the heart of a handsome young soldier who enjoys the General's favor," Peggy said. "In no time at all, he will be an officer, and even better looking in his new uniform and able to grace our salons and balls."

Elisabeth sensed the a barb in Peggy's comment, a criticism of Will's present low rank and an implied disparagement of his lack of culture. The Shippens were among the wealthiest families in Philadelphia, after the Morrises, and while they proclaimed their neutrality, it was whispered they were closet Tories.

"His letters to me are warm and heartfelt," she replied curtly. "And he has his moments of eloquence," she said with more candor than she had wished to reveal. "However, as one deeply committed to our cause, he will be doing his duty in the field rather than attending to me at drawing room soirees." She looked at Peggy and smiled sweetly.

The familiar sounds of beating drums and fifes and the reedy strains of the Hessian oboes signaled the start of the parade. The crowd hailed "their Hessian band," smartly dressed in powder blue uniforms as they marched by in unison. Next came a color guard, carrying the flags of the various Pennsylvania and New Jersey militias, and the newly adopted red and white striped flag- thirteen five-pointed stars within a blue rectangle. The men in the crowd cheered loudly and brandished their tri-corns above their heads in appreciation. [5]

General Knox followed on his large dappled English saddle horse, waving to the crowd. Behind him rode the officers of the Artillery Regiment, smiling and acknowledging the cheers of the people. Then, two mounted cavalry units and finally the cannons. Will was in the forefront on Big Red. The horse was brushed and groomed so that one could see its muscles rippling under the deep rich color, like strong currents in a stream. The stallion pranced as he pulled a light brass cannon, the metal glinting in the late afternoon summer sun. Will sat upright in the saddle, confidently looking straight ahead, the reins clasped loosely in his hands.

"You beaux is so handsome on that magnificent animal," Peggy gushed. "He could pose for a statue to be placed in the most prominent square of the city."

Elisabeth smiled at the thought of a statue being erected to Will, but placed in Albany where her family and friends would see it. She pushed the silly thought from her mind and waved her handkerchief at no one in particular, Will having already passed from view.

—⟫—

It was dark when Will accompanied General Knox to his home. He waited impatiently in the hallway until Elisabeth appeared at the top of the stairs. She was so graceful, it seemed to him she flew down the steps with her feet whispering over the wood. Outside, the streets were filled with celebrants enjoying the festivities. She clung closely to him and Will wanted to think it was due more to her wanting to be with him, than the crush of the crowds.

The sky was illuminated by a fireworks display. Bright balls of red and orange burst above them. No sooner had they finished, to the applause of people in the street, then individual fiery streaks of rockets, launched from the Commons soared upward, before exploding in red fury. The people cheered and counted out loud for each rocket, screaming "thirteen" as the last one rose into the darkness. They paused and watched a militia unit firing from one end of the line to the other, the men obscured by the gun smoke blown back along their ranks. Bonfires burned at major intersections as people danced and milled around them, singing and shouting in celebration.

"There is so much noise, I will become deaf by evening's end, and unable to hear your voice," Elisabeth said. Will knew his own hearing had already suffered from serving in the gun crew. During drills, shouted commands no longer seemed as sharp and clear to him, and afterwards, he frequently found he spoke louder than normal.

"Then, I would have to lean down even more and whisper into your ear, which I enjoy very much."

She smiled at the thought of his face close to hers. "Let me show you the places I have come to know through the graciousness of Mrs. Knox and the friends I have made during my brief few months here."

Bells pealed in noisy chiming from the nearby Anglican Church, as they ambled along Market Street, one hundred feet wide with the now closed and shuttered wooden market sheds running down the middle of the street ahead of them.

"Lightning struck that very steeple at the beginning of the month," Elisabeth said, pointing upward. "Some took it as a sign of Heaven's approbation of the King. Others said it was God's punishment for the British destruction and desecration of Presbyterian and Congregational houses of worship in New Jersey. [6] Will?" she asked. "Do you believe Kind Providence favors our cause?"

Will looked at her in amusement. "I have seen too many lightning storms to believe them to be Divinely inspired." Sensing she thought his answer did not seriously respond to the religious implications of her question, he added quickly, "However, I have also seen the hand of Providence in two instances when weather protected our army." He told her of the cloaking fog on the East River when the army had escaped to Manhattan, and the sudden drop in temperature at Trenton, enabling the troops to make the quick night march on newly frozen roads to attack Princeton.

They passed row after row of homes, each window illuminated by candles, as part of the city's celebration of Independence. Will noticed the buildings had become larger and more imposing, signifying people of wealth lived within.

"This is Mr. Powel's house," Elisabeth said cheerfully, pointing to a large red brick three-story building. "His wife is related to the Shippens and I have frequently been invited within for tea, to dine and once to a ball. Can you imagine a room so long eighteen couples may dance together and with room for others to watch and applaud."

He could not imagine it, he thought somewhat sourly. Nor could he see himself within, dancing with Elisabeth before an elegantly attired crowd, fearful of embarrassing himself and her too. However, with her now on his arm, neither could he imagine Elisabeth in this grand mansion dancing without him.

"And this elegant building belongs to Dr. Benjamin Franklin himself," Elisabeth said in a softer, awestruck voice. "Although I have not been inside," she admitted.

As they continued walking on Market, she leaned her head against his shoulder. He smelled the freshness of her hair and the scent dispelled his gloomy thoughts.

"Would it not be nice Will, to live in such a grand city and partake of all it had to offer?"

He had been thinking at the moment of Sergeant Merriam reunited with his family in Boston, home with his darling daughters and secure from the immediate dangers of war.

"I am sorry Elisabeth, but when one is a soldier who has experienced battle and seen dead and wounded men, my mind does not dwell on elegant homes nor grand balls and dancing." He paused, wanting to choose his words carefully. "I long to be with you, forever if that is possible, and wherever it may be. But I cannot see past this war."

She reached up with her free hand and placed her fingers on his. "I do not wish to seem flighty. I am light-headed because we are together and it is a joyous occasion. I too dread our separations and the anxieties they bring. I only imagine better times to escape from my present worries."

He was about to reply when she pointed ahead.

"Look. There are Captain Hadley and Miss Mercy. Hurry. Let us join them."

Still holding her hand, Will quickened his pace, moving slightly ahead of Elisabeth so as to protect her from being jostled by passersby. "Captain," he called when they were closer. Hadley turned, smiled and removed his tri-corn while bowing slightly to Elisabeth. Will did the same for Miss Mercy and the two ladies embraced and chose to walk together, leaving Hadley and Will to amble ahead.

"There has been a fair amount of powder used today to celebrate an independence which is not assured so long as General Howe can take the field," Hadley said. "Would that some of the barrels had been transported to Morristown or held in reserve for when the need arises."[7]

They had turned north off Market, where the streets were less crowded. People were heading home after the long day of celebrating, eating and drinking, anticipating the official celebrations were coming to an end. Sporadic fireworks and discharge of muskets sounded from the area of the wharves along the river, together with drunk singing and shouting. The windows of the homes on this street were unlit. Will recalled he had seen a flyer, posted at the City Tavern notifying all of the Council's decision that festive candles were to be extinguished at eleven o'clock. It did not seem it was already that hour.

Ahead they heard the shattering of glass followed by loud shouts of anger. Several men carrying torches and armed with wooden clubs were methodically breaking the first floor windows of homes and pulling up cobblestones to heave at the glass on the second stories. A tall man was framed in an open doorway, confronting the thugs as they approached his house.

"You obstinate Tory bastard. You had your chance to light up your windows. Now you will pay," one of them shouted. They became more incensed by his presence and crowded in front of his doorstep.

"I am not a Loyalist. It is the spirit of Christ which moves me not to take up arms against anyone."

"Christ be damned," one of them yelled, picking up a cobblestone and throwing it at the red brick front of the house. Several others bent down, pried up the large stones, and launched them with vigor. Most pounded against the building but one smashed a window causing a jagged shards of glass to fall to the street.

"You are either with us or a damned Tory. None of this bloody Quaker double talk," their leader said, shaking his club in the man's face.

Will ran forward with Hadley close behind. "Stop," Will shouted. "In the name of Congress and General Knox." He climbed the two steps and stood in front of the man. Hadley roughly shoved one of the men aside and drew his sword.

"A patrol of the local militia and watchmen are nearby on Market Street. They will be here any moment. Disburse immediately," Hadley commanded. Will reached inside his uniformed jacket as if to bring a pistol to bear.

"And who are you to order us around and protect this scummy

Tory," their leader asked, holding his club across his chest with both hands.

"I am Captain Samuel Hadley of the General Knox's own Artillery Regiment," he said loudly. "And this is General Knox's aide-de-camp." The men hesitated although it was the just the two of them and one admittedly pacifist Quaker against an enraged group of ten or so.

Out of the corner of his eye, coming from the end of the street Will saw others carrying torches and advancing toward them. At first, he feared they were more patriotic thugs coming to join their compatriots. Anxiously, he watched them approach. The mob in front of the two steps hesitated. Will caught the glint from a musket and brass buttons of a uniform and recognized a squad of the town's militia.

"You there," the man leading them called out. "Put down those stones and leave this area immediately. By order of the City Magistrates. Or I will place the whole lot of you under arrest."

The mob's leader weighed the chances of confronting the militia and thought better of it. Reluctantly, he motioned for the others to drop the stones.

"Why do we pay taxes to protect the likes of them," he said gesturing with his club toward the Quaker. "It is the Magistrates who should be seizing the property of these secret Tories, instead of threatening we true patriots," he said directing his comments to passerbys who had stopped to watch the confrontation.

"Yes," another shouted. "They are either for us or against us. And if they straddle the fence, then they should ride the rail with a coat of tar and feathers," he said to the laughter of the other ruffians and cries of "quite right" and "tar and feather them."

The town militia's officer had heard enough. "Disband now or you will spend this Independence night in jail," he ordered. After some muttering and more cursing of "damned Quakers," the mob dissolved into surly groups of twos and threes, all going in the same direction, angrily jostling other pedestrians as they made their way down the cobblestoned lane.

"I thank you for your assistance," Captain Hadley said to the officer. "Perhaps you should follow them to ensure they do not engage in more mischievous thuggery," he suggested.

Will turned and looked back up the street. He saw Elisabeth emerging from the shadows. He ran forward and held her in his arms, his chin resting on her head, breathing in the lavender scent of her hair.

"I was so afraid for your well-being," she said, looking up at him. "When I ran to seek assistance, you were framed in the doorway by the light from within, confronting those terrible men holding stones and clubs." She shivered, recalling the image and wrapped her shawl more tightly around her shoulders. "Fortunately, I encountered these militia not too far down the street."

They walked the half block quickly toward the Quaker's home, ignoring the curious looks of those on the street who had been attracted to the scene. Captain Hadley and Miss Mercy had crossed the threshold. The door was open but Will knocked before entering. The man, who was placing Captain Hadley's tri-corn on a prong of a curved wood coat tree immediately inside the door, stepped forward to welcome them.

"My name is Edward Lewis," he said "and this is my wife, Mary," gesturing to a short woman who smiled warmly at Will and Elisabeth. They made an odd pair, Will thought, the man much taller than his wife, with a boney, mournful face, a grim line of a mouth beneath a sharp nose. She was petite, cheery, almost doll like, with round cheeks, flushed red as if the color had been painted on. Her auburn hair was tucked modestly under a circular, white embroidered cap. Will and Elisabeth joined Miss Mercy in the front parlor, near the windows still devoid of candles, while Mary retreated to the kitchen to instruct the servant to prepare some refreshments. Will held a chair for Elisabeth next to Miss Mercy so both ladies were seated safely away from the darkened windows.

"You are Quakers," Hadley said, more as a statement than a question, "which is why I assume you have chosen not to display candles in your windows. But surely, simply showing such support for our cause on this, our celebratory day, is not taking up arms against other human beings and thus contrary to your religion?"

"I am grateful for your intervention and protection of my home," Lewis said, "and your young gentleman friend as well," he nodded toward Will. "However, as a member of the Society of Friends, which is what we prefer to be called," he said, as a polite reprimand to Hadley, "I am bound by the direction of the Philadelphia's Yearly Meeting of last September to observe strict neutrality."

"And the reason for interpreting such direction to include not even placing a single candle in a window on this particular day?" Miss Mercy inquired.

Lewis sighed, reluctant to explain anymore about his religious beliefs but feeling politeness and gratitude required a more detailed response. "We are committed to nonviolence by our Peace Testimony. We interpret that not to take any overt action to support either side, although I do admit, there are some of us who have renounced this requirement and actively sided with your cause. I am not one of them," he said with finality. [8]

"Not yet," his wife added, having rejoined them in the parlor. "My dear, by confronting the ruffians, however peacefully, you provoked them to further violence. Had they attacked you, are you so certain of thyself that you would not have raised a hand in defense, or had they entered the house, to defend me?"

"We have had this discussion between us, many times," Lewis said by way of explanation. "My dear wife drives the carriage up to the point where I may be compelled to commit violence and then she reins in the horse of her reasoning short of taking up arms."

"And if the mob had attacked my Will and Captain Hadley and blood had been spilled protecting you and your home without your ever raising a hand? Does that preserve your mantle of non-violence," Elisabeth asked. Will heard Elisabeth's words and was seized with an overwhelming desire to be alone with her and have her call him "my Will," over and over.

"Violence is the product of the lusts of men, out of which lusts the Lord hath redeemed us," Lewis replied quickly.

"We are perceived and condemned by both Loyalists and Patriots, as being for the other, when we are directed to be for neither," Mary said. "In a situation in which violence is forced upon and done to us, non-violence condemns us to destruction by both sides. Our Lord did not . . ."

Lewis interrupted her. "You are deviating from our religious precepts which are not for you to question," he said severely. Mary looked fiercely at her husband and then smiled.

"You are right Edward. We are thankful for the intervention by these good people who are guests in our home. It is the duty of both of us," she emphasized, "to be gracious." The timely arrival of tea and sweets ended the argument between husband and wife.

"You assisted without any obligation to do so," Lewis said.

"Sergeant Stoner has an aversion to mobs, drawn from personal experience," Hadley said. He recounted Will's beating at the hands of patriotic thugs in Boston and nearly being tarred and feathered. Will remained silent while Elisabeth gasped at some of the details Will had not told her.

Miss Mercy demurely finished her cup of tea and with her lips still barely above the rim, mirthfully noted that the tea being served was of the patriotic flavor made from local herbs rather than British tea sometimes still available in the city. Mary's eyes lit up at the jest.

"I do my best, my dear, to support a worthy cause," Mary replied, winking at both young ladies. "Although I hear, down at the wharves, one may still purchase British tea masquerading as Dutch, for more than twenty shillings a pound. And that is for Bohea rather than the better Hyson leaves" she added knowledgeably.

It was after eleven when the two couples left the Lewis home, the time when all candles, by direction of the Executive Council were to be extinguished.

"Now, Quaker, Patriot and Loyalist homes all appear alike," Miss Mercy commented, as they passed the darkened windows of the homes on the street.

"Would that more would join our cause, for we sorely will be outnumbered when General Howe takes to the field," Hadley said.

Will felt Elisabeth tremble. He let his arm drop and took her hand in his. "We have prevailed before when we were fewer," he said to calm her. He knew she feared the perils he faced on the battlefield.

For him, it was different. He found it unbearable to be apart, neither knowing the duration, nor the dangers she faced while they were separated.

## Chapter 10 – A Death Wish and Close Encounter

The scream began as one of fear of anticipated horror. It rose in a pitch of agony and continued as a shriek of pain before descending into uncontrollable wails of misery.

Bant and McNeil stood up with some of the others in their scouting party, sixty men strong, turning their heads toward the piercing sound. They had been lying hidden amongst the shrubs of this lightly rolling hill country, grateful for the limited shade and respite from the hot August sun, watching the dusty road winding down toward the flat coastal plain below and waiting for some sign of the enemy. They were part of a newly formed corps of light infantry, riflemen all, composed of one hundred volunteers from each Continental Brigade. The corps, under the command of Scotch Willie had left the main army and marched south to gather intelligence and harass the advance guard of the British Army. [1]

"That is not the cry of a woman being ravished," one of the men said quietly.

"How would you know?" another asked.

"Tis true," another said "It is more the cry of hopelessness."

Lieutenant Patten asked for volunteers and Bant and McNeil stepped forward, together with six others. Quickly, they left their camp and loped away, using the shrubs that sporadically bordered the road as cover. Around the second bend, they came upon a clearing with a roughly built one story stone house, tucked in amongst a copse of scraggly pine trees. A woman lay motionless on her back with a boy, no more than ten, kneeling next to her, holding her right arm straight up in the air. Blood covered the white cloth bandage wrapped around her hand. The boy started when the riflemen appeared, but remained defiantly by the woman's side.

"We are Continentals," McNeil said. "Who did this?

"Some soldiers came," the boy said bravely trying to contain a sob. "They broke into our house. My mother could not take off her ring fast enough. They cut off her fingers," he said breaking down and pointing from his mother to a thin line of fresh blood on the dark brown, desiccated pine needles. It formed a pool below a wooden stump chopping block near her feet. The woman's four fingers lay at its base, like pale white grubs revealed when one turns over a rotting log.

"In which direction did they go? How many are there?" McNeil asked. "Quickly, boy if we are to catch them."

"Four or five, I think," he said hesitantly, and pointed to a narrow path to the left of the house, which disappeared into the bushes heading uphill. "They are after our cow."

The eight riflemen ran up the trail in single file. They had gone less than half a mile when they heard laughter and the guttural language of the Hessians. Creeping closer they found four of them in the shadows, on the edge of a sunlit meadow, squatting in a semi-circle around their pile of plunder- cups and plates, pewter candle holders, some clothing - laughing and holding different items up to the light. Their muskets and brass hats lay haphazardly nearby. From the amount of booty, it was clear they had looted more homes than the one of belonging to the woman whose fingers they had cut off.

McNeil motioned for the riflemen to wait. After a few minutes, a fifth Hessian emerged from the woods at the top of the meadow, leading a large dark brown cow, her udder full, trailed by a young calf. His comrades greeted him with shouts followed by loud laughter and sucking sounds. The man grinned and tied the cow to a thicket and leaned his musket against a tree trunk.

McNeil nodded and the riflemen emerged from the underbrush and motioned for the Hessians to stand up. They rose confused and then, one by one, smiled and held their arms open, signaling they would not resist.

Bant stepped forward and motioned for the first one to unbuckle his sword. The man glanced down at his waist and nervously fumbled with the strap before handing it to him. Bant unsheathed it, and threw the sword on the ground behind him. Standing in front of the second prisoner, he made the same gesture and so on down the line. When he came to the fifth one, the Hessian had already unbuckled the sword and waited with a look of bemusement on his face for Bant to stand in front of him. He was at least a foot taller than Bant, even without his brass cap. He grinned, revealing two broken front teeth and handed the dull black worn scabbard, hilt first to Bant. The Hessian tugged his own ears and said something that made the other Hessians laugh. Bant knew the soldier was making fun of his knobby curled ears. He said nothing and drew the short blade from the sheath. It was stained with fresh blood.

Bant, looked up at the Hessian's eyes, smiled and thrust the sword deep into the man's chest. He collapsed with a look of dismay on his face, changing to fear as blood frothed from his mouth. The four other Hessians raised their hands higher and began imploring Bant, in words and gestures not to kill them.

McNeil nodded at Bant. "It could have been the blood of someone else," he said. "Or even an animal."

"It was the woman's," Bant replied with certainty.

"Well, it is done with. We need to bring the other prisoners back to camp for the Lieutenant to question. No more killing," McNeil said.

They made their prisoners carry the plunder wrapped in their own field blankets, holding them in front of their chests. The woman came out to the broken front door as the riflemen marched the four prisoners past her stone house, leaning weakly against the door frame, her good hand resting on her son's shoulder.

"Cut off their hands and feet and let them bleed to death," she screeched after them. "They do not deserve to live. Kill them all, kill them all," she yelled and her words followed them after they were out of sight. [2]

It was late in the afternoon when they arrived back at their makeshift camp and delivered the four cowering Hessians to Lieutenant Patten. Some of the newer men, who had never seen Hessians close up, left their dinner fires and wandered by out of curiosity. Others listened to McNeil as he explained the reason for the terrifying shrieks and the ordeal of the woman. Some voiced approval of Bant's killing of the fifth Hessian and several thought the remaining four should be done in as well.

Lieutenant Patten drew some marks in the dirt on the ground and with the assistance of a Pennsylvania rifleman who spoke some German, questioned the Hessians. The four agreed their lines were no more than a few miles away. They had passed through their own sentries, ostensibly to forage for food for their Company, but that had only been a pretense to go plundering on their own. They openly named the Regiments they knew of and indicated there were many more British soldiers quartered in the camp. They had no knowledge of the Army's proposed line of march although they hoped to capture Philadelphia because they had heard the city was among the richest in the colonies. Lieutenant Patten sent a scouting party out to ascertain the veracity of the Hessians' information. The prisoners were placed under guard, their hands tied behind their backs and made to sit cross-legged on the ground.

Bant and McNeil joined a few of the men around a cooking fire, preparing to share two rabbits one of the men had caught with a snare in the woods. One of the soldiers slowly turned the carcasses, pierced through with the long rifle ramrods, over the flames evenly browning the dark flesh. Another, used a thick stick to shift a pan in which some quick bread was baking.

"I say we slit their throats," one of the soldiers said, pointing with his skinning knife at the others around the fire. "Bant did right and the others deserve the same."

"It is up to the Lieutenant to decide," another man added. He took a long drink from his canteen. "This damn watered cider is barely fit to drink. Would we had some of that strong rum we tasted before parading through Philadelphia. A gill now would do me some good." [3]

Bant squirmed uncomfortably, recalling the citizens of Philadelphia staring at him as he marched by. He knew by the way they looked at him, they knew his secret. He could see it in their faces. He was responsible for the militiamen being hung. He had witnessed it and to save his own hide had remained hidden. If only he had jumped down from the tree limb and surrendered, those twelve men would still be alive. One Philadelphia street had been lined with tall fan shaped chestnut trees, the rough brown husks protecting the not yet ripe lustrous mahogany colored nuts hidden inside, mocking him as they hung from the branches. He almost bolted from the line as he saw the faces of the dead militiamen appear in miniature on each husk, the stem turning into a hempen rope noose. He had lowered his head, watching the cobblestones and walked faster, bumping into the man marching in front who had snarled at him to keep his proper distance.

A Hessian called out loudly to the soldier who had translated for Lieutenant Patten.

"Essen, bitte. Essen und Trinken."

"What does he want?" one of the men around the fire asked.

"Food and water," the soldier translator said.

"What for," the man next to Bant said. "They will be dead soon enough." The riflemen around the fire, eagerly tore into the roast rabbit, smacking their lips and licking their fingers to torment the prisoners.

"Is it better to die on an empty or full stomach?" McNeil asked to no one in particular.

"My preference would be to have enough rum in me so as to feel nothing."

"Whiskey would be even better," another added.

"Before we came here, my old Brigade marched for an entire night and most of the next day without a morsel to eat," the man who favored rum recalled. "Twenty four miles at least, it was, before we made camp. I had found some half a dozen turnips along the way and stored them in my haversack. I was pinched with hunger. Those turnips were the best meal I had that entire month," he reflected, lazily sucking on a small rabbit bone. [4] "A lot better than this rye and Injun meal they give us instead of real flour."

Bant listened as their voices merged with the noise of crickets, cicadas and the croaking of frogs from a nearby creek into a pleasant, soothing buzz blotting out their individual words. He was in a hypnotic trance-like sleep, stretched out near the fire and did not notice when the scouts returned to report to Lieutenant Patten.

He awoke to a nudge from McNeil's booted foot just before dawn. His first thought was to marvel that the nightmares had not come to him during his sleep.

"The Lieutenant is giving our patrol the honor of hanging the four prisoners before we move on."

Bant shook his head in disbelief, thinking he was not awake and this was a different nightmare. He stood up and grabbed his rifle. Its comforting weight felt real enough, the long barrel cold and coated with a thin layer of dew. To calm himself, he did routine things, strapping on his large handled hunting knife and shouldering his haversack. He followed McNeil to the clearing where the Hessians stood, their hands still tied behind them, their lightened bags of plunder hanging from their chests. They stood with heads bowed as Lieutenant Patten's words were translated.

"General Washington himself has proclaimed and his orders have been read to all our troops- the penalty for Continentals caught plundering innocents is death. You, as our enemy, must be held to the same account. [5]

You will be hung and your bodies left as a warning to others who may be tempted to terrorize the civilians living in your army's path."

Patten turned and led the fifty odd riflemen in the early dawn down the road toward the British encampment, leaving McNeil and the others who had captured the Hessians to execute them.

"Well, let us get to it," McNeil said, nestling a noose around the neck of one of the Hessians, who was trembling uncontrollably.

Bant let out a terrible wail, rivaling the scream of the poor woman they had heard the day before, in intensity of anguish and fear, and fell to his knees. The other riflemen stared at him in disbelief.

"You stabbed one of them yourself yesterday, with his own sword, and rightly so," a soldier said. "This is less bloody and will be over faster."

McNeil waved the man away, bent down and helped Bant to his feet.

"Start walking slowly after our men," he said softly. "We will finish the business here without you."

Bant shuffled down the dusty road, the foliage glimmering in the rising sun, afraid to look back and terrified they would return on this very same road. For the first time since his nightmares had begun, he no longer thought killing British soldiers would ease his mind. Instead, he knew with certainty the only peace for him was death. He hoped a musket ball would kill him in the coming battle.

—⁓—

The sounds of musket and rifle fire on the west side of the river, that had begun at dawn increased in intensity. Will paced back and forth behind the brass twelve-pounder, more nervous for Big Red's safety, tied to a tree behind the battery, than the approaching Redcoats and Hessians. Two light six-pounders were spaced about twenty feet apart from his position.

All three guns were on a tree-lined slope opposite the main road leading to the ford. During the night and into the early morning, the gun crews, with the help of some Continentals, had constructed rough breastworks of earth and cut trees and branches. After that work was done, they waited as the morning sun beat down on their shoulders, stiff from swinging axes and wielding shovels.

From his vantage point, Will could clearly discern by the cloud of smoke that hovered over the skirmishing line of the Continentals and the oncoming enemy, where the two forces met. Thick woods ran down the rolling hills toward the river, bordering newly ploughed ground and cultivated fields of buckwheat and corn, and apple and peach orchards, the ripe fruit visible to him even at this distance.

"If they come upon us soon," Corporal Chandler said, standing next to Will, "the sun although higher in the sky will still be behind us and in their eyes." Will grunted. He was pleased Captain Hadley had assigned Chandler to his gun crew. He appreciated the former bookbinder's calmness and reliability. It occurred to Will there was another reason for Hadley adding Chandler. He would be a competent replacement to take command, in case Will was killed. Not a pleasant thought, with the British and Hessians slowly pushing the Continentals back toward the river.

The core of the old gun crew was together again, Will, Chandler now as wormer and loader, Levi Tyler for the sponge and ram, and John Baldwin, vent tender. All except Sergeant Merriam who was with his family in Boston, and poor Simeon Webb, dead with his chin blown away at the Battle of Brooklyn, one year ago this past August. The new powder handler, Private Mordecai Grayson was a Massachusetts man, like the rest of them. He had been with Sergeant Otis' gun crew and under fire at Trenton and Princeton. He was short and stout, barrel chested with narrow eyes peering out beneath thick, black eyebrows and a sag to the flesh above his upper lip which gave the appearance of a drooping mustache. He had placed the powder box about fifteen paces behind and to the left of the twelve-pounder and piled some stones in front of it for protection. When the battle began, Grayson would be in motion the most, dashing forward first with the canvas bags of powder and then rushing to the row of cannon balls closer to the gun and handing them to Chandler for loading.

They could see the men of the rifle regiment being pushed back, giving ground slowly, ambushing the onrushing orderly red lines of enemy troops, withdrawing under covering fire and taking new positions amongst the trees and shrubs at the approach to the river ford. It took another thirty minutes or so before the outnumbered riflemen were forced to concede and cross the Brandywine. They retreated in good order up the sloping hill toward the gun batteries. The enemy's ranks continued to swell as they massed in preparation to cross the shallow ford and assault the slopes manned by the Continentals. They were like so many red birds roosting low among the trees and shrubs lining the river, interspersed with light blue uniformed Hessian units, their brass hats reflecting the late morning sun.

Will opened the flap of his quill holder and felt the smooth stems lying neatly on the bottom. Although he was commanding the heavier gun, he waited for a signal from Sergeant Otis at the six-pounder to his immediate left. He wondered, now that the enemy attack was imminent, whether Captain Hadley would reappear and take charge as battery commander.

"Gun crews, prepare for action," Sergeant Otis yelled, looking to his right. Although the twelve-pounder had not been fired recently, Chandler first wormed the cannon, Tyler dipped the sponge in the water bucket, plunged the dripping pole down the muzzle, withdrew it and stepped nimbly aside as Grayson handed Chandler the long canvas bag of powder. Almost before Tyler had rammed it home, Grayson was back cradling the smooth twelve pound ball in his thick forearms. Will listened to it rumble down the brass barrel, waited until Tyler had rammed it home and then stepped forward. He pricked the canvas charge through the vent, inserted the quill in the touchhole and shouted "primed," surprised at how steady his voice sounded. He waited for Otis' command to fire, yelled "Give Fire," inserted the slow match into the quill and took one step back. The three guns boomed almost simultaneously with a crashing roar. Soldiers further down the slope cheered. The slight breeze was behind them and he was unable, until the smoke dissipated, to see the damage the three cannon balls had done, plowing into a concentration of redcoats, massed on the road.

After several more rounds, Will noticed the thick red lines of arriving troops step off the road to make way for their artillery. He judged they were all twelve-pounders, six of them, being pulled by teams of two horses each, the supply wagons with gun crews following. As they approached the ford, the horses veered to the right into an open ploughed field. The line of their artillery was broadside to Will's battery now, as the red-coated riders hastened to get their guns further into the field.

"Quick," Will ordered. "Turn the tiller. We want to catch the horses in their traces." He shuddered at his own words but Captain Hadley had drummed the soundness of the strategy into him, regardless of Will's inhibitions about maiming the animals. Wounded horses in traces made it harder for the gun crews to get their cannons into position and afforded more time to destroy the artillery.

Grayson, Tyler and Chandler swung the twelve-pounder to their right. Will determined to leave the barrel at the same elevation, wishing he had Sergeant Merriam to affirm his judgment. They loaded the charge and ball and fired. This time, the breeze blew from their right and their view was not obscured. Their aim was true. The ball landed just short of the team pulling the second cannon. It skimmed across the ground, struck the closest horse in the legs and threw its rider, and bounced into the gun carriage, shattering its wheel and yoke. Will heard the terrified whinny of the wounded horse and watched as the British riders struggled to control their panic stricken mounts pulling the other cannons.

While the two six-pounders continued to bombard the massed troops, Will kept up a steady fire on the artillery. If they had another twelve-pounder, they could have destroyed all of the British artillery before they even fired a shot. As is, his one battery was able to smash two guns, which lay askew in the field, surrounded by their dead or wounded gun crews, like red flower petals that had fallen off their smoldering stalks.

It took a while for the four remaining British gun crews to mount a counter barrage. They were at a disadvantage being exposed in a low, open field firing up at Will's battery, protected by the breastworks of trees and branches. Their first shots, which either fell short or went wide, killed some of the Continental skirmishers dug in further down the slope. To their right, Will noticed a large body of British light infantry and Jaegers had avoided the ford, and were wading across the river, the water chest high, holding their muskets above their heads. Continental riflemen hidden in the woods were picking them off. Will hoped there were enough of them to hold the enemy back. If the British at the ford attacked now and charged up the slope, Will feared the battery would be over-run.

Chandler tapped Will on the shoulder as Grayson ran up with another charge. "I have noticed their gun crews wait for our cannon flash and then leave their positions. They move several yards away and return after our ball has struck. Perhaps we can take advantage of their subterfuge."

Will ran over to Sergeant Otis. "Can you train the two six-pounders on their artillery? Aim not for the guns but wide. Their crews move on our flash. A few yards to either side of their own guns. Listen for my command, wait to the slow count of five and then fire."

Otis nodded. "It will give the Redcoats a respite from our bombardment. Hopefully they will not seize the moment to attempt to cross."

The twelve-pounder was loaded and waiting. Will pricked the canvas bag, inserted the quill, lit the powder and shouted "Give fire." The boom of the gun was followed quickly by the lesser roars of the two six-pounders. The wind blew the smoke from the heavy musket and rifle fire back toward the British artillery in the open field. Before it enveloped their position, Chandler reported he had seen a few fallen redcoats.

"One more round," Will yelled to Otis. The six-pounders delayed their firing again.

Only two guns in the British battery of four were now engaged in counter fire. Chandler stepped up on the breastworks and shaded his brow. "'Tis a temporary victory until they bring up replacement gun crews."

"Good enough for the moment," Will said. "We will redirect our fire at the main body and respond when they engage us again."

Will lost sense of time. It seemed as if the enemy remained frozen in position across the river, neither advancing nor retreating out of cannon range. From their vantage point up the slope, he could see some of their troops had crossed the river and were hiding behind what cover they could find and firing at the woods sheltering the Continentals. To the left of the ford, he heard heavy musket fire but saw nothing because of the trees and haze that hung over the battlefield. Their three-gun battery was at the center of the line.

He realized there had been no British counter fire for some time. He looked around puzzled. Sergeant Otis motioned to him. Below them, the ranks of redcoats on either side of the road leading toward the riverbanks were withdrawing. The sound of fife and drum and the wail of bagpipes wafted over the fields. The occasional pop of a rifle from their skirmishers seemed louder now because of the overall silence. Puffs of gun smoke dotted the hillsides on the other side of the river where buckwheat fields in bloom abutted against a wall of green forest.

"It appears the Redcoats are consolidating their positions on the opposite hills," Otis said, pointing to columns and columns of troops appearing on the slopes across the river. "Good thing there is a lull. My two guns are running low on charges and ball. You should take stock for the twelve-pounder. We may have to send one of the crew back to the rear and return with a supply wagon."

Will heard the Sergeant's words as if through a porous wall. His ears rang from the roar of his cannon. He stood only a few paces away from the explosions throughout the bombardment of the redcoats and the long artillery duel. He nodded and ordered Grayson to inspect the powder boxes and balls and report back, unaware that his voice was loud.

"You are shouting," Chandler said, grinning at Will. "Your hearing will be normal in a few hours. That is unless they resume their attack before then."

Will looked to both sides of the battery. When had these additional troops arrived? He was aware of the sun past midpoint in the sky and beginning to cast its rays into his eyes when he observed the British massed on the opposing hills. They probably will attack when the sun is behind them, he thought. He wished they had more cannons to defend the center and Captain Hadley to command them.

—⁂—

Bant steadied his breath and felt a calmness take hold. In the early morning he had fought the kind of fight he enjoyed. Taking advantage of nature's cover and ambushing British regulars and then skirmishing with their light infantry and the more sensibly uniformed green coated Hessian Jaegers in the woods on the west bank of the river. The deeper explosion of the Jaeger's shorter barreled but heavier caliber rifles, intermingled with the sharper, lighter cracking of the Continentals' long rifles.

His eyes were keen and he could see patterns where most others could not. He had picked off unsuspecting Jaegers confident they were hidden amongst the dense September foliage, their faces and eyes giving them away to Bant who had blown their heads off. It was the only target they presented.

But then, when Maxwell's rifle regiment had retreated across the river into their own lines, and he had lain there, inactive with his mind returning over and over again to the hanging of the Hessian plunderers, it was all he could do to prevent himself from screaming. And the cannon fire and howitzers which burst overhead made him feel exposed and vulnerable. He wanted to die but not be maimed or horribly wounded by some iron ball or burning metal. He wanted to die crawling through the underbrush, hunting a British skirmisher or Jaeger and in turn being hunted by them.

He was the first to volunteer, when Lieutenant Patten asked for skirmishers to creep up on the Hessian Jaegers hiding amongst some newly cut trees. They were engaged in sniping at Continentals along the far right of the line. Their accurate fire was taking a toll. McNeil and about ten other riflemen came with him. They snaked down the slope but separated at the rail fence bordering the cultivated field. While the others crouched and headed toward the cover of shrubs and brush, Bant, without hesitating, entered the blooming buckwheat field and slithered on his stomach directly toward the Hessians position at the far end. He could hear them rustling, the leaves' movement telling Bant where they were. Their short hunting rifles, with their silver metal were easy to spot, even if their green coats with brown facing blended into the undergrowth.

He waited before crawling closer, moving carefully, using his elbows for leverage and keeping his belly close to the ground. The breeze masked his movements and blew the faint pink, not yet withered flowers on the four-foot high buckwheat stalks. When he was a little more than one hundred yards away, he settled comfortably on the warm earth, with the stock of his long rifle nestled against his cheek. Peering out, he sighted just below the black tri-corn of the Jaeger who was kneeling and appeared to be directing the others. His ball blew part of the soldier's head away. Fortuitously he fell backwards, giving his surviving comrades the impression he had been struck from the front.

Bant rolled to his side and, lying in the dry depression of a furrow, bit the end of another cartridge. He poured some powder into the pan, quietly closed the pan cover, and then, on his back, with the stock clasped between his mocassined feet, rammed the rest of the cartridge and ball down the long barrel and refixed the ramrod. Slowly and carefully, he turned onto his stomach and peered through the leafless stalks at the Jaegers. They had moved forward several feet and spread out. He was deciding to shoot one of those closer to him who was reloading, when he saw another Jaeger, further away, rise up next to a stump and take aim. Bant fired and saw the man crumple, this time falling to his left from the impact of the ball striking him in the throat. Bant rolled over to reload and wondered how long it would take the Jaegers to realize he was in the buckwheat field. He heard the sharp bark of rifles and assumed McNeil and the others were engaging the Hessians from further up the hill.

Patiently, he waited for the breeze to shift the tall buckwheat stalks before moving. This time, he saw two Jaegers facing toward him, scanning the field, both having taken cover behind one of the fallen trees. They were slightly uphill from him and not too far apart. After shooting one, the other might be better able to determine where Bant had fired from and catch him while he reloaded. Then again, the Jaeger had no idea he was alone and might be hesitant to charge into the field. Bant arbitrarily selected the one on the right. He aimed at the forehead of the green-coated soldier who lay behind the thick log, exposing only his head from the neck up. It was enough. Bant fired and was certain he had killed him.

Instead of reloading, he lay flat and motionless, his chin resting on the soft earth and waited. Fortunately for Bant, the smoke from his rifle stayed low to the ground and dissipated in the light breeze. He smiled, enjoying this cat and mouse game. The other Hessian seemed only to move his eyes, methodically scanning each row for any clue of Bant's location. Bant breathed slowly. He watched the soldier's gaze pass by him and continue on to his left. Bant took this moment to roll over on his back and reload. The rifle fire and the Hessian's sniping made it hard for Bant to hear whether the Jaeger had entered the field with his gun loaded and ready. He lay quietly with his own rifle resting on his stomach before cautiously turning to face uphill. The Hessian who had been searching for him was not where he had been. Bant waited, confident he would reveal himself. He scanned the logs lying horizontal to the field, looking for telltale signs of a human. Behind the dark gnarled twist of the trunk, he spotted the black hair and the dirt-smudged forehead of the Hessian. The soldier had taken his tri-corn off and was doggedly waiting for Bant to reveal himself. His hunting rifle pointed over the log like an uncut branch. Unaware he had been spotted, the Hessian remained motionless. Bant sighted just between his eyebrows and pulled the trigger. The head disappeared.

Bant cautiously reloaded, aware of the shouts of men and heavier rifle fire. He stood in time to see the men of his regiment sweeping down the slope and into the woods with the Jaegers rapidly giving ground. They retreated across the Brandywine with Maxwell's rifles in close pursuit. Bant raced to join them, splashing across the creek at the shallow ford and beyond the tree line along a road paralleling the river. He found McNeil and the men under Lieutenant Patten's command resting behind a line of shrubs bordering a fallow field. On the slopes ahead of them, some of the retreating Jaegers had taken cover and begun a sniping fire. Masses of redcoats lined the tops of the hills. Bant rested with his back to the enemy. At least three regiments of Continentals were crossing the ford in good order, fanning out to their left and right and forming lines three deep in preparation for the attack.

"I suppose we will be tasked to clear the Jaegers again," McNeil said taking a long drink from his canteen.

Bant licked his lips and realized how thirsty he was. Biting cartridges and having black powder blow back in his face from the pan had made his throat dry. He had not retrieved his own canteen, left at the edge of the buckwheat field. McNeil offered him his. Greedily, he emptied it. The warm water tasted pleasant going down his throat but made him crave for more. He loped the short distance to the river, filled McNeil's canteen, drank half of it, and refilled it before returning.

Supply wagons were passing along the road and Bant lined up behind McNeil to get more cartridges. He took a handful of hard biscuits although he was not hungry and wished the suttler had brought extra canteens. The bottoms of his pants legs had already dried in the September heat, although his feet chafed in his wet moccasins.

McNeil drank some from his canteen and refilled it with cider from a barrel on the wagon.

"Some of the men, those that have heard you scream at night when your 'demons' possess you, speak openly of you as a lunatick," McNeil said, slipping the canteen strap over his shoulder. He put a large hand on Bant's shoulder as they walked back to the shrub line. "Now those who know of your wailing when we hung the four Hessians will believe it too. You may be crazy, but you are the calmest soldier under fire I have ever seen and braver than most. Not one man in a hundred would have entered that buckwheat field for fear of being spotted and picked off by those Hessian hunters." He wiped the sweat from his grimy forehead with his sleeve. "There. I have said my piece."

Bant nodded. He had felt good in that buckwheat field, killing those Jaegers. Maybe, if he killed enough of them, the heavy, dark burden of guilt would be lifted, eventually. If not, he could always seek out the musket ball to bring him final peace of mind. Today was not the day, however. He was eager to get back into battle.

—◊◊—

"The whole God-damned British army and their bastard Hessian mercenaries are across the river and we are riding to God knows where," Private Grayson said loudly to the rest of the crew. "This is the main ford. Any dolt can see that. Why we are leaving. . ." He stopped in mid –sentence and grimaced as the supply wagon hit a hidden tree stump in the grassy field. The men were bounced into the air and then viciously slammed down on to the rough wooden bench. Behind the wagon, the twelve-pounder, weighed down by the side-boxes, twisted on the hitch but remained upright.

Will was going to say, orders are meant to be followed and Grayson should not question them. General Maxwell's aide had ridden up to the gun crews  and shouted to Sergeant Otis- the battery was to follow the troops already departing through the pastures behind the lines and get on the road in the distance and make utmost haste to support General Stirling's Division.

Before Will could reply, Baldwin rebuked Grayson. "We have never taken the Lord's name in vain in this crew and I suggest to you whilst we are not certain the day's battle is over, now is not a particularly appropriate time to do so." Sergeant Merriam had not tolerated any blaspheming. Will was surprised that Baldwin had spoken up, being the one who had gently mocked Merriam's religiosity.

"It does not seem to me we will need the Almighty's divine protection since it is we who are leaving the field," Grayson grumbled to no one in particular.

Will felt the moment for him to say something had passed. He was disturbed by his lack of decisiveness. Later, he thought, he would consult with Chandler about whether he had been right to remain silent. He clicked his tongue and lightly tapped Big Red's haunches with the reins. In the distance, misty brown clouds of dirt lay close to the road they were supposed to take, marking the soldiers' path almost directly north meandering away from the ford. It seemed to Will there were a lot of soldiers on the move away from the river.

The air was warm and muggy. After the repeated rounds of cannon fire, the comparative quiet as they left the trenches and barricades behind them seemed eerie to Will. His hearing had returned. He could perceive the clop of Big Red's hooves, the creak of the leather traces, the dull rumbling of the iron clad wagon wheels and the occasional scree of a hawk, peering keenly from aloft to spy any prey flushed from the fields by the soldiers marching through. He was sure they were leaving one battle for another. But for that ominous thought, he could have enjoyed the pleasant warm mid-September afternoon, surrounded by peaceful verdant fields, neatly lined with proper fences.

Once they reached the road, they made better time. The soldiers of the regiments trotting along in good order made way for the horse drawn artillery, all heading toward the sounds of rolling musket fire ahead. After reaching a T, they headed almost due east as the road became steeper. Big Red, without any urging from Will maintained his pace. Will saw Continentals dug in a field to the right, flanking the sides of a steep hill, which bristled with more troops. The sounds of rolling musket volleys filled the air.

"Cannons to that hill," a Lieutenant shouted, riding down the line directing Will and Sergeant Otis to leave the road. The ground in the field was soft and almost swampy. Big Red strained to pull the cannon and wagon through the muck.

"Gun crews out," Will ordered and the men jumped out of the wagon to lighten the load. The horse, freed from their extra weight, surged forward onto solid ground and almost galloped up the narrow path, worn through the wooded slopes by the troops and guns that had preceded them. Two six pounders were already in place, surrounded by a shield of felled trees and low earthen works. The smell of gunpowder was strong with the wind blowing toward them from the fields and woodlands below.

"Will. Over here." Captain Hadley waved his tri-corn in the air.

"When they sent for more artillery, I had no idea you would be among them," he said offering Will his hand as he dismounted. Together they unhitched the twelve-pounder before the rest of the gun crew arrived. Baldwin, Chandler, Tyler, and Grayson quickly pushed the cannon into position behind a protective embankment and unloaded the side boxes. Grayson set up the powder boxes and began piling loose stones around them, while the others carried the cannon balls close to the piece. Will waited until Sergeant Otis' crews had the two six-pounders unhitched before he remounted Big Red and led the other two horses back down the far side of the slope. Will tied the horses to the trees, patted Big Red and hoped he would be safe. Then he sprinted back up the hill. The wagons were hidden amongst the trees, well behind the summit. Their battery consisted of four six-pounders and his twelve-pounder with Captain Hadley in command. Will felt both a sense of relief of not having to make decisions and also a surprising twinge of disappointment of not being in charge.

The noise of musket fire was constant. The cannons although loaded, were not yet engaged. Hadley led the men to the edge of the embankment. Below them, lay a sloping hill, the green fields shimmering in the late afternoon sun. At the bottom, along a road running parallel to their position, a bright red British battle line had been drawn up behind a fence. After firing a volley up toward the lead American skirmishers, they were busily engaged in tearing down the rails.

"That road below our hill leads to the Birmingham Meeting House. Our right flank is protected by General Sullivan's Division. Ahead, on our left, Smallwood's Marylanders are heavily engaged. When the British appear in force, we are to rain down on them a furious fire to break their ranks and stop their advance." He pointed to a large dust cloud about a mile and a half away, in the direction of the Meeting House. "I believe the King's minions are approaching. Man your guns and hold your fire until I give the order."

The sounds of musket fire intensified although Will was uncertain as to the direction. He studied the approaching cloud extending back in a long column. If the dust was created by marching troops, there were many indeed on the way to assault the American lines. At approximately a mile away, he could discern the soldiers. They came steadily on, their muskets at shoulder arms, bayonets glinting, their regimental flags fluttering in the light wind blowing toward them. Here and there, a few field officers on horseback rode alongside.

"God save us," Grayson whispered. "They are Grenadiers."

"God has better things to do than save those who have taken his name in vain," Baldwin said, spitting on the ground. "Let us hope, Providence will look with favor on our cause this day. Do your duty Grayson and hope for the best."

Will saw the tall, dark bearskin caps almost at the same time as he heard an aggressive jaunty tune, the high pitched fifes projecting above the menacing steady beat of many sheepskin drums. [6] Their regiments came on in massed, compacted units. At an order, more sensed by Will and the gun crews than heard, the Grenadiers broke from their marching units and crisply formed a long battle line, two deep with each Redcoat an arm's length from his companion. Will heard the thunder of many drums as the Grenadiers quickened their pace. To Will, it seemed that the quick charging troops would overwhelm and roll up the American lines at either end and the battery would be captured. He pushed that thought from his mind.

"Gun crews ready," Captain Hadley said quietly. Will pricked the charge, inserted the quill in the touchhole and shouted "Primed," slightly before the Sergeants of the other two gun crews.

"On my order." Hadley raised his sword. "Steady. Fire," he shouted.

Will lit the slow match, dropped it down the quill and shouted "Give Fire." The twelve-pounder roared. It was a long distance shot, maybe fifteen hundred yards. The ball landed short but with enough remaining energy, it bounced into the line of the advancing Grenadiers. Will and the crew fell into a frenzied routine of worming, sponging, loading the charge and ball, inserting the quill and firing. They worked, in the excessive heat with precision and efficiency, the smoke and powder particles burning their eyes, their tongues thick with thirst. Will no longer watched to see where the balls went. It would not matter anyway as a bluish haze enveloped the fields and fences below. He lost count of the number of rounds fired, only noticing that the noise of muskets and artillery seemed duller inside his head. Through all of this, he heard Captain Hadley call for grape shot for the entire battery.

As the twelve-pounder was being loaded with the canvas bags holding up to forty iron balls, Will surveyed the sloping hills and road below. Through patches in the smoke, the green fields were dotted with Grenadiers repeatedly attacking and retreating before the Continentals dug in behind fences and firing down from a few rocky promontories, protecting the hill and his battery. Will estimated the enemy soldiers were about six hundred yards away. The grape shot tore into the advancing Redcoats, cracking into bone and fence posts alike, tearing gaps in their ranks, as Grenadiers fell dismembered or gutted. They recoiled, regrouped and returned to the attack. After firing several more rounds, Will noticed the Continentals on the slope directly below had been forced to give ground and were closer to the summit. The rocky promontories, forming a curving arc thirty yards below the battery, as fortified as a man-built palisade, was the last line of defense for the troops. Looking to the right of the hill, he saw other Continental units falling back, with a long line of red extending far beyond the Americans' lines. They were about to be surrounded. He fought down a panicky urge to run.

A cannon ball struck just below the top of the earthen works, splattering Will with dirt. Another ball crashed into a tree behind him, shattering branches, raining down leaves and scattering splinters of tree trunk everywhere. They were taking fire from British field artillery. Will heard a scream of pain and fear as he held the slow match to the quill. He steadied the hand holding the match with his other and shouted "Give Fire." The musket fire, whether from the attacking Redcoats or the Americans was incessant. Balls were pinging off the brass cannon barrels and ricocheting through the air. Will saw the Grenadiers were now less than sixty yards below the summit, maintaining their long battle line, the waning sun glinting off their lethal bayonets, as they clambered over the remaining obstacles of felled trees and reformed their ranks. A thin line of Continentals manned a fence line between the advancing Redcoats and the rocky outcroppings. They were about to be over-run. Will looked to Captain Hadley, who was standing behind Sergeant Otis' six-pounder, his sword arm raised high above his head. Will was about to shout and ask for orders to retreat, when he saw a spurt of blood emerge from Hadley's upper arm. He dropped the sword and fell backwards.

"Take charge as gun commander," he yelled to Chandler and threw him his quill pouch. He dashed to Sergeant Otis' gun position where Hadley had fallen. The Captain lay unconscious, sprawled on his back, his head lying at an odd angle on a rock. Blood pulsed through his blue jacket sleeve and pooled on the ground. Will knelt down next to him, aware of increased hail of musket balls in the air and thudding sound they made as they struck the tree trunks and boughs behind the battery. He ripped a piece of Hadley's white linen shirt and made a tourniquet, tightening it with a thick piece of a branch, lying among the debris around the six-pounder.

"We have to save the guns," he shouted to Otis. "The Redcoats are advancing on our right." The Sergeant nodded. "The left flank is also crumbling," he said, waving off in the direction of the other side of the summit. "You go for the horses." Will took one more look at Captain Hadley's inert form and left the embattled battery on the hill.

When he returned mounted on Big Red and leading the other horses, the last of the Continentals, perhaps eighty men, had been forced back from the promontories and had taken cover behind the earthen works surrounding the guns. For the moment, their musket fire and the cannons' grape shot were holding the oncoming Grenadiers at bay.

Will hitched Big Red to the wagon, while Grayson, Tyler and Chandler turned the brass twelve-pounder around and attached it to the wagon's rear axle. Baldwin ran to Sergeant Otis' position and hoisting the limp body of Captain Hadley across his shoulders, ran with him and laid him none too gently in the wagon bed.

Will raced in a crouch to Sergeant Otis' gun. "You fire first followed from right to left in one minute intervals by the others- fire one round of grape and then hitch your cannon to the horses and retreat,"

Otis looked at him and smiled grimly. "First, the bulldogs assault us from the front, then the curs join in for the kill. Well, we will deprive them of their prize." He turned back to the touchhole and inserted a quill. "Primed," he shouted hoarsely.

Will sprinted from one gun commander to the other, repeating the instructions. Musket balls buzzed menacingly through the air around him. They were taking fire from both sides of the summit now as well as from below. The rays of the setting sun, broke through the battle's haze and cast paths of light pointing toward the Americans' crumbling positions.

Before mounting Big Red, he looked in the wagon, where Captain Hadley lay, crowded with other wounded soldiers moaning or crying out piteously for water. Baldwin and Grayson sat hunched on the side bench. Chandler and the rest of the crew clung to the gun carriage. Musket fire severed a large branch that fell in front of Big Red. The horse snorted and shook his head. Will tightened the reins to prevent him from rearing, and aware that he was now a more prominent target, crouched low over the horse's tangled mane and urged him down the far side of the slope, away from the advancing Grenadiers. He hoped the light infantry flanking the battery were not yet close enough to aim accurately or that Jaeger skirmishers had not already cut off their retreat. He had already resolved, if he had to, to abandon the cannon and move the crew into the already crowded wagon. Save the men to fight another day, he thought.

A hail of musket fire, from his left whipped through the low-lying branches, knocking twigs and a shower of leaves to the ground. The balls struck the sides of the wagon with a sharp crack, splintering the pine slats, pinged off the metal latches and hitting human bodies with a soft dull thump. Will felt a sharp pain in his left hand and saw blood ooze from a hole just below his thumb. Big Red staggered and Will cried out, thinking the horse had been shot. He recovered his stride. Will realized he had involuntarily jerked back on the reins when the fragment of wood or metal had struck his hand. He grabbed the reins firmly with his other four fingers and urged Big Red forward, ignoring the screams of pain from behind him.

They galloped down a well-worn dirt path through the wooded slope. At that speed, Will knew the wagon would overturn if it hit a low tree stump in the path. But he was more afraid of an ambush. They had to get away as quickly as possible. Using his good right hand, he pressed his sleeve against the bloody hole just below the thumb joint. The pain was intense, radiating up through his wrist. He hoped nothing had struck bone. He looked back over his shoulder. Some of the wounded lying in the wagon were bleeding profusely. At quick glance, it appeared they had been hit by the last volley of musket fire as they lay helpless in the wagon bed. Baldwin was cradling Grayson with one arm, both of them, now sitting among the wounded. The front of Baldwin's coat was covered in blood. Behind the twelve-pounder, through the trees, he saw one or two of the brass six-pounders from their battery and thought it was Sergeant Otis on the lead horse.

Ahead, through a clearing was a road. With the sun low in the sky behind him, he knew it led southeast, well inland from the ford he had been at that morning. Blue clad Continentals, running as fast as they could, emerged from the woods on his left. He heard musket fire but did not turn in the saddle to see if Redcoats or green clad Jaegers were in pursuit. He reached the road. On either side, clumps of disorganized troops jogged along.

Further down the road, they came upon remnants of a baggage train, some wagons carrying a grim cargo of wounded, maimed and dying soldiers, blood dripping through the floor boards and staining the dusty ground beneath. A body of troops, about one hundred in number led by a few officers, left the road, and marched resolutely through an orchard toward a rocky hill and back toward the enemy. The loud high screech of bagpipes and the drums signaled the relentless pursuit of the Redcoats.

Will kept Big Red at a fast trot. He switched the reins to his right hand and found the four fingers on his left were cramped in a curled position and blood still flowed freely from the torn flesh below his thumb joint. Guiding Big Red with his knees, he fumbled for and found a piece of cloth for cleaning his ramrod in his saddlebag. He tied the dirty grey rag around his thumb, let his left hand rest on the saddle pommel and held the reins in his right.

At dusk, they passed several houses clumped around a crossroads. Weary and exhausted men lay everywhere and those able to stand were crowded around the one or two wells, eagerly drinking and dousing their heads in the buckets while those behind them clamored for their turn. Will decided there would be no help for the wounded and the place would probably be overrun by British troops in the morning. They continued on, following wagon loads of wounded, accompanied by the sounds of insects, the soft moans of soldiers and the occasional piecing scream of a man unable to bear his pain any longer.

After another three miles in the gathering dark, they came to a crossroads and headed almost due east. Lights from the windows of several buildings twinkled ahead. Whatever this place was, Will determined they must rest here. Lanterns hung from tree branches illuminated several fenced in yards. It was quickly clear, from the pile of amputated limbs and the screams of agony from within, that two of the out buildings were being used as field hospitals. Will wearily eased himself from the saddle, stiff and exhausted and limped back to the wagon.

"Grayson is dead," Baldwin said, still cradling the powder handler in his arms. "Took two musket balls through his back. He passed about an hour ago."

Will sighed. He wondered whether he could have done anything differently during the retreat from the summit to better protect his gun crew. Hadley lay with his head on the thigh of another wounded soldier. His eyes were closed and his chest moved slightly as he breathed.

"Help me get the Captain out of the wagon," Will said. Baldwin gently leaned Grayson against another man, bent down and lifted Hadley upright. The Captain's face, even in the dim light looked ashen gray. His eyes fluttered open and he moaned softly. Will draped Hadley's good arm over his shoulder and with Baldwin supporting their Captain from the other side by his waist, they moved slowly toward the light of the shed.

"Do not let them take my arm, Will. Promise me," he said hoarsely, his chin almost resting on his chest.

"I will do my best," was all Will could say to reassure him. The Captain's mouth formed a small smile. "I rely on your promise."

Mercifully, Hadley, lost consciousness and did not see a bloody hand and forearm sawed off below the elbow sail through the shed's window onto the pile of already amputated limbs. [7]

# Chapter 11- Philadelphia in Turmoil

"I will not remain idle in this city one day longer," Mercy Ford said vehemently. Elisabeth nodded in agreement. They were sitting in Mrs. Knox's large drawing room, sorting through bolts of linen and cutting them with sewing shears into strips for bandages. With the rich draperies pulled back, the mid-morning sun streamed through the floor to ceiling glass French doors, which were opened a crack to permit some fresh air to enter. The busy work barely distracted Elisabeth from thinking about Will.

"Dr. Rush himself has left to tend to the wounded, as have several other medical men. Or should I say, men who claim to have the necessary experience," Mercy added. "As if there are no women who have set bones, stitched wounds, staunched blood and God knows what else to repair the damage men have done to others or to themselves." [1]

Elisabeth had not been taught those skills at her family's home in Albany. Will had told her of Miss Mercy's efficient and capable help in tending to the wounded in Morristown. She was certain she could learn from her, or at least be of some help. Anxiously, on September 11th, she along with the people of Philadelphia heard the sounds of the battle. Some wondered what it meant for their cause. The cannonades and musket fire seemed to ominously boom throughout the entire day. When the firing ceased, around 6:30 at night, it was as if the entire city held it's collective breath.

News of the disaster reached Philadelphia mid-morning the next day. Tidbits of information, from those who had heard something from someone who had read a dispatch, grew into the most dire accounts, as rumors first spread among the wealthy in their mansions on Society Hill down to the laborers at the wharves by the river. [2] The city was divided between grim patriots fearing the worst and Loyalists barely concealing their joy.

"I am anxious for my dear Harry, perhaps horribly wounded or lying dead in an open field, unburied and left for crows and . . ." Lucy Knox's voice trailed off as she dabbed at her eyes with a handkerchief. "I had such vivid nightmares with ghastly images of him." Elisabeth had heard her crying in the night, alone in the canopied bed. Her red puffy eyes were proof of her distress this morning.

"Surely, if General Washington penned a note to warn the Congress, my dearest would have had the time to inform me of his status. Unless he is dead or suffering from some awful wound," Lucy said. She rose anxiously at the clattering of hooves on the cobblestones outside, stopped despondently as the sound of the rider passed by down the street and sank her large rear back into the sitting chair. "It tries my very being to be so near to a battle in which my beloved Harry is involved. Better to be far away in Connecticut or even Boston where his letters would reach me the same time as news of victory or defeat," she bemoaned.

"Writing is usually not an activity one immediately engages in while in retreat," Mercy observed. "He may have been captured," she added to soften her reply. "I am sure it will only be a matter of time before you hear from him. The British will treat a general officer with courtesy."

Elisabeth glanced at Mercy. She, like Elisabeth was worried about the fate of a loved one but would not reveal her inner feelings. Elisabeth now thought of Will as one whom she loved. Dear God, having recognized her love would it now be destroyed by this terrible battle. Mercy was right. Sitting idly by doing nothing except accumulating bandages for soldiers in need was intolerable.

"We must go to the wounded to help treat them and not wait for them to be brought here," Mercy said, waving her arm around the room and rolling her eyes at the luxury surrounding them- silken wall paper and matching embroidered drapes, a tea table, a massive highboy, and a dining room table, all made of polished dark mahogany highlighted with lightwood inlays adorned with brass handles. "We need transport- a carriage or wagon," Mercy said, giving voice to Elisabeth's thoughts.

"I will ask Judge Shippen," Elisabeth said, abruptly standing up from the bright yellow upholstered Grecian couch.

"Yes," Lucy said bitterly. "A man who does not hide his Loyalist leanings very well will have no need to flee the oncoming British Army."

"He will not refuse transport of medical supplies and assistance. Philadelphia has not yet fallen and if it does, our cause will still triumph," Mercy said. "He will be shrewd enough to prepare himself for that day as well. While Elisabeth calls on Judge Shippen, I will seek help from another quarter."

"Be careful, my dears," Lucy said. "With all this uncertainty, rough sorts may be emboldened to take advantage and the streets may not be as safe as usual. I would join you but I must remain here with our daughter and word may come at any moment from my dear Harry."

By the mid afternoon, Elisabeth and Mercy left the city in one of Judge Shippen's carriages, not his finest but well suited to the road, and driven by one of his employees, a brawny teamster who would discourage any mischief. They were accompanied by Mary Lewis who, when asked by Mercy had without telling her husband, gone to one of his warehouses and simply commandeered a horse, driver and wagon which was now filled with crates and trunks of bandages, blankets, new and used, and clean clothes for the wounded.

As Judge Shippen had insisted, they did not proceed directly toward the Brandywine battlefield, a distance of fifteen miles to the southwest. The Judge's information was that the army had retreated in the direction of Chester, more to the north. The largest concentration of wounded would be there. Mercy was no longer certain of that. Before they left, a rider had delivered a letter to Lucy Knox, sent from a "Camp near Schuykill" assuring her Harry was safe. [3] It bore that day's date, the 13th of September. With the army on the move, Mercy said, the wounded may have been sent away and perchance were on their way to Philadelphia.

"Perhaps, we should stay and tend to those who do arrive," Mary suggested.

Mercy shook her head. "We have begun the journey. There definitely will be wounded to attend to and a need for our supplies when we arrive. We must continue on."

Elisabeth only vaguely heard them as she sought to quell her desperate panic. General Knox had not mentioned Will as he had in prior correspondence. The absence of a comment was an ominous sign for her. The General was kindly sparing her the worst of all possible news, she concluded. Will must be dead. No, she thought. Until I am told I must believe he is alive somewhere.

Just before dusk, they arrived in the small town of Darby and learned that the army was indeed on the Schuykill and had left the wounded in this place and in small hamlets and at farms stretching from here south to the battlefield. A light rain had begun to fall as the three women, raising the hems of their dresses, walked through the mud of a churned up yard, toward the barn that served as a makeshift hospital. Wounded men lay outside, shivering the cool evening air, seeking any available bit of shelter. Some huddled against a horse trough, others had burrowed into a hayrick, their boots protruding like well shod scarecrows.

Two men with a wheelbarrow emerged from the shadows and passed them, pushing their grisly cargo of dead soldiers, their arms and legs hanging over the sides of the wooden barrow. Lanterns in the field beyond the fence indicated the burial detail at work. Elisabeth noted the dead soldiers were barefoot, their shoes having been removed to serve the living.

Inside the barn, lanterns hung from wooden pegs or nails, illuminating the stalls crammed with the worst of the wounded lying on the hard dirt floor, more than two dozen to a compartment. Some were covered with blankets. Most were not. The wider passageways between the stalls were also filled with those able to sit, their backs against the rough wooden siding of the stalls, their heads lolling to the side in pain wracked sleep.

Mercy approached one of the local women who appeared to be in charge. "We have come from Philadelphia to help," she explained, gesturing to Elisabeth and Mary. "I have some experience in tending to wounded."

"There is one doctor and his two assistants making the rounds from barn to church to home to wherever they are housed," she replied softly. "These men were last seen by him a few hours before sunset. Some need attention now. Others have died in the interim," she said wearily. "The ones in the stalls need the most care and warmth. They are amputees or have chest or stomach wounds. Those here," she said pointing to men on the floor in the passageway, "are at least able to eat although God knows we have little to feed them." She shrugged. "As for the ones outside, we simply do not have the room. Do your best. Holding the hands of those in pain may be all that can be done for these poor souls."

Mary left quickly to have the drivers bring the trunks of bandages and blankets. Elisabeth followed Mercy as she proceeded from stall to stall assessing the soldiers' condition. They lay in rows, so close together it was difficult to walk for fear of stepping on one of them. Some moaned quietly awake, others called out in their sleep. Some labored in their breathing. The breathing of others was so shallow, Elisabeth feared they had passed. Bright fresh blood oozed from the stump of one soldier's leg, wrapped tightly below his knee. He tried to sit up but was too weak to raise himself. Awkwardly, in the narrow space, Elisabeth knelt next to him and supported his back. The man smelled of gunpowder, sweat and urine. He looked wild-eyed at her and then to his bloody stump.

"I must find my leg," he muttered. "I must find it. Mother would want me to." He sank back, exhausted on the dirty straw, still mumbling to himself.

Elisabeth put one hand on the soldier's brow. "His skin is as if it is on fire, and yet he shivers."

"It is the fever after amputation," Mercy said. "They need to be covered. I will ask if there is any hot broth. They require nourishment to keep up their strength." She moved on toward the stall entrance and Elisabeth rose to follow.

She felt a tug on the hem of her cloak. Elisabeth turned and looked down at the face of a young soldier, his unkempt light brown hair, matted to his forehead, his eyes sunken and pleading. His dirty blackened bony fingers held tightly to the dark blue fabric of her hem as if it were a lifeline to his continued existence. A bandage wrapped around his chest and his torn blue jacket was encrusted with dried blood.

"Please, Miss. There is much pressure on my heart." Weakly, he raised his arm. "Could you lift it off?"

She was about to plead she did not have the time. Staring down at him she could not discern where his dried blood ended and the crimson facing of his jacket began. She gasped, realizing Will's uniform was the same color blue with dark red facing.

"Mercy," Elisabeth called softly and then louder. Mercy Ford's head appeared around the stall entrance. "I am tending to those in the corridor."

"I need to remain here," Elisabeth said simply. "With this soldier." She shook her head overwhelmed by the maimed men surrounding her. "And these others."

Mercy quickly assessed the situation. "Very well, someone needs to remain here until the doctors return. Take this stall, the next one and the pathway in between. I will ask Mary to come by with blankets, linen and at least water."

Elisabeth knelt by the young soldier and gently lifted his jacket away from the massive bandage wrapped completely around his chest. "Is that better?" He nodded. "I must tend to others but I will return." She tucked the tail of his blood stiffened jacket under his hip and rose.

Elisabeth went from soldier to soldier, passing the still ones hoping they were deep in an exhausted sleep and not dead. For those who tossed and moaned, in the throes of a high fever and breathing rapidly, she would wipe their sweating brows with a wet linen cloth; for those that cried out, she would reassure them softly and hold their hands in hers. She carried a pewter pitcher and poured water into a cup, offering it to those who implored her with a weak outstretched hand or asked in hoarse whispers. For those with stomach wounds, she dipped the linen cloth in the pitcher and wiped their cracked lips, and let some drip into their mouths, blackened on the right side from biting the powder filled cartridges during the battle. [4] She did not know what to do about those with head wounds and on her own, decided a sip of water would do no harm. One soldier alarmed her with an ear splitting scream as she tried to lift his head for him to drink from the cup, so she simply dripped water into his open mouth.

Over the next few hours, Elisabeth returned, whenever she could, to the young wounded soldier in the uniform like Will's, and Captain Hadley's. He seemed more pale each time. She managed to convince herself it was the candles in the lanterns that had burned down to almost stubs. Every time she was next to him, holding his hand, he managed a wan smile as he looked deeply at her eyes.

As the night wore on, Elisabeth's neck and back ached from constant bending. She was nauseated by the stench of unwashed men, helplessly lying in their urine and excrement with vomit dribbling down their shirts and drying on their chins and necks. Most of all, she was overwhelmed by the sight of so many of them, young men who had been whole and energetic a few days ago and who now were broken, maimed and maybe dying. And she knew, Will could be one of them, lying unattended in some home or barn, perhaps even in Darby. She would not permit herself to think of him as dead. She clung to her resolve- she would only accept his death when told by someone who had seen him. Until then, she would continue to hope.

A local woman joined her and together they dispensed soup from an iron pot with a ladle, the soup being hot when they started in one stall, warm by the second one and fairly cold for those lying in the passageway between the stalls. Her young wounded soldier had been one of the lucky ones to receive two ladles of the warm broth. She smiled encouragingly as she lifted the dipper to his cracked lips. Then, before she could stand up, he had reached out and covered her hand holding the ladle in both of his, like one protects a small bird that has fallen out of its nest. Involuntarily, she brushed his light brown hair back from his forehead. When she next returned to the stall, he was dead.

She watched with horror as two townsmen, beads of rain dripping from their hat brims, one holding the young soldier under the shoulders, the other his feet, carried him out of the stall. She heard the thump as they dumped his body in the wheelbarrow in the yard. They returned carrying another wounded soldier on a makeshift stretcher of a blanket stretched between the long handles of a hoe and rake. The man gave out an inhuman groan of agony as they lowered him on to the stall floor and pulled the blanket out from underneath him. This soldier's hip and upper thigh down to the knee were swathed in bandages. His right arm was missing just below the elbow with a thick woolen cap covering the bandaged stump. The man's eyes were sunk deep in their sockets and his skin, stretched tight across his forehead, was a light grey, like the color of dirty water. Judging by his clothes he was of a militia, but which one she could not tell. She took the blanket that had covered the young soldier and laid it over the militiaman, careful, as she knelt next to him, not to touch his bandages. He tried to speak but his words were more a wheeze.

How long she continued ministering as best she could to the wounded crammed about her, she did not know. The barn buzzed with the constant sounds of moans, soldiers calling out in their feverish hallucinations, the occasional high-pitched scream of someone in horrific pain and the persistent, piteous cries for water. It was those lying listless, comatose and she feared close to death, who received whatever extra attention she could give. And she realized, she did not know the single name of any of the men she was attempting to care for.

Elisabeth was so fatigued she did not notice Mercy, until she felt a hand on her shoulder. "Other women have arrived to relieve us. Come it is long past midnight."

Elisabeth followed Mercy outside. A cold mist enveloped the yard, yet the air was clean and fresh. She took a deep breath. In the dim light of the lanterns, the ground around the barn and sheds seemed to move with those wounded waiting their turn for space inside. Dark shapes tossed and thrashed, calling out for help, for water, for comfort, for any kind of relief from the pain, the fever, the cold, their fear of dying alone. Mary Lewis caught up with them and the three women walked slowly away from the barn and yard, toward the farmhouse.

"I met the surgeon in charge," Mercy said. "He assures me some of the wounded have already been sent to Philadelphia and beyond." Mercy paused and wearily pinched her nose between her eyes. "I have decided to return to the city immediately. I can help there as well as here. If Samuel is alive and wounded, he will send a message to me there." And so would Will, Elisabeth thought. "I will go with you," she said quickly. "And I also," Mary Lewis added. "My husband would not prevent me from tending to the wounded housed in Philadelphia. If I thought otherwise, I would remain here."

The three women were so exhausted, they fell asleep in the carriage despite the jolting ride through the night on the rutted road. Arriving in Philadelphia in the early morning, it was clear the city had changed. There was a tenseness about the people, an air of nervousness and apprehension. The normal business of markets and manufacture seemed to have come to a halt. Nervous crowds clustered on corners discussing the latest news or reading aloud from freshly printed broadsheets. It was evident some people had decided not to wait any longer for bulletins of another defeat and the arrival of the British army. Several wagons loaded high with household furniture and drawn by tired horses plodded by. Angry workmen milled about, some carrying cudgels, calling out obscenities and threats to those they deemed cowards for seeking the protection of the countryside.

Mary left them at Mrs. Knox's and rode with her husband's driver and wagon to her house north of Market Street. Mercy and Elisabeth, despite their weariness ran into the house anxious for news. They found Lucy in the drawing room at her writing desk. She put her quill down and rose from her chair, surprisingly quickly given her ample size.

"Oh my dears. You look so wearied. I was this very moment penning a response to my dear Harry. Please sit and I will tell you my news." She rang a small brass bell on the desk. "Have some tea and nourishment while we talk."

Elisabeth sat on the Grecian couch with her back arched to lessen the stiffness in her lower spine. She kept her legs away from the yellow upholstery, conscious her stockings were bunched and spattered with mud. Mercy took a chair at the tea table.

"The wretched wounded have been arriving in the city in a continuous stream. The Pine Street Church, St. Peters nearby and Christ Church, I am told are all filled to overflowing. Down by the river, warehouses have been turned into hospitals. The very numbers of our poor wounded soldiers have frightened people to believe our army is destroyed and our cause lost." She motioned for the servant to place the tea tray on the table and pour. "Mr. Paine has written an essay calling us to act with more resolve to defend our freedom. All the Philadelphia papers have printed it." [5]

"Judging by the number of wagons we saw being loaded with household essentials, Mr. Paine's essay does not seem to have had the desired impact," Mercy observed.

"The gentlemen of our Congress have remained," Lucy said. "They are setting a fine example for the populace. It is rumors that our now our enemy."

Elisabeth noted her change in attitude and resolve, now that she had received word from her husband that he was unharmed.

"There is no further word from the General or a mention of Will?" Elisabeth asked.

"No, my dear," Lucy replied, reaching over and patting Elisabeth's knee. "My intuition tells me your young man is well and with the army in the field."

"Then why did not the General mention that in his letter to you?"

"Oh, do not be a silly," Mrs. Knox said, taking another piece of toast and spreading it with jam. "Harry wrote his brief note to me in haste. Will may have been on another part of the battlefield or assigned to a different Regiment. When he is once again in the General's company, I assure you my thoughtful Harry will include a word about his wellbeing. Indeed, I will add to my letter you are anxiously awaiting word from your Will."

As she and Mercy hurried to the Pine Street Church, Elisabeth was not greatly reassured by Lucy Knox's words. She had seen so many wounded, it was difficult for her to believe, Will had escaped this slaughter unscathed.

The street in front of the two-story church, with its high windows and four rows of double Greek styled columns lining the entrance way, was crowded with wagons loaded with food and barrels of water, thin mattresses filled with straw, stout ceramic chamber pots of all sizes and crates of linen and sheets. Men and women bustled in and out, like busy ants tending to a partially destroyed nest. Mercy took Elisabeth's hand and together they pushed through the press of onlookers, and through the tall double doors.

Inside, the pews had been moved and lined the walls, one stacked upon the other in wooden piles taller than a normal person. The wounded lay on the stone floor in orderly rows from the entrance up to the carved wood presbytery in the rear. Sunlight streamed through the glass windows on the eastern side, illuminating with its rays the soldiers on the opposite side lying pale on their makeshift pallets. Women moved among the wounded, some sat on low stools or inverted boxes or baskets. It was much more organized than the barn hospital in Darby Elisabeth thought, but the suffering and the stench of excretions and festering wounds was the same. So were the bloody stumps, the fevered looks, the violent shivering of bodies under blankets, the screams of agony and pain and the mumbled words of gratitude or hallucinatory cries of those who had lost their reason. And then, there were those who lay so still, their breathing so shallow, it was difficult to determine if they still lived.

"Elisabeth. You proceed on the right side and I on the left. Wave to me if you find Samuel or Will." Elisabeth nodded and began her grim promenade moving along the rows, thinking of the last time she and Will had walked together on the streets of Philadelphia that summer night in early July.

Lost in her thoughts, she almost did not notice the few soldiers lying quietly in the dim area in the chancel behind the altar. Had one not uttered a soft moan, she might have passed them by. A cloud covered the sun, now past its zenith, and the half circled portion of the floor was in shadows. Her shoe caught on an irregularity in the large rectangular stones and she reached for the wooden railing of the altar to steady herself. One of the men, unshaven with the beginnings of a thick beard, lay unconscious on his pallet, his booted feet extending beyond the thin mattress. His head was swathed in a bandage that pressed his hair to his skull, leaving only an unkempt long brown tuft sticking up from the top. The sleeve of the right arm of his uniform had been cut away, revealing the pale skin of his forearm, resting outside the blanket. His hand, from the wrist down was black with dirt and gunpowder. A bandage with an irregular blotch of dried blood encircled his bicep. It was his uniform that caught her eye- dark blue with red facing, the same as the Massachusetts Artillery. She knelt down for a better look and stared at the face before her.

It was Samuel Hadley. He lay breathing with bubbles of spittle trapped in the nascent beard around the corner of his mouth. She could not tell whether or not he was conscious. Elisabeth came from behind the altar and looked around for Mercy. She was walking slowly down the far side of the church peering at the rows of wounded. Elisabeth thought it would be unseemly for her to shout, although there was enough noise from both the wounded and those tending to them. She lifted her dress so as not to trip and hurried down the center aisle of the Church.

—⁂—

Hadley knew it was not a dream when someone turned him on his left side and pushed a blanket beneath him. The pain in his head was intense, as if a large stone was rolling around inside. He had dreamed Mercy was there, kneeling beside him, washing his face and neck with a wet cloth, then his wrists and fingers, then the forearm, oh so gently. The woman behind her, to his blurry vision, looked like Elisabeth. And in his dreams before, when he been in the throes of a high fever, his wounded arm had been attached, something he fervently wished for but was unsure it was true. One time when he had awakened on his litter in the dark, he thought he saw his hand, wrist and forearm in the candlelight but that could have been an hallucination, brought on by the fever. He almost cried out from the intense pain when they lifted him onto a stretcher. He bit his cracked, parched lower lip so hard, he could taste the blood.

He must be awake, he thought, if he felt the pain while being moved and could taste his own blood. And he could see his own right hand. Thank God it was true. He uttered a sigh of relief. Mercy was walking beside him. She squeezed his good hand. He sensed he was being carried in the street. He heard voices around him and closed his eyes to the bright sunlight that made his head ache more. They had stopped, a horse snorted and stomped its hooves, Mercy admonished someone to be careful and he was tilted and lifted up unevenly, the weight transferring to his wounded shoulder. This time, a loud groan escaped his lips and then he was lying flat, still on the blanket, another blanket on top of him. The warmth felt good. He could smell the fresh straw underneath. Mercy placed something soft under his head and shoulder, he felt her sitting next to him and then the jolting of the wagon on the cobblestones sent shattering white hot flashes of pain through his skull. He wanted to pass out, for this to be over with, but she squeezed his hand to comfort him and her presence kept him conscious. When they carried him off the wagon and he was on level ground, he could see Mercy more clearly. He squeezed her fingers in reply. "No angel in heaven was ever more lovely," he said, and lost consciousness again.

When he awoke, he was lying in a soft bed in a darkened room. She was asleep in a rocking chair in the corner. He stared at her a long time, remembering when he had first seen her in Morristown, administering to the wounded and then their long talks in her father's house. And now, it was he who was in her tender care, recovering from his own wounds. He remembered his surprise at being hit by a musket ball, the impact blowing him backwards and then, little else. As he rested in the quiet, his memory returned in fragmented images: the bright lanterns in the operating room of the field hospital, Will hovering nearby, the surgeon raising the bone saw, Will standing by Hadley's side as he lay on the table, shouts of anger, the intense pain of the metal probe searching for lead and bone in his arm, biting down on a linen cloth as the searing pain of a forceps removed the fragments of the British ball, and then simply darkness. Followed by the incessant pain, fever, chills and hunger, lying in his own filth. He realized the smell of his own excrement was gone. He lay on clean cloth sheets, clad in a nightshirt open at the collar to his chest, his right arm still bandaged and throbbing. Mercy must have cleaned him, he thought gratefully.

When she awoke and they could talk, he would tell her he had nothing to hide from her now. He grinned and drifted off to sleep, warm under the quilt for the first time since he had been wounded. [6]

—⁓—

Elisabeth was awakened by a pounding on the door, followed by the familiar deep booming voice of General Knox. She thought she heard the tall clock in the entryway strike the quarter hour before three in the morning. As servants rushed to let him in, Elisabeth heard the baby crying. She went to Mrs. Knox's room and picked up baby Lucy just as the General came up the stairs. Elisabeth drew her shawl around her nightgown, more for modesty than warmth.

"The British are less than twenty-two miles away and could be here in three to four hours," he said, embracing his wife. "General Washington has alerted Mr. Hancock and recommended that Congress immediately leave the city."[7] He caught his breath from the exertion of running up the stairs. He held out his arms and Elisabeth handed him his daughter who was no longer crying but looked dazed and sleepy. "Lucy. You and the household must pack your essentials in haste and be prepared to leave."

"And by when shall we need to be ready?" Mrs. Knox asked, thinking practically.

"By no later than one hour before dawn. I must assess what may be salvaged from the munitions works and casting factories along the river and that which must be destroyed. I will return to you as soon as possible." He kissed Lucy, hugged the baby and stomped down the stairs.

Mrs. Knox was now all efficiency. She ordered the men servants first to light all the lanterns in the house, make sure there were extra candles, bring up the trunks from the cellar and position a wagon on the street. She directed the maids to begin packing, bustling from room to room, supervising their activities, and for the cook and her assistant to bake bread and prepare a cold breakfast for the General when he returned. Upstairs in the Knox's bedroom, Elisabeth removed bedding and quilts from the long, low drawers of the mahogany and satinwood high boy and laid them in the open rough pine wood chest on the floor. She kept one eye on baby Lucy who was wandering around the bedroom pointing at everything with her chubby little finger and asking her to identify what each item was.

Hearing noise outside, Baby Lucy took Elisabeth's hand and toddled toward the open window. "Watch," she said. "Lucy watch." Elisabeth lifted her up in her arms and pulled back the curtains.

The scene outside was pandemonium. A steady stream of horse drawn traffic rushed by, with the occasional balky cow tied to the back of a wagon piled high with cooking pots next to crates of squawking chickens, the birds oblivious to the irony they were traveling beside their ultimate destination. Large onion shaped cloth bundles stuffed with whatever their owners thought essential sat precariously on top of tables and chairs.

People rushed about, loading carts, wagons, drays and all manner of other wheeled conveyances. In the moonlight the city seemed as busy as if it were already day. There was the constant clatter of iron wheels and horses hooves on the smooth cobblestones accompanied by the sounds of children crying, parents shouting, women screaming. [8]

She jiggled Baby Lucy in her arms to keep her interested. While abandoning Philadelphia was distressing, Elisabeth knew she would manage the trip to Lancaster or York or wherever in Pennsylvania they were going. Now that she knew Will was alive and unharmed. The day after they returned from Darby, Captain Hadley still feverish and but now lucid told her it was Will who had brought him to the field hospital. Upon hearing these words, if she had sprouted wings she would have soared into the September skies. Her euphoria continued to the present, but she vowed the next time she wrote or saw Will she would tell him of her love. She was now sure of it and could not bear the agonizing thought of him going into another battle without knowing this.

Staring out of the window, Elisabeth recognized the figure of Mercy Ford going against the flow of the fleeing citizens. She dashed across the street in front of a pair of oxen slowly pulling an overloaded farm wagon and ran up the steps to the Knox home.

"I have come to bid you farewell," Mercy said standing on the landing before the bedroom, her cloak still bearing the dirt from the night in Darby. "The wounded are being evacuated and I am taking Samuel to Morristown."

"And how is Captain Hadley faring?" Lucy Knox asked holding up her hand to shush a servant in the middle of her report on the packing of some household items.

"Well enough but still very weak. The blow when he fell is disturbing his vision and gives him unbearable headaches. I am optimistic that continued application of whiskey to his open wound and clean dressings every day will ward off infection." [9]

"And his arm?" Elisabeth asked, remembering seeing the torn flesh with the large exit wound at the back. "Will he be able to use it?"

"He can already move his fingers. With proper nourishment, he will regain his strength," she said embracing Elisabeth affectionately. "Please convey to Will how grateful Samuel is for preventing the surgeon from amputating his arm."

"I plan to write Will once we arrive wherever we are to stay," she said, having already begun composing the letter in her mind." She watched from the doorway as the driver helped Mercy into the carriage and then waved for no reason as it disappeared down the street, with several large trunks strapped to the back. She imagined Captain Hadley inside, leaning against Mercy, grateful to be in her presence on the long jolting journey.

General Knox returned a little before dawn. He took a few moments to play with his daughter, making faces and singing a few verses in his deep voice. She held his large tri-corn in both of her tiny hands and giggled at the funny rhymes. Knox undid the top two buttons of his dark blue jacket, as well as several on his buff colored waistcoat and sat down at the dining room table with the toddler on his lap. Lucy took a chair beside him and brushed some dirt from his sleeve as cold ham, freshly baked bread, cheese butter and jam, were carried into the room along with a pitcher of hard cider.

"Make sure my men are adequately fed and given drink," he said to the serving girl.

"I will see to it, myself," Lucy said and followed the girl into the kitchen.

"Your men were speaking of this most recent battle as if it were a victory," Mrs. Knox said when she returned.

"Lucy my dear. We acquitted ourselves well at Brandywine. Our lads stood up to the most fearsome of soldiers, reputed to be the best in the British army, and we held our own. That is to our credit." He took a long swallow from his tankard.

"It was those who seek to profit from this war for our own independence who snatched our victory from us three days later at White Horse Tavern. The very heavens opened up while the battle was still in progress." He paused to put another forkful of ham in his mouth. "True the rains were torrential but our cartridge boxes were defective and we lost upwards of 400,000 rounds. The mud was so thick the British could not take advantage of our lack of ammunition. I'd hang the scoundrels who sold the Army these shoddy supplies." [10]

"For me, my dearest Harry the most important victory is you emerged unscathed, although you look worn and tired from this constant fighting." She patted his hand affectionately and raised it to her cheek.

"Your safety and happiness and that of our babe is the sole object of my heart," he replied. "I am only able to perform my duties in the field knowing that you are well behind our lines, ensconced in comfort and secure from any danger."

Lucy withdrew her hand and snapped her fingers. "I would relinquish the luxuries of life as quickly as that and be willing to taste nothing but bread and water if I could only be with you. When the Army goes to winter quarters I shall share whatever hardships you will endure. I am nothing without my dear Harry."

"My dear. I know not where or when we will go to quarters but if it is safe from attack, then you will be my constant companion."

Knox pushed back his chair from the table, held little Lucy in one meaty hand over his head and shook her gently so that her brown curls swirled around her face. He handed his little daughter to his wife.

"Lucy. Permit me to have a word alone with Elisabeth." Mrs. Knox clutched little Lucy to her bosom and reached up to kiss the General. "Promise me you will ride with us for as long as you are able before departing to rejoin the army."

"I give you my word I will not put spurs to my horse one moment sooner to depart from your company and that of our darling daughter."

Elisabeth remained where she had been sitting at the far end of the dining room table, having thought it more discreet to leave the General and his little family with as much a sense of privacy as possible.

"Come sit closer," Knox beckoned. When she was sitting next to him, he said, "I am known to have a loud voice and it would be better if others were unable to hear what I am about to say."

Elisabeth shifted slightly and waited, unsure what was about to transpire. She feared it was about Will. Maybe he had been wounded after Brandywine. Or worse, she thought. He is dead. She sat rigidly composed, prepared for the worst news possible.

"My dear. You know I am as fond of Will as if he were my own natural son. I would do nothing to jeopardize his happiness. And he appears to be happiest when he is with you." He paused and Elisabeth thought for once the General was at a loss for the appropriate words.

"Will has spoken often of all you have done for him, and thus for me," Elisabeth said struggling to control her apprehensiveness. "Do not have a concern that I will take ill of anything you may say."

"We all risk something in fighting for our noble cause. Will and I on the battlefield. Some may do more behind the lines and take perhaps even greater risks. We know the British will occupy Philadelphia. We cannot prevent it by force of arms." He sighed deeply and unbuttoned his waistcoat further.

"It would be useful, nay vital to our cause to have information about General Howe's intentions, his troop dispositions, the number of sick and able bodied men, the size and direction of his foraging parties, the morale of his troops, whether there are shortages of ammunition and supplies - anything of major importance or seemingly of no matter whatsoever."

He leaned forward, his blue grey eyes fixing on her. "I am asking you to remain behind in Philadelphia and provide us with such crucial information as you may obtain." [11]

"You are asking me to become a spy," Elisabeth whispered incredulously, taken aback by the request. General Knox nodded. "But I am not skilled at secretive activities and know nothing to convey...."

General Knox waved his hand to interrupt her. "My dear. The British Officers enjoy the company of pretty young women, at balls and dances, performances and the like. Your friendship with the daughters of Judge Shippen, who has known Loyalist predilections, will be certain to involve you in their vibrant social life. By virtue of that association you may be especially well positioned to learn of information others may not be able to obtain."

She thought of one of the many Shippen's soirees, she had attended. Now, in her mind, all the young men wore Redcoats and not Continental blue. "If I am to consort with the enemy, it will be difficult for me to play the part of enjoying it, knowing Will is facing their bullets and bayonets."

"You will have to exercise caution and be discreet in your behavior. I must in honesty represent that my request places you in extreme danger if you are discovered. However, if you accept, I will provide you with the safest means for communication."

"I will do it," she said. "If one scrap of information I provide saves a soldier's life, it will be worth it. How do you propose I divulge what I learn and to whom?"

"Why my dear. It is obvious," Knox chortled, his eyes twinkling at the thought. "By your letters to Will. And we will communicate to you through his letters in reply. Only Will and my dear Lucy will know why you have remained in this city."

There was a knock on the door and a trooper entered. "General. Sir. It is getting light. All is ready. Your wife's luggage has been loaded and the carriage is outside."

Knox sighed and stood up. He opened his arms and embraced Elisabeth, kissing her affectionately on the top of her head.

"A messenger from me will deliver more details within the week."

"Is there some sign this messenger will give so I will know him," she said feeling conspiratorial and foolish at the same time.

"I plan on sending Will," the General said, smiling broadly.

# Chapter 12 - Two Lives Entwined

Will thought their group was an odd mixture- eighty Light Horse Troopers and two dozen artillery men like him, drawn from Colonel Sargent's Regiment, as drivers of the empty wagons taken from the Army's encampment on the west bank of the Schuykill. After a hard days ride, they were camped around the Boatswain and Call Tavern, less than twelve miles from Philadelphia and south of Ardmore.

It was a balmy night for late September, too cold for gnats and mosquitos but still warm enough to be outside. Will sat on the edge of a cider press in the yard between the stable and the tavern and breathed in the fresh sweet smell of apple pulp. He preferred to avoid the noise and heat of the main room of the crowded tavern. He was not entirely alone. Troopers went back and forth to the stable, tending to their horses or on some other personal mission. In the moonlight, he could see the glimmer of the pickets' fire down the road toward Philadelphia.

Soon he would be with Elisabeth. He was worried for her safety and wished it were possible they could leave the city together. General Knox had explained she had voluntarily agreed to remain behind and now it was Will's task to teach and give her the tools to function as safely as possible. Any risk of her capture, no matter how small, was too much for him to bear. He would have to get used to this anxiety, a new feeling for him. After all, he reasoned, Mrs. Knox coped with it.

He wondered if Elisabeth worried about his safety when the Army was in the field. She said she did, but was it the same as his gnawing worm of fear, imagining the worst happening to the one he loved.

Will mopped the last of the dregs of his dinner with the remaining piece of bread and licked his fingers. Their commander, Lt. Colonel Alexander Hamilton, an aide-de-camp to General Washington himself, had paid the tavern keeper in sterling for the meals provided to the men. Probably more to buy his silence and to compensate for restricting the keeper, his family and all who worked there from leaving until the following day, than for the quality of the food. It was a thin gruel, with a few pieces of gristly beef, not worthy of the name of stew.

The tavern door opened and Will recognized the Colonel and two other officers as they strolled around the yard. When they were closer, Will thought it appropriate to stand up. He adjusted the haversack across his shoulder. It had been with him ever since his meeting with General Knox. He intended it would never be away from his person.

"Sergeant Stoner, is it?" the Colonel asked. "From General Knox's Artillery Regiment?"

"Yes sir." Will answered as the three men stopped in front of him. Hamilton's tri-corn was under his right arm, pressed against his ribs. The Colonel gazed intently at Will as if trying to place him. Will stared back at Hamilton's determined, almost commanding face with its firm chin, eyes set deeply above a long nose with a slight bent near the bridge and his reddish brown curly hair swept back away from his forehead.

"I was with your artillery at the Raritan above Brunswick," Will said, responding to the unasked question.

"Ah, yes," Hamilton paused, as if recalling the scene. "Quite the hot action was it not?" he said in his clipped, quick accent. "Gentlemen, excuse us for a moment. I desire a word with our young Sergeant."

Hamilton placed an arm around Will's shoulder and ushered him away from the cider press.

"General Knox has spoken very highly of you. I have been instructed by him to give you leave to do whatever you must in Philadelphia and assure your safe return." Will nodded, not knowing what else to say. "Your wagon and horse will be at my disposal for the supplies we intend to requisition. I expect to leave the city by no later than dusk two days hence."

"Sir. In apportioning the loads, my horse is stronger than most. If some of the materials are heavy, place them in his wagon. He can pull it."

Hamilton arched an eyebrow assessing whether Will was merely being boastful.

"Our wagon held more side boxes by half than the other two, when we arrived at the Raritan," Will explained.

Hamilton's tight lips formed into a smile. "I will keep it in mind. General Knox intends for us to bring back bullet molds, unformed lead and pig iron."

Hamilton donned his tri-corn and turned back to the two officers waiting for him in the shadows. "Be efficient about your business," he cautioned. "I will not wait." [1]

"Yes, Sir," he answered wondering whether the Colonel knew what Will's mission was.

—⚏—

By mid morning Elisabeth knew Continental cavalry had arrived in Philadelphia. She hoped Will was among them but feared he would be unable to find her. After Lucy, the baby and the wealthy patriotic merchant, in whose home the Knox family had resided, had departed with General Knox, Elisabeth moved in with Mary Lewis who was now living alone. Her husband, along with many other prominent Quaker leaders had been arrested, by order of the Philadelphia Supreme Executive Council, the day after Mary returned from tending to the wounded. The Quaker men had been removed from the city as a threat to public safety and security. How unfair, Elisabeth thought. Everyone knew the worst that could be said about Quakers was they would not aid either side, neither the Patriots nor the British. And how, she thought, could the authorities justify the fight for liberty from the Crown when they infringed the rights of an entire group on ignorance and false accusations. [2]

Philadelphia had changed remarkably since the alarm had been sounded. Half the city's population had fled along with the Members of

Congress, leaving less than twenty thousand souls behind. Throughout the city homes were abandoned, the windows shuttered, the carriage houses empty, the servants'quarters uninhabited. [3]

The men were gone, not only the young Militia Officers and soldiers of course, but those who would be seen as Rebel sympathizers, or whose occupations would be suspect- the gun smiths and gun powder makers, iron masters, river pilots and port collectors. The tavern keepers had stayed as did those who could profit from the businesses the British would need and hopefully pay for-tallow chandlers and grocers, suttlers and carpenters, shoemakers, horse farriers, and glassmakers. Mostly women and children remained, grim lipped and frightened, hurrying about their necessary business and then returning to what they hoped was the safety of their homes.

There were plenty of Loyalists who strutted about the less crowded streets, relishing with anticipation the arrival of the British. They congregated in the city's finest taverns and inns, formerly patronized almost exclusively by Members of Congress, savoring every moment of their new-found prominence. As for the Quakers, they remained stoic and forbidding, prepared to endure persecution from the British and hoping it would be no worse than that by the Americans.

Elisabeth sat in the very room she and Will had been in, with Captain Hadley and Mercy Ford on Independence Day. How quickly their situation had changed in three months. Lost in her musings she vaguely heard the knocking on the door and then Will's voice asking Mary if she knew where Elisabeth was. She jumped up from the side chair and ran into the entrance hall. He stood there, framed in the doorway, the worn strap of his haversack across the deep crimson facing of his blue jacket and a broad smile on his face at the sight of her. She walked slowly toward him holding out her hands. She felt the roughness of his palms and the linen bandage wrapped below his thumb and circling his wrist.

"You have been wounded," she said with alarm, as Mary closed the door behind Will.

"It is a small gash which does not impair the use of my fingers, although I must take care that it does not get infected."

Elisabeth led him into the sitting room and looked at the bandage stained with grime and dirt. "You have not changed the dressing as frequently as needed," she admonished. "Let me do it for you." Mary brought a basin of water, clean linen strips and a wedge of soap. Elisabeth undid the old bandage and gently washed the angry raw skin puckered around the linen sutures.

"My husband kept a bottle of whiskey in our house although he disapproved of drinking spirits," Mary said, using her thumbs to force the cork from the neck of the dark bottle. Elisabeth poured a small amount in a shallow bowl and took Will's wrist, turning his hand palm up and placed it so the wound was immersed in the alcohol.

Will had been recounting the battle and retreat and of being sent to Philadelphia to help requisition supplies before the British arrived. He winced and sucked in his breath as the alcohol burned and seeped between the sutures. Elisabeth noticed the lines around his eyes and the discolored skin under them. Gone was the carefree and youthful Will she had first met in Albany. He was more solemn and considered in his mannerisms but she saw his eyes still sparkled with the delight of being with her. She was certain of that. After tea, Mary said she had to go to the market with their cook and purchase what was available for their larder.

Elisabeth and Will moved from the front parlor to the kitchen which had only one small window facing the alley at the rear of the house and a solid wooden door, barred from the inside. Elisabeth sat down on one side of the small table and Will on the other, with his haversack resting against his leg.

"Elisabeth," he said, reaching out for her hand across the table. She sensed his nervousness as he hesitated to speak. "I must say this before . . . ."

"Say nothing," she said abruptly, withdrawing her hand from under his. "I have made up my mind and do not need to be lectured by one who risks his own life for our cause, as to why I should not risk mine." She saw the hurt in his eyes but continued. "I am cognizant of the perils of my endeavor and confident of my abilities," she said in a severe tone. "Now Will." She returned her hand to touch his fingers. "No more talk of this, I implore you. How am I to send the information I obtain?" she asked brusquely.

Will stared at her still momentarily confused by her stern tone and change of mood. "I was prepared to say something different from what you anticipated and condemned me for. However, you are correct. We have little time and must discuss the business at hand. We will need paper, a quill and ink and milk if there is some or vinegar will do." When she returned, Will instructed her to write on the paper. "Pretend you are writing to me but only about your normal activities, teas you have been to, what meals you have eaten, innocuous everyday matters that will not arouse suspicion."

She addressed the salutation "My Dear Will," which reminded her she had wanted to tell him she loved him before he again went into battle. She wrote a few lines concerning the stalls on Market Street, the high prices of eggs and flour and the weather turning colder. She felt Will's eyes on her, watching her hand move fluidly across the paper creating small cursive lines of print. Her words covered half the page, when he told her to stop.

"We will use invisible ink. The words may be written in lime juice, vinegar or milk. You must write them between the lines of the ink and be careful not to get them wet or smudged." Will took the half written letter and blew on it to dry the coarse ink.

Elisabeth reached for the vinegar. "No. No. Use a different quill or the residue of the ink will show," Will cautioned. She took a small bowl, poured a little vinegar into it and took up another quill. She wrote quickly and confidently filling the spaces between the inked lines.

Will held the paper carefully by the two top corners. "See, Elisabeth. It appears to be a normal letter. Now, when it is exposed to heat, the invisible writing becomes apparent." He took a candlestick from the mantle, made sure the candle was fixed firmly on the pricket and lit it with a stick from the fireplace. She watched his face as he waved the paper back and forth causing the candle's flame to flicker. [4]

I love you Will Stoner with all my heart. My love for you strengthens my own resolve to hasten the end of this cruel war. May Providence always protect you, my love.

He dropped the sheet on the table and pushed his chair back. Suddenly, Elisabeth was in his embrace, holding him tightly, feeling his arms around her, his hand on the small of her back pressing her closely to him. He kissed her gently at first on the top of her head, then on her cheek and finally his mouth was on her lips. She broke off and buried her face in his neck, smelling the salt and the faint residue of gunpowder. Somehow, he found her fingers and they stood, she did not know for how long, with her arms at her sides, his fingers in hers, their bodies pressed together. He alternately kissed her hair and whispered repeatedly, "I love you Elisabeth. I love you."

It was Will who first stood back. She saw the joyous expression on his face. With a smile, he took her hand and led her back to the table. This time, they sat next to each other, holding hands under the table, his leg casually pressing against hers.

Her draft letter lay in brittle fragments on the table. "You see the problem with invisible ink," Will said. "It crumbles once it has been heated. When I receive them I will have to quickly transcribe your messages." He raised her hand to his lips and kissed it gently. "But now, I have no proof of your professed love. It has disappeared," he said with mock sadness.

"Do not treat my love so carelessly that you imagine it to be of such short duration," she said, pretending to be insulted by withdrawing her hand. Will leaned over and rubbed his lips gently against her cheek.

"I will write your father and ask for your hand so you will not withdraw it again."

"Papa will be pleased but may suggest we await the outcome of the war."

"I cannot endure waiting on General Howe and his mercenaries to surrender."

"I also," Elisabeth said, "will not wait one day longer than necessary."

"When I return to camp, I will seek General Knox's advice and support."

"And when must that be?"

"No later than tomorrow before evening."

They sat in silence. The thought of their imminently being separated forced them to focus on the business of spying.

"Are you ready for the second lesson?"

Elisabeth nodded.

Will took a blank piece of paper and drew two horizontal and two vertical lines, creating a grid of nine square boxes, three across and three down. "Write the letters of the alphabet, beginning with 'B,'" he instructed. "Three letters per compartment with the last box in the lower right having only two- 'Z' and 'A'."

Elisabeth wrote out the letters and looked at the page. "That does not appear to be very secret. We have changed only one letter in order."

"It is a cipher," Will explained. "Each letter of the alphabet, when placed in a message is represented by a dot, in the same position as that letter in the box. The absence of a dot is the first letter, one dot for the second and two dots for the third letter. You must draw the lines of the box so the reader knows the position." He motioned for her to try it. [5]

Elisabeth took up her quill and drew a series of lines, frequently looking at the diagram Will had made. She handed the paper to Will. The first box had only one dot, the second the same, as did the third. He broke into a broad grin, needing only the first three letters to guess at the message: "I love you."

"I am certain General Knox expects more strategic and useful information will flow from your quill once the British arrive."

"For now, these messages are for your eyes only," she replied.

"All you need to remember is how to draw the diagram, begin with the letter "B" and the dot system for each letter in the box. If you make the diagram, be sure and burn the paper afterwards." Elisabeth nodded her understanding. "And how are these messages to be sent. They cannot be part of a letter. It is obviously a code."

Will tapped the cipher message Elisabeth had written. "The dots and boxes take up but a small space on a paper. You will write your messages on tiny strips and sew them into a seam of clothing or slip inside a book's binding." [6]

"Then I will have to send you many scarves and perhaps some cloth covered buttons," she replied, "as well as books, if they are still available after the British arrive."

"There will be tradesmen and farmers returning from selling to the British, who will be on the roads and will carry the post from tavern to tavern. I will receive what you send," he said. "We must clear the table. We do not want Miss Mary and her cook to surprise us."

Elisabeth returned the vinegar bottle to the cupboard and threw the scraps of marked paper in the fireplace.

Will lay his haversack on the table and unbuckled it. "There is one final method with a gift from General Knox." He removed a book and handed it to Elisabeth. "It is Entick's New Spelling Dictionary. The General and I have copies of this very edition." Elisabeth opened the cover to the title page. It was inscribed "To my dear Elisabeth" and signed by HK.

"Open to the last page," Will instructed. "It is numbered 468. That will be page one and the title page with General Knox's inscription shall be page 468. One dot shall signify the first column on each page and two dots the second. Select a word at random," he instructed. [7]

Elisabeth opened the dictionary to words beginning with the letter A. "I choose 'absent,' because you will be absent from me."

"But you are always in my thoughts," Will replied.

She nodded in appreciation. "As you are in mine."

"So on what page does the word appear?

Elisabeth saw it was page 34 and subtracted that number from 468. "So it becomes page 434."

"And the column?" Will prompted.

"Since it is the first column and the fifth word I would write it as 5.434."

"Correct," said Will. "Tomorrow, we will go over the three methods again before I leave the city."

"Why are there three?" Elisabeth asked, suppressing the thought that they would be together for only one more day.

"I posed the same question to General Knox. He responded it was in your discretion to choose which method to use. He suggests the invisible writing for general descriptive information of no immediate urgency such as the morale of British troops and where they were quartered. The cipher and Entick's would be used for messages we need to receive quickly in order to act upon or . . ."

"You mean to warn of imminent danger" she said.

"Yes, that would be one such instance."

"In that case, I would carry it myself."

"No you would not," Will said firmly. "You shall not under any circumstances reveal yourself as . . ."

"A spy? That is what I am. You must trust me to exercise my own judgment and . . ."

They both heard voices in the entrance hallway. Mary and the cook found them in the kitchen seated across from each other with the closed dictionary on the table.

"Look, Mary what Will has given me as a gift," she said, smiling, holding up the dictionary.

"Oh, Sergeant Stoner. There was no need to have brought Elisabeth a dictionary. My husband has an edition of Entick's in his library. I myself have found it quite useful in writing letters to my relatives. You will of course stay for dinner," Mary said cheerily.

The meal was a torture for both of them, trying to be pleasant and sociable while unable to say anything meaningful to the other. Elisabeth desired to be alone with Will, to either talk or simply to be in each other's company. They remained with Mary chatting in the sitting room and once it was dark, by mutual understanding they expressed a desire to take a stroll.

There was a mild autumn chill in the night air. She secured her light wool cape around her as they unconsciously retraced their walk of Independence Day, passing first the shuttered sheds in the middle of Market Street and then the fine Georgian style homes on Chestnut, many of which were dark with no signs of being inhabited. A convoy of wagons driven by troopers clattered down the street, one loaded with tanned leather hides, another blankets and assorted clothing, several incongruously carrying church bells, resting on thick wooden blocks and securely lashed down. [8]

"We have orders from General Washington to requisition supplies for the Army. We can only give receipts or Continental currency," Will said as the wagons disappeared down the darkened street. "I am afraid we will make no friends here with such payments."

"This is truly a different city from when we last walked these streets together. It will be more so once they arrive," Elisabeth said, emphasizing the word with distaste but refraining from calling them British. She saw Will frown. "Do not worry. I will be charming. I will be sociable. I will be flirtatious. All the while I will think of you and how every little bit of information may be of help to our cause."

They passed a well-lit Georgian mansion on Chestnut and heard dance music from within.

"That is the home of the Norrises. They are related by marriage to the Shippens," Elisabeth explained. "Staunch Loyalists, as you can see and hear for yourself. Nor are they reticent tonight about showing their true colors."

Will ignored the bitterness in her tone. "Elisabeth. There is one more matter to discuss," he said, holding her arm more tightly. "In the event I am wounded or killed, and you learn of this, you are to address your letters to Mrs. Knox as if she were with the Army in the field or winter quarters. In that way, your news will still be of use."

She stopped abruptly and turned to face him, her hands on her hips. "This is not your own thought, Will Stoner. It is a calculated plan by someone who is more concerned with valuable information than my feelings for you. If you are dead I have nothing more to live for. I cannot tell you now what I will do." She spoke quickly, a tinge of anger and fear in her voice. "I will not spoil our precious time together by discussing what I am to do if you are dead." She took his hand in hers, aware of the disapproving look of two Quaker women, who hurried by, one uttering a loud "tsk, tsk."

"You must understand it is harder for me than for you. You know where I live and can see my surroundings in this city in your mind. I only am aware you are with your Regiment, not knowing whether you are in camp or in the field." She squeezed his fingers hard and held his hand tightly. "At the very moment when I am having tea or returning from market, or why even writing a letter to you, you may be in the thick of an artillery duel or major battle. I have seen the carnage cannons and musket balls wreak upon our soldiers. I have been to field hospitals where men scream in pain, blood flows along the floors and piles of amputated limbs are stacked up outside operating rooms like so much cordwood. I will be in constant fear for your well-being." She shook the clasp of her cape. "Please do not treat this lightly as if I am simply to address letters to another as I would change this light cape for a heavier woolen cloak when the weather requires." She tucked her arm in his as they continued walking. "Now, let us renew our promenade and set aside these grim thoughts."

They turned toward the river and walked in silence past shuttered auction houses. The smell from the few operating small breweries blended with the stronger animal smells from tanneries and acrid, sooty coal fires, still smoldering from the now abandoned smelters.

Will hurried her along past the doorway of a tavern, with a wooden insignia whose faded arcs of paint announced it was "The Sign of the Rainbow." From the raucous shouts within, it was clear some laborers were drinking heavily to ward off the reality of the impending British occupation.

When they reached the waterfront, Will wrapped his arms around her to protect her from the sharp wind blowing from the Jersey shore. The docks now were a hive of grim, hurried activity in contrast to the festive air of Independence Day when flags had festooned the ships of the Pennsylvania Navy. Torches illuminated those who had waited until the end to flee, loading crates, furniture and merchandise on to sloops and small river schooners, ready to cast off at a moment's notice.

Elisabeth and Will stood in the shadows, solemnly watching the desperate, disorganized scene unfolding on the docks.

"All of these people hurrying to escape before the British Army arrives and I have chosen to remain," she said softly. Will rested his chin on the top of her head. He bent down so that his mouth was next to her ear.

"None of them know of your courage, and none staying behind will either. It is our secret and unifying bond, giving us strength for whatever will come," he whispered.

She turned her head and rubbed her cheek on his hand, feeling the warmth of his skin. She almost believed if they could stand in the darkness close together viewing the scene on the waterfront, they would remain here forever with the moment never changing. What a silly conceit, she thought to herself. Their separation was imminent and of undetermined duration. She knew her anxiety for Will's safety would be with her every waking hour of every day. It was time to recognize that reality.

"I will miss you my love," she said taking his arm in hers and turning away from the river.

—∿—

John Stoner angrily brushed the flanks of his mare with the currycomb. The pleasure of being allowed to ride with two select squadrons of the 16th Light Dragoons and escort General Cornwallis into Philadelphia dissipated with each rough stroke. Colonel Harcourt and the other officers had grooms and servants for this work. The fact that some troopers were currying their own mounts did not lessen the affront to his sense of dignity. Worse in his mind, without a batman, he had been compelled to clean his own uniform, brushing the dirt from his red coat and the dark green facing, a uniform that set him apart from the other Dragoons. Nor did he wear a crested brass helmet with the death's head insignia on the black front plate and a red crest on the top. He had taken care to make sure his black knee high boots were highly polished as well as a sword he had purchased from a Hessian, booty captured by the guttural speaking peasant in some battle or other. The shorter one he owned seemed like a toy compared to the Dragoons' lethal looking sabers.

He was angry for a deeper reason. After the Battle of the Brandywine, he had seen the accolades accorded to those who had excelled in the field. He had observed the easy, almost careless friendship afforded to those who were heirs to landed estates and titles, Earls and Dukes of this or that, sons of powerful men in England. How naive of him to believe he would garner favor with them and enter their world of privilege, where one sat down at a table with Lord Cornwallis or Colonel Harcourt. If they treated John Stoner as a lower class Colonial, then he would make them take notice of him as a Loyalist. How he would do this he was not yet certain, but he was resolved to succeed.

With Colonel Harcourt in the lead, the two hundred Dragoons trotted along three across, each trooper with his saber drawn and held vertically at their right shoulders. John now felt he had made a poor choice with his sword resting on his shoulder. It was obviously too long. As he was in the middle line, he hoped no one would notice. Behind the Queen's Dragoons, came Lord Cornwallis himself, accompanied by his staff and several wealthy Loyalists from Philadelphia. They had caught John's attention as the Dragoons rode past them. He knew they were extremely important men to be accompanying Cornwallis himself on the triumphal entry into the city.

Regiments of British and Hessian Grenadiers followed the General's entourage, flags waving in the breeze, muskets at shoulder arms with bayonets flashing, marching in unison ahead of the horse drawn gun carriages, the highly polished brass cannons gleaming in the sunlight. [9] John's mood brightened as the horses hooves drummed on the cobblestone paved streets, and they were greeted by smiling people, mostly women, many of them well-dressed and good looking and small boys cheering and waving enthusiastically. He took note of the vacant elegant homes along their route and decided these places were likely ones to be expropriated for officers. He would see about finding appropriate quarters for himself and a servant as well. His days of being treated with disdain and indignity by others were over.

They formed up in front of the State House and remained mounted as Cornwallis, escorted by two bewigged and smiling Loyalists walked ahead of the General's staff and entered the colonnaded brick building.

"Do you know who those two men with our General are?" John asked one of the troopers next to him.

"I have no idea," he said unhelpfully and deliberately concentrated on staring resolutely straight ahead as if that was more important.

"I heard Colonel Harcourt mention their names," the trooper to his right said.

"Thank you," John replied, smiling.

"But I have forgotten them," he said provoking a loud guffaw from the one John had first asked. John turned red and bit his lower lip in anger. *I will find out soon and by God end this constant humiliation.*

For two days, John was quartered with the 16th Dragoons at Schuylkill Stables, a mile or so outside of Philadelphia. Lt. Chatsworth had assigned him and a few other troopers to arson patrol that first night, commenting that John had some experience with fires in New York. It was meant as a personal joke between the two of them but John took it as another slight, a reference to when he had not "acted like a gentleman," as Chatsworth had put it.

However, he played the part of an obedient soldier and pretended to go gladly. From the local Loyalists who joined the troopers on patrol from midnight to six a.m., John learned the city's streets and more importantly the locations of the homes of the prominent and wealthy Tories of Philadelphia. The next day, Lt. Chatsworth in casual conversation gave him the precious information- the names of Joseph Galloway and Andrew Allen, the two distinguished gentlemen who had accompanied Lord Cornwallis and escorted him into the State House.

On the third day John rode alone into Philadelphia and called at Mr. Galloway's home. A servant informed him that Mr. Galloway was attending a meeting at The City Tavern. John boldly decided to present himself.

He entered the meeting hall and noted he was the only one of those present in uniform. The others, dressed in fashionable, prosperous but civilian clothing were seated at a long table. Galloway looked up at John, his dark eyebrows accentuated by his powdered and curled wig, appraising him carefully. John had providentially decided to wear his sword that morning, signifying he was an officer and a gentleman. Galloway inquired as to his identity.

"I am Lieutenant John Stoner, formerly Aide-de-Camp to General Timothy Ruggles of the Massachusetts Loyal Associators and currently attached to Colonel Harcourt's Queen's 16th Light Dragoons," he replied in a measured steady and clear voice.

"Ah. General Ruggles. I made the pleasure of his acquaintance when I was in New York City," Galloway said smiling at John. "And Colonel Harcourt I know passingly well. You are welcome to attend this meeting and perhaps you can aid us in our work." He paused as servants entered carrying pitchers of ale and cider and trays of cold meats, cheese and bread, and waited until they had left and closed the doors behind them.

"Gentlemen. I have been appointed by General Howe to establish the civil administration of our city. To this end, His Excellency has made me Superintendent of Police and the Port," he announced to the group. John leaned back and loosened his sword belt and the bottom buttons of his waistcoat. He studied Galloway as he spoke and guessed he was a man in his mid- forties, with a mature and confident air, and obviously experienced in addressing influential people. Galloway stated he needed loyal, competent men in his administration to help fulfill the great trust General Howe had placed in him. John recognized the emphasis was to rally the men in the room to do their utmost with the underlying message that Galloway had the General's ear. A sound and efficient civil government would not only restore order Galloway continued, but lead the good citizens of his city to enthusiastic support of the Crown and end this unfortunate war which was destroying the prosperity of Philadelphia and his beloved Pennsylvania. [10]

One by one, Galloway called upon the men to offer their ideas as to how they could contribute to a competent well-run administration of Philadelphia. John found the responses of some egotistical and pompous while others were more practical. During a self-serving and particularly lengthy declaration by one merchant of how he would run the port, John suppressed a smile that provoked a conspiratorial smirk from Galloway.

"And you Lieutenant Stoner. Do you see any manner in which you may be of assistance to my administration?"

"Sir," John replied, surprised by his own audacity. "With all due respect to the loyal gentlemen in this room, I believe the description of my talents are best reserved for your ears only."

Galloway stared at him a long time with his hands folded in front of his thin, tight lips, the tip of his small nose resting on a knuckle. "As you wish, Lieutenant Stoner. Tarry a moment after the meeting."

When they were alone, John recounted his serving as liaison with the Dragoons on orders from General Ruggles, expanding on his role in ferreting out rebels on Long Island and exaggerating the encounter with the rebel spy, Van Hooten at the Rising Sun. He related his efforts in New York City and New Jersey to confiscate rebel property and to discover their sympathizers and supporters, again exaggerating his part in various skirmishes and battles.

"So, you see Sir. I too have held positions of trust to protect Loyalists, encourage others to see the advantages of supporting the Crown, and punish those who continue to stand against us. I hope that some of my experience may prove useful to you."

Galloway studied John. "Answer me this, Lieutenant. When we entered the city, how would you describe the reception by the people?"

"Some were genuinely enthusiastic, most in my opinion were merely pretending to warmly welcome us."

"Precisely," Galloway said slamming his hand down on the table. [11] "The city is filled with rebel sympathizers and spies who will do everything in their power to undermine both the civil and military governance of this city. We will need to ferret them out. And," he added, " keep a watchful eye on the Quakers as well. You Lieutenant," he said, pointing an elegant long finger at him, "with your experience and of course having been in battle with the Dragoons, will help me do just that."

John permitted himself a small smile and nod of acceptance, although he did not see how his relationship to the Dragoons fit into Galloway's plans.

"I cannot give you a title more than Aide to the Civil Governor, but in reality you will be my chief assistant with broad responsibilities for preventing subversion and uncovering rebel spies. I will more than match your pay and I can provide for handsome lodging together with other advantages, shall we say. Report to me at my house tomorrow. I will speak to General Cornwallis about your transfer to my office."

John left The City Tavern and it was all he could do to suppress a shout of joy. He could only imagine what some of the advantages of his position would be. Whatever they were, he was certain, one would be a man-servant and perhaps even a cook. It was as if all the bad luck, slights and indignities he had suffered were being erased by one stroke of good fortune.

As he approached the Schuylkill Barracks of the Dragoons, he put on a long face. When he met with Lieutenant Chatsworth, he would appear disappointed and unhappy about the assignment but there was nothing he could do about it. The Civil Governor, acting upon a directive from General Cornwallis himself, had insisted.

# Chapter 13- Difficult Tasks Fulfilled

Bant struggled to keep pace with McNeil, his short legs putting him at a disadvantage, even without the weight of their haversacks and blankets left at their camp, now eleven miles behind them. Each man in Hand's Regiment carried nothing more than their rifles, forty rounds and two day's cooked rations of "Injun," roasted potatoes and a small piece of beef. Many of the men had filled their canteens with whiskey or rum, saving their ration for the march and battle. Bant's held his usual- hard cider diluted with water.

The Orders of the Day, which had been read to all of the troops and to which Bant had paid scant attention, urged the men to be firm and brave in attacking the British at Germantown and victory would be theirs. After that, General Washington promised to lead the Army into Philadelphia. [1]

Bant did not give one whit for going to Philadelphia. In fact, he thought there would be no fighting for the city - the British would either burn it and retreat or simply leave it intact. Either way, there would be no opportunity for his sharpshooting skills.

The Officers, from Colonel Hand on down had stressed the need for silence on the march and no lights of any kind. They left camp, in the early evening, when there was still a remnant of the sun's rays toward the west under ominous grey clouds. No moon rose that night and the darkness was almost impenetrable. Some of the men had attached pieces of white paper to their tri-corns, which Bant even with his keen eyesight was barely able to perceive in the gloom. Marching along in silence, sensing the presence of McNeil on the road to his right, Bant thought it was much like the night march from Trenton to Princeton. Although he was not a talker, he would have preferred to exchange an occasional word with McNeil, instead of every soldier marching along in wordless self-imposed muteness, broken only by the coughs, sneezes and farts that escape all men, even those under orders to maintain silence.

Bant estimated they had been tramping on nameless roads for five hours when they stopped to rest. Although they were now presumably closer to the enemy than before, the officers gave permission for the men to talk in low voices. No fires were to be lit. Indeed there was no need. The night was mild and the men had left their cooking pots, pans and food behind. Bant leaned against the tree where McNeil and a few others from their Company had settled. He pulled off his moccasins and ran his fingers inside, feeling for the small stone that had irritated his right heel for the last mile or so. He found it wedged against the stitching and held it between his fingers feeling its one sharp edge, before throwing it on the ground behind him.

"My guess is not too much further to go," McNeil said. Bant, who had been eager for conversation during the march, merely grunted. But McNeil was undeterred by his reticence.

"This darkness makes our chance for surprise greater but slows our progress at the same time," he observed. "With a little moonlight we could get there faster. What say you, Bant?"

"No sense engaging him in conversation," an unseen soldier answered from the far side of the tree. "Might as well be talking to a post."

McNeil came to his friend's defense. "Bant talks when he wants to and that is good enough for me. As for engaging, it is engaging with the enemy that he is good at. For me, I would rather be alongside him in any battle than one who is amiable to a fair the weather but runs at the first sign of trouble."

"Are you saying I am a coward?" the unseen soldier snarled.

"No," McNeil replied. "Not speaking about anyone in particular.

Just saying that Bant is one of the most reliable of men in battle. That is all."

The soldier seemed mollified. The men sat silently listening to the noises of the night- the hooting of a nearby owl, twigs cracking as men returned from relieving themselves away from the road, farm dogs barking in the distance.

"No moon helps to hide us from British patrols," Bant said, as if McNeil had just asked his question. "Our scouts will know where their pickets are by their fires so we have no need of light." Thinking he had said too much, he kept quiet.

"I heard our Regiment is to hold back and the militia will advance and silence their pickets with cold steel," a voice said in the darkness. "Serves them right for what they did at Wayne's affair," another replied. [2] "No quarter for any of the British bloodhounds," added a different voice more vehemently. The men were silent as they thought of the slaughter of the Continentals in the surprise British night attack, and the prospect of advancing in silence and gutting the Redcoats in reprisal.

Bant ignored the sentiments being expressed as more of the soldiers joined in. He was motivated both by thoughts of revenge against the troopers as well as a desire to rid himself of his demons. Night marches suited him. No sleep meant no revisiting the horrors, no feelings of regret and guilt at having survived while twelve others were hanged. The certainty of an attack in the morning gave him the opportunity to kill more of the enemy. Afterwards, he would fall into an exhausted sleep during which his demons might be assuaged by his bloodletting and leave him undisturbed.

Dark shapes passed among them with orders to resume the march in silence. Bant plodded along, the respite having stiffened his legs rather than revitalized him. He kept close to McNeil, taking two steps to the tall man's one. His mind was empty of any thoughts, good or evil. Occasionally, his left hand touched his cartridge box to reassure him the ammunition was there, waiting for him when the battle commenced. He noticed with surprise that he was able to make out McNeil's face, the jutting chin and the over-riding brow. It was near dawn. Ahead, he heard the deep bangs of the Jaegers' short heavy caliber rifles answered by a concentrated volley of musket fire.

"Well, no one is sneaking up on those Jaegers and giving them cold steel," McNeil said as Lieutenant Patten shouted for the company to form ranks and dog trot forward. The air was clear but as the road sloped down toward a river, all Bant could see was a heavy fog blanketing both shores and a faint blue haze hanging over the area. One hundred yards below, the Pennsylvania militia was arrayed along a fence line midway down the slope, firing volley after volley at the Jaegers hidden alongside a wooden bridge across a narrow river. The militia's two light three-pounders were to his right on the heights, firing down on the Hessian positions.

"If the fog lifts, there will be enough smoke from all those volleys so we still will not be able to see a thing," McNeil said, appraising the field below.

Lieutenant Patten ordered his company to halt in the woods and wait. As the sun rose higher, part of the fog dissipated but still enshrouded the Hessian positions immediately abutting the river. The riflemen were slightly more than two hundred yards away from the enemy's lines. Bant could make out individual green-jacketed Jaegers running through the shrubbery before taking cover behind a stone mill and its surrounding outbuildings. The Americans advanced further to the edge of the woods. The tall cedars and evergreens provided a cool shaded refuge from the morning heat.

Bant heard the Lieutenant calling for volunteers and together with McNeil arose and walked up to their officer.

"Some of you men ascend these tall trees. From that height, lay down a sniping fire on the Jaegers foolish enough to show themselves. There is a battalion of Hessian Grenadiers moving up from their camp. Pick off their officers if you are able."

McNeil motioned for Bant to follow him and select two trees to climb. Bant stood rooted to the spot. He saw images of another tree a long time ago; saw himself lying flat along a branch, unarmed, watching British troopers hanging militia men below. Wide eyed, he looked up as a breeze rustled the limbs above him, beckoning him upward.

He shook his head, seeing men clawing at the tightening nooses, swinging from the branches.

"No, no" he shouted, putting his hand before his eyes. He fled from the tree line down the slope toward the militia, running blindly into the brightly lit field. He tripped, rolled over and lay there on his back, his eyes tightly closed his fingers wrapped around his rifle barrel. Gradually, the open space above him, the warmth of the earth and the clean smell of fresh grass still wet from the fog and dew, soothed him. The noise of musket fire did not disturb him. It was the sound of Jaeger rifles that aroused him. Cautiously, he stood up and saw he was mid-way down from the heights, between the riflemen above and the militia less than fifty yards ahead. Without thinking, he loped down to the fence line. He would kill Jaegers from there. And maybe a few Grenadier officers as well. [3]

—⁂—

Will was in the middle of a large column of regulars rushing down a broad dirt road leading to the town. Ahead, in the fields, several Regiments were racing through the knee-high grass, fanning out in a long line of battle. As he rode forward on Big Red, who was easily pulling a light six-pounder and a wagon with the gun crew, Will saw the tents, baggage wagons, sacks of provisions and even a few field guns, hastily abandoned by the British units. They had been over-run by the advancing American divisions now flanking the stone houses of the town. The troops on the road, sensing the collapse of the British line, let out a roar of triumph that to Will's ears was louder than the heavy volume of musket fire. He was eager to join the battle, afraid that it would be as at Princeton where, obstructed by other troops, he had arrived too late to partake in the assault on Nassau Hall.

The columns in front of him slowed and parted for a rider approaching from the front. Will recognized an aide to Colonel Sargent, who to his surprise reined up alongside Big Red.

"General Knox's orders. You are to join the assault on this fortress that is impeding our advance. Follow me."

Will followed the aide to a low stonewall that bordered the road. There were four six-pounders firing at a massive two and a half story solid grey stone house. The building sat like a castle on dominating high ground, with a clear field of fire for about thirty yards all around. Will hurriedly dismounted. Chandler, Tyler, Baldwin and the new man, Ezra Davenport who had replaced Grayson, killed at Brandywine three weeks ago, had already unhitched the gun carriage. Will helped them manhandle the six-pounder into position. They unloaded the side boxes with the canvas charges. Will decided the powder box would be safer closer to the stone wall than further behind the gun where it could be struck by the steady but errant musket fire coming from the second story windows of the building. A ring of smoke hung around each of the stone framed windows as the British troops inside laid down a hail of fire, both at the troops along the stone wall and those marching past and on toward Germantown. The soldiers on the road were barely within effective musket range. It was almost one hundred yards to the house. Nevertheless, the whiz of balls in the air, whether aimed or not, caused the troops to increase their pace as they passed.

"Who is in charge of this gun?" an officer asked to no one in particular.

"I am Sir. Sergeant Will Stoner of the Massachusetts Artillery."

"I am Colonel Proctor in command of this battery. You are to direct your fire at the doors and windows. Our balls seem to do no damage to the stone front." As he spoke, Will saw a cannon ball glance off the wall causing a shower of sparks and a small cloud of pulverized dust, barely leaving a mark to show where the ball had struck.

"Sergeant, wait for my order. The New Jersey boys are preparing to assault this building. We will lay down covering fire." He noticed the powder box near the wall but said nothing. "After the first round, fire when ready until our troops advance."

Will nodded, thinking grape shot might be better if they were aiming at the windows but the Colonel had already moved to another cannon in the battery. "We will use grape shot," he said to Davenport. They inserted a wooden wedge under the breach to elevate the cannon. Once it was loaded, Will reached into his pouch and removed a quill, pricked the canvas bag through the vent and waited. The Jersey Regiments formed into compact columns and hunched down behind the stonewall, both for cover and to conceal their imminent charge.

"Prime your guns," Colonel Proctor shouted. Will inserted the quill in the touchhole shouted primed and lit the slow match. "Give fire," the Colonel yelled again and Will dipped the match in the quill and stepped back. The five guns roared, almost simultaneously. Multiple puffs of dust peppered the tall second story window and a cheer went up as a six-pound ball shattered part of the front door.

"Have at them again." Will thought it was the Colonel who shouted the command but with the ringing in his ears, he was not certain. The crew worked efficiently together, with Baldwin closing the vent, Tyler quickly sponging the barrel, Chandler inserting the long worming pole and Davenport bringing up the canvas charge and then the grape shot. They fired several more rounds. The wind was behind them, blowing their cannon smoke up toward the grey fortress. Through the haze, Will saw some of the British had closed the thick wooden shutters of the windows before a round was fired and opened them to pour musket fire down on the Americans while the cannons were being reloaded. He determined to switch to a six-pound ball and put an end to that ploy when Proctor ordered them to hold their fire. With his cannon already loaded but not primed, Will placed the quill back in his pouch.

The two Jersey Regiments clambered over the wall, spread out in a battle line and charged up the driveway and grounds heading toward the shattered front door and first floor windows with their shutters hanging askew. The British opened up with a deadly rain of fire from the second story windows and there were flashes of musket fire from the cellar just at ground level as well. The volleys were incessant as the British soldiers who had fired stepped away to allow those with loaded muskets their turn. The effect was continuous sheets of lead balls. A few of the Jersey men reached the cellar windows and were bayoneted as they tried to climb in. Several died on the narrow steps leading to the front door. The lucky wounded were dragged or carried back out of range as the troops retreated. The others lay where they had fallen, motionless blue clad mounds amidst the deep green grass.

The troops behind the wall kept up a harassing fire but from that distance it was largely ineffective. Will moved away from his battery and found Proctor conferring with an Officer from a Jersey Regiment.

"Yes, Sergeant. What is it?" Proctor said, whether annoyed at Will's presence or at the failure of the assault, Will could not determine.

"Sir. I have fired all except my first round with grapeshot at the second story windows. The time such fire is needed is not before our troops attack but during the assault. I ask permission to fire while the men are advancing."

Proctor studied Will as if he were a strange species of beast he had encountered in the woods for the first time.

"And why do you suppose Sergeant, all our artillery manuals do not advise such a practice? Because of the risk of hitting our own men in the back."

"Yes, Sir. But in our current situation, the building is on higher ground, the second story windows higher still and it is from there the British pour down a deadly fire on our men."

Will noticed the New Jersey Colonel nodding in agreement. Proctor saw it as well.

"If a single soldier suffers grapeshot in the back, I will see you court-martialed and hung for that soldier's death."

"It will be easy to know, " the New Jersey Colonel added. "All of my men, killed or wounded, bear their bloody marks on their fronts, suffered while advancing."

"So be it, Sergeant. Support the attack before with cannon balls and grape during the assault," Proctor said, dismissing him.

Will returned to the gun crew and relayed their orders, leaving out the part about the threat of court martial. After several rounds, one of which blasted through the closed shutters of a second floor window, causing his men to cheer, they were ordered to hold fire. Will made certain the wedge elevating the cannon was firmly in place and called for Davenport to load with grapeshot. The Jersey Regiments rose again and charged the building. Will saw several British at the window with the now shattered shutters, fire and drop back to be replaced by several more leaning forward over the sill, the flashes of their muskets bright pinpoints of light through the smoke.

"Give fire, he shouted. He watched with satisfaction as the grape struck home and several soldiers fell backwards from the stone sill into the room.

"Quickly now men. They are back at the window." Will pricked the charge, poured powder down the touchhole and shouted primed, followed by the slow match and the command of "Give Fire." Again the lethal lead balls found their targets, one soldier falling forward over the sill before being dragged back by his comrades. As the gun crew readied the cannon again, Will noted that no more soldiers appeared at the targeted opening. Instead, a heavy concentrated fire continued from the windows to its left and right. The deadly hail of lead took its toll and the Jersey soldiers retreated, with far fewer in their ranks than had advanced.

Will lost count of how many times assaults were mounted and repulsed. The battle became a blur of cannonades and rounds of grape shot at windows, and then sporadic musket fire and regrouping for the next attack. Sometime in mid-morning, they were ordered to hold their cannon fire. Through the smoke and haze, Will observed a small force of blue clad men, led by an officer with a sword, coming from the direction of a barn about fifty yards behind the main house, with armfuls of hay and straw. They disappeared behind a low stone building to one side of the house and then rushed forward toward the now shuttered first floor windows on the front. The few who had made it that far huddled against the thick walls, trying to light the hay while the Americans kept up a heavy musket fire against the British in the second floor windows. Will thought he could see flickers of flame take hold, a few of the brave souls rose up and were shot as soon as they pulled the shutters open and climbed over the sill. A solid ring of smoke emerged from the cellar windows as the defenders fired a musket volley and the last of the brave men fell. The troops to the left and right of Will's cannon let out a roar of helpless rage and renewed their generally ineffective musket fire at the stone fortress.

Will knocked the wooden wedge from under the breech. "I want to skip a ball into that cellar window, second from the front door," he said to no one in particular.

"The ball will most likely strike some of our men lying there," Levi Taylor observed. Will could not hear him. "What did you say?" Levi repeated it in a loud voice. Will looked confused and turned toward Chandler for advice. The Corporal put his arm around Will's shoulder.

"They are most likely dead already," he said. His lips were pressed grimly together as he nodded in agreement with Will. The men grabbed the handspikes and moved the six-pounder until it was directly in a line with cellar window. When the general musket and cannon fire resumed and their cannon was loaded and primed, Will put the slow match to the quill, shouted "Give Fire," and jumped up on a side box to see better. Their ball hit the ground about twelve feet from the fallen blue clad soldiers, there was a spray of blood as it plowed through the human barricade made by the American's bodies and smashed directly through the stone framed window.

Hard of hearing as he was from the constant cannon fire, Will thought the noise of muskets and artillery had increased. A blue haze rose from behind the house as more of the American troops thickened the lines encircling the bastion. The firing was constant, another indicator to Will that as one line fired and stepped back to reload, another line let loose a volley of musket balls. After all of the hours of bombardment, it was clear the cannon balls were having no success in battering down the massive walls. He wished he could leave his post and probe the other sides of the house where the walls may not have been as thick or as well made, but he knew he needed permission from Colonel Proctor. He looked around for the Colonel and saw a substantial body of troops marching up the road from the town toward the rear. More troops followed, emerging out of the haze and fog in an orderly and quiet procession, some curiously looking at the troops lining the stonewall facing the massive house on the hill. Will saw the New Jersey Militia shoulder their arms and leave the wall to join the columns marching away from the battle that had been going on in the town and beyond.

An officer moved through the battery shouting for them to secure the cannons and proceed to the road. As his gun crew loaded the side boxes on the carriage, Will retrieved Big Red and the wagon from a shed in the field  now filled with marching men. The horse raised his head as he smelled the gunpowder and blood but trotted forward obediently. The crew wrestled the cannon into position as Baldwin and Tyler hitched the tongue to the back of the wagon. The New Jersey troops had withdrawn and Will found himself surrounded by a Maryland Division that marched by quietly, their muskets at shoulder arms. He turned to look back at the stone mansion and was surprised to see a swarm of Redcoats, about one hundred in number, emerge and form up on the road. They fired a volley at the rear of the retreating column.

A company of Marylanders turned and formed into a defensive line as the rear guard. Will dismounted and together with the crew, unlimbered the six-pounder and pushed it down the road toward the British troops. He felt a fierce spirit of vengeance and anger, mixed with the pleasure of being able to kill those who had hidden in their fortress for all these hours. He sensed the same emotion amongst the crew, Baldwin was shaking his leather encased thumb and fist at the Redcoats and Tyler's mouth was drawn back in a vicious anticipatory grin. Only Chandler looked remorseful as if he had to perform this distasteful duty one more time this bloody day. Without an order from Will, they loaded the light field cannon with grapeshot and waited. The six-pounder was to one side of the road, aimed at the center of the British line, with the Marylanders to the crew's left. At the command, the Marylanders let loose a volley. A few seconds later, Will shouted "Give Fire" and the deadly hail of lead balls tore into the ranks of the British soldiers kneeling to fire and those reloading in their rear. One more round and they hitched the cannon to the wagon and retreated unhindered back up the road they had so enthusiastically marched down at dawn. [4]

—⚏—

Will followed the Corporal sent to fetch him by General Knox to the Red Bull Tavern on the Old York Road. In the surrounding fields soldiers settled down in the chill October night. Here and there, bonfires consumed the rail fences laboriously erected by the few local farmers who were now unwilling hosts to the army that had uninvited, descended upon them. The wounded from the most recent encounter, initially housed in the tiny hamlet of Jenkintown, had been moved west by circuitous route toward Reading and Lancaster.

The Corporal escorted Will through the noisy tavern drinking room, filled with boisterous officers loudly recounting their roles in the previous fight or reviewing tactics and opining as to how the battle might have gone differently. He led Will up a dark stairwell in the rear and paused at a closed door on the second floor. A seam of light peeked out from where the door jamb and floor sill did not quite meet. The General's familiar booming voice answered the quiet knock.

"Ah, there you are Will." Knox was seated in a wide, spindle-backed chair that barely contained his corpulent frame. Two candles burned in wall sconces behind him and one on the small desk before him was low in its holder. His jacket was laid out on the bed and a pair of tall black boots, newly polished, stood beneath, as if waiting for the stout legs to fill them.

"Have you noticed the high spirits of our men after Germantown," he asked, motioning Will to a chair, without expecting him to answer. "We only lost the victory we possessed for much of that morning due to the confusion of the unusual fog. Now, we are less than a dozen miles from Philadelphia and I have yet tolerable prospects and hopes for the army to winter in that city." [5]

Will himself was confused as to why the army had retreated when all seemed to be going so well, although he had only seen the part consisting of the assault on the fortress like mansion. The thought of recapturing Philadelphia made him smile.

"There is a letter addressed to you from Elisabeth. My secretary is transcribing it and will return momentarily. It was delivered to me by an officer of our Light Cavalry on patrol who gathered up the posts from some taverns closer to the city. Why, it is only dated the 10th and here we are on the 14th, almost as expeditious as the official post between Boston and Salem. Would you not agree, Will?"

"Sir, I have no experience with the post over that route but accept your conclusion. However, the letters from Elisabeth to me are of a personal nature and . . ."

"You doubt the discretion of my secretary?" Knox asked, effecting surprise and hurt. "I assure you he is a most trustworthy fellow. Enter," he shouted in answer to forceful rap on the door.

"Why here he is now."

Will turned in the chair and saw William Knox with a sheaf of papers under his arm.

"Brother Billy," Knox said chortling at his little deception. "We were just speaking of you." [6]

"Will, it is good to find you well," he said before handing several pages to his brother.

"Here Will is the letter from your dear Elisabeth, unfortunately not in her own hand but rather my brother's. She has given us much information by pretending to prattle on and gossip." He handed three sheets to Will. "Let me read the matters revealed by the invisible ink and we can then discuss your response."

"There is no original?" Will asked.

"Only ashes and fragments once I applied heat," Billy replied.

"I would treasure even such a burnt fragment," Will blurted out in such a heartfelt manner that the General looked at him sympathetically.

"Observe Brother how strong an emotion true love is in the heart of a brave soldier. I cannot make amends for your loss other than to offer you a copy of the words she has written and intended for you. Even those fragments of the original must be committed to the flames. It is to her protection that must be our utmost concern."

Will nodded and read the transcription of Elisabeth's letter.

*10th October, 1777*

*My dearest Will, -- It has been five days since we heard the terrible incessant sounds of cannons and muskets six miles from our city. It seemed to continue for hours. I pray that you have not been injured at this place called Germantown and are well. Please write to reassure me so my anxious heart will return to normal and only be pained by our being apart.*

*My life in Philadelphia since the British have arrived is one of Contradictions, so much as to make my poor head swim in confusion. During the mornings, together with Mary L and other Quaker Ladies who suffer daily from the forced and Unjust Exile of their husbands by order of the Congress and Council, we attend to the wounded at the Pine*

*Street Church, the very place where I found Captain H. The pews have been removed and broken up for firewood to warm the horribly maimed men who lie within. They are all Hessians, almost Four Hundred of them. I am told they are casualties from the most recent two battles. Their dead, unfortunately of whom I have seen many, are buried in the Church's Graveyard, interred four to a plot poor souls, stacked one on top another, deprived of the Privacy and Dignity of their own grave and headstone.*

*Other wounded are in the Pennsylvania Hospital where I will visit tomorrow to be of some assistance, although the wards are said to be terribly overcrowded. I have been told and have no intention of visiting the neighborhood near the Barracks, that many more lie in filth and pain in tanneries and brickyards converted into Hospitals for the sick and wounded. Many soldiers are sick but from what I know not.*

*I have no apprehension of the Hessian Grenadiers quartered in the Barracks but instead fear the denizens of the neighborhood, common laborers who populate the grog shops and tippling houses, and the lower class women who associate with them.*

*My daily morning tasks take me past the Walnut Street Jail where now many Prominent Persons suspected of being against the Crown are incarcerated, including those transferred from the State House, now converted after the most recent battle to a Hospital for British Officers.*

*The Prisoners have been arrested on orders of Mr. Joseph G who has taken a decisive role in the administration of our city for which I am thankful. We enjoy peace and order from dawn to dusk with a curfew enforced by Loyal Private Citizens.*

*In contrast to my mornings, my afternoons are filled with gaiety and culture. I have attended on a daily basis, afternoon teas with Peggy S. and her sisters, at their home or others. Everyone is competing with one another to attract the most eligible, handsome young Officers on Generals C's and H's staff. I have noted that a certain Major A. has definitely been taken by Peggy S. even though she is the youngest of the Judge's daughters.*

*She denies it vehemently but blushes at his attentions. Our afternoons are wiled away with brief Concerts by the young ladies and recitations of Poetry by the Officers, some of whom are quite accomplished in their dramatic presentations, all performed in the most admirable manner from memory.*

*I was present at one dinner hosted by Mr. and Mrs. A at which Lord C's entire staff were there. Mrs. A. fortuitously seated me next to Captain JM, an engineer and accomplished artist as well. He told me of his maps and drawings of battlefields and wished to show them to me on an appropriate occasion. He expressed a desire to escort me to a play, to be performed next week at The City Tavern, but unfortunately later sent me a note advising that he must attend to surveying and supervising some fortifications along the Delaware. I will not lack for company however. An Artillery Major, with whom I chatted at one of the S's teas, will do in his stead.*

*The pleasure of my evenings is not in one bit impeded by the curfew. After Dinners and Concerts, I am escorted home by a brilliantly uniformed High Ranking Officer through the very streets we walked together. My escort imperiously waves off the patrols appointed by our own Mr. John S.*

*I am afraid that Mary L. strongly disapproves of my companions and attendance at these galas. I have done all in my power to assure her that my conduct is beyond reproach. We did have angry words one evening and I pointed out to her that one of her close Quaker acquaintances, a Mrs. Lydia D, houses many of General H's staff across from his own Headquarters, formerly owned by General Cadwalader. I apologized promptly on the morrow and she accepted it with grace.* [7]

*A Mr. James R, originally from Boston, and recently arrived with General H has begun publishing a vibrant newspaper, the Royal Pennsylvania Gazette. It has not only the latest news of events in New York but also advertises the finest cloths as well as middling and lower priced materials in the most wonderful of colors- whelks blue, pea and grass green, claret, cinnamon and white. I plan to make a purchase and ask a Tailor to fashion a Neck Stock for you. I know you will need one for the Winter.*

*Peggy S has the most wonderful Seamstress who is making her gowns in the latest fashion. She has promised to give me some clothing from her Wardrobe and even to have her Seamstress alter them on my Behalf. She and I have become close since you left and I greatly enjoy her Company.*

*I must close now my Dear Will as the hour is late. I pray you are well and that this letter, which I will post with a rider tomorrow will reach you soon. Please write to me frequently as no word from you causes my heart to ache.*

*Your dearest friend- Elisabeth.*

He was reading it for the second time when Knox interrupted.

"She is a clever girl, observant and quick to learn. There is much valuable information here," he said tapping Billy's transcription of the hidden invisible words that filled one page and part of another.

"She writes two hundred wagon loads of wounded were reported to have entered the city after this last battle, the Hessians quartered in the Barracks suffer greatly from bloody flux and many are too weak to muster; laborers from the city are employed by Captain JM, who we know is General Howe's chief engineer, John Montresor, to build a floating bridge across the Schuylkill; our naval blockade on the Delaware is causing food shortages amongst their troops necessitating large foraging parties that leave the city for the west toward Chester; she gives the names of those imprisoned by the local Loyalists and that their loved ones are unable to provide them with food for their own sustenance."

"She has promised to send me a neck stock but she herself gave me one in Morristown."

"She must mean to alert you that the neck stock she sends will contain a cipher. You must write her," Knox continued. "Inform her of the high spirits of the army and your hope to march into Philadelphia before winter sets in, wearing the neck stocking she is to send you against the bitter fall chill. Tell her about your daily life, exaggerate our strength and situation but give away nothing. If the letter is opened and read, as it very well may be by those disloyal along the road to Philadelphia, it will give our British friends pause and confuse them as to our intentions. I trust your discretion."

Will stood up to leave.

"I want you to write only one message in invisible ink, Will. Tell her any more information of Captain JM's plans and the fortifications the British are building will be most useful."

Billy ushered Will into his own private room and gave him two sheets of paper, a quill and ink. He sat on the only chair in the room, using the broad flat interior windowsill for his desk. He was at a loss as to where to begin. The thought occurred to him that the General would probably read his letter before it was sent. Or worse. Others, who did not have his best interests at heart, would intercept it. No matter. He would write what he felt and reaffirm his deep love for her. He comforted himself by visualizing her in Mary Lewis' home, sitting in the front parlor, reading and re-reading his letter, smiling at his turn of phrase and his expressions of devotion. He took up the quill, dipped it in the inkwell and began to write. He would add the secret message once Billy supplied him with the appropriate liquid.

# Chapter 14 - The Confrontation

John Stoner sat with his back toward the fire in the dining room of Joseph Galloway's Georgian home. Around him, the other invited guests, gentlemen of wealth and distinction chatted amiably as two liveried servants poured after dinner brandies.

It was a cold November day, almost two months after the Army had first entered the city. These were advantageous times John thought to himself, placing one hand on his stomach bulging against his waistcoat. He had gained weight, too many hearty breakfasts and dinners, frequently with the city's elite and occasionally with Chatsworth, recently promoted to Captain Lieutenant and the condescending Colonel Harcourt and his staff. He would have to have that tailor on Third Street the one who catered to high-ranking British Officers, alter his uniforms. The food shortages that had existed in the early days of the occupation were over. Hessian foraging parties had brought back herds of cattle and once the flour millers and farmers in the surrounding areas discovered they would be paid in sterling for their goods instead of the near worthless Continental currency, they flocked to the city on Fridays for Market Weekend. It never ceased to amaze John how easy it was to purchase people's allegiance with hard money. Of course, with increased commerce and the free passage of merchants between the contending armies, there was the danger of spies.

By his diligence in gathering information and preparing reports for Galloway, John was now the Superintendent's indispensable aide. He knew how to play the game. It was his mission to make Galloway's administration efficient, maintain law and order and ferret out any planned rebel disturbances, all to enhance his superior's reputation with General Howe. As Galloway's standing improved with the Commander-in-Chief, so did John's with Galloway.

It was Galloway who decided the authorities needed a census of the population, the occupants of every house, the owners of every business and the vendors at every market. It was he, John Stoner who refined it and gave the concept a sense of urgency. He proposed to begin in those areas of the city where General Howe, his staff and the other senior officers were housed. After all, he argued persuasively, where might the threat from Rebel sympathizers be the greatest than from those closest to the high command? Galloway agreed and authorized him to implement the census plan immediately.

John was tireless in his efforts, initially going out with the squads of armed men from house to house, showing them how to interrogate the occupants, compile the information and then poring over the names and locations to prepare summary reports for the Superintendent. He prowled the city day and night, familiarizing himself with every street and alley and learning every detail. Who really owned that tavern on the south side of Market between Third and Fourth, near that Rebel scoundrel Franklin's elegant home, now the residence of Major Andre. There were large numbers of Quakers remaining in the city. Although an unreliable population, he deemed them as dull as beetles but clever enough to disguise their Rebel sympathies by claiming their religion required them to be neutral. Many of them lived near the Quaker Meeting House and Assembly. However, there was a cluster near General Howe's residence at Sixth and Market, and even one or two across from the General's Headquarters at South Second Street. John thought those occupants were deserving of special attention.

He listened to the buzz of conversation around him, letting the pleasant warmth of the fire and brandy take hold. Paid by Galloway well above his Loyal Associators' Lieutenant's salary, residing in a pleasant two story brick house he shared with three light infantry officers, he smirked thinking of the other benefits to his position. In his obsession to learn the city streets himself while supervising his census squads, he had observed, on several occasions, many British officers entering the home of a Mrs. McKoy on Fifth and Chestnut. Upon further inquiry he discovered the attractive widow was the matron of a high-class brothel. He personally called upon her for purposes of verifying the census information and accepted her generous offer of his choice of any of the young ladies for an afternoon. It was a much more refined experience than being pleasured by the cheap harlots who frequented the Sign of the King of Prussia near the Barracks close to the wharves.

Galloway's voice calling from across the room drew him from his reverie.

He rose unsteadily, either from the three brandies or stiffness in his knees  and made his way to the Superintendent who was standing with Joseph Stansbury, the head of civilian patrols for the city.

"John," Galloway said grabbing his arm warmly. "We have been discussing the excellence of your reports in connection with the census." Stoner bowed his head slightly in acknowledgment of the compliment. "You are so clever analyzing information, I suggested that you peruse Mr. Stansbury's patrol captains' nightly reports. Conceivably, you may see patterns in behavior, suspicious persons frequenting neighborhoods where they do not belong, persistent violators of the curfew, material such as that." [1] He waved his hand in the air aimlessly, the cuff of his sleeve encased in ruffled white lace. John smiled, staring at a blotch of red claret staining Galloway's cravat, which the Superintendent was unaware of. Not his place to point it out, John thought.

"Yes, sir," John responded. "An excellent idea." He looked at Stansbury, a head taller than him. This man also had General Howe's ear and his influence could be of benefit. "It would be my privilege to review whatever reports you choose to send me," John said. "Perhaps the knowledge I have gained from our census to ensure the security of British military officers and staff will also be of some use." John heard his words and realized he had struck the wrong note- too obsequious and self-important at the same time.

Stansbury's grey eyes narrowed. "Of course. Your review may supplement our own efforts. I will have one of my assistants provide you with the most current ones." He gazed over John's head at another person in the room.

John acknowledged the comment with a slight bow, accepting that the meeting with the two men was over.

Once home, he removed his boots, undid his waistcoat and breeches and lay down for a nap. He awoke refreshed, called for the woman servant to brew him some coffee and sat down at the desk in the sitting room to review what he called the Quaker Census. The woman knocked on the door and carried in a silver tray. He motioned for her to place it on the side table and pour the cup. She placed it on his desk and stepped back.

"Will that be all, Sir?"

He reached down and noted the coffee was the color of light muddy water.

"What is this?" he said in disgust. "There is a pound of real coffee in the pantry. I brought it here no less than three days ago. Have you stolen it?"

"Oh no Sir. I thought we were saving it for when you gentlemen entertained." Her hands nervously wrung her white apron.

"No. We are not saving it," John answered angrily. He swept the cup and its diluted contents off the desk, breaking the saucer and spilling the contents on the rug. "Clean this up and brew me a proper pot of coffee as I asked. One more mistake like this and you will be out on the street."

"Yes, Sir. Sorry Sir." She bent down to pick up the shards and he had the thought to put his boot to her rear. The coffee had been a gift from a grateful merchant of fine foods and spices who had appreciated John's willingness not to probe too deeply into the captains and mates who, when in town, lived in a garret above the store. They were only transients and good coffee was so hard to find these days. Besides, it had endeared him to his other housemates and there was no telling when that could redound to his favor.

He opened a file entitled "North of Market," and perused the names of the Quakers listed. The homes were organized by street and house number, their occupants' names written unfortunately by people with varying skills of penmanship. John held the cup in his right hand, inhaled the aroma of the hot coffee before savoring its taste while his left index finger ran down the list. The name Elizabeth Van Hooten stared back at him. Could that be a relative of the spy Van Hooten he and the Dragoons had encountered on Long Island? Or a coincidence. How common is the name Van Hooten, he asked himself. If she is a Quaker she would not be related to the spy who certainly was not of that faith. Well, it certainly required further inquiry. It would have to wait a day or two. This weekend there were dances and dinners to attend. He would make the tailor work all night if necessary to alter at least one of his uniforms. He wanted to look his best.

—⁂—

Elisabeth acknowledged that her good looks and the interest of Captain Montresor, together with the Shippen sisters' friendship, had gained her an invitation to the exclusive dinner at Major Andre's house. Judge Shippen and his wife, together with Peggy and the oldest sister had arrived in one carriage, Sarah and Mary Shippen, together with Elisabeth and two friends in another. They had driven through a high brick arch in the center of the residence into the inner courtyard.

As Elisabeth alighted she was greeted by Captain Montresor, cleanly bewigged, the gold buttons on his uniform sparkling in the flames from the  torches in the iron scalloped sconces. He was not as tall as Will and old enough to be her father. However, she had to admit, he was a handsome man with a strong chin and piercing eyes. He carried himself well, as one experienced in the world with an air of earned self assurance. Peggy had told her in whispered confidence that Captain Montresor had the reputation of being a rake. [2] Elisabeth was not deterred. Indeed, she was pleased the Captain had fastened his eye on her and become her regular escort. He took a genuine interest in not only her appearance but in Elisabeth's seemingly insatiable desire to learn about plays, poetry and literature and her interest in his drawings. Sometimes, when with him, she acted her part of charming companion so naturally and absorbed the information he revealed so easily, later she would question whether she had performed her part because she enjoyed it or because it was her duty as a spy to play that role.

Without being able to say how, she knew the Captain was too much of a gentleman to force the matter and she would never be his mistress. She shivered guiltily imagining how it would be, and wrapped her cloak more tightly around her throat, affecting it was the chill night air.

Montresor gallantly linked his arm in hers and escorted her up the stone stairs, through the double doors and into the reception room. Major Andre was standing next to Peggy Shippen, petite and stunning in a deep blue beaded gown consisting of a plunging bodice and skirt joined together. Where her skirt opened in the front, her outer petticoat was baby blue with an intricate iridescent design of darker threads. Her pale skin, in comparison to the weathered faces and hands of the officers, made her seem like a porcelain Chinese sculpture.

Elisabeth herself had chosen a dark green gown and an embroidered petticoat from a wardrobe of clothes Peggy had insisted she could no longer wear as being too familiar to Major Andre. The bodice of Peggy's gown was raised for modesty so that it ended slightly below her collar bones and was less revealing when she curtsied or sat. Her arms were covered with long sleeves set off by lace-trimmed ruffles at the elbow. Elisabeth deemed her gown to be reasonable and appropriate but Mary Lewis had expressed her severe disapproval when Elisabeth had departed.

The dinner was sumptuous, course after course of fowl, fish and meat, grilled, steamed and boiled vegetables, some delicately carved and cleverly arrayed in bouquet-like designs on large serving platters, cheeses hard and soft, breads still warm from the oven, and wines and ales poured almost as soon as one took a small sip.

Elisabeth was moderate in her intake of both food and spirits. She listened with a practiced semi-bored look, as Montresor described to another officer across the table the status of the construction of the Tete de Pont and redoubts on the west side of the Schuylkill at the Middle Ferry, an earlier one having been carried away in a storm at the end of October. She waited until he had finished and stifled a laugh.

"What is it my dear that causes you to smile so?"

"The British and French are the greatest of enemies, not only on the Continent but here in our part of the world. Yet, you use their words to describe your own fortifications. It seems the French have won the war of language."

Montresor laughed heartily. "You could say the same about me-the Chief Engineer to General Howe has a French name. The Rebels use the same terms and seek an alliance with the French. The word trench comes from the French 'entrenchment.' Do you really desire a lecture on the origins of fortification terminology at this splendid dinner?"

"No, Captain. I am merely pointing out the irony of it. As for your name, I like the way it sounds and would tolerate no other." He raised his glass to her.

"Gentlemen. To all the lovely ladies who grace our table with their presence, to their beauty and their wit." To a chorus of agreement, Elisabeth lifted her wine glass and took a small sip, her blue eyes sparkling with delight, thanking the Captain for his toast.

After dinner, instead of the men adjourning for the usual brandy while the women went to a separate sitting room to chat and freshen up, the entire party by design, led by Major Andre and Peggy Shippen moved to the spacious ballroom. It was festooned with red and blue bunting that partially obscured the decorative white plaster motifs above the light yellow walls. The concave ceiling was segmented by carved wooden faux beams, making the room seem higher than it actually was. At one end, a chamber orchestra of professional musicians selected from the regimental bands sat on a rectangular raised stage. The dinner guests arranged themselves on the settees and couches along the walls. Major Andre announced there would be a brief concert until those who had been invited solely for the dance arrived. After the musicians had played one or two short pieces, Peggy Shippen, clearly tired of sitting and doing nothing, rose and took Major Andre's hand. The Major motioned to the orchestra and they began to play a minuet.

"One of the most popular in London," Captain Montresor whispered in Elisabeth's ear. After the first dance, he extended his hand to her and they joined other couples on the floor. They were third in line, the Captain aggressively asserting his position as Chief Engineer to General Howe regardless of his rank. Elisabeth blushed slightly, knowing many who had not chosen to dance were watching her.

"You see, my dear," Montresor said quietly as they waited for the music to begin. "Here we have another example of French triumphant not only in our language but in our pleasurable activities. As you know, the first eight bars are for the Deportment," he said giving the word a heavy French accent. "And then, we begin to dance," he paused for effect- "a Minuet." He smiled at her and she lost in the moment, straightened her back and reached down to hold her skirt between her thumb and four fingers, and stared upward into his face, cognizant that his eyes were taking in her entire body.

John Stoner arrived at Major Andre's ball together with Captain Lieutenant Chatsworth. The sounds of music and a dance in progress floated through the open doors as they followed Colonel Mawhood and a rather matronly looking lady up the stone stairs, her full figure made seemingly more bulky enveloped in a heavy cloak. John detested the Colonel. He was conceited with an absolutely idiotic sense of duty that had almost resulted in John being killed at the Battle of Princeton. Mawhood would have done better to bring his two dogs he thought, as the woman handed her cloak to a servant and turned to smile at Chatsworth who bowed slightly. She stared at John, determined she did not know him and favored him with a slight nod of her head. John forced himself to bow but did not smile. Nor, fearing a slight from the Colonel, did he wish to step forward and introduce himself.

He had hoped, as Superintendent Galloway's principal assistant, Major Andre would invite him to the dinner. After all he reasoned, it was he, John Stoner, who was essentially responsible for detecting Rebel plots and establishing security in the city. He had performed admirably. Galloway himself had recognized it and thus, it was proper in John's mind that he should be acknowledged by entry into the elite circles. Still, he had to admit, he was among a select group invited to the dance. There was some consolation in that but he remained in a sour mood as they entered the ballroom.

"That is the renowned and most beautiful Miss Peggy Shippen," Chatsworth said, motioning to the stunning young lady dancing with Major Andre. "I have been told Captain Hammond of the H.M.S. Roebuck, invited her to dine with he and his Officers and they all are in love with her. One can see why," Chatsworth said wistfully, accepting a glass of claret from a servant.

John was content to observe from the relative anonymity among the guests lined along the wall. He became part of the group of young officers waiting for their opportunity, hoping to have at least one dance with an attractive young lady. Most of the young women were truly stunning, several dressed in gowns revealing much of their bosoms accentuated by the stays beneath. The overall effect of so many striking females, swirling around the dance floor and the scents of their perfumes intermingling in the air, created an intoxicating sensuous atmosphere, enlivened by the pleasing sound of women's voices and laughter.

After a few more dances, during which John's eyes roved from one elegantly dressed beauty to another, the music ceased. Servants circulated with trays of cheeses and little sweets while others carried glasses of claret and tankards of ale. John roamed the room, glass in hand, listening for snippets of conversation and found himself drawn to a cluster of officers and young ladies standing near the musicians' stage. A Major of a Light Infantry Regiment was discussing a play in Covent Gardens his mother and sister had attended. John listened as the Major recalled, in his clipped accent, when he was in London dining with this Lord or that Duchess. He hated the condescending tone, the assumption of upper class entitlement and most of all, that these beautiful young ladies of Philadelphia appeared mesmerized by his every word.

"Pardon me, Major Howard. While I admit our English comedies are well written, they lack the sharper bite of French playwrights, whom I prefer."

"Ah, Captain Montresor. How delightful to see you again," Major Howard responded welcoming him and his companion. John fixed his gaze on the slender blonde with bright blue eyes whose hand rested lightly on Montresor's forearm. He was smitten by the white skin of her throat. Her curls flowed down her neck to her shoulders and contrasted with the dark green fabric of her gown. She was familiarly comfortable with the Captain, and seemed amused as he discoursed on a play by Moliere, as if they shared a joke between them.

"And who is this lovely young lady you have brought to grace our presence," Major Howard inquired.

"Major. Please, forgive my manners. May I present Miss Elisabeth Van Hooten." Elisabeth curtsied slightly and the Major bowed deeply in reply. John was dumbstruck. He tried to imagine Elisabeth as a spy. No, perhaps she was unrelated to the man they had encountered on Long Island. There was a series of introductions made by the Major and his young lady, then by the other couples, followed by the single officers in their group. John realized it was his turn.

"Lieutenant John Stoner, Aide to General Ruggles of the Massachusetts Loyal Associators and now Aide to Superintendent Joseph Galloway." He bowed slightly to Montresor and Elisabeth, pleased that he had compelled that miserable tailor to alter his uniform for tonight. While his appearance was smart, he knew his accent immediately betrayed him as a colonial with no pedigree. He straightened from his bow and thought he caught a glimmer of alarm in her eyes.

"Miss Van Hooten. Permit me to inquire whether you have family in the vicinity of Albany?" He watched her carefully for any reaction, emboldened by the wine and the sense that she regarded him with some apprehension.

"Yes, I do, Lieutenant." Her composure had returned but John was certain there was more to this. "My father is a merchant there."

"I met a Mr. Van Hooten from Albany in Long Island just before the campaign. He said he was a merchant, but in actuality he was a spy for the Rebels. Are you also a Rebel spy, Miss Van Hooten?"

"Lieutenant," Major Howard said harshly. "Remember where you are."

Captain Montresor took a step toward him but was restrained by Elisabeth.

"Surely, Lieutenant Stoner," she said gently. "You must be aware of divided loyalties among families in this cruel war." John was taken aback. His mouth opened in shock. She could not know about his brother. That was impossible. Yet the way she stared directly at him, her ice blue eyes now devoid of any sparkle, he felt somehow she knew about William.

She smiled at him demurely. "Why the uncle of my very good friend Miss Peggy Shippen is a surgeon for the Rebels," she continued. [3] "Perhaps you would like to ask our host, Major Andre, if tonight, he is dancing with a Rebel spy." This time her eyes danced with mirth.

"Enough of this sir," Captain Montresor said. "You have shown abysmally poor manners. Your accusation is not only baseless but an affront to Miss Van Hooten. On her behalf, I demand an immediate apology or you will have to answer to me." John was aware more officers and their ladies had surrounded them, curious to learn why Captain Montresor had raised his voice.

John mumbled words of apology for causing Miss Van Hooten any distress. He tried to explain himself by recounting the attack on the 16th Light Dragoons at the Rising Sun. Major Howard brusquely interrupted him.

"We have no need to hear from you further. Miss Elisabeth has accepted your apology and that is the end of it."

Humiliated, John walked from the ballroom, his face red with embarrassment, hearing every murmured comment as he passed.

"He accused Peggy Shippen of being a Rebel spy," he heard one say.

"That is what comes of inviting lower class people to these events," were the words that followed him down the stone steps.

He threw his half empty glass of claret vehemently down on the cobblestones. The shattering glass did nothing to assuage his anger. Fuming, he walked under the brick archway and out onto Market Street. That Dutch bitch will pay for this, he vowed. He will have his men watch her house, her every movement and he will find her out. Then, he thought smirking, I will decide whether or not to expose her or make her beg for my silence. She would pay dearly for that. Oh yes, he would have his way with her, whenever he wanted. The thought pleased him as he made his way to Mrs. McKoy's on Chestnut Street. He needed to relieve his rage tonight with one of her girls.

—⁓—

At three in the morning, Elisabeth lay in bed, awake and troubled, revisiting the events at Major Andre's dinner dance. Even though her window was closed and she was covered by a quilted comforter, she shivered at the recollection of her confrontation with John Stoner. She had acquitted herself well, she thought, making light of his accusation. Her repartee would give rise to gossip all over the city, likening her situation to that of Peggy Shippen's, who was much in favor with the officer corps. Still she recognized she had made a dangerous enemy.

John was so different than Will it was difficult to comprehend they were brothers of the same mother. A mean face like a ferret, avaricious looking and pock marked, on top of a torso going to fat. Shorter than Will, who carried himself modestly without airs, John exuded self-importance like a dressed up poppy-cock acting out the part of a real soldier. Well, it is said that the uniform does not make the man and that is certainly proven in his case, she thought with some satisfaction.

She shivered again, recalling his slight malicious smile when he had introduced himself. She knew with certainty he was unaware of her relationship with Will. She would be more careful in addressing her letters in case they fell into Loyalist Militia hands. There were many such patrols guarding the roads from the city. Perhaps she could ask Captain Montresor for a pass requesting that her letters not be interfered with. Would that invite his suspicion? She would have to contemplate that further.

She considered how to counter the threat from John Stoner. For a moment she thought of provoking him to insult her again. Montresor would challenge him to a duel to protect her honor and his. No, as much as she feared him, she would not have John Stoner's blood upon her conscience. There were other precautions she could take. In the morning she would give Mary an account of the evening. She would warn her friend to never reveal to anyone, her relationship with Will. She could trust Mary but should she go further and inform her of her real purpose of remaining in Philadelphia. She needed to think more before taking that step.

# The Confrontation 281

Almost at noon, she was awakened by the sound of angry voices. She dressed quickly and moved quietly to the top of the stairs. Flattening herself against the wall, she caught a glimpse of John Stoner, standing in the alcove, his hat disrespectfully still on his head. Mary stood before him, looking matronly in her small white cap and apron, short, rotund and immovable, with her hands on her hips.

"I ask you again, is Miss Elisabeth Van Hooten at home? I demand to see her."

"She went to a dinner and dance last night with Captain Montresor. I did not remain awake for her. For the sake of her chastity I presume she returned late and is still asleep."

John snickered. "Oh, it is her chastity you are now concerned with? I believe her to be a rebel spy. I can have you arrested for harboring such a person."

Mary stood her ground. "She is no more a spy than you are General Howe," she retorted. "My husband was arrested by order of the Rebel Congress in late September. He is still imprisoned somewhere in southern Virginia. Do you seriously believe I would support a cause that has given me so much grief? Now, leave my house. You have taken up too much of my time already."

She took two steps forward and John retreated to the open doorway. "I will be watching you and your Miss Van Hooten," he said pointing a finger at her. "The slightest misstep and you will be inside the Walnut Street Jailhouse. You may write your imprisoned husband from there."

"One more threat from you and I will report you myself," Mary snapped back.

"Oh? And to whom would that be?" John said, as he leered placing his face closer to hers. "Superintendent Galloway? You forget, you Quaker traitoress, I am his most trusted aide."

"Not Galloway," she replied, barely hiding her contempt for the Superintendent. "I will report you to General Von Knyphausen. I have treated many wounded Hessians and he is deeply appreciative. As are his officers. Perhaps some of his Grenadiers may accost you on the street one night and teach you some manners." She made a shooing motion with her hands and barred the door behind Stoner.

Elisabeth met Mary coming up the stairs and embraced her. "Let us have some tea together and you can tell me what has brought this about," Mary said. Elisabeth kissed the older woman on her cheek. "You are a dear, dear woman and friend," Elisabeth said, resolved and greatly relieved to be able to tell someone of her secret and cease pretending even for a little while.

# Chapter 15 - The Return of Friends

Will reread Elisabeth's letter, dated the 28th of November. He was puzzled and confused. Addressed simply to Sgt. W of the Massachusetts Artillery it contained no tone of love and affection. She had not even referred to him by name, beginning with a rather formal sounding "My Dear." She might as well have been writing to a maiden aunt, he thought. There were no hints of information, nothing written in invisible ink, a regretful comment about a dance being cancelled and some silliness about lights in the sky as an omen of a great battle to come. [1] The only part that made sense to him was the repetition of her intention to send him a neck stock and, she added this time, some buttons for the knee bands of his breeches.

Two days later, he was asked to report to General Knox' tent. Billy Knox showed him a package, wrapped in a week old edition of the Royal Pennsylvania Gazette. Inside were the promised neck stock and ten cloth buttons in a small embroidered pouch.

"My brother desires that you examine this immediately." Will laid out the contents on the General's camp desk. Billy produced a razor and Will carefully cut the neck stock along the seam and the cloth from each of the buttons. He laid out several long strips of paper, all in the pigpen cipher. With quill and paper he set to decoding the boxes and dots.

One strip revealed: *first battalion of loyalists raised in city
queens rangers under maj simcoe enlisting new companies
four hundred men to date* [2]

Another, when decrypted stated: *one hundred and eighty
waggoners hired beef and flour bought up by suttlers
farriers working night and day shoeing horses
carpenters repairing wagons*

Still another strip read: *abled bodied wounded taken from
hospitals for sentry duty in city
soldiers in redoubts reduced in number*

Billy became more and more excited as Will laboriously decoded the
messages and handed them to him.

The one hidden in the neck stocking read: *from mrs l friend
several long staff meetings at gen howes headquarters
more dispatch riders than usual
on the 27th light infantry left city in direction of germantown
much activity at hessian barracks* [3]

Will handed him the piece of paper and lowered his head to the thin
strips to better see the number of the dots, some of which were tiny
and barely visible. He smiled at the thought of instructing her to write
her cipher in bolder ink.

*your brother is asst to supt g
accused me of being rebel spy because of my father
has visited mrs l home
believe i am being followed and watched
he knows nothing of you and i
protected by maj a and capt m
be careful in your responses
best not to include your name
sign letters capt h*

Will reread the message he had translated and almost crumpled it in his hand in frustration. They were twenty-two miles from Philadelphia. He could be there in less than three hours. Billy read the last slip of paper.

"I must bring these to my brother," he said and rushed out of the tent. Left alone, Will overturned the canvas campstool in frustration and paced back and forth within the tent. He went outside into the cold and then remembered the cipher papers. He rushed back inside, burned the narrow strips of her coded messages in the candle flame and brushed the ashes to the ground, crushing them with his heel into the dirt. Then, he scooped the buttons up in his hand, wrapped them in the neck stocking and wandered the camp aimlessly, distraught and anxious for Elisabeth's safety.

On the second of December, the Army moved out of the gloomy, wet woods and occupied a series of high ridges, only sixteen miles from Philadelphia. The next day, British troops arrived and took up positions opposite them.

Will stood on the heights of the ridge for a second frigid night, staring across the valley at the fires of the British Army. The campfires of the Americans flickered to his right and left for a continuous line extending three miles. The day had been marked by only light skirmishing in the valley below and probing attacks by British Light Infantry on the Americans' right flank. I pray to God they come on tomorrow, Will thought, clenching his fists. Let them storm up the hill and be annihilated. Then we will drive them back through Germantown and from there to Philadelphia. He intended to ask General Knox to be reassigned to some forward unit. He could be among the first to enter the city. Once there, he would search for Elisabeth.

He fingered the new neck stock Elisabeth had sent him, feeling the rough replacement stitching he had made along the seam. It was hard for him to concentrate, so great was his fury at his brother and his fear for Elisabeth. May it please God to direct the British to leave their fires in this coming morning and assault the ridge, he prayed. He did not sleep that night and at dawn, Chandler found him staring across the valley. A light fog and smoke from the campfires obscured the British lines.

"They will not attack here," Chandler said, pointing to the battery of ten cannons at the center of the line. As if to prove his point, they heard the sound of musket fire on the far left of the American lines from the densely wooded area sloping down into the valley. "Light volleys those," Chandler said. "More probing I suspect."

By mid-morning, when no general attack had been launched, Will became increasingly irritable. He paced the battery from one cannon to another like a caged wild animal. The combination of musket and rifle fire had continued on the left flank but the volume remained the same, a clear indication that no massive assault was underway. When the firing petered out shortly after noon, Will was beside himself. A victorious shout erupted from the American lines as it became clear the British were abandoning their positions across the valley.

Will could not believe his eyes. The entire British Army was marching back toward Philadelphia on this clear bright December day, as if they were returning from field exercises. Perhaps it was a ruse he thought. To draw our army after them. Into the open. He waited for the orders to hitch up the cannons and give pursuit. There were no such commands. By nightfall, when the temperature plummeted, the soldiers emboldened by the British retreat from the field, tore down the barricade of sharpened tree trunks and branches in front of their own lines and used the logs as fuel for their cooking fires.

For Will, the next several days were an agony of dashed hopes, freezing rain and hunger. Each time the Army marched, he hoped they were moving into battle. Instead, they seemed to aimless roam the barren countryside, already despoiled of everything edible by the strong foraging parties the British and Hessians had sent out from Philadelphia. Every time, when he realized they were moving further away from Philadelphia, Will fell deeper in despair, imagining John knocking on Mary Lewis' door, pushing her out of the way and grabbing Elisabeth to drag her off to some prison. His brother's face dissolved into a caricature of evil, his eyes burning bright with lust and power, his mouth open in an triumphal laugh, with Elisabeth screaming for help all the while. Chandler, noticed Will's wild eyed, gaunt face and once asked him what was wrong. Will could not respond without revealing his secret, so he rudely told Isaiah to mind his own business. The rest of the gun crew, aware of his sour mood, left him alone. Will felt he would go insane from anxiety over Elisabeth and his overwhelming sense of helplessness. Only an accidental meeting with Billy saved him from his severe depression.

Will remembered being seated inside the General's tent, relatively dry on that cold, rainy day and listening to Knox's deep voice, gently tell him, the information Elisabeth had sent corroborated that received from others. The planned surprise attack at Whitemarsh had been thwarted, the Americans had held the field and it had been the British who had retreated. The morale of the Redcoats and more importantly the Loyalists in Philadelphia was low. The depredations of the British in wantonly destroying crops and orchards, setting fire to homes and barns and leaving nothing standing, had alienated those who were undecided and strengthened the resolve of those already committed to the cause.

"Your Elisabeth has helped to preserve the Army to fight another day."

"My Elisabeth," Will said miserably, "is in immediate danger of being found out by my brother John and thrown into prison. And I can do nothing to protect her." He broke down crying. "Worse things will be done to her, I know," he shouted, in anguish.

Knox waved away a sentry who had burst into the tent at Will's loud voice.

"Will, my boy," the General said. "Elisabeth is an extremely clever and resourceful young lady. You cast doubts upon her intellect and ability by worrying so. That your brother has revealed himself, and she knows this, is something she will turn to her advantage."

"That is a comforting thought, Sir, but does little to alleviate my immediate misery and sense of foreboding. My brother is more vindictive and mean spirited than my father whom you last met in Great Barrington."

"True, Will. I did meet your father and bested him in the bargain having gained a fine young soldier and one I now regard as my own son." Will looked up and managed a smile through red-rimmed eyes.

"Let me go to her, Sir," he pleaded. "I will disguise myself as a farmer, drive a wagon to Market Street this Friday and bring her to safety. It will be an easy matter to reach our pickets."

Knox leaned back in his camp chair and shook his head. "Your plan has little chance of success, Will. There are Loyalist Tory patrols on all the roads. If you are captured, it will further endanger Elisabeth." He looked at Will sympathetically. "I understand your feelings of fear and desperation. I too felt that way when my dearest Lucy and I fled Boston and again when the British fleet arrived off of New York. Yet, distraught as I was, I placed my duty above my love for her, which I readily admit has no limits and can never adequately be described in my letters. You must do the same, Will and persevere."

He knew the General was right. There was no other practical course other than to wait. "Sir. Is there nothing else to be done?" he asked.

Knox contemplated Will's miserable expression. "I am at liberty to tell you we have others in Philadelphia who can be of assistance to Elisabeth if necessary. I will instruct them to contact her and make their presence known. We can bring her to safety when necessity demands it. For now, with the high ranking protection of Major Andre and Captain Montresor, I truly believe she is above and beyond reach of your brother."

The next day the Army moved to its winter encampment, a valley with a creek and the ruins of a burned ironworks, destroyed by the British before they captured Philadelphia. The urgency of constructing shelter channeled Will's pent up anger and frustration from his mind to his shoulders and arms. The shrapnel wound in his hand, received during the retreat at Brandywine, had healed although there was residual stiffness in his thumb. He ignored it. From dawn well into the December winter darkness, Will led a squad of twelve men felling trees to construct log huts, each one built to the same specifications-fourteen feet wide by sixteen feet long, with slab shingled roofs. [4] He swung his axe in a steady rhythm, the long arcs biting huge, thick wedges from the trunk, occasionally seeing his brother's head in the bare white wood before landing the blade either in a slashing blow across John's skull or a straighter cut across the throat. His anger obliterated his hunger through the first few weeks, even though they were on half rations and sometimes for periods of four or five days, without bread and the another week, without beef or pork.

By mid-January, the Army camp at Valley Forge was laid out in neat rows of log huts, with the officers' cabins at the front of each row, kitchens at the rear of the line and behind them, the latrines. [5] Will still kept mostly to himself. On some clear, cold days he would take Big Red and ride out towards the forward pickets and beyond where he knew there were skirmishers in hopes of seeing a glimpse of the spires of Philadelphia, twenty-five miles away. In the absence of any further letters from Elisabeth, he imagined her seated in Mary Lewis' front parlor, writing to him in guarded terms and glancing nervously out the window at the approach of each red-coated patrol.

He returned one day in the late afternoon before dusk from his melancholy ride and led Big Red into a stable the Regiment had constructed for the artillery horses.

"Will Stoner. They told me I would find you here," a familiar voice said from the darkness within. Will immediately recognized the broad Bostonian accent.

"Nat. Nathaniel Holmes? Is that you?'

"It is indeed, trying to keep warm while waiting for you." Nat emerged from the shadows and grabbed Will by the shoulders.

"It has been a long time, almost an entire year since we last saw each other." Will looked down at his friend's smiling face, a little more careworn but still the same genuine, straightforward countenance he remembered. "Tell me, are you now a father?"

"My son will be a year old in three weeks. He has been christened John Henry Holmes," he said, the pride obvious in his voice. "Named for Colonel Glover and General Knox. I hope he will grow up with their attributes of character. More good news is that Anna is expecting our second. I left her in Salem almost three and a half weeks ago, in excellent health but dreading our being apart. And you," he said, grabbing Will's forearm in his two hands. "You look more gaunt and haggard. You must tell me of the battles you have been in since Trenton but first, do you still correspond with your dear Elisabeth?"

At the mention of her name, Will croaked, a sound between a sob and acknowledgment. He looked around at others in the stable tending to their horses. "I will tell you everything," he said determined to reveal Elisabeth's service as an American spy and the helpless anguish he felt. "We need privacy. Saddle your horse and ride with me a ways."

Nat looked reluctantly at his mare picking at some moldy hay in her stall. "My sea faring bones are still jarred by the long trip from Massachusetts." He covered his reddish brown hair with his tri-corn. "Yet," he sighed, "for the friendship I bear you, I will accept this additional pain." Will patted Big Red on his shaggy mane and led him outside where they waited in the cold.

They rode past the newly constructed redoubts and beyond the first line of pickets, huddled around a log fire that illuminated the frozen road. Will talked quietly of the joy he felt when Elisabeth professed her love for him, his fear when she agreed to remain behind in Philadelphia, his daily agony, knowing his brother was watching her every movement, intent on arresting her as a spy, and his overwhelming feeling of helplessness and inability to protect her.

Nat listened. Without responding directly, he recounted his three voyages as Captain of a privateer out of Salem. At the start of each cruise, leaving Anna behind on the dock waving until his fast twelve gun sloop was out of sight, of days spent searching for unescorted British merchant ships coming down from Halifax, of outrunning armed British schooners and hiding from the faster twenty-four gun frigates that prowled the Atlantic sea lanes. They had captured five ships in those three voyages and his share had made him a wealthy man.

"Yet every time I sailed away from the dock, seeing my Anna standing there, I was filled with a fear that if I were killed or hung as a pirate, she would be alone in the world, without me to protect her and our infant son." He reached across the space between their two horses and gripped Will's arm with his gloved hand. "I could not bear that thought any longer. I spoke with Colonel Glover. He has remained in Massachusetts, in command of a militia to be near his wife who is in poor health. [6] He recommended I do the same and offered me a position in his regiment."

Will stopped Big Red and peered at the flickering flames ahead, marking the position of the outer line of pickets. "Obviously you did not take his advice"

"No," Nat said. "I did not. I am still motivated by a sense of duty to our cause that requires me to fight. For me, privateering no longer warrants the risks taken. I have made enough to provide for Anna and my son for a while. At least if I am taken prisoner on land, I will not be hung on the spot as a pirate. I suppose that makes me a coward, but so be it."

"You are no coward," Will replied quickly. "I have seen my share of them at many battles. But what has this to do with me and Elisabeth?"

Nat ignored his friend's exasperated tone. "All of us who serve suffer from being separated from those we love. The only difference is you know the dangers facing Elisabeth and I do not know what perils confront my Anna. The human imagination, Will is a wondrous instrument. I am witness to it daily. I fear for the health of my infant son. Winter is upon us. Will he catch a cough and succumb before he has lived even one full year? The church graveyards in Salem are marked with small granite slabs for those babes who died in their infancy."

Will recalled the tiny grave of his infant brother, born and buried behind their farmhouse, not one month old. It had been a long time since he had thought of the farm in Scholarie.

"I will not list the dangers I envision. You know the familiar diseases of smallpox and measles. I know of many more and the perils of childbirth are not far from my mind. Anna is of a delicate and frail physique." He paused, shook his head to rid it of some dark vision and wiped his nose on the back of his glove.

They turned back toward the camp and rode in silence for a while.

"I tell you Will, you will never know real fear, horrible, helpless, terrifying fear, until you hear your beloved scream with the pain of childbirth and know there is nothing, absolutely nothing you can do to help, other than to drop to one's knees and pray, as hard as you have ever prayed, to the Almighty. Fortunately, Anna was attended by an experienced and skillful midwife."

Will recognized there was some truth to Nat's mournful confession. "You have hardly given me any consolation, other than the opportunity to unburden myself to a friend. Yet, truly I do feel somewhat relieved."

"Perhaps I can brighten your countenance more with the news that Privates Adam Cooper and Titus Fuller, who served with me on my sloop and also felt compelled to cease being privateers, have accompanied me to Valley Forge. I left them to seek out shelter while I went to find you."

"Adam and One-Eyed Titus here?" Will said. "That is indeed good news." He urged Big Red forward eager to see his old friends. "However, you have chosen a most inopportune time to join us. We shall all starve together. We know not from one day to the next whether or not we will eat or even if what is provided is fit to be eaten."

"Starving together with friends is better than hanging alone from a yardarm," Nat replied as he bounced high in the saddle. "Besides, we are Massachusetts men and used to harsh winters."

And Will thought, this winter will end and give way to the resumption of the war and a spring campaign. A campaign to drive the British from Philadelphia. If her father consented, he and Elisabeth could be married there. He resolved to keep that idea foremost in the days ahead, waiting for the time when the army would march out of Valley Forge and move on Philadelphia.

## Part One- Trenton and Princeton

### Chapter 1- The Taking of Trenton

1) After the initial surprise, the Hessians rallied. Two three-pounders were arrayed in front of Colonel Rall's headquarters on King Street. As the Hessians engaged the American artillery at the top of the street, a Virginia unit, under the command of Captain William Washington, (a relative of George Washington), and Lieutenant James Monroe (later President of the United States), attacked the two guns. The Virginians captured both guns, although Captain Washington and Lieutenant Monroe were wounded. They were among the few American casualties of the battle. (William M. Dwyer, "The Day Is Ours!" p. 256.) Captain Washington was wounded in both hands and Monroe took a musket ball in his shoulder, which severed an artery, causing him to bleed profusely. (Richard M. Ketchum, "The Winter Soldiers," p. 260.)

Colonel Knox also ordered Sergeant White of the Massachusetts Regiment and others, whose own cannon had been disabled by a broken axle, to join in the attack, shouting: "My brave lads, take your swords and go up there and take those two pieces they're holding. There is a party going; you must go and join them." (Dwyer, p. 256.)

White stated "I hallowed as loud as I could scream to the men to run for their lives right up to the pieces." (Ketchum, p. 260.)

I have given the fictional characters of Lieutenant Hadley, Will and the gun crew the honor of capturing the Hessian brass three-pounder and turning it on the fleeing enemy.

2) Among the American troops attacking Trenton on December 26th were Colonel Nicholas Hausegger's German Continentals, Regiments from Pennsylvania and Maryland, totaling about 375 men. They shouted, "in German and in English," for the Hessians to surrender and lay down their weapons. (David Hackett-Fischer, "Washington's Crossing," p. 251.)

3) The enduring myth of the Battle of Trenton is the Americans surprised the Hessians, sleeping off their drunken stupors of Christmas Day and took the town. This falsehood diminishes both the American Army's accomplishment and the Hessians' brave and stubborn defense. Historians agree the Hessians were not drunk but tired and worn down by the incessant patrolling, sentry duty, and harassment of their supply lines.

Accounts of the numbers of Hessians, killed, wounded and captured differ. Dwyer states the Americans captured 868 Hessians, killed or wounded 106, took six field pieces, fifteen regimental flags, one thousand muskets, and other equipment including a full set of band instruments and forty hogsheads of rum, some of which was drunk by the victorious Continentals on the spot. Among those captured were twenty-five musicians, who ironically became favorites in Philadelphia and provided music on July 4, 1777, the first anniversary of independence. (Dwyer, p. 270.) General Washington wrote to Congress only "two officers and two privates were wounded" on the American side. (Dwyer, p. 271.)

David Hackett-Fischer states the Hessians lost 918 men, 22 killed and 83 seriously wounded. The Americans captured 896 officers and men and enough supplies and "material to equip several American brigades," including "six double fortified Brass three pounders with carriages and ammunition wagons." Hackett-Fischer points out, correctly, the American casualties were higher than Washington reported. He speculates that although there were not many battlefield casualties, many of the exhausted and starving men died of exposure, malnutrition, hypothermia and other illnesses, either on the march to Trenton or on the way back, or even in barracks when they returned to Pennsylvania. (Hackett-Fischer, pp. 254-255.)

Regardless of the actual numbers, the Battle of Trenton was a significant and important victory and a disaster for the British. American morale soared. An English journalist, reporting from Virginia, wrote: "The minds of the people are much altered. A few days ago they had given up the cause for lost. Their late successes have turned the scale and now they are all liberty-mad again." (Dwyer, p. 279.) General Howe's report to Lord Germain, Secretary of State for America in the British Cabinet, stated, 'the unfortunate and untimely defeat at Trentown has thrown us farther back than was at first apprehended, from the great encouragement it has given to the rebels." (Dwyer, p. 278.)

## Chapter 2- Keeping the Enemy at Bay

1) Although the victory at Trenton buoyed the spirits of patriots, and many young men may have joined local militias, many other units term of service expired at the end of December. On December 30th, a cold snowy day, one day before the expiration of their service, Washington spoke to some Regiments of the Continental Army. Eyewitness accounts report that after the General's first appeal, in which he offered a $10 bonus for the men to remain in the army for an additional six weeks, not a man stepped forward. He tried again, stating:

"You have done all I asked you to do, and more than could be reasonably expected, but your country is at stake, your wives, your houses, and all that you hold dear. You have worn yourselves out with fatigues and hardships, but we know not how to spare you. If you will consent to stay only one month longer, you will render that service to the cause of liberty, and to your country, which you probably never can do under any other circumstance." He concluded this is "the crisis which [will] decide our destiny." (Ketchum, p. 278.)

Nearly all who were fit for duty stepped forward. Hackett Fischer noted that one of the veterans who agreed to stay on "remembered later that nearly half of the men who stepped forward would be killed in the fighting or dead of disease 'soon after.'" (Hackett Fischer, p. 273.)

Brigadier General Knox appealed to another body of troops. General Thomas Mifflin's appeal was described by a Rhode Island Sergeant as follows: "Monday the 30th in the afternoon our brigade was sent for into the field where we paraded before the General. . . and after making many fair promises to them, he begged them to tarry one month longer in the service and almost every man consented to stay longer who received 10 dollar bounty as soon as signed their names. Then the General with the soldiers gave three huzzas and was with clapping of hands for joy amongst the spectators and as soon as that was over the General ordered us to have a gill of rum per man. . ." (Dwyer, p. 289).

The bounty was paid in "hard money," raised by Robert Morris in Philadelphia, that is "Spanish silver dollars, French crowns and English shillings," and not Continental paper. (Dwyer, p. 294.) The Spanish milled dollar, the "peso duro" or hard dollar was also known as a piece of eight. Five Spanish dollars equaled one English pound sterling. (Ketchum, p. 280.)

The end result was a total of 1,200 poorly clothed, hungry, shivering "animated scarecrows," agreed to stay. The Fourteenth Continentals, the Marblehead Mariners, who had served so well since March 1775, elected to go home, probably infected with "privateers' fever," that is the opportunity to become wealthy by earning shares of the cargo seized from British vessels captured by American privateers.

2) Among the patriots, 1777 was called the "year of the hangman" because the number seven resembled a gallows. Soldiers and statesmen alike knew the Crown regarded them as guilty of treason. If the Revolution failed and they were arrested, many thought they would hang for their rebellion.

3) The weather favored the Americans. The army needed time, after crossing the Delaware and marching through Trenton to dig in on the south side of Assunpink Creek and form defensive lines. Washington had between 6,000 and 7,000 men, including untried militias and thirty artillery pieces. They crossed the Delaware at Trenton, marched through the town and began digging in on the sloping heights above the creek. Most of the troops arrived on December 28 and 29. Washington arrived on December 30, with General Sullivan's troops, their crossing having been delayed by ice floes in the Delaware. The artillery reached Trenton on December 31, 1776. (Dwyer, p. 292).

There had been an early thaw on New Year's Day with temperatures close to 50 degrees by the afternoon, followed at night by a heavy rain. On January 2nd, the abnormally warm temperatures continued. The melting snow, together with the rain had turned the main road from Princeton to Trenton into mud, knee deep in places. (Dwyer, p. 314.) This hampered the British Army's advance from Princeton, making their march a tough, slow slog and bogging down their field artillery and baggage train.

Washington's plan was to delay the British Army's progress for as long as possible so it would be dark when they reached Trenton and unable to launch a full scale attack. At eleven a.m. the British Army, 9,500 strong, reached the town of Maidenhead. They were about seven miles from Trenton.

One thousand or so American troops blocked their way. Led by Colonel Hand, the riflemen of the First Pennsylvania Continental Regiment, hidden by thick woods and aided by field artillery, ambushed the advancing British and Hessians, forcing them to form battle lines before the Americans retreated and set another ambush closer to Trenton. When the outnumbered Americans were a little more than half a mile from Trenton, Generals Washington, Greene and Knox, rode out to encourage Hand's outnumbered Americans, now down to six hundred or so, to delay the oncoming British for as long as possible.

It was past four o'clock when Hand's troops were finally forced to retreat into Trenton. The sun set about a half an hour later. They had successfully impeded the British Army's advance. (Dwyer, pp. 315-317; Ketchum, pp. 288-290; Hackett-Fischer, pp. 294-298.) When the British entered Trenton, there was little daylight left and the opportunity for a decisive daylight battle was gone.

4) It was not unusual for young men to become officers or hold rank above that of Private in the Continental Army. Captain-Lieutenant Winthrop Sargent of the Massachusetts Artillery was 23. Sergeant Joseph White, who was promoted on the orders of General Knox for his role in the first battle of Trenton was, at age 19, a gun commander at the Battle of Princeton. Lieutenant James Monroe, second in command of the Third Virginia Continentals, at the same battle, was 18. Alexander Hamilton, a battery commander at the first Battle of Trenton, was about 20. The fictional battlefield promotion of Private Will Stoner to Corporal, almost 17, is in keeping with the actual practice of the times.

5) General Washington, on his white horse waited, "at the far end" of the bridge across the Assunpink, for the men of Hand's Regiment and the troops sent to provide cover for them to enter the American lines. (Ketchum, p. 290.) At the time there was general cannon and musket fire from both sides. The bridge was barely wide enough to allow a horse and carriage to pass.

A private in a Rhode Island Regiment, retreating across the narrow bridge wrote: "The noble horse of Gen. Washington stood with his breast pressed close against [the] end of the west rail of the bridge, and the firm, composed and majestic countenance of the General inspired confidence and assurance in a moment so important and critical. In this passage across the bridge it was my fortune to be next to the west rail, and arriving at the end of the bridge rail, I was pressed against the shoulder of the general's horse and in contact with the general's boot. The horse stood as firm as the rider, and seemed to understand that he was not to quit his post or station." (Hackett-Fischer, pp. 300-301.)

6) As the sun began to set, but before it became completely dark, the Americans could see the British and Hessians troops, battalions of

them, clearly outnumbering the defenders, assembled on the upward slope toward the top of Trenton. Enemy regiments of grenadiers, jaegers, and light infantry moved through the town in plain view, marching to assault the bridge across the creek. Behind them, came columns of Redcoats. British artillery began bombarding the American lines.

The troops recognized the crisis. There was no safe way to retreat. An Ensign in the center of the line, across from the bridge noted, "no possible chance of crossing the River; ice as large as houses floating down, and no retreat to the mountains, the British between us and them." (Hackett-Fischer, p. 303.) If the American lines broke, it would be a rout.

An American officer, recalling the battle years later wrote, it was "an awful moment [when] Cornwallis displayed his column and extended his lines. . . . If ever there was a crisis in the affairs of the Revolution, this was the moment; thirty minutes would have sufficed to bring the two armies into contact, and thirty more would have decided the combat. . ." (Hackett-Fischer, p. 303.) A Rhode Island Private observed "commencing at the moment when the British troops first saw the bridge and creek before them, [until their attacks were repelled] depended the all-important, the all absorbing question whether we should be independent states or conquered rebels." (Dwyer, p. 319)

7) The Hessian Grenadiers began their charge at the bridge from about sixty yards away. The American artillery and troops opened fire and although the Hessians made it to the bridge, their column "moved slower and slower until the head of it was gradually pressed nearly over, when our fire became so destructive that they broke their ranks and fled." (Dwyer, p. 323.)

At that point, the American troops yelled. "It was then our army raised a shout, and such a shout I never since heard; by what signal or word of command, I know not. The line was more than a mile in length and from the nature of the ground the extremes were not in sight of each other, yet they shouted as one man." (Dwyer, p. 324.)

The Hessians and British assaulted the bridge two more times. Each time when they were driven back, the Americans spontaneously shouted in defiance, victory and perhaps with relief.

Sergeant White described the effect of grape shot on the advancing troops: "We loaded with canister shot and let them come nearer. We fired all together again, and such destruction it made, you cannot conceive. The bridge looked red as blood, with their killed and wounded in their red coats." (Dwyer, p. 324.)

8) General Knox noted that after the fighting stopped, the artillery fire ceased, "except for a few shells we now and then chucked into town to prevent [the enemy] enjoying their new quarters securely." (Dwyer, p. 325.)

### Chapter 3- A Cold Night March

1) While General Cornwallis waited in Trenton, confident his attack in the morning would overwhelm the American lines, Washington left the entrenchments around one a.m. on January 3rd and led most of his army around the British left flank and on to Princeton by a little known path through dense woods until they reached a road roughly paralleling the Trenton to Princeton Post Road. It was a distance of twelve miles. The troops were cautioned to march in silence, while a skeleton force remained behind, stoking the bonfires and attempting to make the usual camp noises of an army still in place. (Hackett-Fischer, pp. 318-321; Dwyer, pp. 328-331.) The freeze that night worked in the American's favor, hardening the roads making for faster marching and the passage of the gun carriages. (Dwyer, p. 331.) Washington's army of about 6,000 men approached Princeton by the Saw Mill Road in the early morning.

2) Colonel Charles Mawhood, in response to an order from General Cornwallis, delivered by courier the night before, left Princeton early in the morning with two regiments, some cavalry, artillery and a heavy baggage train with supplies for the army in Trenton. Around 8 a.m., slightly more than a mile southwest of Princeton, they spotted elements of the oncoming American troops. (Hackett-Fischer, pp. 329-331; Dwyer, pp. 337-338.) The opening shots of the battle took

place when Mawhood's regiments, numbering around three hundred troops attacked the advancing units of General Mercer's brigade, also about the same number, and drove them out of an apple orchard. The charging British troops broke the American line and caused panic among the militia reinforcements moving from the Saw Mill Road toward the fields. (Dwyer, pp.341-344.) Washington rode into the field to rally the troops and led them forward while the Virginia Continentals and Hand's riflemen fired on the British left. (Ketchum, pp. 306-309.)

3) The phenomenon of blood flowing down the icy surface of the fields, instead of sinking into the soil was recorded by eyewitnesses. "The ground was frozen," Sergeant R noted, "and all the blood which was shed remained on the surface, which added to the horror of this scene of carnage." (Dwyer, p. 352; Hackett-Fischer, p. 332.)

4) In launching their attack and driving the Americans back toward the Saw Mill Road, the British troops gave no quarter.

Lieutenant Bartholomew Yeates, an eighteen-year-old member of the First Virginia Regiment, 'received a wound in his side which brought him to the ground. Upon seeing the enemy advance towards him, he begged for quarter. A British soldier stopped, and after deliberately loading his musket by his side, shot him through the breast. Finding that he was still alive, he stabbed him in thirteen places with his bayonet, the poor youth all the while crying for mercy. Upon the enemy being forced to retreat, either the same or another soldier, finding he was not dead, struck him with the butt of a musket on the side of the head.' Yeates would impart these details to Dr. Benjamin Rush before dying a week later. (Dwyer, p. 344.)

5) Captain Alexander Hamilton was in charge of the two cannons which supported the assault by General Sullivan's forces on Nassau Hall of Princeton College. One cannon ball indeed rebounded off an outside wall and almost struck a mounted American officer. Legend has it, the other ball beheaded a portrait of King George II, which hung in the prayer hall. (Hackett-Fischer, p. 339; Dwyer, p.354.)

6) The British lost approximately 450 soldiers, killed, wounded, captured or missing. The Americans claimed to have taken 200 to 300 prisoners. (Hackett-Fischer, p. 340.) Estimates of American losses were sketchy, with Washington claiming six or seven officers and twenty-five to thirty privates killed. (Dwyer, p. 353.)

Although Washington may have originally intended to continue on the offensive and attack Brunswick, "the biggest British base in New Jersey, 'with all their stores and magazines,' and 'a military chest' of seventy thousand pounds sterling," the Army was too exhausted to continue and the British army in Trenton was rapidly coming up the Post Road. At the time, Brunswick was defended by only one regiment.

Nor was there any pursuit of the British baggage train fleeing Princeton. The capture of several wagons by Captain Hadley, Corporal Will Stoner and two others is fictitious. Instead, the victorious Americans plundered Princeton, claiming that the town was full of Tories. (Dwyer, p. 356.)

Cornwallis had the British army on the move from Trenton to Princeton by 8 in the morning and "the advanced guard entered Prince Town as the rear of the enemy [the Americans] left it" (Dwyer, p. 360.) Once the bulk of the Redcoats arrived, the troops were issued three days rations and began the quick march to Brunswick. The Americans proceeded, exhausted but unmolested from Princeton northwest through Somerset Court House and Pluckemin, finally arriving at Morristown on January 6th, where they set up winter quarters.

## Chapter 4- The Education of King George

1) Surprisingly, it was the old women of Philadelphia who displayed the greatest hostility toward the Hessian prisoners. One Hessian wrote: "We arrived at the front entrance to the city [Philadelphia] at noon and as we marched through the city, many people, big and little, young and old, stood there watching sharply, seeing what kind of people we were. Some of them came up very close to us. The old women screamed fearfully and started to threaten us. They cried out that we ought to be hanged for coming to America to rob them of their freedom. Others, however, brought us liquor and bread but they

were not allowed by the old women to give them to us. At one time the people pressed on us with such force as to nearly break the guard over us. The old women were the worst. If the American guards had not protected us, the women would have killed us." (Dwyer, p. 298.)

Such vehement hatred could be attributed to the well-publicized accounts of numerous rapes committed by the Hessians troops. Whig propaganda, in the form of broadsheets and gazettes, exaggerated Hessian atrocities to whip up support for the cause. George Washington was aware of the propaganda value of parading the Hessians through the streets of Philadelphia to emphasize the magnitude of the victory at Trenton and to show that the Hessians could be and were defeated. (Lecture by Daniel Krebs, June 14, 2014, at the Society of the Cincinnati, Washington, D.C.; Daniel Krebs, "A Generous and Merciful Enemy-Life for German Prisoners of War during the American Revolution, pp. 78-79.)

2) On December 29, 1776, General Washington wrote to the Pennsylvania Council of Safety that Hessian "officers and men should be separated. I wish the former may be well treated, and that the latter may have such principles instilled in them during their Confinement, that when they return, they may open the Eyes of their Countrymen." (Hackett-Fischer, p. 276.) The author goes on to point out that Washington "often reminded his men that they were an army of liberty and freedom, and that the rights of humanity for which they were fighting should extend even to their enemies."

One Hessian attributed their better treatment to a proclamation from General Washington, posted throughout Philadelphia that stated: "the Hessians were without blame and had been forced into this war. The Hessians had not come of their own free will. They should not be regarded as enemies but as friends of the American people and should be treated as such. Because General Washington had full authority and he gave his honest word, it became better for us. All day long Americans. . .came to the barracks and brought food to us and treated us with kindness and humanity." (Dwyer, p. 298.)

Many of the Hessian prisoners worked on farms in Lancaster County, Pennsylvania for the duration of the war. Hackett-Fischer reports that of "the 13,988 Hessian soldiers who survived the war, 3,194 (23 percent) chose to remain in America." (Hackett-Fischer, p. 379.)

3) Many of the troops had learned trades either before entering the Army (most young men started learning a craft around age fourteen) or when they were furloughed during garrison duty while still in their home provinces. The most common skills were tailoring and shoemaking. Others were linen weavers, millers, smiths, joiners, cloth makers and carpenters. (Krebs, pp. 63, 68-70.)

4) A Housekeeping Book, by Nelly Custis Lewis described Martha Washington's remedy for worms as follows:

"1 oz seeds of wormseeds
half an oz rhubarb
1 tablespoon small cloves of garlic

Put the ingredients into a pint bottle. Fill it with best wine or whiskey, let it stand a few days, shaking it well, then strain it." (Cokie Roberts, Ladies of Liberty, p. 395.) Wormseed is an herb and its flowers were used to make medicine. It is believed to contain a chemical that kills intestinal parasites.

5) The description of the Kierney family farm is based on Eric Sloane's "Diary of an Early American Boy, Noah Blake, 1805." On page 8, there is a marvelous illustration of their cabin's dirt floor, swept and decorated with a floral design by Noah's mother. This book describes in beautiful detail the evolution of the Blake farm from 1790 to the early 1800s, the self-sufficiency of the family in making much of what they needed and used, as well as neighbors helping each other with planting and harvesting, barn raisings and bridge building.

## Part Two – Winter Quarters

### Chapter 5- The Happiest Man in Camp

1) Martha Washington actually arrived at the Morristown winter camp of the army sometime in March 1777. She significantly improved her husband's morale. "Everyone watched the commander in chief visibly brighten in her presence. . ." (Ron Chernow, "Washington, A Life,"p. 295.)

2) In February 1777, Lucy Knox was in Boston while the Army was at winter quarters in Morristown. (While there, she introduced General Benedict Arnold to a young lady whom he assiduously but unsuccessfully courted). (Nancy Rubin Stuart,"Defiant Brides-The Untold Story of Two Revolutionary Era Women and the Radical Men They Married," p. 30.) Henry Knox refused to let his wife visit winter quarters, writing: "Your safety and happiness is the sole object of my heart. . . I however anxious to have you with me cannot consent to a step which will most inevitably . . . reiterate . . . the disagreeable situation" [referring to when Lucy had been in New York City when the British invaded.]) Stuart, p. 32 Lucy's visit to Morristown in 1777 is fictitious.

3) Knox, upon orders of General Washington, left Morristown in January 1777 for Springfield to "see to the casting of cannon and the establishment of laboratories, [for the manufacture of gun powder]. (Francis S. Drake, "Life and Correspondence of Henry Knox," p.41; Noah Brooks, "Henry Knox, A Soldier of the Revolution," p. 87.)

4) The song, "Battle of Trenton," consists of six verses, six lines each, and tells the story of the freezing night march, storming the Hessian pickets, winning the battle and capturing an exaggerated number of Hessians and their equipment. The song appears in Poetry and Prose of the Revolution, edited by Frederick C. Prescott and John H. Nelson. The section of Revolutionary Songs and Ballads begins with the following introduction: "Perhaps nowhere, . . . is 'the complexion

of the times' better shown than in the popular verse of the Revolution. In songs, ballads, satires, epigrams and patriotic hymns, the colonists proclaimed their opposition to tyranny and royal aggression; while in the manner, but frequently with more dignity, the loyalists upheld their side. . . . Most of          them were printed (in colonial newspapers or broadsides) almost as soon as they were composed; but frequently the author's name was withheld, and is unknown to the present day. (Prescott and Nelson, p. 83.)

### Chapter 6- Hunting the Foragers

1) General William Maxwell, known as "Scotch Willie," because of his strong Ulster accent, having been born in County Tyrone, was one of Washington's more aggressive Generals in the "Forage War" or "petit guerre" from January to March 1777. (Hackett Fischer, pp. 348-349)

Maxwell, with regular units of the Continental Army, including Colonel Hand's riflemen, joined with New Jersey militias to engage in a series of harassing raids, ambushes, sniping and attacks on the British when they sent foraging parties out from their New Jersey bases. The British and Hessian troops at these bases, stretching from Brunswick and the Amboys in the south to Elizabethtown across from Staten Island, were adequately supplied with food and provisions. The problem was lack of firewood and hay and forage for their animals, necessary to pull their artillery and supply wagons and baggage trains.

2) The actual battle of Spanktown, or Rahway, began on the morning of February 23, 1777. Two thousand British troops, consisting of a battalion of grenadiers, one of light infantry and a company of Scottish Highlanders were scouring the countryside hoping to surprise Jersey militia who were attacking British foraging parties, or engaged in foraging of their own. Using a foraging party as bait, General Maxwell enticed the British troops to attack a small force of New Jersey militia on a hilltop, while keeping the main American force, including Colonel Hand's riflemen out of sight. The Americans flanked the Highlanders as they began their assault, and routed the

entire British force, pursuing them as they fled a distance of more than twenty-five miles to Amboy which they reached at eight p.m. at night. Total British casualties were between seventy-five to one hundred men, with the Americans suffering five killed and nine wounded. (Hackett-Fischer, p. 356-357; Thomas J. McGuire, "The Philadelphia Campaign, Brandywine and the Fall of Philadelphia," p. 18.)

I have placed Colonel Hand's riflemen in the principal flanking position and given them the task of pursuing the British the entire day from the battlefield to Amboy. This is speculation on my part.

3) In 1777, some British officers were equipped with light muskets that were shorter than those carried by the regular troops and thus, more easily raised and fired when ambushed. These light muskets were called fusils because of their French origin and nicknamed "fuzees" by the British. (McGuire, p.18.)

4) Another battle was fought on March 8, 1777 again involving General Maxwell and about two thousand British troops. (Hackett-Fischer, p. 357.) Maxwell directed his troops to attack a smaller segment of the Redcoats attempting to reinforce part of the British line and the British fled in disarray. Hackett-Fischer states the British lost about sixty men and the Americans about twenty. (Hackett-Fischer, p. 357.)

I have no documentation establishing whether Colonel Hand's regiment of riflemen or the British 16th Light Dragoons were present on the field but have chosen to include the Dragoons for purposes of the plot.

The Forage War sapped the strength of the British forces, wearing down the troops and reducing the number of effective soldiers able to take the field. Hackett-Fischer estimates that "more than nine hundred men were killed, wounded, captured or missing. . . [and] the true numbers were higher. Altogether, from the Christmas campaign to the beginning of spring [this includes the first and second battles of Trenton and the battle of Princeton] Howe's army suffered at least 2,887 killed, captured and seriously wounded, after losing [only] 1,510 men in the New York campaign." (Hackett-Fischer, p. 359.)

When General Howe took to the field in the summer of 1777, with a plan to force the Americans into a full scale battle in defense of the Continental capital of Philadelphia, Hackett-Fischer speculated "that campaign. . . might have had a different outcome if the British and Hessian regiments had not lost so many of their best troops before it began." (Hackett-Fischer, p. 360.)

Chapter 7 – Resurrection in the Spring

1) After the Army had been in its Morristown camp for about two weeks, General Washington ordered Knox to explore and establish arsenals in New England. In mid to late January, Knox traveled to Hartford, Connecticut and Springfield, Massachusetts, further up the Connecticut River and assessed the locations for casting of cannons, making gunpowder and storing arms and munitions. (Puls, p. 84; Brooks, pp. 86-87.)

2) John Locke, (1632-1704), the English political philosopher, wrote "Two Treatises on Government," in 1689. They were highly influential on the political thought of those colonials who first argued their rights as Englishmen and evolved their theories to demand full independence. Locke was the intellectual mentor of the Whigs in the colonies. His Second Treatise was reprinted in Boston in 1773.

Benjamin Edes was a prominent Boston printer. I have attributed the printing of Locke to his shop, although I have no documentary evidence to support it.

3) John Hancock, then President of the Congress, was insistent that the magazines and laboratories be located in Brookfield and Hartford, Connecticut as well as Carlisle, Pennsylvania. Knox believed Springfield was a superior location, both because it was further up the Connecticut River than Hartford and was thus less vulnerable to British naval attack, and it was better suited to supplying American troops in upstate New York. Metals used for casting cannons, copper, tin and brass, were also more accessible near Springfield. Washington threw his prestige behind Knox and asked Congress to approve his

artillery General's change in congressional plans. Ultimately, they did, but John Adams recorded Hancock's "great resentment against the book binder [Knox]. (Puls, pp. 84-85,) Before the war, Henry Knox was a bookseller not a bookbinder.

4) After he arrived in Boston, Knox wrote Washington on February 1, 1777, that he was gathering materials "necessary to carry on the various branches connected with the laboratory and ordnance establishment" in Springfield. He commented on the rapid rate of enlistments and the "very extraordinary bounty offered by the State ($86) for recruits for the service." (Drake, p. 41.)

5) By letter dated March 14th, Washington wrote Knox, still in Boston: "I have for some time past most earnestly expected you, to arrange matters in the artillery department. . . As you see how necessary your presence is here, I hope you will make as much haste as possible to join." (Puls, p. 87.)

6) The descriptions of the construction of the bridge and mill, the carpentry and ax work are depicted in wonderful drawings in The Diary of an Early American Boy. (Sloane, pp. 26-27; 36-38.)

7) "Rog Sunday" is short for Rogation Sunday, the day farmers and their families prayed for a bountiful harvest. In the evening, the families "walked the boundaries of their property; it was both inventory and time for giving thanks for their land." (Sloane, p. 33.)

## Part Three- The Campaign Renewed.

### Chapter 8 - Return to the Jersey Shore.

1) The New Jersey Constitution, adopted in 1776, entitled all heads of households, owning property over a certain value, to vote in New Jersey elections. This was interpreted to include unmarried widows, who by the death of their husbands and inheritance, became heads of households. (Blog-"Boston 1775," September 27, 2014.)

2) In the 1790s, an estimated 10,000 women were heads of households in New Jersey and entitled to vote. In 1807, New Jersey passed a new election law, restricting the right to vote to "all taxpaying white male citizens." (Blog-"Boston 1775," August 27, 28, 2010.)

3) The Congress Minuet, like other minuets "was a dance of ceremony and ritual." It was danced "in order of descending order of social rank" and was one that "any two dancers could safely perform without previous practice together." (Charles Cyril Hendrickson and Kate Van Winkle Keller, "Social Dances from the American Revolution – Music and Instructions for country dances from the personal notebook of an officer in General Washington's Army," p. 9.) For example, at a dance and party hosted by General and Mrs. Knox at Pluckemin, the artillery encampment in 1778-1779, General Washington danced the opening minuet with Mrs. Knox as the hostess.

4) Washington was anxious to learn General Howe's intention as the troops embarked on ships at Amboy. One American spy reported horses were being loaded on board and "Their Stalls are all Cover'd and the Sides lined with Sheepskins with the Wool on to prevent the Horses Chafing- they would not make Use of Such precautions if they Intended up the North (Hudson) or East River." ((Thomas J. McGuire, "The Philadelphia Campaign, Volume I- Brandywine and the Fall of Philadelphia," p 70.) In other words, Howe did not intend to sail up the Hudson and attack Continental Forces in the upper Hudson Valley but his destination was Philadelphia.

5) General Howe finally moved his 17,000 strong force out of New Brunswick on June 13, 1777, against an estimated Continental army of 7,000-8,000 soldiers, encamped in the relative security of the Wachung Mountains at Middle Brook. The British officers had every expectation that after six months of inaction, they were marching to capture Philadelphia. However, to the confusion of both British and American officers, the British Army stopped, made camp and dug trenches and three earthen redoubts, as if expecting a frontal assault.

General Knox wrote, "It was unaccountable that people who the day before gave out in very gascondading terms that they would be in Philadelphia in six days should stop short when they had gone only nine miles. . . . In the course of a day or two [we] discovered that they had come out with the intention of drawing us into the plain." (McGuire, pp. 36, 39.) Some of the British Officers disagreed with Howe's entire strategy. ". . . the idea of offering these people battle is ridiculous; they have too much caution to risk everything on one action, or rather too much sense to engage an army double their numbers, superior in discipline, and who never make a show of fighting but upon the most advantageous ground. If we wish to conquer them we must attack him." (McGuire, p. 39.)

After a few days of skirmishing and plundering of the surrounding areas by British and Hessian troops, the entire Army decamped and was back in New Brunswick by June 18th. John Adams wrote from Philadelphia, "We are under no more Apprehension here than if the British Army was in the Crimea." The marauding troops "began to burn, plunder, and waste all before them." (Drake, p. 45.) This in turn ignited the rage of the local population who flocked to join militias and engaged in raids, sniping and harassment of the main retreating British force. General Knox, in a letter to a friend wrote "Nothing could exceed the spirit shown on this occasion by the much injured people of the Jerseys." They were "all fire, all revenge." (Drake, p. 45.)

6) As the British retreated to Amboy, General Washington, who had initially moved his army from the winter camp at Morristown to Middlebrook to be in a better position if the British forces marched on Philadelphia, continued to follow the enemy. On the night of June 25, 1777, Howe ordered two columns to advance, one to attack General William Alexander's (also known as Lord Stirling) forces of about 2,500 men and the other to get behind General Washington as his men advanced to support Lord Stirling's troops, dug in on low lying hills. The 16th Light Dragoons were part of the flanking column. Their participation in the attack on Stirling's fixed position is fictitious. (McGuire, pp. 53-55.)

General Howe's plan to draw the American army out of the protection of the Wachung Mountains and force them to do battle on open terrain, almost worked. The proximity of the British Army to his, they were about two and half miles from the Continental Army's headquarters in Quibbletown, caught Washington by surprise. He pulled his forces back into the mountains. Alexander Hamilton wrote: "It was judged prudent to return with the army to the mountains, lest it should be their (the British) intention to get into them and force us to fight them on their own terms." (McGuire, p. 57)

Chapter 9 – An Independence Day Celebration

1) By the beginning of the American Revolution, with the influx over the prior decades of different immigrant groups of varied religions and ethnicities, the rise of a propertied class and the development of shipping, Philadelphia had ceased to be the tolerant, pacifist leaning, Quaker dominated City of Brotherly Love and instead had become a vibrant port and the political capital of the newly independent nation.

Robert Morris, one of the city's most prominent citizens wrote: "You will consider Philadelphia, from its centrical situation, the extent of its commerce, the number of its artificers, manufactures and other circumstances, to be to the United States what the heart is to the human body in circulating the blood."

The population was between 30,000 and 40,000 and before the war, the farms of Pennsylvania fed the port city flour and lumber, the chief exports. Philadelphia, the largest port in British North America, "had a large, rough, working-class population of dockworkers and laborers. . .Transportation of goods into and out of the city required porters, carters, draymen and teamsters- rough able-bodied characters who slaked their thirst at some of the more than 150 licensed taverns in the city. Others patronized illegal "tippling houses" or taprooms in the back alleys and waterfront areas, where 'persons of evil name and fame and dishonest conversation' were know to congregate, according to city court records." (McGuire, p. 126.)

2) In May 1777, when General Knox was with the Army in Morristown and Lucy was staying with General Heath's family in

Sewell's Point (now Brookline) outside of Boston, he responded to her letter in which she said she had not received a letter or word from her family by stating: "Though your parents are on the opposite side from your Harry, yet it's very strange that it should divest them of humanity. Not a line! My God! What stuff is the human heart made of? Although father, mother, sister, and brother have forgotten you, yet, my love, your Harry will ever esteem you the best boon of Heaven." (Noah Brooks, Henry Knox- A Soldier of the Revolution, p. 90.)

3) John Adams called it the "most genteel tavern in America." It was the favorite meeting place of many members of the First Continental Congress. The City Tavern was built by subscription in 1773 at a cost of more than £3,000. On May 20th, 1774, over two hundred men gathered in the long gallery of the City Tavern to respond to the request for assistance from Bostonians against the British, following the passage of the Boston Port Bill. (Wikipedia, The City Tavern, Philadelphia.)

4) Strange as it seems, given the propaganda about Hessian atrocities and the angry, harsh and even violent reception of Hessian prisoners captured at Trenton when they were paraded through the streets of Philadelphia, the Hessian musicians became part of the social life of the city and performed for hire for Congress and others. Musicians were considered noncombatants "by the rules of eighteenth-century warfare." The list of prisoners taken at Trenton included ten oboe players, as distinguished from fifers and drummers. (McGuire, p. 342, note 8.)

The Hessian Band, "the most popular musical group" in Philadelphia, perhaps joined by some local musicians, provided the entertainment for the diners at the Independence Day celebration at City Tavern.

Congressman Thomas Burke, of North Carolina, who attended the dinner observed, that the Hessian musicians "performed very delightfully, the pleasure being not a little heightened by the reflection that they were hired by the British Court for purposes very different from those to which they were applied." (McGuire, pp. 64-65.)

5) The Independence Day Parade took place on Second Street. There were two troops of cavalry from Maryland, horses drawn artillery and "about 1,000 North Carolina infantry who were en route to join Washington's army in New Jersey." One observer, was not that impressed with the infantry and wrote: "the troops paraded thro' the streets with great pomp tho' many of them were barefoot & looked very unhealthy." (McGuire, p. 65)

I have not found any evidence that General Knox attended the Independence Day Celebrations or participated in the military parade. Since some artillery were part of the event, I have inserted General Knox, his officers and some men of the Massachusetts Artillery Regiment into the parade.

6) On June 9, 1777 during a severe thunderstorm, lightning struck the steeple of Christ Church, then the tallest structure in Philadelphia. "Gracing the point of the spire was a gilded crown, symbol of royal authority over this Anglican parish. The lighting bolt 'carried away some part of the Ornaments of the Crown at the top of the rods.'" (McGuire, p.65.)

7) Not everyone approved of the lavish celebration. Connecticut Congressman William Williams criticized the waste of gunpowder as well as the excessive consumption of alcohol. Reverend Henry Muhlenberg also condemned the lavish displays and thought it invited Divine retribution. "The air was filed and shaken by artificial fireworks and thunderclaps. Empty skins were bloated with food and drinks of health. Houses with their artificial illumination outshone the moon and stars. . . In connection with all this it occurred to me in the words of the common saying, 'The birds that sing early are easily caught by the cats.'" (McGuire, pp. 66-67.)

8) Quakers, like others living in the colonies, were forced to choose between allegiance to England and the King or the patriots, home and colony. "For Pennsylvania Quakers (members of the Society of Friends), decisions about whether to support or oppose the war were further complicated by the inherent conflict between two deeply held

beliefs: their pacifist principles and their desire to protect and support the colony founded by William Penn. . . In September 1776, the largest organization of Quakers in America- the Philadelphia Yearly Meeting- formally directed its members to observe strict neutrality. This meant that Quakers should not vote or take oaths of loyalty to support either side, should not engage in combat or pay for a substitute (a not uncommon practice in that era) and should not pay taxes to support the war effort. (Karin A. Wulf, "Despise the mean Distinctions [these] Times Have Made:" The Complexity of Patriotism and Quaker Loyalism in One Pennsylvania Family," revolution.h-net.msu.edu/ essays/wulf).

Wulf speculates that "the majority, torn by conflicting loyalties, sympathized with both sides. Many remained tacit Loyalists. . . Other Quakers renounced neutrality and actively sided with the Patriots. . . .[T]he perception among both Patriots and Loyalists was that Quakers could not be fully trusted. In the Delaware Valley, where for most of 1776 and 1777 first the British and then the Americans held sway, Quakers were punished by each side for their supposed allegiance to the other." (Wulf, The Complexity of Patriotism and Quaker Loyalism in One Pennsylvania Family.)

The city magistrates of Philadelphia were aware of the possibility of mob violence on July 4, 1777. The town militia, wardens and watchmen were all instructed to prevent riots from 8 until 11 pm and "a Bellman be sent round to give notice to the inhabitants, that the Council do expressly order all the lights ... be extinguished at Eleven O'Clock." McGuire, p. 67.)

However, the presence or absence of candles in the windows indicated the occupants' political preference- illuminated windows in patriots' homes and windows without candles in the homes of loyalists, or Quakers who wished to remain neutral.

As a result, the celebrations at night included smashing darkened windows all over town, including the area "north of Market," where many Quakers resided.

"In the Evening, the whole City (except Torry Houses whose Windows Paid for their Obstenacy) were Illuminated with Lights at every Window," an observer wrote. Another stated, "I conclude much Tory unilluminated Glass will want replacing." (McGuire, p. 67.)The Quakers on the receiving end of the riotous behavior were not so delighted. "We had 15 broken, N[icholas] Waln 14, T[homas] Wharton a good many more, and Uncle [James] Logan had 50 cracked & broken & all this for joy of having gained our liberty." (McGuire, p.68.)

## Chapter 10 - A Death Wish and A Close Encounter

1) On August 29, 1777, after Howe's army landed at Head of Elk, Maryland on the Chesapeake Bay, Washington ordered the formation of a "corps of light infantry. . . , made up of 700 chosen marksmen, 100 each from the Continental brigades, and supplemented with more than 1,000 militia from Delaware and Pennsylvania," with Brigadier General William Maxwell in command. (McGuire, pp.143-144.)

2) Savage plundering by regular troops and stragglers was not limited to Hessians. In fact, it was a British soldier who amputated a woman's fingers to get at her rings.

"A soldier of ours was yesterday taken by the enemy beyond our lines, who had chopped off an unfortunate woman's fingers in order to plunder her of her rings" (McGuire, p. 147.) Plunderers caught by the Americans were hung with their plunder upon their backs as a warning to others. (McGuire, p.147.)

3) Washington deliberately spaced the regiments and artillery, in some cases 100, 150 or 200 yards between units, so that the troops extended for ten miles as they paraded through the city. His purpose was to impress upon those who thought the Rebel Army weak and decimated, that it was in fact a fighting force to be reckoned with.

"I am induced to do this from the opinion of Several of my Officers and many Friends in Philadelphia, that it may have some influence on the minds of the disaffected there and those who are Dupes to their artifices and opinions." (McGuire, p. 130.)

The eight thousand strong army were accompanied by four

hundred field musicians and took more than two hours to pass through the city. John Adams observed the parade and wrote to Abigail: "They don't hold up their Heads, quite erect, nor turn out their Toes, so exactly as they ought. They don't all of them cock their Hats- and such as do, don't all wear them the same Way." (McGuire, p. 131.)

The lack of straight lines and orderly parade steps that caught John Adams' eye, may have been the least of it. According to another historian, "[The] troops were not only insufficiently clothed but there were practically no uniforms and the pitiful expedient was adopted of having each man in the ranks wear a sprig of green in his hat to give a touch of uniformity as the army marched through Philadelphia. . . The baggage and camp followers which would have ruined whatever little effect the nondescript equipment could produce, were not permitted to move through the city with the troops but were sent around it." (John C. Fitzpatrick, "George Washington Himself," pp. 303-304.)

4) Hunger was a constant companion of the soldiers of the Continental Army. Rations of one pound of flour and one pound of beef were usually short on the flour and always for the beef. A typical experience for the soldier continually marching, fighting, and marching again was described by Private Martin following one battle as follows: "I now had to travel the rest of the day, after marching all the day and night before and fighting all the morning [a distance of about twenty four miles.] I had eaten nothing since the noon of the preceding day, nor did I eat a morsel till the forenoon of the next day, and I needed rest as much as victuals. . . . . I was tormented by thirst all the morning, fighting being warm work; but after the retreat commenced I found simple means to satisfy my thirst. 'I could drink at the brook' but I could not 'bite at the bank.'" (J.P. Martin, 'Private Yankee Doodle Dandy," pp. 74-75.)

5) As a result of some "reputable" civilians of Wilmington lodging complaints for plundering and worse against a regiment of American soldiers, Washington wrote the commander ordering him to return to Wilmington. "If any of the people who have been injured can point out the particular Persons, either Officers or Soldiers, they shall be

made examples of." (McGuire, p. 148.)

On September 4, 1777, the Commander-in-Chief stated in the General Orders: "Notwithstanding all the cautions, the earnest requests, and the positive orders of the Commander in Chief, to prevent our own army from plundering our own friends and fellow citizens, yet to his astonishment and grief, fresh complaints are made to him, that so wicked, infamous and cruel a practice is still continued. . . [T]he Commander in Chief requires, that these orders be distinctly read to all the troops; and that the officers of every rank, take particular pains, to convince the men, of the baseness, and fatal tendency of the practices complained of; and that their own safety depends on a contrary conduct, and an exact observance of order and discipline; . . .the Commander in Chief most solemnly assures all, that he will have no mercy on offenders against these orders; their lives shall pay the forfeit of their crimes. Pity under such circumstances, would be the height of cruelty." (McGuire, pp. 148-149.)

6) The British Grenadiers were perhaps the most formidable of the British Regiments. They were elite troops and were the tallest soldiers in the army. Their bearskin fur caps added a foot to their height. They were awesome and their approach was a mixture of pageantry and mesmerizing lethalness. McGuire described the 1,200 Grenadiers beginning their attack as follows: "The senior drum major inverted his mace and raised it vertically to his chest, upon which the drummers silently lifted both sticks horizontally to their nostrils, waiting for the word of command. 'GRENADIERS!' bellowed through the ranks. 'By battalions!' The drum major raised his mace high. 'To the FRONT!. . .QUI-I-CK. . .MARCH!' Mace and drumsticks dropped in one crisp motion, and a visceral thunder of drums rumbled out . . . [They advanced with] muskets at the shoulder and flags streaming, the battalions swaying rhythmically forward. . . the late-afternoon sun glinting from hundreds of bayonets and musket barrels in double ranks." (McGuire, pp. 210-211.)

They marched into battle to the fifers playing their Regimental song- "The British Grenadiers." The soldiers may have even sung it as they advanced, adding more menace to their approach. The front plates of their bearskin caps, above the lion and British Crown, bore the Latin motto "Nec Aspera Terrent- Hardship does not deter us."

The Colonel of the 1st Battalion of Grenadiers in his speech to them before they began the assault said: "Grenadiers, put on your caps; for damn'd fighting and drinking I'll match you against the world!" (McGuire, p. 210-211.)


7) The Battle of Brandywine was fought on September 11, 1777. It was a terrible defeat for the Americans, unfortunately the first but not the only disaster to occur on that date in our history.

General Howe repeated the overall tactics he had employed successfully at the Battle of Brooklyn in August, 1776. He kept Washington confused as to the main point of his attack, pinning down the bulk of the American Army at Chadd's Ford across Brandywine Creek with a sufficient force of British troops under General Grant and Hessians under General Von Knyphausen (the very same units which had menaced the American Army at the Shore Road in Brooklyn).

Howe himself, led several thousand men in a wide sweep of the American lines, crossing the Brandywine well up from Chadd's Ford and falling on the American right flank around four p.m. in the afternoon. Basically, after fierce fighting, with the Americans putting up stiff resistance although there were gaps in their lines on the right due to hasty positioning and inability of the Continentals to maneuver quickly while under fire, the right flank was turned and the Americans were forced to retreat. At Chadd's Ford, the Americans also were forced to retreat before the advancing troops of Generals Grant and Knyphausen as their position was untenable with their extended right flank crumbling.

Accounts of the losses vary. According to one source, the Americans suffered 200 killed, 500 wounded and 400 captured, along with eleven cannons, including newly arrived guns from France. More importantly, the British were now in position to capture Philadelphia. British losses were estimated at 89 killed, 488 wounded and six missing. (Savas and Dameron, "A Guide to the Battles of the American Revolution.") Chernow, in his voluminous biography, "Washington, A Life," gives the same numbers. (Ron Chernow, "Washington, A

Life," p. 305). General Henry Knox, in his account of the battle to the President of the Council of Massachusetts, wrote on September 18th that from "the most particular inquiry I have been able to make, [the American losses] will not exceed seven hundred or eight hundred killed, wounded and missing, and ten field pieces." He assured the President that "from my own observation and the opinion of others, their loss must be much greater than ours." (Drake, "Life and Correspondence of Henry Knox, pp. 49-50.)

McGuire states the official British and Hessian casualty lists claimed 93 dead and together with the wounded and missing a total of 587 casualties. Howe reported the American casualties were 300 killed, 600 wounded and nearly 400 captured. Other British sources estimated American losses at close to 2,000. (McGuire, p. 269.) One British officer wrote: "Orders Wass Given for to Review the ground and Beruie the dead and the Surgens to attend the Wounded. The Enemy had 502 dead in the field. We had 39 beried the Next Morning. The Wounded In not as yet asserted. We took 400 Prisners that Night and the Next Day." (McGuire, p.269.)

General Grant observed: "General Sunset saved the Rebell Artillery & prevented a pursuit, but they retreated in the utmost confusion to Chester & many of them never stopt till they got to Philadelphia." (McGuire, p. 261.)

Chapter 11 - Philadelphia in Turmoil

1) A few days after the battle, Dr. Benjamin Rush, under a flag of truce, was admitted to the British camp, along with other surgeons to treat the wounded American soldiers now held prisoner. It was General Howe who initially proposed doctors be sent, due to the large number of American wounded. (McGuire, p. 270.)

Rush was a signer of the Declaration of Independence and a prominent physician. During the Revolutionary War he wrote "To the Officers in the Army of the United States: Direction for Preserving the Health of Soldiers," which was published and widely used.

While in the British camp he met with some of their Army Officers as well as Philadelphia Loyalists who had joined the British.

One British Officer wrote that after acknowledging the completeness of the Americans' defeat at Brandywine, [He] "declared that all possibility of accommodation much less satisfaction was as remote the day after the battle as it ever had been since the declaration of independence; before which they all (both whigs & tories,) agree that a few concessions on our side [the British Government] would have put an end to the whole business." (McGuire, p. 271.)

2) Around midnight on September 11th, General Washington having brought the retreating Army to Chester, wrote to John Hancock in Philadelphia: "Sir: I am sorry to inform you that in this day's engagement, we have been obliged to leave the enemy the masters of the field." (Chernow, p. 305.) He tried to cast the defeat in more positive terms and advised Hancock, and thus the Congress, that:"Our loss of men is not, I am persuaded, very considerable; I believe much less than the enemy's. . . Notwithstanding the misfortune of the day, I am happy to find the troops in good spirits; and I hope another time, we shall compensate for the losses now sustained." (Chernow, p. 305.)

3) General Knox's letter began: "My dear girl will be happy to hear of her Harry's safety; for, my Lucy, Heaven, who is our guide, has protected him in the day of battle. You will hear with this letter of the most severe action that has been fought in this war between our army and the enemy. Our people behaved well, but Heaven frowned on us in a degree. We were obliged to retire after very considerable slaughter of the enemy: they dared not pursue a single step. If they advance, we shall fight them again before they get possession of Philadelphia; but of this they will be cautious. My corps did my great honor: they behaved like men contending for every thing that's valuable."
(Drake, p. 47.)

How could both Generals Washington and Knox have so grossly overestimated the enemy's losses? While Washington may have been tempted to over state the casualties to Congress, Knox surely had no such reason in writing to Lucy. And there was a wide discrepancy between the British casualties reported by the Americans and the British count of their losses. McGuire suggests that the American commanders were misled due to the manner in which many of the British troops fought. Soldiers in some British Regiments repeatedly dropped to the ground on a signal from an officer's whistle as the Americans took aim, got up once the musket volley had been fired and charged with bayonets. (McGuire, p. 209, 259.)

4) McGuire has a fascinating description of the ammunition used by soldiers during the War.

"The ammunition was made up in paper cartridges, which had to be bitten open, resulting in the blackening of the soldier's mouth, especially at the right corner as the teeth held and tore the cartridge while the right hand pulled it away, smearing the gritty powder across the face and hands. In the haste and chaos of fighting, powder also spilled into the soldier's mouth, sometimes in large amounts if the biting was not done carefully- hardly possible in the heat of battle. A compound of potassium nitrate, sulfur, and charcoal, black powder is very salty and astringent. Together with the marching, shouting, and stress produced by battle, a maddening thirst was a constant companion of the combat soldier." (McGuire, p. 265.)

5) Thomas Paine wrote a stirring essay the day after the Battle of Brandywine which he signed "Common Sense." It was published in the local papers and became known as "The Crisis # 4." A clarion call for greater resolve and effort, Paine urged his fellow patriots not to despair, even though the ground where the battle had been fought was lost. He reminded his readers the Americans were fighting for a cause, not territory.

"Those who expect to reap the blessings of freedom, must, like men, undergo the fatigues of supporting it. . . The event of yesterday was one of those kind of alarms which is just sufficient to rouse us to duty, without being of consequence enough to depress our fortitude."

After characterizing the British Army as "a band of ten or twelve thousand robbers, who are this day fifteen hundred or two thousand less in strength than they were yesterday," he ended with a warning to General Howe:

"You sir, are only lingering out the period that shall bring with it your defeat. . . . We are not moved by the gloomy smile of a worthless king, but by the ardent glow of generous patriotism. We fight not to enslave, but to set a country free, and to make room upon the earth for honest men to live in. In such a case we are sure that we are right; and we leave to you the despairing reflection of being the tool of a miserable tyrant." (McGuire, p. 272.)

6) Infections and disease were the major causes of death of wounded soldiers. First, infections were caused by the musket ball, bayonet or shrapnel. The balls were made of lead that expanded upon impact making the exit wound larger than the entry point and leaving lead fragments inside the soldier's body. Second, the surgeons themselves contributed to the spread of infection. They used the same saws and instruments over and over again on all the casualties being attended to. The need for sterilization of surgical tools was unknown.

In addition to the wound becoming infected, diseases in hospitals were rampant. The overcrowding in unsanitary conditions, led to the spread of typhus, typhoid fever, yellow fever, and measles and whooping cough. Straw bedding was not changed, even when the patient died. Soldiers lay in their excrement. Casualties were usually fed mush, soups or broth, from wooden bowls with the same spoon used for an entire ward.

Dr. Benjamin Rush stated: "Hospitals are the sinks of human life in the army. They robbed the United States of more citizens than the sword." While a soldier had a two percent chance of dying in combat, this increased to twenty five percent if he was wounded and hospitalized. One statistic claimed that there were nine deaths from disease for every one from a wound received in battle. Eichner, L.G., MD, "The Military Practice of Medicine During the Revolutionary War (A paper presented at the October 2003 meeting of the Tredyffrin Easttown History Club.)

7) Washington indeed did send "an express" message delivered by one of his aides to John Hancock around one o'clock in the morning of September 19th, recommending that the Congress leave "as the

Enemy had it in their power to throw a party that Night into the City." (McGuire, p.298-299.) Hancock wrote his wife that he "instantly gave the alarm, Rous'd the Members [of Congress] etc and after having fix'd my Packages, Papers etc in the Waggons and Sent them off, about 3 oClock in the morning I Set off myself for Bristol." (McGuire, p. 299.) General Knox did not ride to Philadelphia to determine what munitions and supplies should be salvaged or destroyed. His fictitious presence is solely for purposes of the plot.

8) There truly was pandemonium in Philadelphia as people prepared to flee. Thomas Paine recalled Philadelphia's streets were crowded by so many people in the "moonlit streets, that the town resembled high noon on market day." (Chernow, p. 306.)

Congressman Henry Laurens described the scene as follows: "Thousands of all Sorts in all appearances past by in such haste that very few could be prevailed on to answer to the Simple question what News?" (McGuire, p. 299.) It turned out to be a false alarm. Two days later, John Adams wrote : "Congress was chased like a covey of partridges from Philadelphia to Trenton, from Trenton to Lancaster." (Chernow, p. 306.) He despaired of Washington's lack of leadership and asked "Oh, Heaven! Grant us one great soul! . . One active, masterly capacity would bring order out of this confusion and save this country." (Chernow, p.306.)

9) Tincture of myrrh or application of turpentine were applied to clean a wound and ward off post-operative infection. Whiskey was more commonly used and other topical applications were basilam powder and quinine. (Eichner, p. 30.)

10) Knox is referring to the "Battle of the Clouds," fought on September 16th about twenty miles west of Philadelphia. The battle, which began around 1 p.m. was going badly for the Americans. A torrential rain saved the Continental Army by turning the fields and roads into a thick mud, making any advance by the British impossible. (Savas and Dameron, p. 124.)

Several days after the battle, Knox wrote Lucy: "After some days' manoeuvring, we came in sight of the enemy, and drew up in order of battle, which the enemy declined; but a most violent rain coming on obliged us to change our position, in the course of which nearly all the musket cartridges of the army that had been delivered to the men were damaged, consisting of above 400,000. This was a most terrible stroke to us, and owing entirely to the badness of the cartouch-boxes which had been provided for the army." (Drake, p. 50.)

11) Washington was well aware of the need for solid intelligence about the British. When he was forced to abandon New York city in September 1776 he had no spy network in the city which became the British winter quarters. He was determined not to repeat this mistake.

Knowing of the British focus on capturing the American's capital, Washington instructed General Thomas Mifflin, a native of Philadelphia to establish a spy network in that city. The spies "are to remain among them under the mask of friendship." The network was in place when General Cornwallis entered the city on September 26, 1777. (Nagy, John A., "Spies in the Continental Capital," p. 41, 46.)

Washington also ran his own spy network directly and individual commanders were encouraged to obtain information about the enemy in all ways possible. I have surmised that General Knox would have taken the initiative and recruited at least one well-placed spy in the city.

## Chapter 12 – Two Lives Entwined

1) At the age of twenty, Alexander Hamilton was promoted to Lieutenant Colonel on March 1, 1777 and became an aide-de-camp to General Washington. Following the Battle of Brandywine the British waited a week before occupying Philadelphia. Washington took advantage of the delay and sent Hamilton into the city to requisition much needed supplies for his army such as blankets and clothing as well as cartridges. (Chernow, pp. 306-307.) Washington acting under emergency powers ordered the taking of critical supplies. The citizens received receipts for their goods but no payment at the time.

I have surmised that Hamilton would also have seized bullet molds as well as the raw materials for making musket balls.

2) The actual arrest of prominent Quakers was ordered by the Congress and the Supreme Executive Council and occurred around September 8, 1777. As the Battle of Brandywine was being fought, they were placed on wagons and transported first to Reading, Pennsylvania and ultimately to Winchester, Virginia. (McGuire, p. 272.) The action taken against them was based upon "false papers allegedly 'found' by General John Sullivan in New Jersey that hinted at a Quaker plot to aid the British Army." (McGuire, p.273.)

John Adams described the need to prevent Quaker treachery in a letter to Abigail Adams as follows: "We have been obliged to attempt to humble the Pride of some Jesuits who call themselves Quakers, but who love Money and Land better than Liberty and Religion. The Hypocrites are endeavouring to raise the Cry of Persecution, and to give this Matter a religious Turn, but they cannot succeed. . .American Independence has disappointed them, which makes them hate it." (McGuire, p. 273.) So wrote the lawyer who had defended the British soldiers accused of firing on innocent civilians in the Boston Massacre on March 5, 1770.

3) According to the British census that they made when they occupied the American capital: "there were 9,423 males and 12, 344 females for a total reported population of 21,767. [The normal population of Philadelphia was approximately 40,000.] The census found 5,360 inhabited dwelling places and 567 uninhabited dwelling houses, which had been deserted by the disaffected, for a total of 5,957 dwelling houses." (John A. Nagy, "Spies in the Continental Capital" pp.46-47.)

4) Both the British and Americans employed various forms of invisible ink for secret communications during the Revolutionary War. The ink formulas used solutions of bismuth, gallo-tannic acid or lead. Ink was made visible by use of reagents such as acid, heat or fire. One of the problems of using heat or fire was that it made the paper

very brittle. The recipient of the secret message would thus transcribe the letter before sending it on. (John A. Nagy, "Invisible Ink-Spycraft of the American Revolution," pp. 29-33.) Milk, lime juice and vinegar were also used when formulaic inks were unavailable.

5) All kinds of ciphers were used by both sides during the Revolutionary War for secure communications and for secret messages. The most basic cipher used a simple substitute of one letter for another in the alphabet. One such alphabetic transposition used the letter n for a, m for b and so on. (Nagy, Invisible Ink, pp. 51-52.)

Another type of cipher used by the Americans, British, French and Hessians was called the pigpen cipher. It looked like a tic-tac-toe grid. The sender and recipient agreed upon the placement of the letters in each of the "pigpens" or boxes. Then, by drawing the position in the diagram where the letter was placed and a dot to indicate the letter in that box (no dot for the first letter, one dot for the second and two dots for the third) the sender could transmit a secret message. (Nagy, Invisible Ink, pp. 55-56.)

6) Nagy refers to an instance in which coded messages were written on "tiny strips of paper. . . one quarter-inch wide and could easily be sewn in the seam of a garment or placed between a book's binding and its cover, making detection nearly impossible." (Nagy, Invisible Ink, p. 57.)

7) Book codes were also commonly used by both sides, the trick being that both the sender and recipient had to possess the same edition of the same book. And a popular subset of book codes were dictionary codes. Entick's Spelling Dictionary was readily available as was the same author's New Spelling Dictionary. Sometimes, a fixed number was added to the page and word numbers in the book for additional security. For example, the first word in the first column of the dictionary appearing on page 139 would be written 149 /11, adding the number ten to both the page and word position. (Nagy, Invisible Ink, pp. 72-73.)

8) The bells of Christ Church and the State House bell, which

later became the Liberty Bell, were carted out of the city to prevent them from being captured by the British and melted down into cannons. (McGuire, p. 327.) I have assigned that task to Lt. Colonel Hamilton's men but there is no historical basis for that.

On September 24th, 700 wagons comprising the baggage train of the defeated American Army, along with 2,000 personnel arrived in the little, peaceful Moravian populated town of Bethlehem. Some members of Congress had arrived two days earlier on the way to Lancaster. Along with them "were the church bells from Philadelphia. . . and the wagon in which was loaded the State House bell [the Liberty Bell] broke down in the street and had to be unloaded. (McGuire, "The Philadelphia Campaign, Volume II-Germantown and the Roads to Valley Forge, p. 23.) [All future references to McGuire in the End Notes are to Volume II.]

9) General Cornwallis led 2,000 to 3,000 marching troops, cavalry, and artillery of six brass twelve pounders, four howitzers and light field guns into Philadelphia. It was a show of force designed to intimidate the remaining populace and display the might of the British Army.

McGuire describes the spectacle as follows: "On command, the column stepped off at the slow-march rate of sixty-four steps per minute, the fifes warbling 'God Save the King,' above the solemn rumble of the drums. The large battalion flags of light silk, each 6' by 6'6" inches on a 10' pike, opened fully, their brilliant red and white crosses on dark blue proudly displaying golden crowns and badges wreathed in roses and thistles." (McGuire, p. 11.)

Earlier, the Hessian Grenadiers had prepared for the entry by whitening their belts and cross straps with pipe clay, polishing "brass buckles, cap plates, and badges to a glow, blackened the leather cartridge boxes and bayonet scabbards and Hessian mustaches- with black-ball wax, and powdered their hair white." (McGuire, p. 7.)

10) Joseph Galloway and Andrew and William Allen, all prominent Loyalists from Philadelphia rode alongside Cornwallis as he entered the city. Their presence was designed to reassure the

citizens that the Army was there to protect them and there would be no widespread pillaging and looting.

Joseph Galloway believed that most Americans preferred to remain part of Britain and loyal to the Crown. In 1774 as a member of the First Continental Congress he proposed a "Plan of Union" which would have guaranteed the Colonists the privileges as Englishmen, as well as the right to representation in Parliament and consent to the laws under which they lived. His plan would have created an American legislature. The King would appoint a President General to administer the colonies and no law would take effect without the approval of both Parliament and the American legislature. (Encyclopedia.Com/ Joseph Galloway.) His Plan of Union was rejected and Galloway continued to oppose independence for the Thirteen Colonies and remained loyal to the King. He quit the Pennsylvania Provincial Assembly and the Continental Congress when they rejected his recommendation to abandon defiance of Britain and went to New York City where he offered his services to the British.

In September 1777, upon occupying Philadelphia, Howe appointed Galloway as Superintendent of Police and head of the civil government. He was an efficient administrator and organized the Loyalists in the city, hired spies and magistrates to suppress revolutionary activity and prevent goods from reaching the American Army in their winter quarters at Valley Forge. (Encyclopedia.Com/ Joseph Galloway; Wikipedia/Joseph Galloway.)

11) Opinion among the British and Hessians about the sincerity of the welcome they had received from the citizens of Philadelphia varied. Captain John Montresor, the Army's Chief Engineer and on Cornwallis' staff remarked, "the army took possession of the city 'amidst the acclamation of some thousands of the inhabitants mostly women and children.'" Captain von Munchhausen reported "The inhabitants of the city. . .came to meet us and showed in various ways their pleasure at our arrival." (McGuire, p. 19.)

Captain Lieutenant Downing was less impressed. "Whether they were pleased or not at our entrance, they must have been struck with the appearance of a body of such fine fellows as the British Grenadiers."

(McGuire, p. 13).

I have made Joseph Galloway skeptical of the outward show of enthusiasm and cognizant of support in Philadelphia for the Rebel cause for purposes of the plot. In reality, on September 26, 1777, the day of the triumphal entry of the British into his native city, Galloway claimed with great exaggeration, "no Roman General ever received from the citizens of Rome greater acclamations than the noble General [Cornwallis] did on this occasion from the loyal citizens of Philadelphia." (McGuire, p. 19.)

### Chapter 13 – Difficult Tasks Fulfilled

1) Washington's Orders of the Day on October 3 were a combination of inspiring rhetoric, "Our dearest rights- our dearest friends- our own lives- honor, glory and even shame, urge us to this fight," a morale boosting reference to the recent victory of September 19th by General Horatio Gates over British General Burgoyne in the Saratoga campaign, as well as practical information that the British had been compelled to send so many regiments to Philadelphia and elsewhere that their forces which held Germantown were depleted and down to less than 6,000 men. (McGuire, pp. 52-53.)

2) The reference is to the September 21st battle of Paoli in which a British night attack on the American camp resulted in the slaughter of many of the troops by a stealthy bayonet charge. General Wayne was unable to rally his troops who were illuminated by their own campfires and shot down by British troops from the surrounding darkness. McGuire, p. 68.)

3) The primary goal of the American engagement with the Jaegers on the right of the British line was to keep them pinned down and out of the main battle taking place in Germantown. Three hours of sniping and skirmishing accomplished this. (McGuire, p. 80.)

4) At the beginning of the battle, the early morning rapid American advance on the British lines caught them by surprise. Approximately

100 to 120 British light infantry under the command of Col. Thomas Musgrave retreated and took up positions in a mansion on the outskirts of Germantown. The massive two-story house, situated on a slope and near one of the main roads through Germantown, belonged to former provincial Chief Justice Benjamin Chew. It was a formidable building made of quarried gray stone with the front walls nearly two feet thick. The British commenced laying down volley after volley of musket fire, which was disconcerting to the Americans advancing down the road into Germantown but largely ineffective at that range.

Many of Washington's staff recommended continuing the main thrust into Germantown and skirting the house, leaving behind a regiment to keep Musgrave's forces contained. However, General Knox cautioned against leaving such a strong enemy position in the army's rear and his advice prevailed. Washington ordered an assault on Chew House and the advantage and momentum of the surprise attack was lost. A dense fog and the sounds of heavy musket fire at the Chew House, that was to the rear of the troops assaulting the British center, convinced the advancing Americans they were being flanked and caused them to retreat. (McGuire, pp. 83-90.)

5) Knox wrote an account of the Battle of Germantown to the President of the Massachusetts Council. He noted that the American troops after marching all night attacked the British around 6 a.m. forcing their troops back. He omitted any mention of his decisive but fateful advice to attack the Chew mansion instead of pressing on, and attributed the dense fog as "the unhappy cause of our losing the victory after being in possession of it for near two hours, and having driven the enemy above two miles from the place where the engagement begun, quite through their encampment." He then optimistically assessed the morale of the army, writing: "Our men are in the highest spirits, and ardently desire another trial. I know of no ill consequences that can follow the late action: on the contrary, we have gained considerable experience, and our army have a certain proof that the British troops are vulnerable."(Drake, pp. 52-53.)

6) William Knox actually joined his brother in July and served as the General's secretary from then on. For purposes of the plot, I have placed William's arrival around the end of September, just before the Germantown battle.

7) General Howe's headquarters was at 164 South Second Street, the former home of American General John Cadwalader. In addition, Howe appropriated the front parlor of the house across the street for staff meetings. The Quaker residents, William and Lydia Darragh, were allowed to continue to live there and in one case, passed on extremely vital information to the Americans. (Nagy, p. 48.)

Chapter 14 – The Confrontation

1) Joseph Stansbury, a Philadelphia merchant was appointed by the British as commander of the watch, the city's civilian guards. When the British withdrew from Philadelphia in June 1778, Stansbury remained behind and in May 1779 was the intermediary used by Benedict Arnold to offer Arnold's services to the British.

2) Captain John Montresor was Chief Engineer to General Howe and responsible for the construction of the new defenses for Philadelphia. When the British occupied New York City, Montresor purchased an island in the harbor. It was initially known as Montresor Island and is now Randall's Island.

His reputation as a ladies man was enhanced in no small part by Charlotte Temple, a novel, allegedly based on his life and written by his first cousin, Susanna Haswell Rowson. The main character, John Montraville, seduces an innocent English young lady and induces her to run away with him to America. This novel, published in 1790 was said to be the most widely read fiction in the new United States until Uncle Tom's Cabin.

3) Dr. William Shippen was Director General of Military Hospitals for the Continental Army and the winter of 1777-1778 served at Valley Forge. He received his medical training in Europe

with a degree from the University of Edinbugh in Scotland. After the war, Shippen taught at the University of Pennsylvania Medical School in Philadelphia,the first such school in the country. (The Pennsylvania Gazette, July/August 2015.)

Chapter 15 – The Return of Friends

1) On Friday night, November 27, 1777 a spectacular display of the northern lights lit the night sky and was visible in Philadelphia. "The sky red as blood interspersed with white streaks & when the Redness grew less, it was as light as when the moon is just risen." This was taken as a sign that a bloody battle was about to be fought. (McGuire, p. 237.)

2) The strength of British Regiments was seriously depleted by casualties and sickness. For example, the Queen's Rangers had lost almost a quarter of their number at the Battle of Brandywine. On October 15, General Howe promoted Captain John Graves Simcoe to Major in command of the Queen's Rangers with exclusive privilege "of enlisting old countrymen (as Europeans were termed in America) and deserters from the rebel army." (McGuire, p. 231.) Simcoe brought the Rangers up to eleven companies including one of Highlanders, consisting of Scottish refugees from North Carolina and elsewhere.

3) General Howe's surprise attack on Washington's army at Whitemarsh, fifteen miles from Philadelphia was thwarted by a spy revealing the plan to the Americans. Lydia Darragh, whose parlor in her house across from Howe's headquarters was used for staff meetings, hid in a closet and overheard Howe's briefing his staff on the impending attack. The next day, under the guise of obtaining flour, she passed through the lines and went to the American outpost at the junction of the Germantown and York roads. According to Colonel Boudinot, the American officer who received the information: "After Dinner a little poor looking insignificant woman came in . . .and put into my hands a dirty old needlebook, with various pockets in it." Boudinot found a rolled up piece of paper on which was written "information that Genl

Howe was coming out the next morning with 5000 men, 13 pieces of cannon, Baggage Waggons, and 11 Boats on Waggon Wheels." Boudinot presented this information to General Washington. (Nagy, "Spies in the Continental Capital," pp. 48-49; McGuire, p. 240.)

In addition to Lydia Darragh's intelligence, there had been other evidence indicating that a surprise attack was imminent. I have given Elisabeth the role of communicating such information in her ciphered messages to Will.

4) Washington issued General Orders for the construction of the Army camp at Valley Forge, with specific instructions as to their construction. (McGuire, p. 268.)

5) Dr. James Thacher, a surgeon with the Massachusetts 16th Regiment described the camp as follows: "The huts are arranged in strait lines forming a regular uniform compact village. The officers' huts are situated in front of the line, according to their rank, the kitchens in the rear and the whole is in the form of a tent encampment. . . The officers' huts are in general divided into two appartments and are occupied by three or four officers who compose one mess. Those for the soldiers have but one room and contain ten or twelve men with their cabins placed one above the other against the walls and filled in with straw, and one blanket for each man. ( Thacher, James D. Dr., "Military Journal During the American Revolutionary War 1775-1783," pp. 189-190.)

6) After a personal appeal from George Washington, Glover returned to service in the American Army and was active in the Saratoga campaign of 1777 and the Battle of Rhode Island in 1778. His first wife Hannah died in 1778, he remarried in 1781 and for the remainder of the war was stationed on the Hudson River to guard against the British sailing up from New York City.

# Author's Note and Acknowledgements

One challenge in researching historical novels is deciding what to include and what to omit. In "Blood Upon the Snow," the scenes of life on the Kearny farm, drawn in large part from "Diary of an Early American Boy- Noah Blake 1805" by Eric Sloane, are a case in point. I learned more about how to extract boulders from a frozen field, forge nails, erect a bridge and construct a gristmill than any reasonable reader would wish to know. It took several rounds of editing to prune that information into hopefully crisp sentences without weighing the reader down with too many snooze-inducing details, while still conveying the essence of the continuous back-breaking labor that was the daily reality of self-sufficiency.

The same is true for the Battles of Brandywine and Germantown. Thomas J. McGuire's excellent two-volume work, entitled "The Philadelphia Campaign," is replete with precise and clear overviews of the battle plans and troop movements. His books are also filled with terrific details taken from letters and correspondence and first hand accounts of the charges, retreats, hand to hand combat, assaults on fortified positions, and close encounters with death or capture. Since ordinary soldiers (such as Will Stoner and his gun crew, Bant and McNeil,) experienced the battle from the narrow perspective of fighting the enemy in their immediate vicinity, all of those specific accounts present a wonderful opportunity to have them happen to the fictional actors. The trick is to first decide what part of an historical battle would most interest the reader and then, like someone moving toy soldiers about, insert the fictional characters at that critical juncture.

I have tried to have it both ways in Chapter 10, A Death Wish and A Close Encounter, by placing Sergeant Will Stoner and his gun crew first at Chadd's Ford. At the beginning of the battle, General Grant and the Hessians were demonstrating against the Americans to mislead Washington into thinking this was the main point of attack, while General Howe led his troops in a wide flanking movement, crossing the Brandywine at an unprotected ford and crashing down on the American left later in the day. I took the liberty of moving Will and his gun crew to reinforce the thin American line so they could shell the advancing British Grenadiers and participate in the climactic end of the battle.

In Chapter 13, Difficult Tasks Fulfilled, although the American troops had advanced well into Germantown, driving the surprised British before them, I chose to focus on the unsuccessful assault on Chew House that ultimately proved to be a major tactical mistake and turned an imminent victory into a retreat, with the Americans leaving the British in possession of the field.

For me, there are so many interesting real historical characters it is a challenge to decide which ones to include in presenting the lives of ordinary people caught up in the war. Bant, the psychologically damaged militiaman is one such person.

I also made a conscious decision, in "Blood Upon the Snow," to develop the female characters of Elisabeth Van Hooten and Mercy Buskirk Ford and introduce a Quaker woman, Mary Lewis. All three give me the opportunity to explore with readers the roles women played during the early years of the Revolution. Mary lets me depict how the Quakers were distrusted by both Patriots and Tories alike, because many of them remained steadfast to their pacifist and religious principles. Mrs. Knox continues to play a supporting role and in much of her dialogue, I have drawn upon words or phrases she used in her letters to her beloved Harry. They really were that affectionate toward each other, and not shy about expressing themselves.

Finally, the more research I do, the more I am convinced of the need to dispel the many myths we have about the Revolution.

In "Blood Upon the Snow," Will Stoner, Nat Holmes and the Massachusetts Artillery and Marblehead Mariners, having crossed the Delaware, participate in the well-known attack on the Hessians in Trenton on December 26, 1776. Virtually every American is familiar with iconic painting by Emmanuel Leutze of Washington Crossing the Delaware. The disparities between historical facts and artistic license were discussed in "Tories and Patriots" in Note 1 to Chapter 16.

Picture that painting in your mind. You can probably describe it from memory. Yet, with that image so prominent in the mythology of our Revolution, very few history teachers or books explore who was that African American in uniform, seated at the gunwale on Washington's right. That was one reason I introduced the Marblehead Mariners in "Cannons for the Cause." I gave Nat Holmes and Adam Cooper prominence in "Tories and Patriots," because of the Mariners' vital role in saving the Army from capture on two occasions in 1776. Since their regiment disbanded at the end of that year, and I am committed to being historically accurate in my novels, Nat Holmes, Adam Cooper and Titus Fuller are basically absent in the story told in "Blood Upon the Snow." However, they return at the end to endure with Will the hardships at Valley Forge and will play a major role in "Spies and Deserters," the fourth in the series, which will explore among other themes, slavery in New Jersey.

Once again, I am indebted to my friends who read different versions of the manuscript and offered many helpful insights and comments. As I have stated before, they know who they are. I value their friendship and continued support.

Ben West, my editor, focused with laser like intensity on character development and plot. In some cases I assumed something was obvious when it was not, or my ideas consisted of confused half-baked thoughts, inarticulately presented. His comments always clarified and sharpened my writing.

I am especially indebted to my friends Dr. Haile Mezghebe and Dr. Daniel Waterman for medical information relating to battle wounds, field surgery and subsequent infections, shock, fever and chills.

I am deeply grateful to David Lyman, a volunteer at Peirce Mill, part of the National Park Service's Rock Creek Park in Washington, D.C. It is a functioning, water-powered mill, grinding wheat into flour in the same manner used in the late 1700s and early 1800s. David was kind enough to spend much of a pleasant Sunday morning explaining the original workings of the mill as well as the later addition of an elevator to carry the raw grain from the basement to the top floor. His patient and detailed account enabled me to better describe the construction of James Kierney's mill.

All remaining errors of fact, grammar or spelling are of course my sole responsibility.

My immediate family has helped in writing "Blood Upon the Snow," in various ways. My son, as always, has given generously of his time and artistic talents to design the cover, format the text, and provide the internal artwork.

My now two years + old grandson has unwittingly served as a model for baby Lucy Knox, as he went from crawling to running and from infant sounds to phrases and questions. He will continue to give me insights into a child's development as little Lucy becomes a three year old in "Spies and Deserters."

My beloved wife, who does not like historical novels in general, and descriptions of battles in particular, has nevertheless meticulously read this manuscript. It was truly a labor of love. She has applied her excellent writing skills to highlight momentum-stopping prose in the past tense, excessive detail and unnecessary digressions to which I was wedded. "Blood Upon the Snow," is definitely a better novel because of her input.

Since she has already performed the same function for the first two novels and knows she will be called upon to do so for "Spies and Deserters," and the remainder of the series, despite her strong aversion to battle scenes, I can only recognize her commitment to my writing by dedicating "Blood Upon the Snow," to her.

Martin R. Ganzglass
Washington, D.C.
December 2015

# Bibliography

The following are books, blogs or websites I have read for historical background. The blog, Boston 1775 continues to offer numerous articles on a wide variety of Revolutionary War history. Thomas J. McGuire's two-volume history of The Philadelphia Campaign provides an excellent and thoroughly research account of the overall campaign as well as personal accounts and details of the soldiers on both sides. John A. Nagy's "Spies in the Continental Capital-Espionage Across Pennsylvania During the American Revolution," paints revealing scenes of life in Philadelphia and the extensive activities of both British and American spies, agents and informants. I remain partial to the self-deprecating tone of Private Martin in his memoir, "Private Yankee Doodle," and the gripping prose of William Dwyer in "The Day Is Ours!."

Since it is easy enough to search a book or article online by author and title, I have omitted the customary reference to publisher and date of publication.

**Brooks, Noah,**
*Henry Knox- A Soldier of the Revolution*

**Chernow, Ron,**
*Washington, A Life*

**Drake, Francis S.,**
Life and Correspondence of Henry Knox

**Dwyer, William M.,**
*The Day Is Ours!*

**Eichner, L.G. Dr.,**
*The Military Practice of Medicine During the Revolutionary War*

**Fitzpatrick, John C.,**
*George Washington Himself*

**Hackett-Fischer, David,**
*Washington's Crossing*

**Hendrickson, Charles Cyril and Van Winkle Keller, Kate,**
*Social Dances from the American Revolution-Music and Instructions for Country Dances from the Personal Notebook of an Officer in General Washington's Army*

**Ketchum, Richard M.,**
*The Winter Soldiers*

**Krebs, Daniel,**
*A Generous and Merciful Enemy-Life for German Prisoners of War During the American Revolution*

**Martin, Joseph Plumb,**
*Private Yankee Doodle: Being a Narrative of Some of the Adventures, Dangers and Sufferings of a Revolutionary Soldier* (George E. Scheer, Editor)

**McGuire, Thomas J.,**
*The Philadelphia Campaign- Brandywine and the Fall of Philadelphia (Volume I); The Philadelphia Campaign-Germantown and the Roads to Valley Forge (Volume II)*

**Nagy, John A.,**
*Spies in the Continental Capital-Espionage Across Pennsylvania During the American Revolution*

**Nagy, John A.,**
*Invisible Ink-Spycraft of the American Revolution*

**Prescott, Frederick C. and Nelson, John H., (Editors)**
*Poetry and Prose of the Revolution*

**Puls, Mark,**
*Henry Knox-Visionary General of the American Revolution*

**Roberts, Cokie,**
*Ladies of Liberty*

**Savas, Theodore P. and Dameron, David J.,**
*A Guide to the Battles of the American Revolution*

**Sloane, Eric,**
*Diary of an Early American Boy, Noah Blake, 1805*

**Stuart, Nancy Rubin,**
*Defiant Brides-The Untold Story of Two Revolutionary
Era Women and the Radical Men They Married*

**Thacher, James D. Dr.,**
*Military Journal During the American Revolutionary War
1775-1783*

**Walker, Paul K.,**
*Engineers of Independence- A Documentary History of the
Army Engineers in the American Revolution, 1775-1783*

**Wulf, Karin A.,**
*Despise the Mean Distinctions [these]Times Have Made: The
Complexity of Patriotism and Quaker Loyalism in One
Pennsylvania Family*

The thrilling saga of our War for Independence

Continues with . . .

# Spies and Deserters

Captain Chatsworth led the detachment of dragoons down the narrow road, their horses' hooves clattering on the frozen ground. Patches of ice glinted in the moonlight. Twenty paces ahead, at a slight bend in the way, their local Tory guide stopped and raised his hand, listening and looking off to his left into the dark gloom of the woods. The twenty-eight troopers waited, their horses snuffling and emitting puffs of warm breath.

It could be an ambush, Chatsworth thought. They were almost thirty miles west of Philadelphia seeking to kidnap the Colonel of the Chester County Militia from his home near Downingtown. Perhaps the militia had been forewarned. Or their stoop shouldered guide, who knew the back roads and was supposedly the Colonel's neighbor, was playing a double game and betraying the 16th Dragoons instead. His Quaker-like outer coat with no pockets, had initially aroused Chatsworth's suspicion. He unstrapped his fuzee, the short-barreled musket the troopers carried, and held it loosely across his saddle. Nothing for it but to wait, he thought.

Suddenly, there was a crashing noise in the dense bushes. The guide let out a yelp and fled, his plow horse clumsily clearing a low stonewall as he disappeared into the darkness. "I hope he breaks his neck," Chatsworth muttered. He held up his hand signaling for his men to remain where they were, then waved four of them forward. The scouting party vanished around the bend in the road followed by silence as the steady clop of their horses' hooves was swallowed up by the enveloping blackness. Clouds passed across the three quarter moon. Chatsworth sat motionless in the saddle, sweating under his helmet despite the cold and felt a chill on the back of his neck. After several minutes the scouts reappeared.

"We saw some stray cattle. Nothing more," the Sergeant said, shrugging as if he had suspected all along there were no Rebel militia hiding in the forest.

Chatsworth led the troopers forward until he could perceive a widening in the road where it was joined by one perpendicular to theirs. According to the guide, the Colonel's house was the closest of the two after the Downingtown crossroads. He could make out a few buildings. If the terrified Tory had not run off, Chatsworth would have asked if there was a way to ride around without going through town and approach the Colonel's house from behind. He weighed the risk of arousing the town by riding on against leaving the horses tethered and proceeding stealthily on foot. Better to remain mounted, he concluded. They could fight their way out on horseback if necessary.

At his signal, they formed into lines of three across and galloped through the crossroads, past several low wooden buildings and the tavern that served as the center of town, and surrounded a large two story stone house just off the road. A horse from the barn whinnied in alarm, but Chatsworth had already leaped down and was pounding on the door with the butt of his fuzee.

"Open up in the name of the Crown. Resist and you will be shot," he shouted. A light appeared in an upper window, the shutters were thrown open and a grey haired woman in her nightcap peered out.

"Who are you to disturb our sleep," she screeched in outrage at the black shadows of the riders below.

"We are the Queen's 16th Dragoons and have come to arrest Colonel Hannum," Chatsworth replied. "Open this door immediately."

The woman held the lantern out the window, the light reflecting on the troopers' brass helmets with their red crests. "He is not here," she responded, her voice betraying her fear as she quickly withdrew leaving the shutters ajar. Chatsworth stood back and motioned for the troopers to break the door down. As it shattered, there was a scream of surprise from outside.

"We have bagged him, Captain," came a triumphant cry from the rear of the house. The Rebel Colonel, shivering and hatless and looking undignified in his nightshirt and boots, was brought around the porch by two troopers firmly holding his arms.

"He attempted to escape through a back window."

Chatsworth looked at the man, his hair unkempt, his thin naked legs sticking out the bottom of his white night shirt like a plucked chicken.

"Take him inside, let him get dressed but watch him closely," he ordered. "Seize all of the horses in the barn and a wagon if there is one. The rest of you, anything you can easily carry is fair to take from this Rebel scum." Chatsworth wiped his muddy boots on the rug in the center of the parlor, while his troopers ransacked the house with Mrs. Hannum following and haranguing them as godless heathens. Her venom increased as her husband's hands were tied behind his back, despite his promise as a gentleman not to try and escape.

"You mean not to try AGAIN," Chatsworth said with a dismissive wave of his hand. "Your word is of no worth to me." The Colonel was led outside and helped onto one of his own horses with a trooper pushing him hard against the pommel and sitting comfortably in the saddle behind him.

"Captain," one of the troopers called. "Behind the barn. Look at this."

Chatsworth followed him. The light from his lantern shone on a shrouded, bare footed corpse, stiff and frozen, laid out on a rough plank. The Captain bent down and pulled the rigid cloth away from the body's face. In the candlelight, Chatsworth saw evidence of a slashing wound on the side of the neck, the eye nearest to the gash was closed as if the man knew it was fatal and had no need to see it. His other eye was open as was his mouth that formed a grimace, revealing several missing teeth. The remaining ones were stained black by gunpowder. Probably one of the Colonel's militia, he thought, dead for some time, and awaiting a proper burial when the ground was no longer frozen hard as stone.

"Load him in the wagon. He may be useful to us," Chatsworth ordered.

They left the Colonel's home to the shrieks of his wife that they were no better than savages. Whether it was because one of his men had taken her gold watch or the corpse in the wagon, Chatsworth had no idea and did not care. /1 None of the homes showed any lights. Good, he thought. There was time then to leave a calling card.

Their local guide had mentioned the house on the far side of the tavern was occupied by a rebel sympathizer, a loud mouth he said who bullied his Tory neighbors. They deposited the corpse of the Rebel militiaman, standing propped up against the bully's front door, facing in. When the sympathizer opened it, he would be greeted by a one-eyed dead man, who would fall into his arms, as a warning to be careful which side he chose.

Chatsworth sent two scouts ahead of the column. This county swarmed with Pennsylvania Militia and patrols of Continental Dragoons who sallied forth from their army's base at Valley Forge. He would breath easier when they reached the burned out homes surrounding Philadelphia. On orders from General Howe, the dragoons had torched several mansions, used as observation posts by the Rebels or staging areas for attacks on British sentries manning the redoubts.

John Stoner, who had ridden with the Dragoons and now was Superintendent Galloway's aide, had told Chatsworth in confidence of the resentment at what some Philadelphians called the shocking massive conflagration. Chatsworth had dismissed the good citizens' approbation. Shock was what these people needed to keep them in line. /2 His dragoons could live with the bitter looks and the whispered words as long as people remained docile and obedient.

Good old "Ramrod John," Chatsworth thought. The only man in the entire British Army to have killed a rebel with his fuzee's ramrod. Speared him like a savage Indian, forgetting to reset it before firing. The man was a contemptible coward and obnoxious as a fawning hanger on. Always reminding Chatsworth that he had saved his life as if it was a note of debt to be collected. It was difficult to tolerate the man. Trying so hard to be the gentleman he was not. Not surprising,

Chatsworth thought. After all, he was only a farmer's son.

Still, he recognized John could be useful to the Dragoons, in his position as aide to Superintendent Galloway. His network of spies and sympathizers knew where the Rebel leaders were hiding. There was talk of even venturing forth into New Jersey to capture them. Chatsworth wanted those long distance forays for the 16th. There was glory to be gained in such raids. They might even bag a few members of Congress. Or a Rebel General as Tarleton had seized the Rebel General Charles Lee the previous year at White's Tavern.

www.ingramcontent.com/pod-product-compliance
Lightning Source LLC
Chambersburg PA
CBHW021527250626
47154CB00006BA/2008